THE ROAD RISING
©2003

A One Year Journey

By Tony R Woods

Marton Publishing
350 Greenbriar Trail
Holly Lake, Texas
USA 75755

The Road Rising

Copyright©2003
By Tony R Woods

ISBN 0-9749841-09
Library of Congress TXU-1-124-247

A special thanks to Andrew, who inspired me to write this, and to Bill, who taught me what to do once it was written. Thank you Carol and Sarah for your incomparable skill as graphic artists! To my wife, Marsha, for her patience and loving support, for my children, Nathan and Nicki, whose honest appraisals kept me going, and for my Lord Jesus Christ, Who set me on the journey and walks with me every step of the way.

Foreword

Impoverished imagination removes the color and the zest in our biblical readings. Because of our environment's usage of the visual, the inner world has shriveled and nearly become extinct. Our ancestors entered into the biblical world and those past experiences became contemporary for them. The utilization of the biblical resource both spoke to and shaped their lives. Biblical stories can become our stories, and the action of God in the past can become a focus to see the action of God today.

Joshua, sharing with those who had settled in the Promised Land, spoke of Moses' generation crossing the sea of liberation from Egypt. Then strangely he said to those gathered before him, --*you crossed the sea* (Joshua 24: 7). But that was generations before. All those who crossed the sea had perished in the wilderness. But Joshua called the people to remember the past in a way that made the past contemporary. When Jesus said, *do this in remembrance of me*, he is asking us to enter into the events of the past in such a way as to make the past contemporary. It is through imagination this is done. We sing "Were you there when the crucified our Lord?" No, we were not there; that was generations ago, but yes, we were there! That tool of imagination in spirituality has waned in our passive visual age.

The Road Rising brings into usage this lost tradition of spirituality. Tony Woods presents the Christian life as a direction and not a blueprint. The "*way*" was the first defining term for New Testament believers. With a rich imagination and the use of allegory like that of Bunyan in Pilgrim's Progress, Woods engages today's believer with the perils and triumphs of our journey of faith.

Each day's story is ended with a selection of Scripture. I was pleasantly surprised that the Scriptures used were true contextually within the Bible, as well as situationally with the narrative. That reflects mastery of the written Word which is also in evidence within the telling of the story itself.

Woods is a renaissance man. His knowledge of the environment, his evident skills in backpacking, his creative writing skills, and his life awareness, all add to his ability in story-telling. I entered the world of his journeyer and was enriched.

Tony and Marsha Woods have been personal friends for more than 30 years. I have observed their journey in Zambia, Liberia, Ethiopia and Japan. I have known their two sons and been with them when they buried the oldest son, Trevor, in 1992. I have met their adopted daughter. They serve now in Sydney, Australia, with a ministry to Japanese living in that country.

As you read *The Road Rising*, you will face virtually every issue of faith in this 12-month trek. It will be a journey you will be glad to have taken.

Stan Nelson
Senior Professor
Golden Gate Baptist Seminary

Prologue

On a Day Before the Journey Began

"Come," He said. "Come out of the darkness and into the light. Come to Me, and learn what real life is all about." With those words, the invitation found its way into my heart, and my heart was ready. My days had become filled with a constant barrage of things which battled each other for first place, and I had fallen, the first victim. The only thing left was unconditional surrender to God; and what followed was a sense of unconditional love, and a peace I never thought possible. It was a feeling I knew I could never understand, not fully. Small wonder then, that those closest to me were unable to grasp it either. My friends, my associates, even my own family were left mystified at the change. I pray every day for their acceptance, but my longing is tempered by an overwhelming desire to know Him better. He had said, "Come." I came, and now nothing else really matters.

But His next word following "Come" only served to increase my ignorance. He said, "Go. Follow the path that I have set before you. Learn all you can about the path, because it is in the journey that you will find Me."

Come. Go. Learn. Strange words indeed. Strange, perhaps, but not difficult to understand, nor to obey. I must go and I must observe all that I am shown. His Word I will carry with me, and each day I will record what I see. I don't know where the journey will end; I'm told that the normal travel time is one year, but that it could come to a close at any point along the way. I'm not to worry about what I can't see, but only to see what I am shown, and in the process to become more and more what I've been created to be. I can't wait to begin.

Come to me, all you who are weary and burdened, and I will give you rest. Take my yoke upon you and learn from me, for I am gentle and humble in heart, and you will find rest for your souls. For my yoke is easy and my burden is light."
Matthew 11: 28 – 29

You did not choose me, but I chose you and appointed you to go and bear fruit— fruit that will last. Then the Father will give you whatever you ask in my name. This is my command: Love each other.
John 15: 16 – 17

....

Prayer: Father I thank you for calling me to Yourself. I'm sorry I stayed away so long. Now You tell me to go, and I go willingly. Only come with me, I pray. May I never be far from Your side nor out of Your heart. Show me each day what You want me to see, and in that knowledge may I become all that You want me to be. In the precious Name of Your Son, Jesus Christ. Amen.

Ask yourself: Would you be willing to take a journey into the unknown, if you could go with someone you trust? Who can you trust?

January 1

Forgetting the Past

There's a smell of waterproofed canvas in the air. The journey has begun, and each step is accompanied by the creak of new leather and the rhythmic rattle of essentials, finding their way to the lowest reaches of my back pack. A quick glance over my shoulder confirms that I am in fact moving, as the signpost marking the trail head grows smaller with each step. I tug on the straps to find that perfect fit. A deep breath.

This is a journey which I've never made before: the journey into the new year. How long will the trip take? My map tells me twelve months, but my heart reminds me that the destination may be around the next twist in the path. I don't know what waits, and that's part of the excitement. The new year brings a sense of freshness to everything, and with it a renewed confidence.

In a way, I guess that's what forgiveness is all about: a chance to start over. Looking back on last year's journey, I can recall a lot of great adventures. But I also see a lot of things I wish I could forget. Mistakes in the things I chose to carry. The side trips I took. Some of the characters I walked with. Without God's grace, I know full well that I would never have made it to the end. But I did make it, and now last year is last year. Past. Forgiven. Forgotten. Now, with the scents and sounds of newness all around me, I lean into the straps and push ahead.

No need to look back anymore.

But one thing I do: Forgetting what is behind and straining toward what is ahead, I press on toward the goal to win the prize for which God has called me heavenward in Christ Jesus.

Philippians 3: 13 – 14

Prayer: Father, today help me put the past behind and look ahead to the new year. Give strength to my steps and courage in my soul. Keep me on the path You have chosen for me to walk, and guard me from those who would lead me astray.

Ask yourself: How do memories of past events affect my decisions today?

A Good Kinda Hurt

Why is it always like this? No matter how prepared I think I am, my body still discovers new muscles at the beginning of the journey. I didn't even know there *was* a muscle there! Getting up alone this second morning was a real challenge.

There was no big "send off" today from well-wishers and admiring onlookers. Even the birds seemed too preoccupied with business as usual to give me more than a second glance as I hoisted my back pack and started up the trail. Whoa. Those nice, new, *essentials* have put on a few pounds overnight.

The excitement I felt yesterday is, well, diminished. I suppose part of it is the fact that I now *know* something about the path I didn't know yesterday. It *is* a path, after all, with its ups and downs; and this morning I'm feeling a little sore. But still, it's a good kinda hurt. The muscles complain, but even as I stretch them out I can tell that they'll soon be back to full strength. Recovery comes quickly, and the trail is still fairly smooth. I can do this, Lord. It may hurt for awhile, but I won't let it discourage me.

No, I beat my body and make it my slave so that after I have preached to others, I myself will not be disqualified for the prize.

I Corinthians 9: 27

Prayer: The pain I feel this morning is a small reminder of my frailty, Lord. While yesterday I was brimming with confidence, today I confess to a certain amount of doubt in my body's ability to meet the challenge. But that's good, isn't it? My strength never was sufficient, and the sooner I learn that, the better I'll be. As the pain eases today, and strength returns, remind me Father that it is You Who are my healer, my strength giver.

Ask yourself: Think of something you can do now that you had to learn. What was it like at the beginning?

January 3

Anticipation

I woke up early this morning, probably because it was so quiet. Most of the creatures of the night were turning in before the coming day, while the "day shift" had not yet begun their morning's cacophony. The air was still and crisp, the silence like a roaring in my ears. Raising my head out of the sleeping bag, I could just make out the shape of the mountain which lay between me and my destination. The sky was dark, but the mountain was darker still, causing it to stand out in subtle contrast.

I lay there imagining what it would be like to stand on the summit of that huge peak. I could see... no... I could imagine that the sky behind it was growing lighter. One by one, the stars disappeared, and finally a definite glow began to form around the mountain's edges. The sun was coming. I found myself wishing I were on the other side of the mountain already, basking in the sunlight which was already warming the far slopes.

Why is it that we want to be wherever we are not? I'm on this journey for the simple reason that something waits Out There, and I want to go. This campsite is a nice place for an evening's rest, but I'm not interested in putting down roots, not as long as that mountain looms on the horizon.

I suppose once I *do* reach the other side, I'll look back with longing to this place and this moment. But I guess that's how God made me: a traveler going... where? To a place where every tear will be dried and every fear and doubt removed once and for all. I'm not alone on this journey, I discover. I can see it in the eyes of every person I meet on the trail: that longing for the Garden, to the time when everything was good.

And they admitted that they were aliens and strangers on earth. People who say such things show that they are looking for a country of their own. If they had been thinking of the country they had left, they would have had opportunity to return. Instead, they were longing for a better country – a heavenly one. Therefore God is not ashamed to be called their God, for He has prepared a city for them.
Hebrews 11: 13b – 16

....

Prayer: This is a beautiful world, Lord, and I praise You for it. But it's not home. Guard my heart and guide until I reach that land my soul so desperately longs for. May the longing in my heart never be diminished until it is satisfied in Your arms.

Ask yourself: Where would you like to go? What are you doing today to get there?

Forgotten

Yesterday morning as I watched the sun come up behind the mountain, I ached with anticipation, wanting to be *there* instead of *here*. I accept that it's natural to harbor that longing and move forward with anticipation. But here's the surprise: as soon as I left camp, the trail descended into a valley, the mountain disappeared from view, and that longing melted away. For the rest of the day, my eyes were trained not on the horizon for another glimpse of the mountain, but downward into the darkening trail.

What waits below me? How far down must I go before the trail starts uphill again? What happened to the aching desire that wrenched me from my sleeping bag yesterday morning? In a word: the present. The mountain is off in the distance, but today's trail is here and now. I'll think later about lofty peaks and noble struggles, but right now I have a stream to cross, a slide area to negotiate, a dark path to reconnoiter.

Someone called it the "tyranny of the urgent." The future is important, but *today* I have things to do, and which must not be ignored. And that's true; if I were to live only for the future I could easily miss something important today. Something good. Something dangerous. I must keep my attention on the next step, the task immediately before me. But what a blessing is memory! By our remembrance we can look backwards, but not just to past events. Today I can remember looking at my future yesterday: the mountain looming ahead. I can't see it today, but my memory tells me it's still there, waiting.

So I will continue to mind my steps today, but at the same time will hold onto the memory of vision: a vision toward which I still move, and which I will see again.

Now faith is being sure of what we hope for and certain of what we do not see. This is what the ancients were commended for.

Hebrews 11: 1 – 2

....

Prayer: Lord You know how I live for the day, and so seldom plan for tomorrow. Once in awhile You give me a glimpse of my future; may I burn those memories deep into my mind. May I never forget what You have done, and what You will yet do. Help me to live for You today, and tomorrow, and for all time.

Ask yourself: Do responsibilities today prevent you from preparing for tomorrow's jobs? What can you do about it?

The Trail Misplaced

This afternoon I came to a slide area. The winter snows had completely obliterated the path and left only a smooth mountainside covered with broken shale. Getting across was the hardest thing I've done yet on this trip. For every step forward my feet would slide downward, then to regain the loss I would have to move up the slope. I finally made it to the trees at the other side of the slide area, but there was no trace of the trail. Was it up the hill or down? Did it continue straight into the woods through the undergrowth? I felt a growing panic as I noticed the fading light. What if I couldn't find the trail? What if I got lost? I started to run directly into the forest but was soon so cut and bruised I stopped, exhausted. Had I come to the end of my journey so near to it's beginning? Looking back the way I came, I tried to make out the place where the trail had stopped. Yes, there it was, at the edge of the trees. And then... wait... I could see it: a faint line stretching out from the edge of the trees, across the shale and into the woods just above where I was standing. What was invisible from the other side was now plain to see when looking back. The trail was there, but could only be seen from a forward viewpoint. Two days ago I was driven by anticipation, looking only to the goal far off in the distance. Yesterday I was distracted by the challenges of the moment, too busy watching my feet to think of anything ahead. Today, I find that in order to move ahead, sometimes I have to look back. The rock-hardened shale did not yield easily to the booted feet of travelers, but there was a mark, and from this angle it was plainly visible. I guess I need to remember to look over my shoulder once in awhile. Those who have gone before me can often show me the path, but only by looking back on the footprints they left behind.

Therefore, since we are surrounded by such a great cloud of witnesses, let us throw off everything that hinders and the sin that so easily entangles, and let us run with perseverance the race marked out for us.

Hebrews 12: 1

Prayer: Thank you Father, for those who have gone before me. Help me to learn from their experience, and to look back on the footprints they left behind. May my tracks be a guide for someone else who follows.

Ask yourself: Have you ever been lost? How did you feel? What did you do?

Scars of the Curse

I moved farther into the valley today. The horizon began to tower over me, as the sides of the valley grew steeper. The sounds of the birds which had been my constant companion now came from far above me. In their place was the growing sound, or I should say, sensation, of flowing water. The trail began to cut through sections of mountainside, leaving open wounds which revealed the strata of a time gone by. I stopped to rest beside one such cut, and ran my hands over the lines in the rock, trying to imagine how they were formed.

Digging through a particularly thick line of soft clay-like material, I caught a glimpse of something with smooth, rounded features. I lifted it out, wiped it on my jeans, and saw that it was a sea shell, about the size of my thumb. I lay on my back, looking at the mountaintops and tried to picture this trail, this valley, this whole earth, covered in water: enough water to make a home for this creature of the sea. I suppose for some it's a mystery, but for me it's painfully obvious. Here is evidence of a time when God said , "Enough," and unleashed the waters of the deep.

What horrible sin could have caused the Creator to destroy His own creation? The Bible speaks of some terrible thing that happened between the "sons of God" and the "daughters of men", but rather than bringing answers to my fears, I'm left with a profound sense of terror: not toward God but toward my own ability to bring such wrath upon the world. God knows my ability as well, and because of it has chosen to limit my span of life. But will shortening our years keep us from the depths of sin? I think about how far down we've come just in my lifetime. How much farther before God once again calls a halt, and says "Enough?"

The Lord saw how great man's wickedness on the earth had become, and that every inclination of the thoughts of his heart was only evil all the time. The Lord was grieved that He had made man on the earth, and His heart was filled with pain.
Genesis 6: 5 – 6

Prayer: Father I too grieve when I see the sin of man, and all the more when I realize that I stand among the guilty. You were surely right to destroy the world as You did; but I praise You for the mercy You showed. Because of that mercy I can lift this prayer to you, and even dare to ask for Your forgiveness. Because of Jesus.

Ask yourself: When have you ever wanted to just "clean the slate" and start over?

By the Sweat of Your Brow

Today was downhill, as I moved deeper into the valley. The sun all but disappeared, if not behind the mountaintops, then behind a thickening canopy of vegetation. In places, the trail disappeared into the undergrowth, forcing me to bend low and raise my arms against the encroaching curtain of green.

The pain wasn't noticeable until I stopped for a drink of water, then I noticed a stinging sensation on my arms and the back of my neck. Apparently some of the vegetation I had been walking through included thorns, ripping my shirt in a couple of places and drawing blood in several others. Patches of bare skin burned with the effects of a stinging nettle which I had never noticed.

Pouring water over my arms and neck, I wondered, "What did Adam think when he first encountered this?" Apparently, this is a post-Garden thing, so he must have made a few painful discoveries. Yesterday, the shell reminded me of the curse which brought death to an entire planet, save the inhabitants of one comparatively small boat. Today I'm reminded that death is not the only result of sin. Even before the time of the Flood, Adam and his heirs had to learn about life outside the Garden: complete with thorns, nettles and venomous insects.

And it's a curse we share today. How many times have I heard the question: "If there is a God, why is there pain and suffering in the world?" The short answer, I suppose is that it beats the alternative. Because of sin, all of creation has begun to die. There is a built in limit to every living thing, and no one can avoid that Final Appointment. But because there is a God, and because He's a God of mercy, death has been given a stay. Yes, we *are* going to die, but until then let's try to discover *why* that has to be. It may take a few thorns, or nettles, or worse, but God will do everything possible to show me both the depth of my sin and the infinite love of His forgiveness.

Cursed is the ground because of you; through painful toil you will eat of it all the days of your life. It will produce thorns and thistles for you, and you will eat the plants of the field.

Genesis 3: 17b – 18

....

Prayer: Lord may our suffering not be in vain. May every cut, every bruise remind me that I live in a world broken by sin. And by that realization, may I seek your forgiveness.

Ask yourself: Has the experience of pain ever taught you anything?

January 8

Dominion

I came across a bear today, a black bear, I think. He had his head down in a patch of berries and didn't hear me coming until I was within a few feet of him. I must have made a sound because he suddenly jerked his head up, saw me and then raised up on his two back feet.

My heart was in my throat, but apparently I wasn't the only one terrified by the encounter. Unlike most Hollywood bears I've seen, this one didn't come at me with tooth and claw, intent on ripping me limb from limb. Instead, he took a quick look around, saw the best avenue of escape and literally, headed for the hills. I could hear him for a full minute after he disappeared, crashing through the underbrush with no thought except to put as much distance between him and me as "bearly" possible.

Not wanting to see a perfectly good patch of berries go to waste, I gathered a few, then sat down to collect myself. Where was I, exactly, on the food chain? And why is it that a hairless, clawless pitifully slow lump of flesh like me could send something like that into full flight? I suppose he may have come across a hunter or two and didn't want to stop and see if I had a gun; but when you think about it, most animals do give men a wide berth.

And then I remembered where it all began: as the Ark was opened and the survivors of the animal kingdom set foot once again on solid ground, they knew at once that things were not the same as before. Indeed, the "fear and dread" of men was placed inside them, and they wasted no time in moving as far away as possible. Noah and his family must have caught the significance of the moment as well, to hear God say, "Everything that lives and moves will be food for you. Just as I gave you the green plants, I now give you everything."

I don't know if that justifies me being carnivorous or not, but it does show me where it all began. Where once we lived in a world teeming with more edible veggies and fruits than we could ever consume, now we struggle in a post-Flood devastation. Food is scarce, especially if you're living at the salad bar. But once again, God in His mercy changes the rules. "Before, you had all the green plants; now you have it all."

The fear and dread of you will fall upon all the beasts of the earth and all the birds of the air, upon every creature that moves along the ground, and upon all the fish of the sea; they are given into your hands.

Genesis 9: 2

Prayer: Lord, don't let me take for granted what all You have given me. Help me take care of this land, and all that lives in it, for in doing so I return to You a portion of what I have received from You. Thank you.

Ask yourself: Do you think Christianity and ecology are compatible?

January 9

Rebellion

After yesterday's encounter with the runaway bear, the last thing I expected today was to be stalked by yet another animal; but that's what happened. Continuing along the trail, I was bothered by a growing sense of uneasiness, as if I were not alone. I kept stopping to look up and down the trail, but nothing seemed out of place.

The feeling persisted, though, and finally I decided to back track, to put to rest once and for all the feeling that I was being followed. After a hundred yards or so, I stopped to look down, and saw the print my boots had made in the mud, where I had stepped gingerly around an area of standing water. A wave of shock moved up my back as I noticed *another* print covering my own. A cat, I could tell, because no claw marks were visible. The track was huge, almost as big as the one my size elevens had made, and as I watched, a trickle of water made its way into the recession the cat had made. Where was he? What was he doing? Did he intend to hunt me down as if I were a tender morsel of the forest?

I looked around for a rock, or a stick, or anything that could be used as a weapon. Scanning the brush for a club-sized branch, my eyes stopped on something. For a moment, I couldn't tell what I was looking at, except that it was subtly different from the rest of the leaves around it. Then I realized that I was looking at two eyes, which were at that moment boring into my own. More out of terror than common sense, I started jumping up and down, waving my arms and making a sound that resembled a chimpanzee. The eyes in the brush suddenly grew larger, then bolted backwards, into the forest.

Tonight, sitting closer than usual to a larger than normal fire, I prayed, "Thank you Lord for protecting me today." It's disconcerting, to be hunted by a predator who apparently did not catch that part about the "fear and dread" of me in Genesis 9. And then I thought, if man is capable of rebellion, are the animals also? In that same chapter of Genesis, God says that He will "demand an accounting of every animal." So does that mean that every "bad dog", every "snake in the grass" and every man eating cat will have to answer for his behavior? Maybe I don't want to go there, except to take comfort in the promise that all *will* be made right, before the throne of God. In the meantime, Lord, keep the firewood coming.

And for your lifeblood I will surely demand an accounting. I will demand an accounting from every animal...
Genesis 9: 5

....

Prayer: Thank you Father for the promise of a full accounting. There is so much in the world that doesn't seem right; and of course it's *not* right, not until You come back and restore Your Kingdom. Hasten the day, I pray. Bring Your kingdom soon.

Ask yourself: Does the suffering of an animal affect you? How do the think the Old Testament's practice of sacrifice affected those who took part?

Beauty in the Valley

After the experiences of the last couple of days, I wasn't sure if I was going to be up for the rest of the trip. It's only been ten days, and already I'm cut by thorns, stung by nettles and stalked by something that wanted to eat me. Is this what it means to walk the narrow way?

Well, God heard my prayer today and brought me into a glen. By now, the valley is so deep that sunlight can't get to the forest floor. The undergrowth has cleared away, and the trees are *huge*. Reaching for the sky, they must tower 200 feet or more. I tried to measure the distance around one, but had nothing long enough to measure with. The sound of running water, which I've heard for the last three days, finally showed itself as a small brook, dancing over rocks and teeming with trout. It was still early in the day, but I had to stop and camp. The place was just too beautiful to pass up.

Once again, I gained a sense of God's mercy in the midst of the Curse. Yes, there are thorns; yes there are predators, but the remnants of Eden are not lacking. Just as an old man can still carry a reflection of his youth, if you look deep enough, the world still surrounds us with wonder and majesty, wisps of memory of a time that is no more. The trees around me tonight must be ancient; they probably sprouted not long after the flood waters receded. The most awesome skyscraper could never match even one of these giants when it comes to photosynthesis, hydrology and structural engineering. And yet how often do we pass by such wonders with not so much as a second thought?

By Adam's sin, the world was caught in the grip of a downward spiral of destruction; a process that will not stop until the Creator Himself brings it to a close. But still the world bears witness to the power, glory and love of the Father, Who would leave us such as this. Thank you.

The heavens declare the glory of God; the skies proclaim the work of His hands. Day after day they pour forth speech; night after night they display knowledge. There is no speech or language where their voice is not heard.

Psalms 19: 1 – 3

Prayer: Lord, open my eyes to the testimony of Your handiwork! Let me see the beauty You have created right here in this valley. May I never lose sight of Your power and grandeur.

Ask yourself: What natural wonder have you seen lately? Could you see the Hand of God in it?

January 11

Across the Brook

The trail crossed the stream today, and so did I. It wasn't too big a challenge; the stream was fairly small, and there were plenty of rocks to step on. I know that there will be larger rivers farther down the trail, and bigger challenges to face; but this was a good beginning. There's an old proverb that says "A man can never cross a river twice; because next time it will be a different river and a different man." I had to think about that. I've been following this river for two days now, and it *looks* the same, but I guess it is different water that I'm looking at. Life's challenges often look like previous ones as well, but there will always be something that makes each one unique. And I'm not the same person now that I was even last week. I've now experienced excitement, longing, boredom, fatigue, pain and un-obliterated fear. Those things have helped shaped me into someone different than I was last week.

Maybe that's part of the real value of this journey: the process itself. We're all being grown into Kingdom children, and part of that growth is the daily routine of life. I had a child who died before he was ever born, and I suppose for him, maturity came in an instant. But for the rest of us, there is that blessing of *process*, whereby we grow, step by step into what God has created us to be. I may come up against this river again, farther downstream, but I know the crossing won't be the same. It will be a different river, and I will be a different man.

Consider it pure joy, my brothers, whenever you face trials of many kinds, because you know that the testing of your faith develops perseverance. Perseverance must finish its work so that you may be mature and complete, not lacking anything.

James 1: 2 – 4

....

Prayer: I don't ask for challenges, Lord; my faith is not strong enough to willingly seek them out. But knowing that challenges will come, I ask for strength and courage to meet them, and in the process to become more of what You want me to be. Thank you for helping me over the river today. Prepare me for the next one to come.

Ask yourself: Do you think there will be babies in heaven? What will they look like?

January 12

An Object Found

I found something today: a pair of glasses. I might have missed them, except that a bird had flown across the path and stopped to rest on a nearby branch. I stopped for a closer look, and as I was marveling at the impromptu concert he was giving me, something on the ground beneath him shimmered in the thin ray of sunlight that filtered through the trees. I hated to interrupt the musical interlude, but this demanded my attention.

They were glasses, all right, and pretty special ones too, judging from the thickness of the lens. How did they get here? I wondered. And then I paused to think about the assumptions that had gone into that question. I knew the glasses in my hand were unique, specially manufactured for a special need. I did *not* think for a moment that this was a quirk of nature. Nothing in the natural world could ever account for a pair of prescription made glasses. There was evidence of design, of intelligence, of a sense of both beauty and usefulness. The question in my mind was not, "How did these glasses come to be?" but rather, "How did these glasses come to be *here*?" And then I thought, how are these glasses any different from the bird sitting above them, giving me a marvelous bird song concert which no other living creature could duplicate?

Sadly, there are those who would look at that bird and assume an incredible series of natural events that would have *accidentally* produced it, and then make no such assumptions about the obviously man-made object below it. How can we be so blind, to spend our lives studying the creature without recognizing in it the Creator? I put the glasses in my pocket, and the bird's song in my memory. Maybe both will come in handy some day.

They exchanged the truth of God for a lie, and worshipped and served created things rather than the Creator – who is forever praised. Amen.

Romans 1: 25

....

Prayer: Lord, forgive me for my blindness, for failing to see Your Hand within Your handiwork. I know you are showing me these things so that I will recognize You and give you the glory for it, but so many times I close my eyes and ears to creation's testimony. Help me see.

Ask yourself: What is the meaning of the word, "irreducible complexity" , and what does that mean to your ideas about the creation of the world?

January 13

A Glimpse of the Stars

The path moved up away from the river today, and by dusk I found myself on an open meadow. I could still hear the sound of the river below, but almost drowning it out was another sound: the wind in the treetops. I had nearly forgotten such sounds, after the last few days along a dark and sheltered trail. The sound was reassuring in a way: telling me that things were still happening above me even when I had been unable to see beyond the forest canopy. I kept glancing up, as if expecting to see something noteworthy; and as dusk settled in, I *did* see something. A sky full of stars, beginning their evening performance as one by one, they made a glimmering appearance, joining the rest until I thought there could be room for no more. But as the sky grew darker still, and as my eyes became accustomed to the distance, even more performers joined the evening stage, no less spectacular for their distance from the viewer.

God knows each one by name, I recalled, and each one travels a course set before time began. Funny, I thought, that as astronomers strain to the heavens in search for life, one of the definitions by which they operate is to be on the look out for "anything which appears unnatural." Does that mean that nature is by definition synonymous with death? Can we not see the awesome design which has gone into the work of the Designer? How can the stars not "declare the glory of God"? May I never be so deaf.

He determines the number of the stars and calls them each by name. Great is our Lord and mighty in power ;his understanding has no limit.

Psalms 147: 4 – 5

Prayer: As I look at the stars tonight, Father, I'm reminded of Your eternal glory. Only You could do such a thing as what I see in the heavens. And, wonder of it all, You have done such a thing in me! Praise your Holy Name.

Ask yourself: How many stars can you name? What do you suppose are the names God gave them?

January 14

Pain's Blessing

I woke up this morning to the sense that all was not right. Before I could give it much thought, I raised up on one elbow to look around, and quickly dropped back down, my arm screaming in pain. Rolling up my shirt sleeve, I saw the telltale redness surrounding patches of white and knew at once that I had an infection. The scratches on my arm from the other day's struggle through the thorns must have let some bacteria through, and now my body was on red alert, fighting off the invasion.

Sifting through the "essentials" in my backpack, I finally uncovered a bottle of antiseptic and grimacing, applied a liberal dose to the infected area. I scolded myself for not treating the scratches when I got them. I could have washed and dressed them last week and by today they would be just a memory instead of a megaphone. Where have I heard that? Oh yes, C.S. Lewis once called pain "the megaphone by which God breaks through our deafness." He was right, after all. If my arm had not sounded off this morning, I would have no doubt gone through another day without once rolling my sleeves up and examining my wounds. The result ultimately would have been something much worse that the stinging I feel now.

And of course, the same is true for all the pain that comes our way, be it the sting of a bee, the burn of a match, or the unquenchable agony of a broken heart. Pain is the only way most of us will sit up and realize that something's wrong and needs to be dealt with. Now. I have to be honest: I don't like pain. But in the words of my grandfather when I cracked my head, "Just think how *good* that's gonna feel when it quits hurtin'!"

> *He will wipe every tear from their eyes. There will be no more death or mourning or crying or pain, for the old order of things has passed away."*
>
> Revelation 21: 4

....

Prayer: I look forward to that time when pain will be forgotten; but in the meantime, Lord, use my pain to show me what I would not otherwise see. In Your mercy, heal my pain; in Your wisdom, use it for Your glory. Amen.

Ask yourself: What has the experience of pain taught you?

January 15

Wasted Pain

I heard him long before he came into view. At first I thought it was the wind in the treetops, but as I drew closer to the sound I could tell it was a cry of agony. For a moment, I feared that the mountain lion was once again on my trail, but then I began to make out words among the screams. Finally, at the top of a rise I could see him off in a field, lying face down.

Coming closer, I could see that his clothes were torn. He had lost one shoe, and his foot was bleeding badly. His face and hands were a mass of cuts. Coming closer, I called out, "Hello! I'm over here. Let me help you!" He paused for a moment, and looked in my direction, but whether he saw me or not, he soon threw himself back onto the ground.

"No! No! It's no good, you see?" he cried. "It's no good! It's no good!"

Laying my hand on his shoulder, I tried to comfort him. "I'm here," I said. "I'll help you. Let me get my first aid kit." The words seemed to soothe him somewhat, and he rolled over and sat up, but still held his head in his hands, moaning softly.

"No, I have to go. I lost the trail, but if you'll show me where it is, I'll be going."

"Don't be foolish," I said. "You're hurt. I have to dress these wounds. What happened to you?"

"I was *there*," said, with a voice of defiance. "I had it! All I needed to do was make the next marker. But then I lost my glasses, and I've been running into things ever since. I have to *go!*"

Reaching into my shirt pocket, I quickly pulled out the glasses I had found back on the trail. "Are these your glasses?" I asked. He looked in my direction, reached one hand out, and I placed them into his fingers. He clutched the glasses, fumbled with them until they were open, then placed them over his ears.

"Yes! Yes!" he cried, and stood up to move away.

"Wait!" I shouted. "You're hurt. I need to..."

But he was gone, stumbling and limping back onto the trail, then on down the hill, crying with pain all the way. What drove him to such insanity? I may never know, but I've known others like him: people who are so intent in reaching the goal, they never experience the journey. The *process* of becoming is in God's sight as precious as the becoming itself. I have no doubt that God could have made us all full grown, just as He did Adam and Eve. But in His wisdom, He included in His creation a plan for maturity, one step at a time. I hope I see every step along the way.

And a highway will be there; it will be called the Way of Holiness. The unclean will not journey on it; it will be for those who walk in that Way; wicked fools will not go about on it.

Isaiah 35: 8

....

Prayer: Lord help me to fully experience every step of the journey You have given me. May my eyes be full of wonder and steps directed by Your Holy Spirit.

Ask yourself: Have you known anyone who was so dedicated to reaching the goal that he or she missed the process of getting there?

A Pause in the Journey

My sleep was troubled last night, perhaps due to the encounter with the poor soul yesterday who had despised the journey in favor of the destination. Several times I thought I could hear his cries in the darkness far below my camp. What would happen to him? Could he possibly find the end of the trail in his condition? Was there nothing I could do to help him? My body finally gave in to fatigue and slept a dreamless sleep which brought no rest.

I woke later than usual, the sun creeping over the treetops finally wrestling me awake. Seeing the late hour, I jumped out of the sleeping bag and threw on my boots. No time for breakfast; I had to be on my way. The day was well spent already. Throwing my sleeping bag into the back pack, I found myself in a state of near panic, as if I were about to miss an all-important plane connection. Then it occurred to me: I was becoming like *him*. The goals I had set for each day of the journey were becoming my gods, to be disregarded at my peril.

But what, in fact, was the point in rushing? I remember now something I was told before the journey began: the travel time would be twelve months, no more no less, except in case of early pick up. The latter, nor for that matter the former, were under any control of mine. All that was expected of me was to take up the back pack and go. Each day would take care of itself. So I paused while lacing a boot. What would happen if I went faster? Or slower? According to the instructions, I would arrive no sooner nor later than expected. That was a difficult concept to take in; I would need to give it some more thought.

Sitting back, I looked around the place where I had spent the night. Could *this* be part of the journey? Is there something here I need to discover, to understand before moving on? And so I sat. Morning came and went. Noon arrived and I pulled out some lunch. Still sitting with my back against my gear, I continued to ask, "Am I missing something? Should I be doing something?"

Evening found me still seated in the same spot, no wiser than I was in the morning. Slightly confused, I unpacked my sleeping bag again and climbed inside. The breeze was nice. Night birds were beginning to tune up for the evening. But as sleep began to overtake me, I prayed once more, "Why Lord? Why did I sit here all day, doing nothing?" Then I fell into a deep well of sleep. And from the depths of the well I heard the voice of One I knew: "It was good to have your attention this day. Sleep well."

Be still, and know that I am God; I will be exalted among the nations, I will be exalted in the earth." The LORD Almighty is with us; the God of Jacob is our fortress.
Psalms 46: 10 – 11

....

Prayer: Thank you for this day of rest, Lord. I didn't go a far distance, but the time with You was so much more. Help me to keep my eye on You, even when I'm moving.

Ask yourself: When was the last time you took a vacation?

January 17

Lighten the Load

What a difference the morning makes when you've slept well! This time I made it out of my sleeping bag and had coffee on the fire before the first magpie realized I was up. Breakfast done and the dishes washed, I whistled a tune as I started putting things into my pack. What a mess things had become! This needed to be straightened up. Emptying everything out for the first time since the journey began, I was horrified to find what I had been a carrying on my back for the last sixteen days. A hammer? Why did I pack that? And what's this? A cast iron frying pan!

One by one, I took each item, considered it carefully, then put it into one of two piles: one to pack, one to leave. Experiences of the past couple of weeks had taught me about what was important and what was not. Most of those "essentials" were in fact not that essential at all. They were merely symbols of the life I had known before the journey began: symbols that I had been reluctant to let go of.

Well, this was the day for letting go. A sizable stack of good but "non-essential" equipment was gathered up into a bundle and left on a rock near the fireplace, along with a note encouraging fellow pilgrims to help themselves to anything they wanted. Who knows? Maybe some of these things *are* essential to someone. With a lighter backpack, I now took a look at myself. Those boots need oiling, that tear in your shirt needs mending. That scratch needs tending. It was approaching noon before I finally hitched up my gear and started down the trail, with a lightness to my step I had not known before.

When evening came, I discovered that I had covered all the ground that I had hoped to cover, and more. It seems that speed it not always the way to win races, but then, who's racing anyway?

Let the morning bring me word of your unfailing love, for I have put my trust in you. Show me the way I should go, for to you I lift up my soul.

Psalms 143: 8

Prayer: Thank you, Father, for helping me remember that You are the focus of my journey. Not the path, not the daily goals I set for myself, but You alone. Thank you for giving me joy in the journey, whether I'm moving forward or standing still.

Ask yourself: What if you lost everything you owned tomorrow? What would happen to your life?

Distant Smoke

It was warm today. The barometer was dropping, and although I could see clouds gathering in the distance, there was no sign of rain anytime soon. Once in awhile I heard the distant rumble of thunder, but it stayed in the distance. Then, as evening approached, I came to a high place in the trail and saw a thick column of smoke off in the distance, ahead and to the left of where my trail was leading. A bush fire. Scanning the skies, I could see that the wind was moving from right to left. If that remained unchanged, perhaps the fire would move on, away from me. But I had had some experience with bush fire. I knew how quickly conditions could change, and if the wind pushes a fire toward you, there's no outrunning it.

A familiar lump formed in the back of my throat. I'd known this feeling before: fear. Not the kind of fear that hits hard and fast, like a crouching mountain lion. If that were the case, the adrenaline would start pumping, and the body would react instantly: fight or flight. But this kind of fear was more like the slowly rising needle on a gas pressure gauge. Danger. But not now... soon.

"What should I do, Lord?" I know now, even as I knew then, that there are several possible answers to a question like that. "Run for your life" is one possibility; and at the time probably the answer I would have liked most to hear. Or if not that, "Fill some buckets," or "Start a backfire," or "Dig a hole." Any of those would be acceptable answers, especially if I knew they came from *Him*. However, it seems that the answer I hear most is the one I'm least excited about: "Wait."

But Lord, shouldn't I be *doing* something? Oh, I am doing something. I'm waiting.

I am still confident of this: I will see the goodness of the LORD in the land of the living. Wait for the LORD; be strong and take heart and wait for the LORD.
Psalms 27: 13 – 14

....

Prayer: Lord You know this is the hardest thing of all for me to do. It was easy when I was repacking and mending, but now, especially now in the face of pending danger, I want to *do* something. But You remind me that waiting is doing, and that You want me to wait on You. Help me be strong in my waiting.

Ask yourself: What frightens you today?

The Work of Waiting

Another day, another time of waiting and watching. The smoke is growing closer now, and I can begin to see flames shooting up the tops of the tallest trees. It's a hot fire, and it's moving fast. The wind is still pushing it to the left, but the back of the fire is finding plenty to burn... in my direction. Throughout the day, I drop to my knees in prayer. Lord, how long must I wait? Did I misunderstand You the first time? Shouldn't I be doing *something*? In answer, I hear nothing whatsoever, as if God is saying, "I've already told you what to do; you don't need to ask again."

But I *do* need to ask again, because my fear is challenging my faith. If I hurry, I could still make it past the fire before it sweeps over the trail ahead. Maybe I should just... "*Wait*." Tonight I lay in my sleeping bag, watching the sky. A full moon has come up over the horizon, but it's blood red, due to the smoke in the air.

If I hold my breath and lay perfectly still I can hear the fire burning. Trees giving way to the onslaught and falling into the maelstrom, adding still more fuel. Cinders sweep up into the sky. In the morning, my sleeping bag is covered with a thin layer of ash. Lord, I'm afraid. What should I do? "*Trust me. Wait.*"

We wait in hope for the LORD; he is our help and our shield. In him our hearts rejoice, for we trust in his holy name. May your unfailing love rest upon us, O LORD, even as we put our hope in you.

Psalms 33: 20

Prayer: Lord teach me the work of waiting. It's so hard, thinking I should be doing something, and yet trying to understand that waiting in obedience is the best thing I could ever do. I trust You, Lord. Help me trust You more.

Ask yourself: Is it easy or difficult for you to wait?

Time to Move

The call came early, before daylight. It sounded for all the world like the single word, "*Move!*", but was more likely the sound of a nearby tree exploding. The wind had shifted during the night, pushing the fire in my direction and across the trail directly in front of me. For a moment, I thought I was staring into the face of my own death, not sure how to feel. Was this the "early pickup" I was given as a possibility? Were my last words going to be "I *told* You I should run."?

But before I could put feet to my fears, I noticed that the wind was at my back, pushing the fire away from me. The overnight wind shift had succeeded in clearing the way in front of me before turning back again to cross the trail and move on to the right. I packed up quickly and moved off the hillside toward the burned out valley. By the time I reached the fire line, it was mostly finished, except for a few logs still smoldering.

The sound of thunder, this time much closer. Large raindrops began to fall around me, hissing as they struck embers close by. The storm which had started the fire three days ago was now gearing up to put it out. With the dawn, I began to see the extent of devastation. As far as could be seen in any direction stood blackened and smoking stumps of once gigantic trees, now reduced to charcoal.

A log lay across the trail ahead. But as I approached closer, I realized that it was not a log, but something else. Something which had been alive and moving just hours before. There was nothing left to recognize except one thing: the twisted frame and thick lens of a pair of glasses. The poor man; in his desperation to reach the goal, he missed it completely.

I suddenly felt a wave of weakness sweep over me. That could easily have been me. I too wanted to move ahead. I too wanted to run. I too almost let fear take me into the jaws of what would in fact be my worst fear.

A prudent man sees danger and takes refuge, but the simple keep going and suffer for it.

Proverbs 22: 3

....

Prayer: My refuge is in You, Lord; not in my own ideas of what is "safe" and "right". Thank you for teaching me daily to depend on You.

Ask yourself: Is there anyone you would trust with your life?

A Sudden Storm

The raindrops which had begun yesterday, today gathered in intensity and soon broke out into a full-fledged storm. The ash I was walking through was soon turned into a muddy soup, turning my boots, and before long my whole body into a blackened mess.

I slipped and fell repeatedly, sapping me of energy with each passing hour. I searched desperately for a shelter of some kind, but the bush fire had done its work well; there was nothing but burned out stumps for as far as I could see in any direction. I tried to think of alternatives, but nothing came to mind. Like it or not, I was in the midst of a storm, and there was nothing to do but keep walking. No need to hurry; just save your energy and find a pace that will carry you on. Think about something else.

My thoughts drifted to days past: to sunny days and nights filled with stars. I remembered the bush fire, and the lesson I had just learned about waiting on God. A clap of thunder brought me out of my reverie, and it dawned on me that I must have been walking for, how long? Hours, I suppose. And while the storm still raged all around me, I went back inside, to the part of myself that has a weather pattern all its own.

Thou wilt keep him in perfect peace, whose mind is stayed on thee : because he trusteth in thee. Trust ye in the LORD for ever: for in the LORD JEHOVAH is everlasting strength:

Isaiah 26: 2

Prayer: Lord I know there will always be storms in this life, and not always when there is shelter to which I can run. Teach me how to find that part of myself which is so in tune with You that nothing from the outside can find its way in.

Ask yourself: Have you ever had to endure something unpleasant by thinking of something else? Did it work?

January 22

Sudden Loss

With no place to camp, and my gear totally soaked by the storm, I walked on through the night, comforted by thoughts and prayers unaffected by what was going on around me. I can't say it was a pleasant night, exactly. The storm *was* still there, after all. No amount of ignoring it was going to take away the possibility of hypothermia setting in. But still, there was an overshadowing comfort throughout the night, as if God were telling me, "*This* is what life is all about. Not the things which assault you from the outside, but what *I* give you on the inside." And so the dawn broke over a blackened and muddy landscape. My stomach was empty, but my heart was full. I would like to say that, at that moment, the sun broke through the clouds, the music swelled and I ran onto a field of flowers, rejoicing all the way.

But what happened instead was much different. The trail had been cut into the side of a hill, and below me a small stream had transformed itself overnight into a raging torrent. I was watching my step, but suddenly and without warning, a whole section of the mountainside slipped and fell into the river, taking me with it. One moment I was walking steadily through the storm; the next, I was under water and fighting for my life.

Somehow I managed to get free of the backpack, which was pulling me under. I slammed into a half-submerged rock, clung to it with every ounce of strength I could muster, and finally pulled myself free, crawling away from the riverbank and collapsing from exhaustion.

> *Although the Lord gives you the bread of adversity and the water of affliction, your teachers will be hidden no more; with your own eyes you will see them. Whether you turn to the right or to the left, your ears will hear a voice behind you, saying, "This is the way; walk in it."*
>
> Isaiah 30: 20 – 21

....

Prayer: Father I know that every day can't be like the movies, with all problems resolved and all faces smiling. But keep reminding me that real life is the life I have with You, regardless of what the world gives me. Keep my soul at peace today.

Ask yourself: What is the source of your peace? Is it the things you possess, or is there something else which cannot be removed from you?

Hunger

I don't know how long I lay face down in the mud, my mind conflicted with the supreme relief of escape from that raging river coupled with a growing sense of absolute despair. My back pack was gone, and with it everything that I had so recently judged to be the barest essentials necessary for this trip. My clothes were wet and muddy, as was my whole body, and I was shivering uncontrollably. But the one sensation that seemed to demand my total concentration came from my stomach. I couldn't remember when I had last eaten, but it must have been yesterday... or the day before.

What I was feeling was more than the craving one gets just before mealtime; my body was screaming at me, "You're going to *die* if you don't eat something soon." Lifting my head and looking around, I could see that food was not an option for the foreseeable future. I lay back down and tried to formulate a plan, but nothing would come. All I could think about was my hunger. Maybe today I might tend to forgive Esau for giving up his birthright for a bowl of stew. If I had a birthright to give, I'd sign it off in a heartbeat.

How could Jesus have gone forty days without eating? He's a better man than I am. And yet what was the first temptation Satan offered him? Food. Eating must have been at the top of Jesus' thoughts as well, else why would the master deceiver have been so quick to bring it up? A blessing and a curse. So wonderful to have food in abundance and yet so tragic when it's either missing or else over-partaken. The rest of the day, I lay there, thinking and praying, waiting for something.

The Israelites said to them, "If only we had died by the LORD's hand in Egypt! There we sat around pots of meat and ate all the food we wanted, but you have brought us out into this desert to starve this entire assembly to death."

Exodus 16: 3

Prayer: Father, how our lives revolve around food. The lack of it causes us to grumble and forsake even You; the overabundance of it leads us into excess and sin. I thank You today for my hunger, Lord, even while a part of me complains. Forgive me for my weakness, and use it for Your glory.

Ask yourself: How big a role does food play in your life? Would you be able to do without it for a time?

A Holy Fast

I must have slept. I was still aware of the sound of rushing water just below me, but it served less to distract and more to lull me into rest. In fact, it was the diminishing sound of the torrent that finally woke me, sometime in the afternoon. The flood had subsided, and the river that had so nearly taken my life was now no more than a smiling trickle finding its way through a narrow gorge. The sun was shining through patches of blue in the sky, and when I sat up I saw that my clothes were steaming, the water being pulled inexorably away and leaving me somewhat dryer than before.

My stomach still ached with hunger, but the sunshine was enough to get me to my feet. The trail was easy enough to see: with no trees or shrubs in the way, I could see it winding ahead for miles, following the course of the creek bed. There was really nothing else to do but walk. With nothing on my back and nothing in my stomach, I turned and started moving, uncertain and stumbling at first but gradually finding a pace which I could maintain. As I walked, my thoughts went back to the events of the past few days: the fear, the panic, the loss, the hope.

What does a person think about when fasting? Food, of course; but there does come a point when it shrinks in significance and other thoughts begin to come into focus. I guess I've thought about these things before, but now somehow, they seem more crisp, more real than ever before. Things like my reason for taking this journey, and what waits at the end. I didn't choose this time to fast, but as long as it's been forced upon me, I might as well take advantage of the fact. It's going to be a good day.

When you fast, do not look somber as the hypocrites do, for they disfigure their faces to show men they are fasting. I tell you the truth, they have received their reward in full.

Matthew 6: 16

Prayer: For someone who loves food as I do, Lord, it's hard not to equate fasting with suffering. But help me see beyond the physical cravings today and look upon Your face.

Ask yourself: What do you think about fasting?

Restoration

Today passed like a dream, and yet unlike any dream I've ever had. The landscape around me was blackened by the bushfire, but my day was filled with color. My stomach kept reminding me that it was empty, but my heart reminded me that it was full: full of the Presence of my Lord. And for the day, that was more than enough. I walked, and with each step I was aware of God's presence by my side.

I wonder if this was how Adam felt when he walked with his Creator in the cool of the evening through the Garden? This was certainly no Garden; not anymore. But for me it was the most beautiful place in the world. I spoke about things that were important to me: things I wanted to do, and know and understand. But more importantly, I *listened*. I heard things I had never heard before. Things like what I had done, and what I already understood. Things which were infinitely more significant than any landscape or empty stomach.

I felt like I could walk this way forever, and actually felt a pang of regret when I noticed than the sun was going down behind the mountain. I knew that our walk was nearly finished for the day. Finally I sat down and looked at the river as it carried away the remnants of the fire, restoring the land to the way it was. Ashes, burnt sticks and leaves were being washed downstream, leaving behind the clear life-giving water which would coax new growth upon the land.

And there, hanging on a snag beside the riverbank, was my backpack. I guess it had been there all day, because the sun had dried it and left it in nearly as good a shape as the day I first hoisted in on my back. Removing it from the branch which had caught it, I carried it back up to the trail and opened the flaps. There were my "essential essentials", not the least of which was a packet of dehydrated meat and potatoes. What I needed now was fire and water to make a meal fit for a king. I almost laughed as I realized that the two things I needed most were the two things that had nearly killed me: fire and water. The pack produced some waterproofed matches and the stream provided the water.

That evening I sat and thoroughly enjoyed the blessing of food, followed by the unspeakable gift of a dry sleeping bag and a night full of stars.

And in their prayers for you their hearts will go out to you, because of the surpassing grace God has given you. Thanks be to God for his indescribable gift!
II Corinthians 9: 14 – 15

Prayer: How easily we go from despair to joy and back again! Tonight I'm filled, and my joy is complete. Tomorrow may find me again in want, but may my joy never be lacking. You are my Provider, my Strength, my All.

Ask yourself: Paul said he could be content in any situation. Could the same be said of you?

January 26

Homesick

So much has happened in the past few weeks, it's hard to believe it hasn't been years since I hoisted this back pack and left the trailhead. There's been a gauntlet of emotions and today is definitely on the "high" side. I'm alive, my stomach is full and I'm moving forward. If only there was someone to tell. It's been rather surprising to find the trail so deserted. Except for the crazy fellow who met his unfortunate end in the bush fire, I've had no opportunity to talk with anyone. My mind drifts back to home, and hours spent with no other purpose than to share stories. "How was your day?" "What's up?" "Wait til you hear this!"

I guess I never really appreciated the fact that one of the true joys of "home" is that it gives a person a chance to share. Even the trivial things of a person's day can become significant if we can't communicate them with someone who will listen. My family has today become one of the most precious blessings I know. A part of me sorely wants to turn around, give up this quest and go home, if for no other reason than for the chance to tell them about what has happened.

But I know that's not possible, not now. Since I made the decision to take this journey, "home" has taken on a new meaning. I still have loved ones, and I miss them terribly, but I'm striving now for a better kind of home, and a better way of relating to those I love. From the deepest reaches of my heart, I hope that the rest of my family will make the decision to take this journey as well. When that happens, then we will be united in a common goal, led by One Who loves us more than we love ourselves, and Who promises a home like nothing I have yet experienced.

But the one unchanging truth is that every individual must make the decision alone; I can't make it for them, as much as I would love to. It's a risk, to be sure: to leave what I knew for something which is as yet a mystery, but which promises so much more. It's a risk I'm willing to take, but it doesn't alleviate the pain I feel today.

"I tell you the truth," Jesus said to them, "no one who has left home or wife or brothers or parents or children for the sake of the kingdom of God will fail to receive many times as much in this age and, in the age to come, eternal life."
Luke 18: 29 – 30

....

Prayer: Lord I miss my family today: those who don't share my passion to know You better. Please watch over them; and while I know that You will never take away their freedom to choose for the sake of their salvation, I pray that by some means they will come to know You as Lord and Savior. Make for us a real family, united in our love for You and for one another.

Ask yourself: Are you close to your family? How is your walk with God affected by your relation with them?

January 27

A Brother

As the excitement of the past few days began to wane, and thoughts of home and family occupied more of my waking thoughts, a kind of melancholy settled over the trail. Every new vista, every field of flowers served only to remind me that there was no one with whom I could share the joy of the moment. Just to be able to say, "Wow! Look at that!" would be for me right now the highest joy I could know.

I remember a man I saw at an amusement park one day. I had taken the kids there for a Saturday outing, and was frankly feeling a little put upon, that I had to blow the whole day on Dumbo and cotton candy. Then I saw a man walking by with a sack of popcorn in one hand and nothing in the other. The first thought that came to mind was, "What in the world is he doing here by himself?" followed by another, less charitable thought: "I wonder if he's up to no good?" Watching him wander along, though, I began to understand that he was simply a man alone, looking for a relaxing day in the sunshine. But rather than envy him for his freedom, I started to feel a genuine sympathy for him, that he had no one with whom to share amusement park moments.

Today I felt what I imagine that man must have felt: loneliness, followed by self-pity. Why do I have to do this alone? Why can't we at least be sent out in pairs? Even as I was beginning to wallow, I came upon a huge oak tree whose shade covered a large section of the trail. And there, sitting on a rock with his back against the tree was an old man. Maybe any other day I might have given him a casual nod and proceeded on; but not today, not now.

"Hello," I said, trying to hide my excitement at the opportunity to greet someone.

"Which way are you going?"

"Same direction you are," he said with a smile. "Stop and sit a spell."

A cheerful look brings joy to the heart, and good news gives health to the bones.
                                                                    Proverbs 15: 28

....

Prayer: Lord, my heart goes out to the lonely. Please reveal Yourself to them, and assure them that they are never truly alone. Give them friends and family with whom they can share life's joys and life's burdens. Bless them.

Ask yourself: Do you know a lonely person today? How could you help that person?

January 28

Conversation

Without even thinking about it, I slipped off my back pack and settled on the ground in front of the old man. "So, where have you come from?" I asked him, desperate for conversation. He looked back in the direction I had come, and smiled. "Oh, from farther back than you, I suspect. But this is my first time on this stretch, too." Seeing my confusion, he added, "No one walks this path more than once, but we can learn a lot from the ones before."

"Like what?" I asked, brimming with excitement. "I feel like there's so much I need to learn, but I don't know how to find out."

The old man laughed, a soft gentle whisper that came from his very soul. "Well, you'll enjoy Rendezvous, then. Lot's of good stuff there."

"Rendezvous?" I asked. This was a new term. "What does that mean?"

He looked at me with an intensity that bore deep. "No one can go far on this trail without it. There's lots of hazards along the way; and from the look of you, I'd say you've already met one or two." Suddenly I was aware of what I must look like. I squirmed a little and looked away.

"Don't be ashamed of the mud and the blood, son. It happens to all of us. That's why we need each other. That's what Rendezvous is all about. Fellow travelers coming together to swap stories, re-outfit, look up old friends. You'll love it, that's for sure."

"It sounds terrific," I said. "How do I get there?"

"Just keep going the way you're going, and you can't miss it. When you get there, tell them Charlie's on his way."

I realized I had stood to go, assuming he was coming with me. "Oh no," he laughed, as if reading my mind. "You go your pace and I'll go mine. Just stay on the trail and we'll meet up father along."

I turned back for one last look before disappearing into the trees. He was still there, moving slowly, with a slight limp, I now noticed. Strange. We hardly spent any time together at all, but already he seems like.. what? A father? Grandfather? Brother? Maybe all of those things. Maybe something altogether different.

"Who is my mother, and who are my brothers?" And stretching out his hand toward his disciples, he said, "Here are my mother and my brothers. For whoever does the will of my Father in heaven is my brother, and sister, and mother."
Matthew 12: 46 – 50

....

Prayer: Thank you for family, for those who bore me and raised me, and for those who by our shared faith are counted as brothers and sisters. Bless our family, wherever they may be, and help me to help them reach the prize that awaits them.

Ask yourself: Do you have brothers or sisters? How are they different from friends?

January 29

An Evil Presence

I camped early last night, hoping Charlie might catch up and spend the evening with me. I wonder if I'll meet more like him at Rendezvous? And what is that, anyway? I started out before the sun had even cleared the treetops, hoping I suppose for something special today. I found it, but not at all what I was imagining.

I saw him from a long way off: the figure of a man, moving toward me. That was strange; I didn't think anyone walked the opposite direction on this trail. Never mind, it was another person, and after meeting Charlie, I was looking forward to another conversation. As the distance between us grew shorter, I began to notice things which seemed out of place. He didn't carry a back pack, but he walked with a stoop, as if holding something heavy. He kept his face to the ground without once looking up, and for awhile I wondered if he even knew I was approaching. Suddenly from behind me, far off in the forest, I heard the high-pitched cry of a mountain lion. I jumped and looked back, then turned around to see that the stranger had come closer – much closer. He had stopped, and lifted his head as if to listen. I saw his face then, and felt a cold chill. He was smiling, but it wasn't the kind of smile you give a stranger on the trail. It seemed to say, "I know something you don't." I called out, "Did you hear that?"

He said nothing, just stood there and kept smiling. It was an awkward moment, so I tried again. "Which way are you going?" Stupid question, and the expression on his face confirmed it. It was becoming apparent that he didn't intend speaking, so I started to move on. He remained firmly planted, his eyes burning their way into me, and that smile never changing. "See you,"

I half mumbled, then realized that was a stupid thing to say as well, since we seemed to be going in opposite directions. I stepped off the trail to get around him, and as I cinched up my back pack to move on, I heard him say, almost in a whisper, "See you." Was he mimicking me? Was that an attempt at civility? I turned to speak, and... he was gone. The trail was empty as far as I could see, and there was no place for him to hide. Suddenly, I felt a surge of adrenalin and a heartfelt desire to use it. I moved quickly down the trail, looking over my shoulder every few steps. Tonight the clouds cover the stars and it seems darker than it's ever been. What did he mean by "See you."? That's the last thing I want.

Be self-controlled and alert. Your enemy the devil prowls around like a roaring lion looking for someone to devour. Resist him, standing firm in the faith, because you know that your brothers throughout the world are undergoing the same kind of sufferings.

I Peter 5: 8 – 9

Prayer: Lord, You never promised us a journey free of danger; only that You would stay with us. I need that Presence now, more than ever. Surround me with Your protection and hold me in Your strong Hand. Help me to be brave.

Ask yourself: When was the last time you were truly afraid? What happened?

January 30

The Morning Light

It was good to feel the sunshine on my sleeping bag this morning. I had lain awake most of the night, imagining sounds and creating scenarios in my mind. What if the stranger, whom I can only think of as the Evil Man, came into the camp? Would I try to hide the terror I felt, or would I just run away into the darkness? What if the mountain lion showed up again? For awhile I sat up and stared into the blackness beyond the fire light; then in total exhaustion I laid down, covering my head with my jacket, as if that would offer some form of protection. When I finally got to sleep, it was only to dream of shadows and evil smiles.

Awakening later than usual, I sat up and looked around the camp. Everything was in its place, and even the trees around me that had conjured up such horrific imaginings during the night now seemed like nothing more than a source of firewood, or a place to hang my back pack. I set about to make breakfast, smiling as I realized I was trying hopelessly to whistle a tune, and frowning to see my hands shaking. Whoever, whatever I had met yesterday, was now nothing more than a bad memory. Something to talk about. A wave of longing swept over me: an aching desire to have someone to talk to. The sun helps dispels my fear; a friend would do even more. What is it about those two things that drive the evil from my mind? The sun gives me light, and helps me see exactly what is and what is not Out There. I'm going to appreciate walking in the sunshine today. Seeing. Knowing. Feeling the warmth. A friend would give me what this journal does: a chance to express my fear and my hope. And a friend would do what no book could ever do: talk back to me. Feel my fear. Share my hope. Add to my strength. Where are you, Charlie?

Do not forsake your friend and the friend of your father, and do not go to your brother's house when disaster strikes you—better a neighbor nearby than a brother far away.

Proverbs 27: 10

Prayer: Thank you for friendship, and for the strength that comes from shared experiences. Send me a friend today, and let us discover the possibilities we never knew alone.

Ask yourself: Do you have a friend? How has your friend helped you? How have you helped your friend?

A Cord of Three Strands

Another uneventful day in the sunshine, with time to think about friends. I made a list in my mind of friends I had known over the years, and tried to place them into categories. There were the jocks: guys who may not have been the sharpest tools in the shed, but were guys you could count on in a scrape. Now that I thought of it, just having them around seemed to *guarantee* a scrape.

Then there were the thinkers: the ones who love nothing better than sitting around anything from campfires to coffee tables and say, "You know what I think?" and then expound for hours on a topic of interest. At least it's interesting to *them*. And so the list went on: jokers, worriers, fixers and mascots.

All in all, I believe I had a better than average roll call of guys who I could count as friends. Then I began to imagine having them on this trip with me, and how that would be. I sure could have used the jocks the other night, although a nagging doubt persists that even they might not have been able to go toe to toe with the evil man. The jokers would have made light of the situation; the thinkers would have analyzed till morning, and I'm afraid the mascots would have deserted me.

The more I thought, the more I understood that none of my past friends would have been a lot of help on this trip, for the simple reason that none of us share what has now become my life's greatest joy: that relationship with *Him*. Knowing that has made what I read today even more meaningful: "A cord of three strands is not easily broken." Until now, I would have said something like "Two is better than one," and pat my friend on the back. Now I see that there's a third element which gives the first two their real strength.

My instant friendship with Charlie the other day was possible because he and I share that third strand already. My friends back home, as great as they are, will never have that kind of resiliency until the third and final strand is woven in place. I spent the rest of the day thinking of my friends, and praying that they will come to know *Him*.

Though one may be overpowered, two can defend themselves. A cord of three strands is not quickly broken.

Ecclesiastes 4: 12

....

Prayer: Please help my friends today. Knowing them has helped make me who I am, and I appreciate them. But something's missing in their lives, and until they find it, we will never be as close as You intended us to be.

Ask yourself: What is the third strand of a strong and lasting friendship?

Another Cord

I was still thinking about my friends as I walked this morning when a sinking feeling settled into my soul. I had not yet considered the one who I would like to think is the best friend of all: my loving wife. More than all my friends, she knows me for who I really am. She's seen me at my best, and I'm embarrassed to recall, at my absolute worst. Even when I'm able to keep up a confident front with my friends and bosses, when I come home at night and close the door, the masquerade ends. And she's there to share it, loving me in spite of myself.

Why then am I out here, devoting my life to this journey, without her? I did ask her to come with me, and though she tried to understand, she just couldn't leave everything behind. I can't blame her, really; anyone who has not felt that call which pierced my heart and set me on this path would think it a foolish endeavor indeed. She promised to listen for the call, and in the meantime to wait faithfully... at home. I miss her terribly, but I keep thinking about that three-stranded cord. As long as she and I weave together the individual cords we brought into our relationship, our strength will only be the sum of our two parts. It's that third part that gives the other two their beauty and invincibility. My heart aches for her, and for my children. What could I have done to help them see and understand what is happening inside me? What have I failed to do as a father? As a husband? My thoughts torture me when I recall missed opportunities with my family. And yet I know that He loves them just as He loves me. He will not forget them nor forsake them. I know that He will not force them onto this journey; that's not His way. But I find strength today to carry on, confident that they too will some day know what I know. Until then, Lord, give me strength.

Believe in the Lord Jesus, and you will be saved, you and your household." And they spoke the word of the Lord to him and to all that were in his house. And he took them the same hour of the night, and washed their wounds, and he was baptized at once, with all his family.

Acts 16: 31 – 33

Prayer: Forgive me when I did not use the opportunities I had to share Your precious love with my family. May they not be condemned because of my sin. Speak to them, Father. Help them to see, and know how much You love them. Rescue them, and make our home a place where You reign.

Ask yourself: Can you talk to your family about matters of faith? Why or why not?

February 2

A Ruin Discovered

Today I started a long, slow climb to the top of a ridge. At least a dozen times, the trail switched back, each time carrying me higher above the valley floor. At the top of the ridge stood a huge outcropping of boulders which reminded me of some ancient castle, looking over a king's domain. My progress was slow, but steady, and I estimated that I could make it to the top before darkness fell, perhaps finding a shelter among the rocks for the night.

Early in the afternoon, I stopped to rest at a place where an enormous stone sat squarely in the middle of the path. It provided an excellent table for an extended coffee break, and I gratefully spread out a few things from my bag. Leaning back with my feet propped up and a warm cup of coffee in my hand, I marveled at the rock: how it seemed almost man made in it's conformity. Then as I looked closer, I noticed what looked like chisel marks all over the rock's surface. Indeed, it was man made: a huge rock which could only have been quarried for use in a wall. Standing to my feet, I looked again at the outcropping of rock that towered above me, and realized that it was not natural, at least not completely. In between the spires and boulders, crafted stones had been set into place, resulting in a buttress which from my position seemed invincible. But if it were, then what was this stone doing down here?

My curiosity piqued, I quickly repacked my gear and continued up the trail, looking for different angles from which to examine the summit. With each switchback, the stones in the wall above grew in clarity and size. It was a fortress, all right, but one which had fallen into disrepair. I wondered who could have built it, and how long it had been there? Ironic, I thought as I strained to reach the top before nightfall. For weeks now, I've been passing the most awesome natural monuments imaginable without much thought given to them. Now, when I find something man made among them, I'm desperate to know of their origins. Why was I not so moved at the sight of the mountain itself? Or the waterfall I saw from a distance? Is it because I am man, that I'm drawn to what men have built, ignoring the far more impressive creations upon which they stand? May I never be so blind.

Since they show no regard for the works of the LORD and what his hands have done, he will tear them down and never build them up again.

Psalms 28: 5

Prayer: Father of all creation, give me an ear to hear the heavens, and eyes to see Your handiwork. Show me anew the wonders of Your world, and let me imagine those things which I cannot yet see. Praise You for Your wonderful works!

Ask yourself: What is the most awesome natural sight you have seen?

A Battle Scene

As the trail climbed higher, the rubble increased, more evidence of destruction. Some of the stones were blackened as if by fire, and some had been smashed, either by the fall from above, or else by whatever caused them to fall in the first place. Large sections of the wall were still in place, but the mountains of debris attested to a past glory. Reaching the top most part of the ridge, I could see that the fortress had straddled both sides of the mountain, commanding a view in all directions.

I looked for a way to get inside the ruin. Moving around the perimeter, I came at last upon a watch tower that still stood, as if looking over the remains. Skeletal woodwork on the top told me that it used to be covered by roof, now burned away. Along one side of the tower, a wall still clung defiantly, strengthened by one side of what used to be an enormous gate. Pieces of charred wood and metal work lay scattered about, and picking my way through it I found myself inside the fortress compound.

There was not much to see; weeds had covered most of the bare ground except for places where stacked stone reached upward as if trying to rebuild itself without human help. Turning around from a point roughly in the centre of the courtyard, I tried to imagine how it must have felt, thinking I was in a secure place and yet seeing the walls falling around me and the gate disappearing in a firestorm. A sudden pity swept over me for the inhabitants of this place. Who were they, and what brought them to this day of defeat and death? And what of the invaders? Were they righteous warriors, bringing justice to a defiant foe, or were they evil men, intent on evil ways?

Could war ever be that simple? I slept there, in the centre of the compound, thinking of the men who fought and died here, and prayed for wisdom.

Rescue me, O LORD, from evil men; protect me from men of violence, who devise evil plans in their hearts and stir up war every day. They make their tongues as sharp as a serpent's; the poison of vipers is on their lips. Selah.

Psalms 140: 1 – 3

Prayer: I lift up those in harm's way, Father. Have mercy on them all. If their cause is just, then surround them with Your might and protection, and give them victory. May peace prevail on earth until the coming of Your kingdom, when all enemies are vanquished forever.

Ask yourself: Where is there a war being waged today? How can you pray concerning that war?

Reading the Past

This morning, I started to pack my gear and move on, away from this place of death and destruction. Suddenly, a crack of thunder invaded my senses, throwing me backwards and onto the ground. I looked up and saw the remains of the wooden roof atop the watchtower flying in all directions, like the star burst of a fireworks display. Another flash of lightening crackled across the sky above my head, the accompanying boom preceded by a high-pitch sizzling sound, the understated testimony of its nearness. I knew I had to find shelter soon. Looking around quickly for a place of escape, I spotted a pile of rubble and made a dash for it, in hopes of finding a place large enough to squeeze inside.

On my hands and knees, I crawled under the debris, even as hail stones began striking my exposed legs. My back pack prevented me from going farther, and I struggled to remove it. Bouncing up and down, trying to get free of the straps, I heard another sound which I thought was the crackling of another nearby lightening strike. But as the sound continued, I realized it was coming from underneath me: the sound of splitting wood. A sudden silence was accompanied by the sensation of falling, and I landed heavily on a stone floor about six feet down.

Lying beside me was the skeleton of a man, his arms and legs pulled underneath him in a fetal position. A few rays of light came into the space where I lay, revealing what must have been a basement room. I looked up and saw the hole I had fallen through, the rotted remains of a wooden floor. Apparently this room had escaped both the invader and the fire, but proved ultimately to be the tomb of the poor soul trapped here. I looked around. The room extended about ten feet in each direction, with the remains of a stairway at one end, hopelessly covered in rubble. Wooden barrels lined the opposite wall, I suppose containing at one time a store of food and wine. Enough to keep this fellow alive for awhile, anyway. One had been set against the wall on the right, directly beneath a tiny opening which permitted a shaft of light. On the barrel was a book, and next to it an ink pen, long since dried up.

Opening the book carefully, I saw that it was a journal, much like my own, separated into days and weeks. The storm outside was showing no signs of abating, and this seemed to be a safe enough shelter, so I sat with my back to wall, just as the book's author must have done. I positioned myself so the light came over my shoulder and began reading.

However many years a man may live, let him enjoy them all. But let him remember the days of darkness, for they will be many. Everything to come is meaningless.

Ecclesiastes 11: 8

....

Prayer: Lord I know my life is short; teach me to learn from those who have gone before me. May I in turn be a source of instruction for those who follow.

Ask yourself: Do you keep a diary? Would you like your children and their children to read what you have written in it?

February 5

An Eyewitness

From reading his account, I soon learned that the man had been a traveler like myself. He had begun his journey at the same place where I had started, and many of the things he described I recognized from my own experiences. However, he seemed to wander off the trail from time to time, and whole days would go by with no journal entries. Finally, his daily reports ceased altogether, as if the whole idea had been abandoned... until I turned to the next page.

From that entry on, the days were recorded faithfully, sometimes several accounts recorded in a single day. Now, it was obvious that I was reading the words of a man with nothing else to do but write: a man trapped in the rubble of a forgotten cellar. I began to piece together the events which had led to this place of death. From one page, in his words:

"How could I forget the day I met my two companions? It was there that fate and circumstance led us to this forsaken mountaintop. But who would condemn us? We were drawn together at once by a common bond: that irreducible terror of *him* and those who follow his counsel. As three, we reasoned, survival might be possible, and we therefore made a pact between us that we would commit ourselves to the defense, not only of our individual selves, but to the union which we had forged that day. By night, two would sleep while one stood guard. By day, our eyes and our weapons were turned in every direction, ready to stand back to back if need be, for that was our only hope.

Then our pilgrimage brought us to this high vantage, and we said to ourselves, *this* is at last a place of safety. *He* can never touch us here. We set to, and soon were joined by others: the lost and terror stricken who were only too willing to come under our authority and bend their backs to the tasks. This, we all felt, was our only recourse. Some foolish ones gave up the cause and moved on, either up the trail or down, as their fears led them. We never saw them again. Still others passed by and urged us to move on with them toward the goal which in the beginning we also sought. But we would not venture beyond the rising walls, for behind them we knew was our salvation. If only we had known the depths of our ignorance."

While people are saying, "Peace and safety," destruction will come on them suddenly, as labor pains on a pregnant woman, and they will not escape.
I Thessalonians 5: 3

....

Prayer: Lord, I look to You alone for my safety and my salvation. I know that all others will fail me, and that there is nothing I can build which will stand against the enemy of this world. Surround me now, with Your mighty army. Let me move with them toward the place You have prepared for me.

Ask yourself: In a world full of danger, how do you protect yourself?

February 6

The Fellowship of Fear

Reading through this poor soul's journal, I was drawn on one hand to his transparent foolishness: that he believed his own security could only come from the alliances he had built with other frightened men. But even as I scoffed, a chill ascended up my spine like the rising waters of the flood I had only recently experienced. The man's talk of *Him* sounded all too familiar. Was it possible that he was driven to this mountaintop by the same faceless terror which I too had met? This fortress had stood ages ago; surely every foe that had made its way into the courtyard outside was now long since dead and buried.

Unless... unless that foe was not human, and so not subject to the frailty of humanity. I pulled my collar around me as the chill reached my trembling jaw. The storm outside had moved on, but in the silence that followed it I felt a fear which went much deeper. Night was coming on, and I had no intention of leaving this shelter. Not now. I read on:

"Work on the walls progressed with an intensity that only driven men can maintain. Fortunately, there were a few among us who knew enough about masonry to advise the rest, and soon a proper fortress was rising out of the rocky peak. We took heart in our labors, and even began to relax and enjoy the camaraderie of a shared burden. Some evenings we sang together, and shared stories of our youth. The laughter was almost as infectious as our fear, and it wasn't long before we all felt a bravado that approached nationalistic proportions. We even began to turn some travelers away: those whom we felt were not "good enough" to join our ranks. We had built this pinnacle with our blood and sweat, and did not intend to share it lightly. A flag was soon devised, and seeing it unfurled above the watchtower was the proudest moment of my life. We will survive, I convinced myself. We will endure."

...and the king said, "Is not this great Babylon, which I have built by my mighty power as a royal residence and for the glory of my majesty?" While the words were still in the king's mouth, there fell a voice from heaven, O King Nebuchadnezzar, to you it is spoken: The kingdom has departed from you.

Daniel 4: 30 – 31

Prayer: Lord, may I never forget the folly of my own making. Remind me again today that You are the strength of my hands and without You I could do nothing. Let pride never rule my thoughts or my words, but let a humble spirit keep me in Your perfect will.

Ask yourself: What is the difference between selfish pride and the pride of a job well done?

The Pinnacle of Pride

Throughout the day, I sat in the cellar and read the diary of this fellow traveler who had ended his journey in darkness and hunger. I still felt an inexpressible fear of venturing back outside, but gradually that was being replaced by an irresistible urge to leave this place. That sensation was transformed into urgency as I read his next to last entry:

"The walls were complete, the gate was set and locked, inside, we congratulated one another on our achievements. Awards were granted all around. No one asked to come inside our fellowship anymore, for no one would dare to venture within our realm. We were all-powerful, and we knew it. There was no force that could overwhelm us, no foreign power which could stand before our might. Why, this place was the finest that ever existed! We ridiculed our own former ignorance, that we would have imagined any other journey's end as superior to *our* pinnacle, *our* kingdom.

"In fact, we said, why not let it be known that this place is worthy of any pilgrim's journey? Who would be so foolish as to suffer any further affliction when here stands before him the ultimate goal? Come! we said. Come and pay homage to us. Bring your tribute to our gates and bow in our presence. We are your Caesar!

"That very song was on our lips, the night we heard the approach of the evil one."

But God said to him, 'Fool! This night your soul is required of you; and the things you have prepared, whose will they be?' So is he who lays up treasure for himself, and is not rich toward God."

Luke 12: 20 – 21

....

Prayer: Lord, I confess to dependence upon things which will not save me. Help me understand that my only hope, my only chance at real joy is with You. If there are things which lead me into a false sense of pride, then please remove them from me, and keep me wholly Yours.

Ask yourself: Have you known of a wealthy person who was truly happy? How many have you heard about who ended their lives in misery?

February 8

Destruction

There was no longer any doubt in my mind: this had never been a place of safety, nor was it now. I had to move on, without a moment to spare. But I couldn't leave until I read the traveler's last entry. My hands trembled, as if I were in the presence of a dying man instead of one long since passed. But his words carried a familiar freshness to them, which the years had not diminished. As if I were opening an account of yesterday's news, I bit my lip and read:

"It began as a high pitched scream from somewhere in the valley below. At first we thought it was a pilgrim being ripped limb from limb. But as the sound continued, we realized that we were not hearing the screams of a victim, but of a destroyer. The gates were locked and bolted. Every man took his place on the wall, weapon in hand. Here was the moment for which we had prepared. Now would come the true test of our mettle. Someone had dared to challenge our authority, and that challenge would be answered. In our banter back and forth along the wall, we expressed a confidence that none of us felt, not with that gut-wrenching sound approaching. Surely the walls would hold. Surely our labor had not been in vain. Surely...

"The end came so swiftly we never even saw our enemy. The walls were down before the alarm went up. Those massive gates, the pride of our city, were consumed in an instant by the fires of hell itself. All the bravado I had pretended melted before the flames. Throwing my weapon to the ground, I ran, looking for some place, *any* place that would hide me from *him*. I found my way into this cellar just as the building above collapsed. Huddling behind the barrels of stores which would cruelly keep me alive through weeks of regret, I listened to the sounds of the dying. It continued through the night, and by the next morning all I heard was the sound of feasting. Well, I shall feast as well. Surrounded as I am with food and wine fit for a king, I shall live out my days in royal splendor, my kingdom all that my eyes take in. If only..."

Because they hated knowledge and did not choose the fear of the LORD , and would have none of my counsel, and despised all my reproof, therefore they shall eat the fruit of their way and be sated with their own devices. For the simple are killed by their turning away, and the complacence of fools destroys them; but he who listens to me will dwell secure and will be at ease, without dread of evil.
Proverbs 1: 29 – 33

Prayer: God of all power, Ruler over all kingdoms on earth and in Heaven, I place myself on Your mercy. I know that true victory will only be found within Your ranks. Put to shame all the intentions of the enemy of this world upon Your people, and restore Your kingdom in my lifetime.

Ask yourself: Can you think any great monuments that have fallen? What does their destruction tell you?

Moving On

I stood this morning at the ruins of the gate, trying to imagine the onslaught which condemned every defender to a horrible death save one: the one who lived to reflect upon his folly and whose journal I now carried in my back pack. A soft rain was falling and I heard thunder in the distance, but the thought of shelter was the farthest thing from my mind. All I wanted to do was leave this place of fear and defiance and death.

"You see what happened, don't you?"

The voice from behind startled me, and I jumped. But even before I could turn to face the speaker I knew who it was and a flood of joy swept over me. "Charlie! It's good to see you! Yeah, I spent way too long here trying to piece it together. But it was worth it, if for no other reason than to give you time to catch up with me!" Charlie smiled and put a gnarled hand on my shoulder. I wasn't sure if he was trying to support himself or if he was lending me a strong hand. Somehow, I knew I was right on both counts.

"Have you ever seen anything like this?" I asked him.

"Too many times," he said, shaking his head sadly. "It's always the same; someone gets scared, then gets the idea that they'd be safer holed up instead of moving on. And the next thing you know... well, see for yourself."

"Charlie," I began, not sure how to put it. "Charlie, I have to ask you something that's been eating at me for a few days now. I've sat here in this rubble and re-lived a man's suffering and death, to the point where I feel physically *sick* now. But, well... this wasn't the Rendezvous, was it?"

Charlie's soft laughter was music to my ears. "Not by a long shot, son. No way. If you don't mind keeping an old man company, I can have you there by lunchtime. I'll even introduce you."

I myself will gather the remnant of my flock out of all the countries where I have driven them and will bring them back to their pasture, where they will be fruitful and increase in number.

Jeremiah 23: 3

Prayer: Thank you, Lord, for a brother, and for a good word in times of discouragement. May I be like that in my old age. Grow me up in the knowledge and certainty of Your loving care.

Ask yourself: Do you know someone who gives you confidence? How do they accomplish that?

Rendezvous

It was a slow day, as far as walking was concerned. Charlie never complained, but I could see that every step caused him pain. I talked and listened to him all day, partly to help him keep his mind off his suffering, but mostly because he was such a wealth of information. As we moved along together, he told me about his decision as a young man to take up the journey, and about the trails he'd seen over the years. He talked about fellow travelers, and the things he had learned from them. He showed me scars of his own pilgrimage, and I could almost detect a kind of pride as he spoke of challenges met and overcome, and the things he had learned in the process. As the sun rose high overhead, I remembered his prediction.

"Charlie," I said, "if you've never been on this particular trail before, how did you know that we'd be there by lunchtime?"

He walked along for a few moments in silence, and I began to think that he hadn't heard me. But then he stopped and studied me for awhile before answering. "Well," he began, "I guess I could say that it's because I'm old and wise." I accepted that, and started to walk again, but he put his hand out to stop me. "But I have to say that in your case, there comes a time when you need to take your eyes off the trail and look up to the heavens."

I thought he was about to make a spiritual application, and I paused and looked up in concentration. There in front of me, not 100 yards away, a column of smoke rose above the trees. At first, the memory of the bush fire flashed across my mind, and I felt a surge of panic. But as I looked closer, I noticed that the smoke was rising in a thin column, the kind a campfire makes. Charlie had noticed it early this morning, and knew we were getting close. I had been so concerned with watching my feet and listening to his stories, I had never looked up. Slipping his back pack from his shoulders, I held it in one hand and smiled. "Come on, old man. Let's pick up the pace."

The glory of young men is their strength, but the beauty of old men is their gray hair.
Proverbs 20: 2

....

Prayer: Thank you for old people. Help me learn from them all that you have shown them. May their scars teach me what I have yet to learn. May I reach out to them in their weakness and learn true strength from their lives.

Ask yourself: Do you know an old person to whom you can be a friend?

February 11

A New Family

Coming into the clearing yesterday, the first thing that struck me was the complete reversal of what I had seen at the ruins. While the fortress threatened those who ventured near, this place seemed to invite any and all. There were no guards, no walls, no security checkpoints. And yet the feeling of comfort and safety was almost palpable as I approached the campfire. There was a smell of stew in the air, and it made my mouth water in anticipation. Charlie had already seen someone he knew, and was directing me toward the fire.

"Well if it's not old Charlie!" an elderly woman spoke up from a group of ladies intent on arranging the wood under a huge pot which was suspended over a bed of coals.

"It's good to see you, Lizzie," Charlie said with a wink and light kiss on her wrinkled cheek. "Does that tantalizing aroma have anything to do with you?"

"Now Charlie, flattery will get you anywhere! Pull up a stump and sit a spell. Who's this nice young man you've taken up with?"

I introduced myself, and when she started dishing up two bowls of stew, I hesitated. "That does smell delicious. Can I pay you for some?"

Lizzie hesitated, as if waiting for me to finish the joke, then laughed anyway.

"Charlie, I do believe you've brought us a newcomer! No one pays for food here. Of course, if you have something to add to the pot, then there will be plenty for the next hungry traveler who shows up." I was glad to be able to drop in a few dried vegetables from my bag, and sat back to the first hot meal I'd had in days.

"You'll be wanting to clean up over there," Lizzie said, pointing with her chin to a large tent on the edge of the clearing. "There's fresh clothes as well; take whatever you need and leave off anything you don't." The idea of clean clothes *and* a hot meal was almost too much to take in. Charlie must have seen the look on my face.

"Son," he said, "look around you: everyone you see has something in common with you. They've felt that call, and they've left everything to make this journey. We're family, you see. Lizzie there is my sister, even though I never knew her till I was... well, almost as old as I am now! You and me, now, we haven't known each other all that long, but I'm proud to call you my brother, and I'll hope you'll do the same with me."

"Nothing would make me happier, *Brother* Charlie," I beamed.

"Is that a fact now?" he said with a look over at Lizzie. "If that's the case, then I'd say this boy needs to get out more! Just wait till you've seen the rest of the place."

Let us hold fast the confession of our hope without wavering, for he who promised is faithful; and let us consider how to stir up one another to love and good works, not neglecting to meet together, as is the habit of some, but encouraging one another, and all the more as you see the Day drawing near.
Hebrews 10: 23 – 25

....

Prayer: Thank you, Jesus, for your Church. Thank you for the joy, the suffering and hope we all share. May we lift one another up daily, so that we can all stand as Body.

Ask yourself: How is a church different from a club?

February 12

The Clinic

With the smell of soap in my hair and the incomparable feel of a clean shirt on my back, I stepped out of the tent a new man. Charlie saw me and gave a long, low whistle. "I must say, you do scrub up well, young man! Come along; I'll show you around."

We walked through the camp, and everywhere we turned, groups of people were gathered. Some were playing games, others were engaged in serious discussion. One group was deep in prayer, surrounding a young woman who knelt on the grass, crying softly. "She's new to the trip," Charlie said in a low voice. "Her husband wouldn't come, and those folks are praying for the both of them."

I felt a tinge of pain as I recalled my own home, and the family I left. Charlie read my thoughts and gave my shoulder a squeeze. "Don't worry; we'll be remembering them, too. Let's stop here, first, though." He pointed to a white tent near the centre of camp. Over the entrance a sign read, "Clinic," and people were coming and going, some on crutches, some with bandages, some coughing and sneezing. "I always like to make this one of my first stops," said Charlie, "Especially at my age!"

We entered the tent together, and were greeted at once by a lady with a pencil protruding from a shock of graying hair tied precariously on top of her head.

"Well, hello Charlie!" she said with a warmth that took me back to my mother. "How's the trail treating you?"

"Oh I can't complain," he said. "But I would like to register a few concerns with the doctor." She smiled and led him back through a curtain, then returned.

"I don't believe we've seen you before, have we?" she asked. "What can we do for you?" Why is that nurses always say "we," when what they mean to say is "I" or "you"? Nurse We must have seen the grin on my face, and continued, "From the looks of you, I'd say a once over lightly with the doctor is about all you need, am I right?"

"That's right," I agreed. "Just a few aches and pains. Nothing major."

Eventually, Charlie and I found each other outside the clinic. I was sporting a new white bandage on my arm, and Charlie held a bottle of pills. We found a sleeping tent with space available, and settled in for a night's rest. Hot food, clean clothes, a change of bandages and great company. How could this place get any better?

Is any one among you suffering? Let him pray. Is any cheerful? Let him sing praise. Is any among you sick? Let him call for the elders of the church, and let them pray over him, anointing him with oil in the name of the Lord; and the prayer of faith will save the sick man, and the Lord will raise him up; and if he has committed sins, he will be forgiven.

James 5: 13 – 15

Prayer: Lord, I confess I don't like the pain and suffering we have to endure. But what a wonderful blessing, to experience Your healing at the hands of Your people! Thank you for allowing us this blessed privilege. Use me, Father, to bring Your healing power to those who so desperately need it.

Ask yourself: Can you remember someone who helped you when you were sick?

February 13

Training Day

My dreams carried me high above the clouds, to a place where the sun always shone and the breeze was soft and gentle. My body was weightless, and for the first time since I could remember, completely free of pain. I found I could soar through the air, and tried a few maneuvers just for fun. A billowy cloud drifted below me, and I dove down, luxuriating in its warmth and the faint scent of... coffee? Gradually, the cloud enveloping me became my pillow, even more inviting than the dream had been. The scent of coffee was still in the air, though, and I finally could ignore it no longer. Cracking one eyelid, I could see Charlie sitting beside my bed, waiting patiently.

"Knew that would get you," he said, offering me a steaming mug. "Time to rise and shine, son. We got our work cut out for us today."

"Work?" I said. "What work?"

"The work of learning the trail, that's what work," he said with enthusiasm. "You didn't think I got this smart just by getting *old*, did you?"

After a hot shower and breakfast, we made our way to a place called the "Training Area". Several groups were already involved in things like packing and sorting, tying knots, building fires and reading maps. This looked like great fun, and I was anxious to get into it. Charlie said, "Okay, let's meet here when we break for lunch." He saw my confusion, and added, "I'll be going to a class of seniors; you're not quite ready for that, son," he said with a grin. "You'll be joining that group over there under the tree."

I said goodbye to Charlie and made my way to the "Foundations" group. I was surprised to find people of all ages. I guess Charlie was right: you don't get smart just by getting *old*. The leader of the Foundations Class was a middle-aged man by the name of Andy. He welcomed me into the group and handed me a shoelace. "Your job today," said Andy, "is to learn to tie this properly."

I thought he was joking. I'd been tying shoes all my life, and lacing boots every day since the beginning of this trip. I started to protest, but Andy went on, "Foundations are the most important part of anything worth doing. Everything else builds on what's below it. Tying shoelaces may seem pretty inconsequential right now, but I can tell you from experience, there are right ways and wrong ways to do it. Get it wrong, and you might suffer anything from a nasty fall to blisters."

I cringed at that, and paid attention. By the end of the day, my fingers ached from the repetitive motion of lacing and tying. But I can say this: I can't wait until tomorrow. I'll have the best-laced boots in camp.

Do your best to present yourself to God as one approved, a workman who does not need to be ashamed and who correctly handles the word of truth.
II Timothy 2: 15

....

Prayer: I'm reminded today, Father, that I am Your child, with a lot to learn and a long way to go before maturity. But praise You for Your desire to see me grow! Teach me today what I need to know.. Make me what You want me to be.

Ask yourself: Have you ever taught a child to do something? How did you go about it?

February 14

Solid Food

I even polished my boots this morning, the better to show off my perfectly tied laces. The New Trekkers were impressed, although I have to admit that their laces looked pretty good, too. We moved quickly through the rest of the classes, until by the end of the day I felt like I'd been through basic training at some military camp. I was confident, and ready for the trail, and said so to Andy as we made our way to supper. "So what comes next?" I asked. "Do I get to teach now?"

Andy grinned and patted me on the back. "That's the spirit!" he said. "Come next Rendezvous, I'll be looking for you to take over my class. There are a few more groups you might want to sit in on, though, before you leave here."

"Andy," I said, "I can tie my boots with the best of them. I can get across a raging river without getting wet and build a fire in a rainstorm. What else do I need to know?"

"Have you seen the Evil Man?" he asked softly.

I stopped and turned to face him. "Have you?" I asked, almost afraid to hear the answer.

"Yes, as well as some of those who side with him."

Suddenly, all thought of supper had disappeared. I wanted to know what Andy knew, and I wanted to know it now. A flood gate of emotions opened, and I started telling Andy about my encounter, and the terror I felt, and would he come again, and what about the ruins I had passed?

Andy laid a hand on my shoulder. "All in good time, Brother," he said. "Tomorrow, look for a man named Jonathan. He'll answer all your questions, and a few more besides." He turned, and we started again for the mess tent. "And don't forget to tie your boots properly," he added with a grin.

Behold, I send you out as sheep in the midst of wolves; so be wise as serpents and innocent as doves.

Matthew 10: 16

Prayer: Lord, I know there are wolves out there, and the thought scares me. But You know my weakness, and You've promised to be with me wherever I go. Teach me to live in this world as Your child.

Ask yourself: When did you first realize that the world was not as innocent and harmless as your childlike heart believed?

February 15

Armed for Battle

No one had to wake me this morning. I thrust a mug of coffee into Charlie's sleeping bag and headed out the door to find Jonathan, the one who would tell me about the Evil Man. I had to ask several people in the Training Area before I finally located his class. They were meeting on a hill overlooking the camp, and as I arrived and found a seat, he was telling the group, "Always seek the high ground. Your enemy will try and engage you when you're below him: in a valley, a depression in the trail, anywhere he can gain an advantage. His strength is in his power of deception. If he can convince you that you're defeated, he's won the battle."

I watched Jonathan as he spoke. He didn't use notes, and obviously didn't need them. The strength in his eyes and the scars on his face told me that he spoke from experience. I wanted to speak up: to ask him all the questions that were burning in me. But now, sitting in front of him, I couldn't open my mouth. He seemed to know my thoughts, and looked at me, those eyes boring all the way to the secrets of my heart. "You've met him, haven't you?" he asked. I nodded. "How did you feel?"

"Terrified," I whispered. "Confused. I felt like he knew something I didn't know, and that fact was going to hurt me."

Jonathan smiled, but not in a mocking way. "That's exactly what he wants you to believe. But he didn't touch you, did he?"

The question startled me. "No, but..."

"He doesn't have the authority to touch you; not unless you allow it." Jonathan turned to the group seated around him. "Remember this well: the Evil Man is vicious, but he's been put on a short leash. He *cannot* lay a hand on you." As he spoke, he placed two fingers along a ragged scar that ran across his cheek. "But that doesn't mean you won't get hurt. The Evil Man's been in this business a long time, and he knows all the tricks. He knows exactly how far he can go, and given the chance will go all the way to the end of the leash."

Breaking for lunch, I walked beside Jonathan as we started down the hill. Rude or not, I had to ask about the scar on his cheek. "Self-inflicted," he said quietly. "I thought I had him, and was feeling pretty cocky. Suddenly he was right there in my face. I pulled my weapon up to fend him away and cut myself. He's never let me forget it."

> *Then I heard a loud voice in heaven say: "Now have come the salvation and the power and the kingdom of our God, and the authority of his Christ. For the accuser of our brothers, who accuses them before our God day and night, has been hurled down.*
> Revelation 12: 10

Prayer: Lord help me endure the accusations of those who want to see me fail. For the times when I am innocent and falsely accused, may I be exonerated; for the times when I am guilty, may I be forgiven.

Ask yourself: When was the last time you were accused of something you didn't do? How did it make you feel?

February 16

Communion

There was an air of expectancy all over the camp today; it was time for the journey to continue. Sounds of packing up could be heard everywhere. One group of men were hauling down the hospital tent. Nurse We (I still had not learned her real name) was organizing medical supplies and placing them in boxes. I could see Jonathan on the hill top overlooking the clearing, obviously deep in prayer. "Well Charlie," I said, as I rolled up my sleeping bag, "I wonder what new things we're going to see today?"

Charlie was laying in his bed, staring quietly at the canvas ceiling. "Yep, son; I just wonder." He sat up, took a sip of the coffee I'd brought him, and turned to face me. "You've never been to a communion, have you?"

"I'm not sure," I said. "What is it, exactly?"

"Meet me over by the campfire in a few minutes. You'll see."

The smell of fresh bread was in the air. Andy met me with a huge grin and offered a seat. We seemed to be getting ready for a meal, but the atmosphere was something I'd never felt before. Joy mixed with overwhelming sadness. Jonathan made his way next to the fire and looked around at us. Taking a loaf of bread in his hands, I thought I could see tears in his eyes as he spoke. "Jesus, on the night He was betrayed, took a loaf of bread, broke it, and said, 'This is my body, broken for you. Eat this, and remember me'"

I almost gasped aloud as Jonathan broke the loaf into two parts and passed it among us. We each took a piece and, with a prayer of thanks, ate it in silence. After a few moments, Jonathan took a cup and held it up. "In the same way, Jesus took the cup and told His disciples, 'This is my blood, which is shed for you. Drink this, and remember me.'" The cup was passed in silence, each of us in our own thoughts, and yet at the same time closer to one another than I had ever felt. Jonathan stood up again and spoke. "Today we leave this place and continue the journey. Not all of us will have an opportunity to gather again like this. But this I do know: we will all meet again at the feet of the One we remember this morning; the One Who makes this journey possible, our Lord and Savior, Jesus Christ."

I looked around at the group which had become my family and said a prayer of thanksgiving for each of them. I saw Charlie and started to give him a word of encouragement, but his eyes were closed in prayer, his lips trembling and a single tear finding its way down his cheek.

For I received from the Lord what I also delivered to you, that the Lord Jesus on the night when he was betrayed took bread, and when he had given thanks, he broke it, and said, "This is my body which is for you. Do this in remembrance of me."
I Corinthians 11: 23 – 24

....

Prayer: Lord, help me never to forget what Your Son has done for us. Give me opportunity often to meet together with brothers and sisters to recall that time. Help me feel the pain, and the joy of that moment when Jesus laid down His life for me.

Ask yourself: What does Communion mean to you?

The Journey Continues

Little by little, the camp cleared out this morning, as Rendezvous came to an end. Some of the more energetic had left before daylight. Others were still packing and saying last minute goodbyes. I made my way back to the sleeping area to gather up my belongings and see if Charlie needed any help. I found him sitting on a log, his things still scattered around him." Hey Charlie," I called out. "Did you forget how to pack? We better get moving if we're going to get out of this valley by nightfall."

Charlie looked around the clearing at all the activity and smiled. "No, son, you go on. You'll make better time without me."

"Don't talk that way," I said, chiding him. "You said yourself it's not the distance as much as the direction that counts. We can move as slow as you want. Maybe we'll see some things I might have missed if I was going too fast."

Charlie sat silently for awhile, as if putting together what he wanted to say. Finally, he looked down at his feet and said softly, "Do you remember hearing something about 'early pickup'?"

I had, and I reacted immediately. "No! I mean, yes, I've heard of it. But that means... Charlie, that means if you die. What are you trying to tell me?"

"I'm not *trying* to tell you anything, son. I just said it. You go on ahead. I'll see you at the journey's end."

My backpack fell to the ground, and I fell to my knees with it. "Oh God, no. Not Charlie. Why?" I reached out and took his grizzled hands in mine. "I won't leave you, Charlie. I'll stay here, until..." My voice failed me, and I broke into sobs.

Charlie squeezed my hands and said, "You need to keep moving. There's so much more out there He wants you to see. Don't worry about me. Lizzie's going to stay behind awhile. We'll be all right."

I didn't move for a long time, my breath coming in rasps. Finally, I got to my feet. "Charlie, I don't know what to say."

"I know, son. I love you too. I'm glad God brought us together, if just for a short while. I'm proud of the way you're growing up. Don't forget what you've learned here, and if you get the chance, teach someone else."

My pack in place, I started out of camp and up the trail. I met Lizzie and said a quiet good bye. She kissed me on the cheek and told me to be careful. The clearing was soon out of sight behind the trees, and the trail was heading up, out of the valley.

Teach the older men to be temperate, worthy of respect, self-controlled, and sound in faith, in love and in endurance.

Titus 2: 2

....

Prayer: Father, teach me to look to those older than I. May I learn from their experience and be for them what they need. May I grow old gracefully, becoming what You want me to be for the sake of those younger, and for the glory of Your kingdom.

Ask yourself: What have you learned from an old person? What have you taught one younger than you?

February 18

The Apple Tree

Coming out of the valley this morning, I found myself in hill country, with open fields and an occasional brook. The walk was pleasant, and I had plenty of time to think about Rendezvous, and the people I had come to know and love there. Especially Charlie. I wondered if he was okay. Perhaps he was already there, ahead of me, waiting with a big grin on his face.

By evening, the trail had started to wind through an ancient orchard. The aroma of fruit trees made my mouth water, and the sound of bees among their branches had a lulling effect. I found a big apple tree, with huge branches reaching nearly to the ground under their load. The trunk was twisted and gnarled – like Charlie, I thought with a sad smile – and I knew this was where I wanted to spend the night.

After a dinner of baked apples, I sat and enjoyed the quiet blues and greens of an apple wood fed campfire and thought about this orchard. The trees were so old. How long had they been here? Who planted them? I could only imagine the men and women who must have labored for years in this place, carefully pruning and harvesting until the trees were mature enough to carry on without the farmer's skill. Could they have imagined that one day, years and years later, I would be here sleeping under these branches and enjoying the fruits of their labors? If they could have imagined it, what would they have felt? Would they have considered something so far into the future to be of any relevance to them?

I think the keepers of orchards and vineyards must have a special gift. They know they will never live to see their work in its competed form, and yet they work a lifetime, patiently trimming and planting so that people like me can stop for awhile and admire the beauty of the place. Before going to bed for the night, I rigged some poles and propped up the sagging branches of the old apple tree to keep them from breaking under the weight. Tomorrow I'll take along some seeds and find another spot like this. Who knows? Maybe some day another weary traveler will stop and camp under a tree I planted.

I planted, Apollos watered, but God gave the growth.

I Corinthians 3: 6

Prayer: Lord, it's hard to work when I know I will never see the fruit. But You remind me that I am part of something much more significant, and if I could only see it through Your eyes, I would understand that what I do is a part of what You are doing. Open my eyes.

Ask yourself: Have you ever enjoyed something that was made before you were born?

A Covered Bridge

The trail continued through orchard country today, and although no one seemed to live here anymore, there were signs of their work everywhere I turned. Then as I descended a hill and approached a stream, I came upon a sight that made me stop in wonder: a covered bridge stretching over the water. The roof was covered with shingles made from cedar wood, carefully split and laid so that not one drop of rain water could find its way into the interior of the bridge. The road bed sat upon two monstrous logs which must have been felled some distance away. There were certainly no trees of that size anywhere nearby. Along each side of the bridge was a railing of three rows, set in an "x" pattern which required much more wood than a simple rail, but sufficient to prevent even the smallest child from accidentally falling through. Each end of the railing was anchored to a hardwood post, buried deep and showing no signs of loosening its grip on the soil. The top of each post was covered in copperplate to prevent water seepage, and into the plate had been engraved a series of intricate designs.

I crossed the bridge in awe of its strength and beauty, and then had to turn around and cross it again, just to fully appreciate it. Pausing in the centre, I leaned on the sturdy railing to look down into the stream, and was puzzled. Why was such an elaborate structure built over such a relatively insignificant river? I appreciated it, to be sure, but, looking at the placid waters below, realized that I could have gotten over it without too much trouble. Even wading across would not have been a major ordeal. And if the water was higher, I could have easily pulled a log over and dropped it in place. Building this bridge must have taken months to complete, and I could only guess at the expense.

Running my hands over the engraving, I began to feel something of the heart of the builder. He was more than a practical person. The copperplate alone would have insured that the posts never rotted, but instead he chose to add a touch of beauty. This bridge was for him much more than a means for crossing a stream. It was an expression of his soul; a desire to make something beautiful as well as lasting. In a way, isn't that like God? The world is full of things that work; but moreover, they work *beautifully*. Like a Master Craftsman, God creates, then stands back and says, "That's good." And on the sixth day of Creation, He produced His pride and glory, made in His own image and imbued with a love for all things beautiful. And here at this stream, a long time ago, a man poured his heart and soul into this bridge, then stood back and said, "That's good."

And God saw everything that he had made, and behold, it was very good. And there was evening and there was morning, a sixth day.

Genesis 1: 31

....

Prayer: Thank you, Lord, for placing within me the ability to appreciate the beauty of Your world. Thank you for Your image, which compels me to seek what is beautiful. Bless the work of my hands. May what I do bring joy to Your heart, so that we both can stand back and say, "That's good."

Ask yourself: Think of something which moves you by its beauty. Why do you think you are able to appreciate it?

February 20

A Labor Unseen

I tripped over a rock today, while looking over the orchards and marveling at the work which had gone into making this such a beautiful countryside. Suddenly my toe caught on a stone in the trail. It didn't look all that significant, but apparently was buried deep and immovable, unlike my unsuspecting body. I landed face down, but suffered no major injury except for my pride. Gathering myself up and checking the contents of the back pack, I looked back at the guilty stone. That was a hazard, all right. I imagine I wasn't the only one to fall victim. Somebody needed to... The thought occurred to me, somebody *Who?* No one lives around here anymore. The only potential victims are travelers like myself. I'll never pass this way again, and neither will anyone else after the first time.

I thought again about the apple trees and bridges I'd been enjoying in this hill country: the results of labor by people long gone. I knew what I had to do: get that rock off the trail. I went back to it and gave it a good kick, with the only result a shooting pain in my foot. This was going to be a bigger job than I thought, but never mind; I was committed to the task. Removing my back pack and rolling up my sleeves, I started digging around the rock with my hands. Smiling to myself, I wished for that shovel I left behind at the beginning of the trip. The project took the rest of the day, as the true size of the offending rock became apparent. Now I understood why no one else had removed it: it was huge. Finally, as dusk was beginning to settle, it began to loosen its hold on the road and I was able to wrench it free and push it off to the side. I looked back and saw that down there was a worse hazard: a hole big enough to take a hiker's leg off at the knee. Finding small rocks and dirt from a nearby stream, I hauled enough up to fill the hole and smooth over the top. Done at last, I stood back to admire my work and saw... nothing. Where once there was a treacherous rock in the path, now there was simply a path, completely insignificant.

A part of me felt a tinge of regret at a whole's day's work I'd devoted to this project. If only there were some kind of, well, monument to mark the occasion. Should I set up a sign saying, "This section of smooth trail brought to you by..."? No, that wasn't the issue, was it? Yes, a part of me wanted to be recognized for my labor. But deeper still was the satisfaction that I had done something worthwhile today. I could look at that "absence of rock" and say, "That's good."

Six days you shall labor and do all your work.

Exodus 20: 9

Prayer: Thank you God, for giving me work to do. Thank you that I can look back on my labor and appreciate the joy of accomplishment. Continue to use me for Your glory. Show me what needs to be done, and give strength to my arms.

Ask yourself: Have you worked hard on something which no one else has seen?

Another Glimpse of the Mountain

Rising from my sleeping bag this morning, I decided to pick several apples for drying. Looking for the best ones in the old tree I had camped under, I found myself climbing up through its branches, feeling like a kid again. Eventually I had plenty of apples and more, but the top of the tree was just a few branches away, so I continued the climb. The view was magnificent. Behind me, I could see the trail winding through the orchards all the way back to the covered bridge. The other direction revealed a slight descent: possibly a large body of water far off in the distance.

And there beyond loomed the mountain I had seen on the third morning of my trek. It had been so long ago, I had almost forgotten about it, but there it was. All the old feelings came rushing back, and I remembered the powerful longing I had felt to be there on that mountaintop. But now there was something different about it. No, the mountain was still the same, but perhaps it was me who had changed. At the beginning of this trip, I was a traveler intent on reaching the goal, somewhere beyond that mountain. But now, after the people and the places I had met, the same mountain now took on a different view.

Clouds covered the peak, and it seemed somehow mysterious, even frightening. I found myself hoping that my trail would take me around it, rather than over it. I worked my way back to the ground and prepared the apples for drying, all the while thinking, just what does lie between me and the end of the trail? Am I prepared for what waits?

Look," they said, "we your servants have fifty able men. Let them go and look for your master. Perhaps the Spirit of the LORD has picked him up and set him down on some mountain or in some valley." "No," Elisha replied, "do not send them."
II Kings 2: 16

....

Prayer: We know full well that our lives will be mountains and valleys. Prepare us today for the road tomorrow. May we face each challenge with Your strength and Your courage.

Ask yourself: To what mountains has God led you?

February 22

Behold the Apple

Since it appeared that I would soon be leaving the orchard country, I decided to stop yesterday and prepare some apples for the journey. Setting up a drying rack in the sunshine, I took my pocket knife and begin slicing the apples into thin pieces.

As I worked, I was reminded of the poor reputation this fine fruit has received at the hands of the "Garden of Eden" story. Most people, I suppose, assume that it was an apple which tempted Eve and which subsequently led Adam and the rest of the world into sin. One thing I learned at Rendezvous was that the Latin word for "apple" and "evil" sound the same, and so when the Bible was first translated, people began associating one with the other.

But where in fact did the evil begin? Certainly not with this beauty, I thought, as I tried a sample from the top of the rack. No, the evil began when Adam and Eve disobeyed God. He said, "Don't eat it." They ate it. Simple. God could just as easily have placed a park bench in the Garden and said, "Don't sit there." All that was required was a means whereby Man could demonstrate his obedience, or lack of it.

The rest is history, and here I am on a journey to try and find something we all lost that day in the Garden. Who knows? Maybe it was an apple tree that Eve found "good for food and pleasing to the eye;" but more than that, it was the place for her and for Adam to examine their lives, consider their freedom, and make a choice.

Today, this lovely fruit is nothing more than another of God's gifts, and I intend to enjoy it. But I also have my places of decision, when I must examine my life, consider my freedom and make a choice. I hope I can always choose wisely.

When the woman saw that the fruit of the tree was good for food and pleasing to the eye, and also desirable for gaining wisdom, she took some and ate it. She also gave some to her husband, who was with her, and he ate it. Then the eyes of both of them were opened, and they realized they were naked; so they sewed fig leaves together and made coverings for themselves.

Genesis 3: 6 – 7

Prayer: I thank you today, Father, for the freedom and dignity You allow me. But it's a fearful gift, for by it, I can choose, and have chosen to disobey You. Please forgive me, and help me make right choices from this day onward.

Ask yourself: Why do you think God created you with the ability to sin? Does this say something about His love for you?

Apple Stems

Climbing my favorite apple tree again to re-supply my drying rack, I had to start being a little more selective in the apples I chose. At first, there were more ripe apples than I could carry, and it was just a matter of getting them off the tree and onto the rack. Now, however, not all of the fruit at my fingertips was ready for picking. While the big, juicy ripe ones came off easily in my hand, others still clung to the tree by a stem which was not about to give up its grip without a fight. When I forced the issue and picked the apple anyway, I was rewarded with a hard, sour trophy.

What an amazing system, I thought, as I tested each piece of fruit with a gentle tug. The tree knows better than I do which ones are ready for harvesting, and lets me know with a resistance I only have to heed.

Jesus spoke a lot about fruit, and compared it to our work as His disciples. We are to be fruit, and we are to *produce* fruit, but none of that can happen without the stem, connecting the fruit to the source. There comes a time when the fruit has reached completion and is ready for the harvest, but until then is held securely to the tree.

How am I like this apple? I wondered. What is the stem in my life, and where is my source? Will there come a time when I will be ready for harvesting, and my stem is broken? I thought back to Charlie, my first real friend and brother in Christ. He had given so much to so many, including me, but the last time I saw him, he was ready to go home. All the pain that I had seen in his old eyes had been replaced with a sparkle of anticipation, as if he could see already what waited for him at the end of his journey. If ever a man was ready for the harvest, it was Charlie. And what was he leaving behind? In the short time I spent with him, he taught me about life, and love and what real joy is all about. He introduced me to teachers who opened whole new worlds to me: worlds of challenge and excitement, and I hope, of spiritual growth. Am I part of the "fruit" that Charlie left behind? With all my heart, I hope so.

I am the vine; you are the branches. If a man remains in me and I in him, he will bear much fruit; apart from me you can do nothing.

John 15: 5

Prayer: I know, Father, that You expect me to produce fruit for Your kingdom. I know that I am expected to grow and mature, becoming all that I am created to be. Show me how to do that, Lord. Teach me the ways of the Gardener.

Ask yourself: What are the characteristics of a "ripe" Christian?

February 24

Apple Skins

Before drying properly, apples need to be peeled, and I spent a good part of the day today with my pocketknife, removing the outer layers and revealing the fruit inside. Some of the skins bore the scars of their battle with the elements. Insects had tried to bore in at places, fungi had tried to establish a foothold in others, and various bruises and scratches told of the struggles which had to be overcome if I were to enjoy this apple.

Just about every living thing has a skin of some kind, I reflected. In fact we humans often use it as a means of describing a person, whether he is "thick skinned" or "thin skinned", talking about how he handles criticism. Skin color is cited as a basis for discrimination, and the hiding or revealing of skin reflects our ideas of both fashion and decency.

Many times skin diseases such as leprosy were the focus of Jesus' ministry, and the healing of those diseases often pointed to levels of relationship which went far beyond the surface. I looked at the skin on my arms as I worked and saw there a history which spoke volumes. The color itself determined in many ways my status in the world, and the way my fellow men greeted me. The leathery feel, along with my newly developed calluses, spoke of days in the sun and hard work. Scars from the thorns I had encountered early in the journey testified to past pain as well as healing. Higher up on my arm I noticed the scar from a smallpox vaccination, evidence of knowledge gained in the field of medicine and of a mother's love, who made sure I got the shot, even against my own wishes.

These apples no longer need their skins; their time of harvest has come. But the stories of their perseverance and usefulness have been etched into that thin covering which I now peel away. God will not forget those stories, just as He will not forget the things which have made my skin what it is today.

I know that my Redeemer lives, that in the end he will stand upon the earth. And after my skin has been destroyed, yet in my flesh I will see God.

Job 19: 25 – 26

Prayer: Thank you, Father, for the protection You give Your creation. Thank you for scars, and the reminders they give us of past struggles. Thank you for the unique qualities of my skin, and how those qualities reflect much of what I am.

Ask yourself: Look at your own skin and think about the history you see there. How has God used your experiences, struggles and scars?

Bad Apples

My apple tree was just about harvested. The big, red juicy apples had been either eaten on the spot, cooked into unforgettable dishes, squeezed into juice or dried and packed away for the rest of the journey. Climbing through the branches, all I could find now were small, hard things not worth the picking, or else apples which had been so bruised or damaged that they served only as food for the birds. I noticed two big apples hanging together and reached for them, but as soon as my fingers closed around the first one, realized that it was ruined. Something had damaged it: an insect or a violent storm, and it had fallen victim to disease, turning soft from the inside out. Reaching for the one behind it, I could see that it too was beyond hope. By virtue of the fact that it hung next to the diseased apple, it too was affected.

I remembered the parable my grandmother had passed along to me when I began to choose my friends and pastimes: "One bad apple spoils the barrel", she had said, and by that meant that I had best take care of the friends I hung around with. I didn't give it much thought until the day I got in trouble at school when one of the guys with me threw a rock at a window, breaking it. I was horrified, but even more so when not only he, but all of us were called into the principal's office for a lecture on respect of property. I tried to proclaim my innocence, but he told me sternly, "You may not have thrown the rock, but by the fact you were with the gang of boys who did, you must share the blame."

I had a hard time accepting that, but in the years since, I've begun to see the wisdom he had. Groups of people often take on a character that is unique to the group. They tend to dress alike, talk alike, and as time goes on, they begin to hold the same values. That was apparent in the journal kept by the victim of the ruined fortress I had discovered: he described a group of people bound together first by fear, and then by pride. As they turned away fellow travelers deemed unworthy, they reflected a group attitude which fed on itself. On the other hand, I had seen the reverse of that phenomenon at Rendezvous. There, people were bound together by love, and it was reflected in the actions of every individual. I picked off the two "bad" apples and threw them to the ground; perhaps they would still accomplish something good as compost.

Blessed is the man who does not walk in the counsel of the wicked or stand in the way of sinners or sit in the seat of mockers. But his delight is in the law of the LORD, and on his law he meditates day and night. He is like a tree planted by streams of water, which yields its fruit in season and whose leaf does not wither. Whatever he does prospers.

Psalms 1: 1 – 3

Prayer: Lord, guide me in the choice of friends I make, May I be a blessing to them, even as they keep me accountable. May our friendship be a source of strength to those whose faith may come under attack.

Ask yourself: Think of your friends. Do they encourage you to do good, or do they lead you astray?

February 26

The Edge of the Orchard

Rested from my break in the journey and with a pack full of dried apples, I set out again this morning. The intricately built bridges and fences were behind me, and as the trail continued I began to see less and less evidence of the caretakers who had made this such a beautiful orchard. Who were they, and where had they gone? I may never know, but I will always appreciate their labors. As I came to the edge of the orchard, the trees were less orderly, less tended. Vines had taken over a few, and there was no fruit visible. Here and there, branches had broken off and were left to rot. Finally, the rows of apple trees stopped altogether, and in their place was a wild and wind swept plain.

Looking back down the trail, I felt a twinge of regret for having to leave this place of beauty and abundance. Why couldn't it be this way always? If only along the path, people would have spent a little time making improvements, the whole journey would be easier. But I suppose, like me, most travelers have their eyes set on the goal rather than the trail. This is a nice enough place to walk through, but I'm on my way to something better yet. Still, if my journey has been made more pleasant by the work of someone before me, then how can I not offer something for those who follow? Stopping near the last apple tree, I took a few moments to dig a place in the soil and plant some of the seeds I had gathered the first day I came into the orchard. Bringing some water up from the stream, I poured it carefully around the spot, then as a sign of my faith in those who would come after me, I pushed a stick into the ground. Hopefully, this would show the next person that something had been planted here; and when the seedling finally did appear, it would have something to cling to until it was strong enough to stand alone.

Perhaps some day, when I reach my destination, I'll be able to sit and talk with fellow pilgrims about the apple tree, and hear how it was a blessing. At any rate, I've been blessed already by the effort itself. Dusting my hands off on my trousers, I take up my back pack and turn to face the future.

He is like a tree planted by streams of water, which yields its fruit in season and whose leaf does not wither. Whatever he does prospers.

Psalms 1: 3

Prayer: Lord, I find it difficult to work for things of which I know I will never see the end product. Please give me eyes which reach to the future: to the time when all things will be brought before You. Let me see with eyes of faith the results of what I do today. Grant me strength, and wisdom, and courage.

Ask yourself: What motivates you to do any good thing, if you know that you will never see the good which comes?

Looking Back

The trail continued in a steady upward slope today. The land is still green and rich, but with no sign of human habitation. Because of the upward slope, it's difficult to see very far ahead. Even the far mountains are out of sight, below the horizon. The view backwards grows more beautiful with each step, though. As the trails climbs, I can see more and more of the orchard country, much like the view I had from the top of the apple tree last week. The roof top of the covered bridge is just visible, and I think I'll be able to see the whole structure by tomorrow, if the trail keeps going up. The stream is out of sight, beneath the trees, but as the distance increases, it becomes easier to see where it flows, by the colors which grow deeper next to the banks.

I made camp tonight, and as I sat cradling a cup of coffee, I was shocked to discover that for the first time I was facing backwards, toward the way which I had come, rather than toward tomorrow's journey. And why not? Ahead of me lies only an uneventful trail which grows more barren with each step, while behind me is that beautifully rich land of orchards and peace.

I confess: a part of me wants to turn back, find a place in that idyllic setting and build a home. Perhaps my family would join me there, and together we could keep that place as wonderful as it is now. We could encourage other travelers as they pass by, and help them on their way. Or perhaps they would stop and settle with us, and we could... but no, that's not right, is it? God did not tell me to go out and make a new home. He told me to go through and *find* my home, which He has already prepared. And as lovely and peaceful as this place appears to be, I'm told that it is nothing compared to what waits.

And so, as I get into my sleeping bag, I make a conscious effort and turn facing the trail ahead, so that it will be the first thing I see when I wake in the morning. Lord, let me dream, not of the past, but of the present, and of the land You have for me.

> *Do not let your hearts be troubled. Trust in God; trust also in me. In my Father's house are many rooms; if it were not so, I would have told you. I am going there to prepare a place for you. And if I go and prepare a place for you, I will come back and take you to be with me that you also may be where I am.*
>
> John 14: 1 – 3

Prayer: Remind me today, Lord, of the promise you made to me: that I have a place with You for all eternity. Don't let me be tempted by the attractions of today, but may my eyes be only for You and Your kingdom.

Ask yourself: Do you spend most of your time looking ahead, or looking back?

Horses

The sound reached my ears this morning through the ground upon which I was sleeping. It came first as a deep rumble which invaded my dreams. I awoke, and was then able to hear the higher pitched sounds of hooves striking stone, and the occasional snort and whinny. I raised my head from the sleeping bag and was greeted by the sight of a herd of horses – thirty or more – running by my camp. There were coal black stallions, white mares, Appaloosa and Paint, even a tiny Shetland trying to keep up. The sight and the sound brought to me to my feet, and I felt the thrill of one standing next to raw power.

Watching the muscles in their legs flex and extend, pushing them forward while the wind blew their manes and tails in a furling, flag-like motion, I felt a sense of what the early men of Jerusalem must have felt as they looked on in terror at the armies of Nebuchadnezzar. Here was a strength that I could only dream of, and I was sure that my dreams would be filled with this moment for a long time to come. How could I blame one for fearing such a display? How could I not despair over my own weakness? For the residents of 6th century B.C. Jerusalem, the sight of Babylon's armies, led by fearsome horses pulling iron chariots was enough to cause their hearts to fail them. Today there are plenty of sources for such displays, from the "shock and awe" of modern artillery to the mind-numbing power of a Shuttle lift off.

But God would like me to know this morning that His power makes all these insignificant by contrast. There is no force in the universe, man made or natural, which can compare to the strength of the Creator who called those forces into existence. I needed that reminder this morning, with the peaceful valley behind me and the unknown before me. If I had any thought of turning back, of running to a place of security rather than forging ahead, that thought was dismissed as I stood and witnessed a taste of God's creation, shaking the foundations of my soul. I can shout today with the Psalmist who, having seen the pinnacle of power in his day, could still declare, "My strength comes from God."

Some trust in chariots and some in horses, but we trust in the name of the LORD our God. They are brought to their knees and fall, but we rise up and stand firm.
Psalms 20: 7 – 8

....

Prayer: I tend to be impressed by power, Lord, and that fact makes me vulnerable to anyone who yields it. Remind me when I'm standing before great strength that the greatest strength is found only in You.

Ask yourself: Does the sight of the night sky make you feel strong or weak? Why?

Tracks in the Heavens

I looked at my watch this morning and realized it was wrong: the date read "March 1st" but since this is a leap year, it's actually February 29th. Interesting, that this day only comes once every four years. Pity the poor child who was born on this day and has to be reminded three years out of four that it's "not really his birthday"! On the other hand, I've known a few ladies who appreciate the fact that they can legitimately divide their age by four.

Why do we have this day, anyway? Simply put, we have to adjust the calendar periodically to account for the actual time it takes for the sun to go around the earth. No matter how much we might correct our watches, we come to the end of each year about six hours after the sun does, and so every four years we have to add a day to keep everything in sync.

Amazing, isn't it, that something as massive as the earth moves with a precision that's measured in microseconds. And that's not the half of it. Spaceships are sent to the farthest reaches of the solar system, arriving exactly where they should, when they should; and they're able to do that because they can trust every heavenly body in the universe to be where it should, when it should. People have marveled at the precision of the planets and stars for thousands of years, but for many, the real wonder is overlooked. Why is everything "just so"? How can we set our watches by the stars, and not realize that a Creator God has made it possible?

The Bible says that "the heavens declare the glory of God" (Psalm 19:1), but that man's ears are all too often closed to hearing it. All day today, I've been reminded every time I look at my watch that everything made by man is subject to what is made by God. Maybe we should have leap year more often.

> Go to this people and say, "You will be ever hearing but never understanding; you will be ever seeing but never perceiving." For this people's heart has become calloused; they hardly hear with their ears, and they have closed their eyes. Otherwise they might see with their eyes, hear with their ears, understand with their hearts and turn, and I would heal them.
>
> Acts 28: 26 – 27

....

Prayer: Thank you Father for reminding me through this special day that the sun, moon and stars move at Your command. We can only observe and marvel, and when necessary, adjust our understanding to match Your own.

Ask yourself: Can you think of other systems which depend upon the movement of the stars for their accuracy?

March 1

The Canyon

The trail continued its upward slope today, the lush fields of grass giving way to sparse, rocky vegetation. The horizon began to stretch out before me, and a low range of mountains was becoming visible off in the distance. Because of the rising terrain, I still couldn't see more than a few hundred yards of the trail ahead, though, and I wondered if I was about to break out onto a desert or a lake.

It was neither. What looked like an approaching low summit proved to be the end of the trail. By that, I don't mean that the path was no longer visible among the scrub; it simply ceased to exist, along with the scrub and the land upon which it grew. I found myself standing at the top of a sheer cliff, looking out over a huge canyon, at least twenty miles across and stretching as far as the eye could see both to the right and to the left. The canyon floor seemed to be covered in low-growing mesquite trees which became thicker as they neared the center, possible evidence of a river. On the far side, I could see cliff faces guarding the horizon, beyond which mountains were just visible through the haze.

Fighting a rising surge of panic, I looked right and left for any sign of the trail. I walked along the canyon edge in both directions, hoping against hope for some indication of where previous travelers might have gone. This *couldn't* be the end, I thought. There must be an explanation. Perhaps I had missed a fork in the trail; leaving my pack on the ground, I hurried back a mile or more, scanning the grass on both sides for any sign, but saw nothing.

Coming back to the canyon, I finally sat down, at an absolute loss as to what to do. Evening was coming on, and knowing that searching in the dark would be both futile and dangerous, I decided to make camp for the night. Gazing over the precipice from my camp fire, the canyon below looked even darker than imaginable. Sounds drifted up on the wind, but whether they were human or animal, I couldn't tell. In a way, I felt a little relieved, sitting here looking down, instead of being down there, looking up. I wasn't really lost, I reminded myself. My sleeping bag lies on the trail which leads back to places I know. If nothing else, I can always return. But even as sleep overtook me, I knew that going back wasn't an option. If nothing else, I would strike off along the edge, with or without a trail. Right or left? Which way would it be?

For this God is our God for ever and ever; he will be our guide even to the end.
Psalms 48: 14

....

Prayer: Father, You tell us in Your Word that You will always be our guide. How precious is that promise when we have no where to turn! May we depend upon You, both on the trail and in its absence. Lead me I pray.

Ask yourself: When was the last time you were unsure of which way to turn? What did you do?

The Way Down

The sound of a hawk woke me early this morning. His shrill whistling seemed to be right above my head, and then the next moment he sounded miles away. It was a perfect morning for flying, I thought, if one happened to be a bird. The sun had just begun to send its rays over the canyon floor, and the rising heat must have been creating massive thermals, evident by the columns of dust swirling in the distance. Suddenly the hawk was swept up from just below my line of sight, darting left and right before banking down again with a shriek. As the sound disappeared below the canyon rim, I understood why he sounded so near one moment, so far the next. Curiosity pulled me closer to the edge, and I crept on my hands and knees in order to see down. This was the first time I had looked directly beneath, and the sight caused my stomach to turn over a few times. The cliff face descended straight to the valley floor; if anything, it curved in a bit before reaching the bottom, about a hundred feet down. But what caused my stomach to churn was not the vertical drop; rather, it was the line of holes carved into the sandstone. Their function was obvious: this was my missing trail, leading straight down.

Crawling backward away from the cliff's edge, I rolled over onto my back and let out a lungful of air I'd been holding for much too long. "No, Lord," I said, more to myself than to Anyone else. I had never been fond of heights. Well, let's be honest; I was *terrified* of heights, and the very thought of lowering myself down that precipice with a heavy backpack and no safety rope was enough to make me consider any alternative. How far would I have to walk until I came to a place where I could get down the cliff safely? Would I be able to find the trail again? Maybe if I just waited here long enough, someone would come with a rope, or at least a better idea than I could come up with. Then there was that beautiful orchard country back down the trail...

I spent the entire day fretting over alternatives, desperate for anything which would not require me to face the inevitable. But as I lay down and watched the stars make their appearance in the skies over the canyon, I realized what I had just said to myself: it's *inevitable*. This whole journey is the result of a conscious decision I made to obey. I said from the first day that I would go, no matter where the trail might lead. Easier said than done, I suppose; and yet, as horrible as the climb down seems, disobedience seems unthinkable. I close my eyes, still fearful of what tomorrow might hold, but with a sense of peace that now at last the decision has been made.

> *This is love for God: to obey his commands. And his commands are not burdensome, for everyone born of God overcomes the world. This is the victory that has overcome the world, even our faith.*
>
> I John 5: 3 – 4

Prayer: Lord, I talk often about obedience, but in the face of difficulty it's not always that easy to follow through. Help me keep my eyes on You, Father, and not on the circumstances.

Ask yourself: Can you think of a time when obeying was especially difficult?

That First Step

Every fiber of my being urged me to stay in my sleeping bag this morning. I knew what waited, and I most assuredly did not want to face it. When I went to sleep last night, I was blessed with a sense of peace, not that the deed was done, but that I had at last resolved myself to do it. Obedience dictated that I continue on the trail, even if it led off a sheer precipice. I had spent most of the day yesterday trying desperately to find any alternative, but there was none. I packed slowly, deciding to wait until I reached the canyon floor to have breakfast, as if the extra weight in my stomach would offset the strength I might have gained from eating. Everything cinched up tightly, I lifted my back pack, then had an idea: walking carefully to the edge of the cliff, I hesitated a moment, then tossed the pack down. It seemed to fall for an eternity before disappearing from sight. I never heard it hit the ground. Now I was committed. Everything I owned was in that pack; I could not easily move forward or backward without it, and now that it was down below, my direction of travel was set. I finally took a deep breath, got on my hands and knees and eased backwards over the edge. It was there that I made a despairing discovery: knees don't bend forward. My right leg was extended straight, but until I lowered myself down farther off the cliff, there was no way I could get my foot into the first hole. Sweat was dripping off my forehead, and my hands were trembling. My body was being held in place by three points: right and left hands and left foot. The other foot had to go. Using my elbows for added grip, I let my left foot slip over the edge. Now there was nothing keeping me from death except my trembling forearms and ten fingers, dug inextricably into the hard packed soil of the trail. My strength was failing; if I didn't keep moving, I would lose my grip. With a desperate prayer escaping my lips, I let my body slip farther down. My right foot touched rock, but where was the foothold? Gingerly, I moved my foot up, then down, then right and left. Nothing but sheer cliff face. Battling every shred of self-preservation, I lowered myself more, until I thought I could no longer hold on. I kicked with my foot. Once. Twice. Then suddenly, instead of my toe striking the surface, I felt a shooting pain as my shin collided with rock. My foot was inside the first hole! I eased weight onto it and was rewarded with a sense of relief that spread from my shaking fingers all the way to my toes. The rest of the way down was terrifying but not impossible. Eventually, I came to a point about halfway where I realized that it was going to be easier to keep going down than back up. Then a few steps later I ventured a quick look down and saw the bottom, about thirty feet farther.

The rest of the way was almost exhilarating, and I reached the bottom totally depleted but laughing with a mixture of relief and joy. Why had this been such a challenge? One step, I realized. After that first effort, the rest came progressively easier.

If the LORD delights in a man's way, he makes his steps firm though he stumble, he will not fall, for the LORD upholds him with his hand.

Psalms 37: 23 – 24

....

Prayer: Lord, You know how prone I am to stumbling. I need Your guiding Hand today to help me past those "first steps" of faith. Hold me. Guide me. Rescue me. Praise You, Father, for walking with me today!

Ask yourself: What is an example of a "step of faith", which I personally must take before understanding comes?

March 4

Into the Canyon

After my initial exhilaration yesterday over the successful descent, I was struck today by the oppressiveness of the canyon floor. There was no wind, and the heat seemed to push down with a palpable force. After so many days of idyllic pastures and apple trees the bare mesquites that filled the canyon were pitiful by comparison. There was not much sign of wildlife, except for the occasional lizard and the constant droning of flies. The trees limited both visibility and sound, and in many ways I felt as though I were walking through a poorly ventilated store room filled with unwanted building supplies. The trail was a faint track over sand, and several times I lost the way, having to back track until something familiar would re-appear. Both sides of the canyon were now totally out of sight behind the surrounding scrub, and if there was a river ahead, it made no sound which I could hear.

I walked all day, but when evening came had no idea how far I had come. Darkness brought a relief from the heat but also a sense of uneasiness, as if there were something I should know but had not yet discovered. Moving closer to the fire and pulling my collar up around my ears, I thought, if only there were a view of *something*, I might be able to gauge my present circumstance. A goal ahead, a familiar point behind, anything which would tell me if I'm moving, and in what direction.

I started to remove my shoes, and remembered Andy's "boot lacing" class back at Rendezvous. He had told us, "Foundations are the most important part of anything worth doing. Everything else builds on what's below it." There was my point of reference. Circumstances around me today could not show me if I had gone anywhere or not, but my boots, still laced to perfection and showing the scars of the day's trek shouted loud and clear, "Great day. Miles covered. All systems go."

I went to sleep, enjoying the fatigue that spoke of hard work. Tomorrow I'll keep moving ahead, regardless of what my surroundings do. The foundation I stand on tells me where I am and where I'm going. For now, that's enough.

The LORD is exalted, for he dwells on high; he will fill Zion with justice and righteousness. He will be the sure foundation for your times, a rich store of salvation and wisdom and knowledge; the fear of the LORD is the key to this treasure.

Isaiah 33: 5 – 6

....

Prayer: Lord may I not be a victim today of my circumstances. Help me keep my eyes on You and the foundations You have laid for me. Keep me moving forward for You Name's sake.

Ask yourself: What kinds of things make up a person's foundations for life?

The Lion Returns

I got an early start this morning, deciding to cover as many miles as possible in the cool of the day, then find shelter to sit out the heat. About midmorning, I stopped for a rest under the shade of a mesquite tree. The insects provided a constant background hum, and occasionally one would pass close enough to my ears to add a distraction. A moment later I became aware of the cries of birds off in the distance: a flock of crows from the sound of it. Funny that they would be so active this time of day, I thought. The sound suddenly intensified, and I could hear the violent flapping wings in accompaniment. But what I heard simultaneously was enough to bring me instantly to my feet, my heart pounding. Something between a roar and scream, which I knew at once to be the sound of a mountain lion, drowned out the cacophony of the birds. I stood with my eyes glued to the area from which the drama had just unfolded. What should I do? Run? Where? Stand and fight? With what? Hope that my presence had gone unnoticed? Most certainly, but I knew it was unlikely that every creature in the canyon did not already know exactly who and where I was. But in fact, who and where was this creature I feared? Could it possibly be the same one I had encountered at the beginning of the trail? It's possible, I thought, that this was merely another of nature's predators who wanted nothing to do with me; but something deep in my heart was telling me differently. Something besides my irrational fear was shouting a warning which I heard loud and clear. This creature is no ordinary lion. It knows me. It's playing with me, and eventually it will come for me. All thoughts of either rest or flight were put aside, and I began to think of defense. How could I protect myself against such an animal? Fire. I looked around and saw enough wood to build a small camp fire, and set out to do just that. The thought occurred to me to set the mesquite forest on fire and walk behind the advancing flames, but the memory of the last fire I had seen on this trip was enough to make me hold back on that plan, at least for now. As I gathered wood for the fire, I spotted a tree branch about as big around as my arm and fairly straight. After some effort, I managed to break it loose and began to fashion a crude spear.

With a glance at the sky, I noticed that it was already growing dark. I stacked up as much underbrush as I could in a circle around my fire. Maybe it wouldn't keep anything out, but at least it would make enough noise to give me some warning.

Lying next to the fire, spear in hand, I listen for anything beyond my makeshift shelter. I'm afraid, but strangely at peace. The warning I sensed earlier today gave me assurance that I'm not alone. And if I can be warned, I can be protected.

Hear, O my people, and I will warn you- if you would but listen to me, O Israel.
Psalms 81: 5

Prayer: Lord, give me ears to hear all that You would say to me. Especially today, as I walk through valleys of darkness, may I hear Your voice, and know of Your warnings to me. Guide me on the path of safety and keep me for Your Name's sake.

Ask yourself: In times of danger, what makes people act bravely?

March 6

Attack

He came before dawn. I had not slept much during the night, keeping the fire going as much as possible and listening for sounds. Finally, as the sky began to lose a few if its stars and dawn seemed fast approaching, I began to relax. Immediately I was asleep, and dreaming of orchards and vineyards. The rustling of brush was at first a part of my dream, as I shook the branches of apple trees to see if the ripe fruit would fall on its own. But another part of my brain knew that the sound was external, and sent urgent messages to the rest of my body: "Wake up! Wake up!" My eyes struggled to focus, and then were snapped to attention at the sight of two yellow eyes, staring at me from across the camp fire. The lion was halfway through the scrub brush fence and was getting ready to pounce over the fire and onto my sleeping bag.

Fumbling for a moment, I finally found the spear and just had time to raise it when he leaped. It struck him a glancing blow, and I felt flesh give way along his side. One paw landed on my shoulder and I was driven back to the ground with a cry of pain, letting the spear slip from my grasp. My hands were shaking uncontrollably as fear, relief and the morning cold surged through my body. He was hurt, I knew, but not badly. If anything, he would be even more determined to make an end of me.

It was time to move out, and I quickly threw my things together and started down the trail, spear in hand. Perhaps there would be a better place of defense farther on. As I walked briskly down the trail, I thought of the words of the man whose journal I now carried in my back pack. Attempting to justify his abandonment of the journey in favor of building a fortress, he had said of himself and his companions, "We were drawn together at once by a common bond; that irreducible terror of him and those who follow his counsel." Who was he speaking about? Is there a connection to this lion whose unnatural desire to kill me escapes all logic? I don't know, but I can say this: I'm less critical now of those whose fear led them into disobedience and destruction. I could use a few friends right now, and if I were to come across a well-built fortress, I'd be sorely tempted to stay awhile.

Fear is a powerful force, and today I'm afraid. I only pray that my fear's power can be directed toward something good today, and not toward my downfall.

My heart is in anguish within me; the terrors of death assail me. Fear and trembling have beset me; horror has overwhelmed me. I said, "Oh, that I had the wings of a dove! I would fly away and be at rest- I would flee far away and stay in the desert I would hurry to my place of shelter, far from the tempest and storm.
Psalm 53: 4 – 8

Prayer: Lord I know that I have no reason to fear, but I confess that I am afraid. Forgive me, I pray, and use this fear for the glory of Your Kingdom. May my trembling become dancing, as I see Your mighty Hand at work. Restore my courage and use me to accomplish Your purpose.

Ask yourself: What are you afraid of? Why?

March 7

The River

The day was spent walking, stopping to listen, walking some more. I was desperate to find some kind of shelter before evening came. The first time I encountered the lion, I'd been able to drive him away by deception and surprise; he was unlikely to fall for that again. But somehow I knew that he *would* be back, and next time he would come at me in a way I wasn't expecting. How could I resist him then?

Another roar filled the air. It seemed to be coming about 100 yards behind me, but it might as well have been within arm's reach; I bolted and ran. My lungs seemed about to burst as I slowed down and looked for a tree to hold onto, lest I fall flat on my face. The timing was good, because just as I reached out to prop myself up, my hand came to rest on a man-made object. It was a graying weathered post, about ten feet high and topped with a rusted pulley. There not six feet away was the bank of a river. I judged it to be about 200 feet across, and flowing swiftly: too deep to wade, and the strong current ruling out the prospect of swimming. On the far bank stood a post much like the one I leaned against, except that a rope was threaded through its pulley and stretched into the water toward me, only to be caught in the rapid current and waved enticingly at me from the center of the river. I could catch a glimpse of the trail winding up the bank on the other side, and knew that this was where I was supposed to cross, but now what could I do?

The question answered itself in the next instant, as I turned back and saw the lion, running full speed toward me. I had only a matter of seconds, and acted out of sheer impulse: With two quick steps and a leap I was in the water. My struggle turned to pain as my back slammed against a log, floating in the centre of the rapidly moving water. Instinctively my hands went up to grasp the branches protruding from the log and held on. Apparently, it was caught on something. As I moved around it in search of a better grip, I saw that what it was caught on was the broken rope I had seen dangling from the pulley on the far side. It wasn't much of a chance, but it was all I had. Kicking my feet and pulling hand over hand, I moved with excruciating slowness up the length of the rope. By the time my feet found the bottom, and I was able to half stand, half crawl the rest of the way to the shore, it was dark. I had never been so exhausted in my life. My mind was still screaming something to me about lions and running, but my body was too tired to care. Without even removing my pack, I fell face down in the mud of the riverbank and slipped into a state of semi-consciousness. Sleep overtook me, and the world was at peace.

Consider him who endured such opposition from sinful men, so that you will not grow weary and lose heart.

Hebrews 12: 3

Prayer: In the midst of my exhaustion, what a joy it is to know that You, Oh God, never grow weary! When my feet can carry me no farther, You lift me up and set me on high. Be my strength when I have none.

Ask yourself: How are a person's rational thoughts affected by fatigue and exhaustion?

March 8

The Evil Man

The sound of the river was a soothing interference to the thoughts which troubled my soul. As dawn began to break, I stirred, tentatively at first, as if recovering from some unknown disaster and as yet uncertain how serious my injuries were. When I was at last able to open my eyes fully and look around, I scanned the far shore and soon spotted the lion. He was pacing up and down the river bank, looking directly at me the whole time. When he turned and walked right to left, I was able to see clearly the wound I had inflicted on his side. It had left an ugly scar, but as I suspected was not life threatening. He seemed tireless in his intensity, like lions I had seen in zoo cages, pacing back and forth, as if there might suddenly be a way out, or in this case, a way over the river and to me. I watched him for a few moments, wondering if he would ever find a way to get to me, when suddenly he stopped in mid stride, turned to face me, and sat down.

I barely had time to consider the meaning of this new action when I became aware of a presence behind me. Turning slowly to my left, I saw him standing on the grass just beyond the river bank, an expression which at one and the same time spoke total indifference and undiluted hatred. The evil man.

"He will find a way over, you know," he said while looking beyond me to the other side of the river. I quickly regained my feet, uncertain what to do but knowing that I would not be staying there.

"Who are you?" I asked, not really wanting to hear the answer but desperate to gain control of the situation. "How do you know what that lion will do?"

A smile broke across his face, but one which did not reflect anything remotely funny. "He and I are old friends," he said. "And we will be here long after you are dead."

I stepped backwards instinctively, barely aware that I was standing in the water. A fear which by now was becoming familiar gripped me and nearly succeeded in making me bolt and run in sheer panic. I remembered now what I had learned at Rendezvous:. "You have no authority," I said at last. "You can't touch me."

For a moment, he seemed to lose his composure, the wicked smile frozen on his face. Then he spoke again. "Been listening to stories, huh? You're right, I suppose. I can't touch you, not yet. But *he* can." With a nod of his head, he pointed to my right, upstream. There, standing on the river bank less than ten feet away, was an image I thought at one time I might be able to forget someday, but no longer. It was a man, or what was left of a man, his features horribly burned away. His eyes were hollowed out sockets, and yet I felt as though he were staring directly at me. He seemed to be smiling, but then I realized it was only because there was not enough flesh to cover his teeth. There was not much to identify, but I knew exactly who it was: the man I had met on the trail earlier, and who had died in the bush fire.

I will turn my ear to a proverb; with the harp I will expound my riddle: Why should I fear when evil days come, when wicked deceivers surround me
Psalms 49: 4 – 5

....

Prayer: Lord I know in my heart that the enemy cannot hurt me unless You will it. But I fall victim so often by his deceptions. Teach me how to know the truth, and how to resist the evil one. Show me Your power when I'm confronted by his lies.

Ask yourself: Can you think of a time when you or someone you know was hurt because of a deception of some kind?

March 9

Escape

In the midst of terror, a person doesn't usually think rationally. Whatever was standing before me, with all expression burned away and yet seemingly alive, could not possibly offer much of a threat, could he? I used to laugh at the old horror movies which showed disfigured and barely mobile creatures bringing terror to whole communities with nothing more than a groan and a shuffling walk.

But now was not the time for rational thought. With the lion on one shore, the evil man on the other and now with this indescribable horror shuffling toward me, there was only one option: the river itself. I leaped into the current and was immediately swept off my feet. Just like before, I struck the log which had become entangled in the rope, and this time my back pack caught on a short branch, holding me securely. This gave me a chance to get a better grip on the log, and see what was happening back on shore.

What I saw was mind-numbing; the creature had a grip on the rope, and was pulling it, and me, inextricably back to the shore. I tried to let go of the log, but because the back pack was firmly snagged was unable to. There was only one other way to go; digging into my jeans, I managed to find my pocketknife. Opening the blade, I started sawing desperately on the rope, all the while drawing closer and closer to the creature. When he was almost an arm's length away, the rope parted and I started drifting away, slowly at first and then picking up speed as the log slipped back into the current. From that point on, looking back at the nightmare I was leaving behind was out of the question; every ounce of my energy was devoted to keeping my head above water. The shoreline sped by, accelerating at a rate I might have found terrifying under any other circumstances, but in this case a welcome situation, since it was taking me farther from them. Eventually I found a balance point on the log, and was able relax somewhat. The river continued its steady course, and I had no desire to reach either shore, not yet. But as my legs began turning numb from the cold water and my back pack threatening at any moment to shift its weight and pull me under, I had to consider: had I done the right thing? The only creature back there that had actually hurt me was the lion, and he was on the far shore. I had been taught that the evil man had no authority to touch me, and his actions seemed to confirm that. The horrible apparition was the stuff of nightmares, but what, really, could he have done to me? Had he been a normal man, I could have faced him and had a pretty good chance of beating him; what was it about him being burned and disfigured that made him seem so much more formidable? I clung to the log as the river took me farther and farther away from them... and from the trail.

When I am afraid, I will trust in you. In God, whose word I praise, in God I trust; I will not be afraid. What can mortal man do to me?

Psalm 56: 3 – 4

Prayer: Father, my fears keep me from thinking rationally, and they keep me from remembering who You are. Remind me just now that You are the Creator of everything: even the things which scare me. You have absolute power over them, and absolute love for me. Keep me safe in that assurance.

Ask yourself: Think of the most frightening scenes you can remember from a horror movie. What would you have done if you had been faced with something like that?

The Boat

I don't know how long the river carried me. For a few hours at least, each passing mile was welcomed, since it increased the distance between me and *them*. As fatigue and exposure took their toll, however, I started wondering if I had made the right choice, after all. At the time, all I could think of was escape, but what had I actually escaped from, and where was I going now? Would I ever be able to find the trail again? If the evil man and the lion could find me so easily there in the canyon, was anyplace really safe from them?

Two distinct fears began to conflict with each other: the fear of where I was going and the fear of where I had been. My exhausted body wanted desperately to kick for the shore and get out of the freezing water, but my terrified mind wanted to keep on clinging to the log and let it carry me even farther downstream. The conflict rendered me powerless to do anything but let the current take me. I could do nothing but pray.

As darkness settled over the river, the current brought me into an eddy, where the water swirled into an easy spiral, slowing my forward progress and allowing me to loosen my grip a little on the log. It was too dark to see my surroundings, and for the first time today I was grateful not to be moving so swiftly downstream. The log I clung to was drifting, but in what direction I couldn't tell. A tree branch scraped across my face, and I could tell that I was moving into a tangle of debris left by some previous flood.

Progress came to a sudden halt when the log collided with an immovable object. It seemed big in the darkness, but what was more intriguing was the fact that it sounded metallic. I reached one hand up and touched a smooth surface. Working my way in one direction and then the other, I finally determined that I was up against a boat which was pressed up against the trees, turned on its side with the bottom facing me. With a renewed hope I had not felt in a long time, I worked at the debris until the boat was freed from their grip and settled back upright into the water. It was an aluminum-hulled row boat, about ten feet long. Feeling around for a grip, I discovered a length of rope still tied to the bow, and knew at once where it had come from: this was a part of the crossing apparatus back at the trail. Some flood had snagged it and broke it loose, bringing it to this eddy where it was finally brought to a stop.

With great difficulty, I managed to get my back pack off my numb shoulders and into the boat. Then by using the log which had been my constant companion all day was able to pull myself aboard. The snagged debris still prevented me from moving, but that was good for the moment. I decided to try and get warm, wait for daylight, then assess my situation. I can't say it was the best night's sleep I've ever had, soaking wet and laying across metal ribs in an unstable row boat, but after the log, it was like a five star hotel.

Therefore let everyone who is godly pray to You while you may be found; surely when the mighty waters rise, they will not reach him. You are my hiding place; you will protect me from trouble and surround me with songs of deliverance.
Psalm 32: 6 – 7

Prayer: Thank You Lord for the things You put in my way to rescue me. Even when I have no control over my steps, You are there to reach out and be my strong right Hand. Help me to see Your mighty works today, and to know that You have never forsaken me, nor ever will. Praise You Holy Name.

Ask yourself: What surprises have come into your life which have helped you through a difficult situation? Was this God's Hand at work?

March 11

Into the Unknown

There's nothing colder than an aluminum water bed. The sun was never so welcome as it crept over the trees surrounding the river where I lay, shivering, in the bottom of the row boat I had discovered the night before. Looking around, I saw that the boat continued to float in an eddy of swirling water, with the main current farther toward the center of the river. The shore was just a few yards to my left: a small sandy area flanked on two sides by huge boulders and against a backdrop of impenetrable undergrowth.

Cold and fatigue overruled any fears I may have had from yesterday's horror, and I paddled with my hands until the water was shallow enough to climb out and pull the boat up onto the shore. The contents of my backpack were soaked, but I found some matches in a waterproof container and soon had a fire going.

With dry clothes and warm food, I was finally able to assess my situation: going back upstream was out of the question, due to the strength of the current and the heavy undergrowth along the river bank. The wall of trees and brush behind me prevent any ideas of going that way. The only alternative, it seemed, was to continue downstream in hopes of finding a way to return to the trail.

Drying my gear as best I could, I repacked and secured everything in the bottom of the boat. Sorting through the driftwood, I found a straight pole which could help with steering, and I thought as I sharpened one end, could double as a weapon if necessary. The sun was nearly directly overhead as I pushed away from the shore and into the current.

A part of me grieved to know that I was putting even more distance between myself and the trail to which I wanted so desperately to return. But on the other hand, I thought, at least I'm going *somewhere*, and with a little help from above, will be able to find some good even in this unexpected detour. The rest of the day, I guided the boat downstream, watching the shoreline for anything, good or bad, and prayed for wisdom to do the right thing.

> *Your thunder was heard in the whirlwind, your lightning lit up the world; the earth trembled and quaked. Your path led through the sea, your way through the mighty waters, though your footprints were not seen.*
>
> Psalm 77: 18 – 19

....

Prayer: Lord, I want to do Your will, but I feel like circumstances have taken me farther away from You. Help me get back to the path You have set before me. Show me which way to turn when there is no obvious way. Lead me back to Your side.

Ask yourself: Do you think the traveler in the story has made the right decision to continue down stream? Why or why not?

Rapids

After I left the eddy and pushed into the main current of the river, I felt a sense of relief that now at last, I had some control over my progress. True, I was still moving away from the trail, but the journey was pleasant and restful. Trees shaded most of the river. Birds sang along the river's edge and the occasional frog would leap into the water as my boat approached. Some areas along the shoreline were less densely packed with vegetation, and had I looked closer I might have found a way through it. However, that would mean leaving behind this idyllic setting and this fantastic mode of transportation, so I hesitated to look too closely. The late afternoon sun warmed my back, and I soon found myself drifting into a semi sleep, lulled by the insects and the sounds of the river. Had I been more alert, I would have noticed that the sounds were changing. Subtly at first, the boat began picking up speed. The insects that were buzzing around my head were soon left behind as the wind started whistling through the straps of my gear.

The first indication of trouble came with a loud "thunk" followed by a metallic scraping sound as the boat was dragged over a submerged rock. I sat up and noticed at once that the shoreline was no longer covered in trees. In their place was a solid wall of rock, pressing closer from each side of the river, and as the channel narrowed, the speed of my boat increased. I grabbed my pole and began fending off rocks as they threatened to disembowel the aluminum hull, but soon gave up the effort and focused instead on holding on for dear life. At times I shot straight down the center of the rapids; at times I was turned backwards and sideways, carried over terrifying drops and swirls, all of which threatened to either capsize me, crush me, or accomplish both simultaneously. All I could manage was to grip the sides of the boat tighter and cry out with each drop, like an unwilling passenger on an untested roller coaster. The sound of water striking rock filled my head, and I was sure that the next sound would be my own body slamming up against a boulder. Instead, the sound began to change, from a high watery pitch, to something deeper and infinitely more ominous. An unspoken terror made its way to my consciousness and I struggled to grasp passing rocks, anything that would stop my forward progress.

But there was no stopping, and no avoiding what waited around the next sharp bend in the river. The foaming waves seemed to simply disappear, leaving only the narrow canyon dead ahead. I didn't have time to wonder where the water had gone, because in the next instant I was carried over the edge of the waterfall, the only sound reaching my ears now, the sound of my own screams.

There is a way that seems right to a man, but in the end it leads to death.

Proverbs 16: 25

....

Prayer: As much as I try to control my life, Lord, I know that there are times when events move faster than I can take them in. Prepare me for those times, or if it is my own choices that take me where I do not want to go, then grant me wisdom to avoid them.

Ask yourself: Has your life ever entered a time when you felt like circumstances were moving faster than you could respond to them? How did you feel?

Maelstrom

I don't know how far I fell. In times of sudden crisis, events often seem to slow down, and as the boat dropped over the waterfall's edge I was gripped with other-worldly fascination. My back pack, which had been securely lashed down, slowly worked its way loose and rose up to meet me before drifting away into the air. The sight of my pole, shooting straight down through the mists as if caught in the lens of a wildlife photographer, was strangely beautiful. My own dependence on the boat seemed to lose its significance, and my hands, which had been holding the sides in a death grip, now floated up in front of my face, unsure of what to do next.

Then the world turned upside down as we struck the water. Darkness swallowed up the rainbow which I had been noticing just above my head, and the silence of the fall was now replaced by a deep rumbling sound which seemed to originate from inside my head. I was surprised to find that I couldn't breathe, and moreover had no idea of where the surface of the water might be. My world was a swirling mixture of light and dark, silence and sound, devoid of air. I struggled, then gave up, then found my head above water, prompting me to gasp and resume the fight. But in the next instant the dark void returned and my struggle was less intense. A second time air found my lungs, only to be deprived again.

Eventually I lost count and simply breathed when I could, relaxed when I could not; and the maelstrom at the base of the waterfall demonstrated its absolute control over my life. At some point I must have been carried clear of the swirling current and pushed onto a sandbank about a hundred yards downstream. I lay there until a mosquito buzzing in my ear compelled me to move. I tried to raise myself up, but was wracked by pain which I could not identify. I lay back down and let the darkness cover me, unable to stand or speak, but only to utter a prayer. Thank you that I'm alive; what happens now?

God has made my heart faint; the Almighty has terrified me. Yet I am not silenced by the darkness, by the thick darkness that covers my face.

Job 23: 16 – 17

....

Prayer: Lord, when the world comes crashing around me I have no eloquent prayer to offer. I can only trust You to rescue me and set me on the rock that is higher than I. Surround me with Your Presence; guide me through the maelstrom for Your kingdom's glory.

Ask yourself: What was the simplest prayer you ever offered to God?

March 14

Picking up the Pieces

The waterfall had taken its toll, both on me and on my equipment. I was bruised and cut in several places, but no bones seemed to be broken. My clothes were torn. Looking up and down the riverbank on both sides, I managed to find my back pack and some of the contents, but not everything. I found the boat up against a rock, and after dragging it out of the water discovered that several holes had been punched in the aluminum hull.

Back upstream, the waterfall seemed to erupt from a narrow cleft in a solid rock face which sat between two rock mountains standing higher yet. If I had entertained any ideas yesterday about returning back to the trail by way of the river, those thoughts were put to rest once and for all. Looking in the other direction, I could see that the river's fury was pretty well spent: the water widened and settled back into a calm journey toward whatever lowest point lay beyond. The trees had disappeared, and the area seemed to be the start of a desert.

I didn't know what lay ahead, but I was in no condition today to find out. Making camp near the water's edge, I started the process of recovering and repairing whatever I could. Foodstuffs were laid out and assessed, clothing was mended, cuts were dressed and wrapped in bandages. The boat seemed to be the biggest challenge of all. Using strips of cloth and candle wax, I managed to make some patches, but they held only loosely. I soon discovered that the best approach was to let it leak and spend my energy bailing the water out, using a coffee cup.

By the end of the day, everything seemed ready to resume the journey. But where was I going? Would there be any way to get back to the trail? How I longed for a map! If only I could know where I was, in relation to where I had been going. I had been told that the trail itself was my map; as long as I kept it in sight I had nothing to worry about. Well, now the trail was far behind me and I felt nothing but a profound fear. Somehow, I could not bring myself to worry about the evil man or those who travel with him. My heart told me that as long as I strayed away from the goal, I was no threat to him, and he in turn would be no threat to me. Pitiful compensation, I thought to myself; two days ago I would have gladly chosen this forsaken place over any territory inhabited by *them*. Now as I lay watching the stars come out I thought, I would take them all on, bare handed if need be. Just bring me back to where I'm supposed to be.

From the ends of the earth I call to you, I call as my heart grows faint; lead me to the rock that is higher than I.

Psalm 61: 2

....

Prayer: Oh God, I know You have a path for me to walk, but in my pride and ignorance I have strayed away from it. Please turn me around and lead me to that place of security and hope: to the place that leads to Your kingdom.

Ask yourself: Would you rather face an enemy in a place where you know you should be, or would you rather be alone somewhere else?

The River's End

The river seemed to hold no major obstacles and I was anxious to make progress, even though I still had no idea where I was going. Nevertheless, it was a slow start.. The coffee cup was painfully inadequate as a bailer, and I had to stay at it constantly. The river continued to widen, and as it did, became increasingly shallow with each mile. Time and again a pole was called to use in guiding the boat into areas of deeper water. In some places, there was no main current to be found, and I had to get out and pull the boat over water that barely covered the toes of my boots. The area was like a huge delta, except that it was still a desert. There was no vegetation except for an occasional weed, and the sides of the canyon had moved away to reveal a plain stretching in all directions. Only the rising heat waves prevented me from seeing all the way to the horizon.

During one rest break, I lowered my bailer/coffee cup into the water next to the boat for a drink. As soon as it reached my lips, I flung the water away; it had become salty. I had seen something like this in two places: the Great Salt Lake in Utah and the Dead Sea in Israel. My river was running into what used to be an ocean but in the absence of an outlet was gradually evaporating, leaving only the salt behind. Pulling the boat up onto shore, I retraced my steps upstream, testing the water until it once again tasted fresh. Bringing every container I could find, I filled everything, knowing that this could be the last drinking water I see for a long time.

Taking a long drink and shading my eyes to scan the horizon, I saw that the lake did indeed spread out. Far off in the distance, I could even see waves, evidence that it would soon be deep enough to navigate again. But what captured my attention and rekindled my hope was the sight which lay beyond the farthest distance over the water. There stood the mountain I had glimpsed previously. The first view I had of it had excited me and drove me on at the expense of what blessings there were on the trail itself. The next time I saw it I felt an uncomfortable fear, not certain why but vaguely aware of something evil about the mountain. Now, however, it brought me the greatest joy I had known in days. Somewhere in that direction was the trail. I now had a beacon to follow. Loading up the boat with my water supply, I set off again, wading and pulling when I had to until finally it would float on its own. It was still not more than about knee deep, and I was able to dig my pole into the mud and push the boat along. When night came and I could no longer see the mountain, I lay down for a rest. Watching the stars come out, I thought, "How wonderful to have a goal again, even if it's far away over trackless desert and lifeless sea." With that thought, I fell asleep.

He marks out the horizon on the face of the waters for a boundary between light and darkness.

Job 26: 8

Prayer: When I lose sight of the goal, Lord, keep me on the right path. When the prize is before me, give me strength to move forward. When I have forgotten my aim, remind me please.

Ask yourself: What goals drive your life today? What will you do if and when you reach those goals?

March 16

Deep Water

A splash of salty water woke me this morning. The wind had picked up and the boat was rocking sluggishly in the waves. It would have been moving more swiftly except for the fact that it was in the last stages of sinking. I hadn't intended to go to sleep last night, at least not for long, and although my makeshift patches held back the worst of the leaks, water had been seeping in for several hours by the time I was aware of it. The edges of the boat were almost even with the outside surface of the water, my back pack was floating over my legs, and it seemed as though any sudden movement would send both boat and occupant straight to the bottom. My coffee cup was floating near my head, so I grabbed it and started gingerly bailing.

It took nearly an hour before I felt that I could dare sit up. Looking around, I saw first that my mountain still rested before me on the horizon, seemingly no closer than the night before. Then I turned to look behind me and was shocked to see nothing familiar at all: no delta, no distant canyon, nothing. Apparently I had indeed drifted farther away from the shore during the night. Good for me, I thought as I carefully stood up and prepared for another day of "poling". Gripping my pole with both hands and lowering it over the side, I soon discovered that the bottom was no longer in reach. What I thought would be an enormous knee deep lake turned out to be simply enormous. Taking a piece of rope from my pack, I tied a metal skillet to one end and lowered it down, measuring the rope as it went. Ten feet, twenty feet, twenty five feet. Not especially deep for a lake, but when all you have is a seven foot pole, it might as well have been the Marianas Trench. Peeling a bit of bark off the pole, I tossed it into the water and compared its drift with my own. If the boat was moving at all, it was negligible. How was I to move? I started rowing with my hands, but soon gave up, exhausted. The skillet proved to be a little more efficient, but not much. I kept up the effort all day, stopping only for brief periods of rest or to bail.

By evening the mountain seemed no closer than it had this morning, but I was measurably more fatigued. I tried to rest, but was afraid that I might sleep too long and awake to find my boat sunk from under me. If I could have found the energy, I would have kicked myself for getting into this predicament. But where had I gone wrong? How far back would I have to retrace my steps until I found the turning point which led me to this impossible situation? The rest of the night, I thought and bailed and prayed, not knowing which would help the most.

I am like a desert owl, like an owl among the ruins. I lie awake; I have become like a bird alone on a roof.

Psalm 102: 6 – 7

Prayer: Speak to me, Lord, during the long nights when my thoughts torment me. Show me the folly of my ways, and then light my path that I may return to the place where You set me. Lead me through the stillness.

Ask yourself: When faced with a difficult decision, which is most important: thinking about it, praying about it, or working toward a solution?

On the Wings of the Morning

In my dream, a bird was flying around me, singing a song which sounded like "Hey you! Hey you!" I raised my hand to wave him away and the resulting splash in the water brought me awake. My boat was once again nearly filled with water, and moving as little as possible I found my coffee cup and started bailing. The bird song sound continued, and I became aware of the wind, whistling over the boat. When I could move around again, I checked my position and saw that the mountain seemed no closer than it had the night before. The wind was fairly strong, however, and blowing from behind. If only I had a sail, I thought. I tried standing in the boat, hoping my body would provide something for the wind to blow against. Seeing my pole, I wondered if it might serve as a mast to which I could tie something. Rummaging through my back pack, I found an extra shirt, a jacket and some trousers. I carefully strung these along the pole, as if it were a clothesline, then set it up toward the bow of the boat. At first everything flapped uselessly in the wind, but by using my rope to secure everything to everything else, a makeshift sail began to take form.. I tossed another piece of bark into the water and watched as it drifted behind, evidence that I was moving ever so slowly. This gave me hope, and I spent the rest of the day refining my sail, tying down loose ends and turning it carefully as the wind shifted. I spent a lot of time going in circles, but eventually discovered that my skillet could serve as a kind of rudder, keep the bow of the boat more or less pointed toward the mountain.

As the sun approached the horizon, I tried to see if I had made any progress at all. A distinctive shape on the side of the mountain which I had noted earlier now appeared slightly higher up, a sure sign that I was closer than before. Encouraged, I tied everything into place, bailed out the boat one more time, and settled down for a short nap.

How interesting, I thought: here I was, stuck in the middle of a dead body of water with no means to move myself forward, and the answer comes from the thing over which I have absolutely no control. The wind blows where it will. I can't see it. I can't command it. All I can do is let it push me; and hopefully by the power of the wind, I will eventually find myself on solid ground again. I said a silent prayer of thanksgiving for the blessing which I would never see with my eyes, but which blew through my hair and drove me forward even as I slept.

The wind blows wherever it pleases. You hear its sound, but you cannot tell where it comes from or where it is going. So it is with everyone born of the Spirit."

John 3: 8

Prayer: Father, I know that some of the most wonderful blessings I enjoy are those which I never see. Thank you for providing the wind, and the changing seasons and all the mysteries of nature which make life possible. Teach me how to see through Your eyes, and appreciate today Your guiding Hand on my life.

Ask yourself: Is seeing a requirement for believing? What things can you accept as true even though they are invisible?

March 18

"Don't You Care?"

The sound of the mast cracking in half and striking the aluminum hull of the boat brought me suddenly awake, and would have brought me to my feet if that were possible. The boat was being tossed so violently that it was all I could do to simply hold on and try to remain inside. The wind, which had been such a welcome change yesterday, today had grown into a full-fledged storm. Visibility was no more than a few feet, and whether the curtain of water around me was being blown up from the lake's surface or rained down from the sky I couldn't tell. Twice I saw my backpack get washed over the side but managed to grab it with one free hand, holding on for dear life with the other.

My mind was a mixture of confusion and terror, and I discovered, anger. Why was this happening? Just yesterday I was thanking God for the blessing of the wind and looking forward to finding my way to shore by it's gentle power. Now it looked as though it was about to kill me, and even as I fought down my terror, I had less success in fighting down the feelings that raged within me. I felt like one of those disciples, finding Jesus sleeping in the back of a storm tossed boat and crying out, "Don't you care if we die?" With each crashing wave, reality slipped farther away from me, much as a drowning man must feel as he sinks beneath the surface for the last time. So this is it, I thought; the "early pickup" which will take me away from this journey and directly to... what? What was waiting for me beyond this place? Was it the land of peace and eternal life I had come to believe, or was it something else altogether different? Suddenly I was not so sure, and as a result I felt what those storm-tossed disciples must have felt: absolute terror. "Lord!" I cried. "Where are you?"

What happened next is difficult to describe, and indeed I cannot, not fully. Even though visibility was not more than a few feet, my eyes were drawn to something in the distance. Rather, I should say, Someone. It was the figure of a man, standing calmly, looking my way. My first thought was that it must be the Evil Man, since he seemed to have some power that I didn't understand. But that thought was quickly put aside, as my heart was overcome by a feeling of peace. The waves were still raging; the wind still howled in my ears; but my eyes were riveted on the figure, standing, it seemed, just a few yards away. A wave crashed over the bow of the boat, and my attention was drawn away. Suddenly the terror returned and I gripped the side of the boat in desperation. But as soon as I looked back at the figure, peace returned, and nothing else mattered.

A furious squall came up, and the waves broke over the boat, so that it was nearly swamped. Jesus was in the stern, sleeping on a cushion. The disciples woke him and said to him, "Teacher, don't you care if we drown?"

Mark 4: 37 – 38

Prayer: Lord I confess that I often let my fear control me. There are times when I can be neither rational nor caring, because I'm afraid of what is happening to me. Forgive me when I take my eyes away from You, Lord, and allow myself to be so victimized. Show me a glimpse of Yourself, Lord, and calm the raging sea within me.

Ask yourself: What is the difference between fear and anger?

March 19

"Come"

The sight of a human standing unperturbed in the midst of a raging storm was both terrifying and reassuring. The storm continued unabated, but looking at the man, I knew that it had no power over him. It's power over me was yet to be decided. Whenever I looked away from him, the terror returned and I fought to stay alive against impossible odds. In the next moment, my eyes were riveted on him and the waves seemed trivial by comparison. Deep inside, I knew that the storm was still all around me. Fixing my eyes in one direction or another had no affect on the weather, but the action had a profound affect on me. As long as I looked at him, I cared nothing about anything else. So it came as no surprise when from deep in my soul I heard the only word I wanted to hear: "Come".

A moment before, I would have insisted that it was insanity brought on by impending death that would urge me to leave the only security I knew and step away from it, into the jaws of an angry sea. But then, a moment before, I would have thought it the mark of an insane man to claim the kind of vision I was looking at now. Vision, insanity, profound deception: no explanation was sufficient, nor did I care to consider any of them. All I knew was that I was being summoned, and I intended to go. Never taking my eyes off the figure who stood a few away, I swung one leg over the side of the boat, then the other, until I sat, feet in the water. Sliding away from the boat, I dropped down and into the water expecting... what? To sink out of sight? To drown? It didn't matter, as long as I was moving toward him. I stood there, lost in awe of the moment, and then realized that I was in fact standing. Was I walking on water, like some Bible story disciple? I looked back at the book and saw that it was tipped slightly on one side as it rested in the shallows. I looked down at my feet as the waves slapped around me, reaching occasionally to my knees. I looked into the storm and could just make out the shoreline, running from my right to my left. Then I looked back toward where the figure had stood and saw nothing. I walked forward a few more steps until I was standing on the beach, straining my eyes in every direction but seeing nothing but the receding storm.

Falling to my knees, I cried out; but whether it was a cry of joy or a cry of despair I could not tell. I had been brought from certain death to solid ground, but the One who brought me here could no longer be seen. I wept and thanked God for my rescue, then I wept and begged for another vision. Face down in the sand, I pleaded and praised until the stress of the last two days overtook me and I slept, dreaming of a Man who stood over me, whispering words of reassurance.

> But Jesus immediately said to them: "Take courage! It is I. Don't be afraid." "Lord, if it's you," Peter replied, "tell me to come to you on the water." "Come," he said.
>
> Mark 14: 27 – 29

....

Prayer: Lord, how I long to see Your face, and yet in Your mercy You tell me "No, not yet." You are near me, I know that. I can feel Your presence and see Your works. Hasten the day, dear Father, when I can see You face to face.

Ask yourself: Why do you think God would refuse our prayers for a direct look at Him today?

The Unseen Friend

By the time I awoke, the storm had passed. My feet still lay in water, but the waves lapped gently over my ankles. The boat was touching the shore not far away, and I could just see the top of my back pack still resting inside. The remains of my makeshift sail were scattered up and down the beach. I sat up, trying to remember how I had gotten here, and then the memory came flooding back. I stood to my feet, looking in all directions in vain hope of seeing Him again. Had it really happened, or had I been dreaming some kind of hallucinogenic vision? I tried to review the facts again: the storm, the fear, the sight of something which prompted me to get out of the boat, only to discover that I was back in shallow water again. I had not really walked on the water, after all, and the combination of hunger, thirst and sheer terror could explain the vision.

And yet, He had seemed so real. Even the dream that I now recalled was unlike any I had ever experienced: He was standing there beside me, encouraging me, sheltering me, loving me. Now that I was awake I saw nothing, heard nothing, but does that mean that what I saw and heard before was not real? As I thought about it, very few people in the Bible ever had face to face encounters with God. Instead, it was dreams, or prophets or burning bushes that moved them to action. The few times He did come close to His people, they pulled away or fell on their faces in fear.

Perhaps it's God's mercy that I don't see Him. C. S. Lewis once said that if Christians ever did really see God, they would be killing themselves in order to get to Heaven immediately. And then there's the fact that even what I see can be a deception, a lesson I've learned painfully on this trek. Maybe God does not appear in the flesh because man would only doubt Him all the more. At the end of the day, the best, most real experience I can have is the one that comes to me by way of the heart.

For this people's heart has become calloused; they hardly hear with their ears, and they have closed their eyes. Otherwise they might see with their eyes, hear with their ears, understand with their hearts and turn, and I would heal them.
Matthew 13: 15

Prayer: Lord, I want to see You face to face, but I know that You will reveal to me only what I am able to bear. Until I can stand before you, work a miracle in my heart; help me see You there and know the power of Your love for me.

Ask yourself: Would seeing something cause you to believe it, or would you still doubt?

March 21

A Place of Worship

I couldn't leave that place, not right away. Even as I gathered my gear and packed for the journey ahead, my mind was re-living the events which had taken place on this shoreline. I had seen *Him* right at this spot. He had visited me here, I was sure of that. I sat for hours and looked around, trying to memorize every detail. Not surprisingly, this was not a place I would have picked for a Divine revelation: a lifeless lake of salty water surrounded by a barren and trackless desert. When I thought about it though, I remembered that some of God's most incredible workings with His people were in such places. The deserts, the wilderness, the oceans, all were not known for their particular beauty or majesty, nor were the individuals He chose particularly outstanding in their own right. Of course, in memorializing those people and places, men have tried to "dress up" the images somewhat. Magnificent cathedrals and colorful paintings command our attention, but the fact remains that it was not the place nor the person which was significant but rather the Creator of those places and those people.

Still, I couldn't help but feel a special stirring in my soul for being here. I hope that some day I can come back to this place and try to re-kindle that feeling. Dragging the boat out of the water, I stood it up so that the bow pointed to the heavens. Then I collected rocks and stacked them around it for support. From the broken mast of my makeshift sail, I lashed together a crude cross and fastened it securely to the top of my monument, like a steeple. On one of the larger stones, I used my knife to carve the words, "Come", the message which I had heard so clearly in the midst of the storm, and which had prompted me to step willingly into what for all I knew at the time was certain death. As the sun made its way to the horizon, I found a vantage point from where I could see both the monument and the lake behind it. I fell to my knees there and worshipped, crying aloud for God's mercy. I thanked Him for saving me from the storm, and I begged Him to reveal Himself again. Then I lay facedown and simply let the mystery of the moment work through me. I don't know how long I lay there, but when I raised my head again, it was dark. The stars on the horizon beyond my structure formed a frame even more beautiful than the setting sun had created. I kneeled and prayed again, until sleep came. My dreams on this second night at this place were not of Him and the words He had spoken to me. This time I dreamed of cathedrals and monuments, of bronze plaques and statues. If He spoke to me while I slept, I was unable to hear.

Peter said to Jesus, "Lord, it is good for us to be here. If you wish, I will put up three shelters-one for you, one for Moses and one for Elijah." While he was still speaking, a bright cloud enveloped them, and a voice from the cloud said, "This is my Son, whom I love; with him I am well pleased. Listen to him!"
Matthew 17: 4 – 5

Prayer: Father, forgive me when I let the things You have done interfere with the reality of Your Presence. Forgive me for turning my attention to the places and forgetting Your works. Remind me today that it is You and not anything You have created and used which is worthy of worship. Touch me anew and help me listen, and feel.

Ask yourself: Think of a famous memorial you have visited. How did you feel, knowing that something significant happened at the place where you stood?

A Reluctant Parting

Leaving my monument by the shore was one of the most difficult things I've ever had to do. My bag was packed, the sun had already risen high above the horizon, but still I stood and contemplated this place, memorialized by the boat/stone structure I had so carefully erected. Walking around it, I saw angles which had yet to be appreciated, stones which needed re-adjusting. I studied the upturned boat and remembered the hours spent racing down the river, poling through the shallow salt flats, tossing on the stormy waves. And I remembered stepping out of the boat, into the midst of the storm and toward the Figure who stood in the distance and bid me come. How could I leave this place of awe and mystery? How could I turn my back on the very place where my Master revealed Himself to me? Perhaps I've come to a kind of Holy Land, where His mighty work is more evident. Maybe if I waited here awhile longer, He would come again, and...

But even as I contemplated, I knew that it was wrong to stay. Just as I could not tarry back in the apple country, as beautiful as it was, I cannot tarry here. The thing which holds me here, I know, is neither the lake, nor the shore nor any of the things I can see and touch; rather, it is the experience with the One who created me and loves me. The fact that it happened here makes this place significant for me, but I must not let the place be a substitute for the experience. My journey will eventually find its end at His feet, and all the places where He has visited me in the past will be nothing in comparison. It's good to remember the places and times when my heart was filled and my soul felt that reassuring electric power of His presence. But it is, after all, the Presence and not the place that's important.

With that thought, I turned my back on the past and set out again. The direction was clear: toward the mountain which still loomed on the horizon. I stopped occasionally and looked back toward the lake and the monument I had built there on the shore. A part of me wanted to return, I confess. But as the distance increased, the sense of separation was not diminished. He was still with me.

Be strong and courageous. Do not be afraid or terrified because of them, for the LORD your God goes with you; he will never leave you nor forsake you.

Deuteronomy 21: 6

Prayer: Thank you, God, for the times and places where You have worked in powerful and obvious ways. May I never forget those times, and may those places always rekindle in my heart the love and devotion I have for You. But protect me, I pray, from the temptation to make of those places shrines which would become a substitute for You. May I never be guilty of worshipping the creature instead of the Creator.

Ask yourself: Do you have anything in your home which you keep as a reminder of a special time in your life? How do feel when you look at it?

A Straight Line

Although there was no trail, the path ahead was abundantly clear. The mountain, which I had seen at the beginning of the journey and which I knew stood between me and the final goal, rose up from the desert floor like a beacon. It was still a long way off; during the weeks I've been moving toward it, it hasn't grown a lot bigger. But distance didn't seem to diminish it's power and it's call to me.

Directly ahead of me stood nothing but trackless desert. Closer to the lake the ground under my feet was an unbroken plain of salt, harsh and unchanging as the sun rose higher. As I moved farther into the desert, the salt was mingled with sand until finally it disappeared altogether, allowing the occasional cactus or desert weed to grow. Determined to make this crossing as quick and efficient as possible, I picked out an imaginary point on the mountain ahead and walked steadily toward it. Once in awhile I stopped and looked back to make sure I was traveling in a straight line, making minor adjustments as they seemed necessary. By early afternoon, an outcropping of rock caught my eye, just off to the right, and I diverted toward it in hopes of seeing something from a higher vantage than I could from below. Climbing up the rock and settling for a rest and a drink, I looked back and was dismayed to see the tracks I had left. They seemed to go straight for awhile, then veered off to the right or left, leaving a zig zag pattern and easily losing a half hour or more in progress.

From this viewpoint, I could see what had happened: each twist in the tracks was made where I had turned to look back. I shook my head and mourned my performance. This was not rocket science, after all. Anyone knows that in order to walk a straight line you have to keep sight of a mark dead ahead. Looking back will cause you to lose your perspective, every time. And to make matters worse, I knew that my looking back was not just in order to check my steering; I was looking past my footprints to try and catch a glimpse of the lake, and the monument, and anything or Anyone else which might be back there. I knew I couldn't stay back there, but today I was hampered by the temptation to *look* back.

Well, no more. From my vantage point on the rock, I drew another imaginary line toward the mountain, and picked out several objects closer to where I stood: a rock, a plant, anything which would hold my attention and keep me moving forward. Now that I've left where I was, I wanted more than ever to get to where I was going.

They have left the straight way and wandered off to follow the way of Balaam son of Beor, who loved the wages of wickedness.

II Peter 2: 15

....

Prayer: There are many things behind me, Lord: things which I want to remember and things which I would like to forget. Help me keep my eyes forward. Let me see the goal You have set for me, and give me strength to move ahead.

Ask yourself: Is there anything in your past which hinders your forward progress?

March 24

Thirst

Many sensations in life can be ignored for awhile, such as a headache, a blister or hunger. But there is one feeling which demands attention and threatens extreme discomfort if those demands are not soon met, and that is the feeling of thirst. This morning, I had just enough water left in my back pack for a reminder that I wanted more. The temptation to go back was now overruled by the fact that the only thing waiting behind me was a lake of salt water. Looking ahead, I could see green forests covering my mountain, and patches of white which had to be melting snow. Forward was the only option now, and the sooner I left this desert the better.

Eyes still fixed on landmarks to insure a straight journey, I tried to occupy my mind with thought. I recalled past adventures and imagined what lay ahead, but to no avail. Like a civil defense broadcast blasting through my classical music program, the words were a constant scream in my brain. "You're thirsty. Get... a... drink... NOW." The demands softened to a gentle pleading, then cranked up the volume again. "You're DYING, you idiot! DO something!"

Finally I compromised with my brain and sang an old country and western song from my childhood: "All day I've faced the barren waste without the taste of water; cool, water." Whether it helped or not I don't know, but as evening came, I kept walking and moved on to the rest of the song: "The nights are cool, and I'm a fool; each star is a pool of water; cool, water."

Fatigue eventually won out over thirst and I fell onto the sand, still warm from the day's blistering heat. I tried to verbalize what I was feeling, but all I could feel at the moment was thirst. Maybe tomorrow, I'll be angry, or bewildered, or dead. Right now, I only want a drink.

As the deer pants for streams of water, so my soul pants for You, O God, for the living God. When can I go and meet with God? My tears have been my food day and night, while men say to me all day long, "Where is your God?"

Psalms 42: 1 – 3

....

Prayer: There are conditions like thirst which move every other thought to a lower priority. Father, may my yearning for You be as powerful and consuming as physical thirst.

Ask yourself: When were you really, really thirsty?

The Sounds of Children

"Tag! You're it!"

"No way! I was it already."

"Timmy! Put that bug down and catch up."

"But he's nice. Can't I keep him?"

My dreams had become surrealistic, moving from a jungle waterfall to a mountain stream, fishing with my Dad. Then suddenly, I was in a playground, surrounded by children. They seemed to be moving past me, but taking no notice of my presence. Sleep began to fall away and the dream became more vivid with returning color and the feel of a breeze on my cheek. But the children were still there. The one that I knew had to be Timmy was standing next to me, holding a grasshopper between thumb and forefinger.

"Hey! Wait for me!" he yelled. The sound brought me fully awake, or at least I seemed to be.

"Timmy," I croaked through parched lips. "Where are you going?"

The boy stopped and looked back at me, a hint of a smile on his face. "I've got a bug," he said. "His name is Elmer."

"Where are you going?" I repeated, still too weak to stand. "Where did you come from?"

But Timmy's attention was pulled away to the group of children, still moving westward. "I have to go," he said, breaking into a run and a shout of "Wait for me!"

I tried to stand, but the world was spinning far too quickly for me to hold on. I fell back down with a feeble cry. "Wait for me, too."

He took a little child and had him stand among them. Taking him in his arms, he said to them, "Whoever welcomes one of these little children in my name welcomes me; and whoever welcomes me does not welcome me but the one who sent me.

Mark 9: 36 – 37

....

Prayer: Remind me today, Father, about childlike faith, and how I need to be like that. Take away my fear and show me where I should go today.

Ask yourself: How is a child's faith different from that of an adult?

Led By a Child

I lay where I had fallen, not fully conscious but not fully awake either. My thirst still ruled all rational thought, which was quickly being replaced by irrational. A grasshopper landed next to my face, and as my eyes tried to focus on him, I wondered if it was the same one Timmy had caught.

Where was Timmy? And the others? Had I dreamed everything? Pulling my knees and elbows up, I managed to raise myself enough to look around. The desert was still there, as I had feared. That much had not been a dream. There was no sign of the children, so that question remained unanswered. But as I looked again toward my mountain, I thought I could see a trail, leading directly to it. Funny, I thought, there was no trail there yesterday. A closer look showed me that the "trail" was actually a line of footprints... very small footprints.

The revelation was enough to get me to my feet again, and I staggered toward the tracks which lay like a beacon, clearly visible in the early morning sunlight. I tried to imagine how a group of children could have gotten to a place like this, and where they might be going with such apparent ease. Whatever the explanation, it was far beyond my ability to comprehend. All I could do was move forward, one step at a time, trying as much as possible to place my feet into the tracks in front of me.

A new strength found its way into my dehydrated body. Even in my delirium, I was able to recognize the fact that a group of children had passed this way, and in fact must be just ahead. If they did it, then so could I.

The wolf will live with the lamb, the leopard will lie down with the goat, the calf and the lion and the yearling together; and a little child will lead them.

Isaiah 11: 6

Prayer: May I never be so proud that I would neglect Your perfect leading, Father, even it be through the leading of a child. Humble my heart and teach me by Your precious children how to trust in You.

Ask yourself: What have you learned from a child?

March 27

Water

Step after faltering step, the miles passed under my feet. At times I would close my eyes and move ahead in a dreamlike existence, but when I opened them again would find that I had drifted off the child-sized footprints which served as my guide. Eventually a routine developed, and I would close my eyes for five steps, open them just long enough to get back on track, then close them again. In this way, I was able to ignore somewhat the searing heat from the sun which was gaining height from behind me. I would pretend that I was sleeping, comfortably ensconced in bed, watching my progress as if it was a "B" grade movie. Not much dialogue, I thought to myself. Not much action either. I'd have to take this video back for a refund. They guarantee their movies, I know. If you don't like it, bring it back. Well, I don't like this one. It's too much like those reality TV programs that have become so popular lately. "Tune in and watch a man walk across a desert until he dies of thirst!" "But wait! There's more: experience first hand his out of body delirium, as he races after a group of imaginary children, leading him to that imaginary water pump."

But there it was, directly in front of me: an old-fashioned cast iron pump, secured to a cement slab and painted bright red. Even as I stared unbelieving, wet spots on the cement evaporated away, evidence that water had been splashing around the pump only moments before.

The children were nowhere to be seen, but I wouldn't have noticed them even if they were. My entire body was riveted on that pump and what it promised. I half-staggered, half fell forward, landing on my knees and grasping the pump handle. With an effort I would not have thought possible, I began pumping the handle furiously, but was rewarded with sound of cool air being brought up the pipe and out of the faucet. It was then that I noticed the words painted on the cement upon which I knelt: "Read this before using."

The poor and needy search for water, but there is none; their tongues are parched with thirst. But I the LORD will answer them; I, the God of Israel, will not forsake them.

Isaiah 41: 17

Prayer: Help me to remember, Lord, where all good things come from. Every time I take a drink, or eat a meal, or talk with a friend, or enjoy a sunrise, remind me that it is You and Your love for me that makes it all possible. Then I will praise You with all my heart.

Ask yourself: Think of any good thing which you know, and try to trace it back to the Ultimate Cause. Is there anything which cannot be traced back to God?

March 28

Faith in the Promise

The words were painted with the same red paint that had not too long ago been applied to the pump itself. Crawling to one side, I rubbed my eyes and tried to read:

"This pump works, but needs priming. Just enough water stored under the door. Please re-fill before you go."

It took awhile to comprehend what I was reading, but one part grabbed my attention: "...water stored under the door." There it was, on the other side of the pump: a piece of wood, painted red and lying recessed into the cement. A hole just big enough for my finger allowed me to lift it up, and reveal a thermos. Taking it in both hands, I brought it up out of the compartment where it rested, and with trembling fingers managed to twist off the cap.

Sure enough, the thermos was filled with water, enough to save my life. I almost had it to my lips when the rest of the message made sense. This water was not for drinking but for priming. I would have to pour it down the well, so that the leather sucker washers below could be moistened enough to make a seal, allowing the pump action to draw the well water to the surface.

But what if it didn't work? What if I poured away the only thing that would save me and get nothing in return? I looked around; the desert extended as far as the eye could see in every direction. There was no way I could make it across without this water. For that matter, even this one thermos would probably not be enough to keep me alive anyway. It was all or nothing. If I poured the water into the pump and it didn't work, I would most certainly die. But if I took the thermos, drink its contents and continued on, I would die anyway.

There was really no decision to be made, but it was left for me to make it.

This day I call heaven and earth as witnesses against you that I have set before you life and death, blessings and curses. Now choose life, so that you and your children may live and that you may love the LORD your God, listen to his voice, and hold fast to him. For the LORD is your life, and he will give you many years in the land he swore to give to your fathers, Abraham ,Isaac and Jacob.

Deuteronomy 30: 19 – 20

Prayer: What great love, o God, that You would allow me to choose between death and life, knowing full well what is the best for me to choose. Yet because you love me and will above all allow me to love You, I stand daily at the point of decision. Grant me wisdom, I pray.

Ask yourself: Is forced love ever real love?

Faith in Action

Like a man possessed, I moved to the pump, cradling the thermos in both hands. Next to the sucker rod which led down through a hole in the cement was another hole, about two inches in diameter. Just so there was no mistake, my mysterious sign painter had carefully lettered the word, "Prime" with a red arrow pointing to the hole.

I knew if I hesitated I might listen to another voice in the back of my head, screaming something like "No! No! Drink it! Drink it!" With a strength that came from outside of myself, I tipped the thermos forward and watched in horror as the contents ran into the hole. The sound of falling water was like the sound of the last train pulling away from the station, leaving you in a very bad part of town.

The world seemed to stop, but my body kept moving, grasping the pump handle and working it up and down like a madman. At first there was only the now familiar sound of cool air rising from below. But the sound was soon accompanied by another, sweeter note which gained in pitch with every downward push on the handle. When it seemed as though the sound had leveled off, a gush of water shot from the faucet.

I stopped pumping for a moment, but the water continued, gradually losing pressure. I grabbed a handful of water and sucked it into my mouth before returning to the handle. The next break, I filled the thermos, just in case, then held my head under the cool flow, letting the water drench me.

With another couple of quick pumps, I opened my backpack and started removing all the containers I could find, filling them, drinking them dry, filling them again. At last I was satiated, every container filled and sealed, the thermos replaced carefully. It was past noon, so I decided to stay here for the night and enjoy the luxury I never until this moment learned to appreciate. With a wet cloth over my head, I leaned back against the pump, thanking God for His provision and trying to recall why I had been angry with Him before.

This is what the LORD says: "In the time of my favor I will answer you, and in the day of salvation I will help you; I will keep you and will make you to be a covenant for the people, to restore the land and to reassign its desolate inheritances, to say to the captives, 'Come out,' and to those in darkness, 'Be free!' "They will feed beside the roads and find pasture on every barren hill. They will neither hunger nor thirst, nor will the desert heat or the sun beat upon them. He who has compassion on them will guide them and lead them beside springs of water.

Isaiah 49: 8 – 10

Prayer: Lead me, dear Father, through the dry times. Take me to the places of rest and refreshment, that I might remember You and Your goodness. Strengthen me when I face difficulties, that I may never forsake You, because You never forsake me.

Ask yourself: Think of a "dry" period in your life. What did you do when things were not going as you had hoped?

Stars' Reflections

I slept through the heat of the day, waking only occasionally to give the pump handle a few more pushes and, reassured by the rising inflection of the coming water, returned to my sleep. By the time evening had come, I was strong enough to move around a bit and even prepare a decent meal. The center point of the meal of course was an endless supply of water.

Rested and refreshed, I decided to push on. The mountain was still visible within a framework of stars, and the cool desert air meant that I would be able to cover more ground, more quickly. There was no moon, but the light from the stars lit up this miracle oasis, giving it a glow which seemed to come from within.

I think the Psalmist must have felt something of the same awe and majesty as I was experiencing now, when he wrote, "When I consider the heavens, the work of your fingers, the moon and the stars, which you have set in place, what is man that you are mindful of him, the son of man that you care for him?"

The last couple of days have without a doubt shown me the depth of my frailty. How quickly we can fall from confidence to despair! And yet, how marvelous God's provision, to bring me to this place of rescue. Suddenly I remembered the children. Where had they gone? How did they get to this place? Were they nothing more than another vision, sent to lead me where I needed to be? Moses had his burning bush, the children of Israel had their column of fire and smoke. Perhaps for me, God's best way of speaking was through a little boy with a grasshopper in his hand.

I guess if nothing else it should teach me to keep my eyes and ears open, and not be surprised to learn that God specializes in surprises.

You made him a little lower than the heavenly beings and crowned him with glory and honor. You made him ruler over the works of your hands; you put everything under his feet.

Psalms 8: 5 – 6

Prayer: As you show me Your wonders today, Lord, teach me where I fit into it all. May I be all that I have been created to be.

Ask yourself: How should a Christian feel about environmental protection?

A Shrub Appointed

As daylight approached, my body told me it was time to rest. I had walked through the night, guided by the dark form of the mountain ahead. The desert air felt cold on my face when I stopped, but I knew that the rising sun would soon drive away all memory of it. It was time to find shelter.

This desert had attached whole new definitions to the word "barren". Except for the first day's rock outcropping and the second day's water pump, there had not been a single feature to catch one's attention. Even as the salt plain gave way to desert sand, only an occasional thistle was able to survive long enough to make a seed, giving hope that the next generation would fare better.

The sky behind me grew from black to gray, and as a deep orange glow promised the coming sun, I scanned the horizon for a sign of anything different. At first, nothing could be seen except for more sand. Then as I looked in the direction I planned to travel, I thought I could just make out a faint shape. It appeared man-sized at first, causing a wave of anticipation accompanied by a nearly-forgotten terror. But looking carefully, I could see that it was a bush, the first I had seen since leaving the river.

It took nearly an hour to get to it, by which time the sun had already cleared the horizon and dissipated any semblance of the previous night's coolness. I couldn't tell what kind of bush it was, but its branches were more than adequate to provide shade for the coming day. I took a few dried twigs and built a small fire: just enough to brew a cup of coffee to go with my dwindling supply of dried apples.

Life doesn't get any better than this, I thought, sipping on my first dose of caffeine in days and taking in the smell and taste of an apple orchard, now many miles behind me. I thanked God for the shrub which would be my home for the day, remembering the time when He had appointed another such plant to shade another of His children. As sleep overtook me, I dreamed of Jonah, and wondered if he had been this comfortable.

Jonah went out and sat down at a place east of the city. There he made himself a shelter, sat in its shade and waited to see what would happen to the city. Then the LORD God provided a vine and made it grow up over Jonah to give shade for his head to ease his discomfort, and Jonah was very happy about the vine.

Jonah 4: 5 – 6

....

Prayer: I thank you Father for the shelter You provide for me today. May I remember that it is You Who shades me from the burning sun and protects me from the wild things around me. May I never take for granted Your constant presence and protection.

Ask yourself: What can you thank God for today?

Ordination

Lying in the shelter provided by the desert shrub, thinking about Jonah and his painful lessons on obedience, I couldn't help but draw a few parallels to my own situation. God told him to go to Nineveh; I was shown a trail and told to follow it to the end. Jonah chose Tarshish instead, and ended up in the belly of a big fish. As much as I might try to justify my actions, I chose to leave the trail in favor of the river, and ended up in the middle of a dead sea, literally without a paddle. Jonah was rescued, and so was I, but just as he complained bitterly about God's mercy on Nineveh, I had trouble dealing with the wind which one day carried me to safety but the next nearly killed me in the storm. At the end of Jonah's story, we see him cooling off under a bush "ordained" by God to give him shade. Then we see him frying again, thanks to a worm "ordained" to eat the bush. All together, including the big fish, there were three things ordained by God in that story, all given a specific job to do so that God's purpose could be carried out.

What's been ordained for me on this journey, and what purpose are these things serving? If Jonah provides any instruction for me, then I must realize that anything and everything, from a monster fish to a hungry worm, has the potential for carrying out something significant in my life. For Jonah, the lesson had to be repeated, and as far as I know he never did get the point.

This bush has been a real life saver today, and sitting here in the shade I've had a chance to reflect. I don't see any worms yet, so I hope that means I'm on the right track of discovery with God.

When the sun rose, God provided a scorching east wind, and the sun blazed on Jonah's head so that he grew faint. He wanted to die, and said, "It would be better for me to die than to live." But God said to Jonah, "Do you have a right to be angry about the vine?" "I do," he said. "I am angry enough to die." But the LORD said, "You have been concerned about this vine, though you did not tend it or make it grow. It sprang up overnight and died overnight. But Nineveh has more than a hundred and twenty thousand people who cannot tell their right hand from their left, and many cattle as well. Should I not be concerned about that great city?"

Jonah 4: 8 – 11

Prayer: Lord, I confess that I don't always appreciate the circumstances in which I find myself. But please keep me from letting those circumstances take over my attitude, so that I am angry and unrepentant. Grant me wisdom to accept and grace to rejoice.

Ask yourself: Have you ever been cruel to someone just because they were close to you when you were upset about something else?

April 2

Desert's End

After one more night of walking under the stars, I could sense a change in the ground under my feet. It seemed a little less sandy; not quite so level. With the coming daylight, I could see that my desert travels were almost over. Shrubs became more numerous and grass even started appearing in places. The foothills in the distance lost their purple hue, and I could distinguish individual trees on the approaching slopes. A line of dark green willows came into view, and as I got closer saw that they were growing along a riverbank.

The river was a gently flowing stream, moving from left to right, and I had no trouble wading across. A grassy knoll perched above the far riverbank, and I decided to make camp there. Everything I owned, including me, was in severe need of a good washing, and this looked like the perfect place.

I soon discovered that the river was not only good for drinking and washing, but was also the home of some beautiful spotted brook trout. A search through my gear turned up a fish hook and some line, and a willow branch made an ideal fly rod. Before dark, I had managed to catch a couple of nice sized brookies, and soon had them roasting over a bed of hot coals.

From my hilltop vantage point, I was able to see the desert from which I had come, and realized that I had not looked back since that first day. Now that this portion of the journey was over, I felt that it was safe to have a look at where I'd been. The lake, the monument, the pump, everything was of course out of sight, but the desert itself lay before me and spoke volumes by its sheer immensity.

Would I go back? Not willingly, to be sure. And yet the experiences, the lessons, even the suffering were part of the journey which I will cherish forever. I don't know what lies ahead, but if what lies behind is any teacher, then I'm ready and willing to face it.

Look to the LORD and his strength; seek his face always. Remember the wonders he has done, his miracles, and the judgments he pronounced, O descendants of Israel his servant, O sons of Jacob, his chosen ones.

I Chronicles 16: 11 – 13

....

Prayer: Thank you Father for memories! Some are pleasant, some not so, but they all point the way to Your love and care for me. May I never forget to praise You for what You have done.

Ask yourself: What did God do for you today?

April 3

Upward and Onward

After an early morning plunge in the icy waters of the mountain stream, I packed my gear and for the first time thought seriously about which direction to proceed. Before it went out of sight behind the approaching foothills, my mountain still lay straight ahead. However, that way seemed impassable. The only other two choices were along the riverbank, either upstream or downstream. Thinking it unlikely that a river would flow toward a mountain, the choice was made: I would turn left and travel upstream until a way was found directly into the foothills to the right.

It was slow going, since I had to make my way over boulders, fallen trees and crevices without the benefit of a trail, but there was a certain comfort in having the river so near. Perhaps my body was still recovering from dehydration, or perhaps it was the sight of more brook trout leaping through the shallow rapids. For the moment at least, the river was my friend and I was enjoying its noisy company.

By calculating my direction with the sun overhead, I noticed that the river had turned a little to the right. This was good news, since that meant I was once again moving more or less toward the mountain. My heart sank, however, when coming around another twist in the river, I found myself standing at the base of an impossibly high waterfall. The cliff rose three hundred feet or more, and a rainbow connected the top to the bottom through a fine mist.

I sat on a boulder and studied the canyon wall ahead. There would be no hidden hand holes carved in the rock this time, since I was still separated from the trail. The cliffs on either side offered no hope, and turning back was out of the question. The only was forward, it seemed, was up the waterfall itself.

You, O LORD, keep my lamp burning; my God turns my darkness into light.
With your help I can advance against a troop ; with my God I can scale a wall.
Psalms 18: 28 – 29

....

Prayer: Sometimes the way ahead looks impossible, but You are my Guide and my Strength. Father, if there is a way around the obstacles I face, then please show me where to go. If my way is to face those obstacles, then give me strength, I pray.

Ask yourself: What obstacles stand between you and where you want to go today?

April 4

Against the Stream

I sat looking at the waterfall until darkness fell, then built a fire and listened to the sound it made. The sunrise lit up the top of the falls first, and as the shadows were illuminated, I picked out a route and tried to memorize every ledge and cleft. I would have to begin on the left side of the falls, climb to a point about halfway up, then traverse to the right, completing the climb through a fissure which was undoubtedly a raging torrent during the wet season. Unlike my descent into the canyon, I would have to do this while wearing my back pack. With that thought in mind, I checked everything again, making sure there was nothing else I could take out and leave behind.

It was mid-morning when I finally decided that it was time to move. An extra conch of the straps, and I started climbing. As much as possible, I stayed out of the waterfall itself. Wet rock could be treacherous under any circumstances, but when combined with the downward force of a falling river, it was like being sucked into a storm drain. Then too, I kept thinking about what night be hurtling over the falling in the water. All those boulders at the bottom of the cliff used to be at the top of the cliff, until one day the constant pressure of the river had its way. I remembered reading David Livingstone's journal, and especially the part where he came upon that awesome sight which he named the Victoria Falls in southern Africa. One of his men thought the base of the falls would be a great place for a shower. However, he was struck by a falling rock, killing him instantly.

Standing against the flow, I reflected, is what this journey is all about. Moving against the current; pitting strength against strength. But it can also be a hazardous adventure. A river's current, especially when it's falling straight down, can be relentless, chipping away at the mightiest boulder, until it lies at the bottom of the falls. Moving through the water as I traversed to the other side, I thought, "I couldn't do this for very long. Either my strength would give out or a rock would find my head." But this won't last forever, I reminded myself. We're not expected to climb a mountain every day of our lives. Torrential floods become babbling brooks. Apple orchards are followed by salt flats. With each experience, another aspect of my life is tested and strengthened. I paused and held out my hand for a drink, taking refreshment from the racing column of water which would drive me off this rock, if it could. Then I moved on.

I know what it is to be in need, and I know what it is to have plenty. I have learned the secret of being content in any and every situation, whether well fed or hungry, whether living in plenty or in want. I can do everything through him who gives me strength.

Philippians 4: 12 – 13

....

Prayer: Lord, thank you for the challenges I face today, and thank you for the strength to overcome them. May I draw from the flood that threatens to overwhelm me and find there a refreshing and sustaining energy.

Ask yourself: How could a problem in your life be a source of strength?

April 5

The Fissure

Having made the traverse through the waterfall, I now began working my way to the right, toward ledges I couldn't see now, but had memorized before starting the climb. I was relieved to find that most of them were much wider than they had appeared from below. Smiling to myself, I thought, that's the way a lot of life's challenges are: formidable when seen from a distance but do-able up close and personal. Well, I was about as familiar with this waterfall as I cared to be, and was grateful to be moving away from it, into the dry fissure I had observed this morning.

The rock along the sides of the fissure bore evidence of a turbulent past. Rough places had been worn smooth by the rushing water and pieces of rock, caught in whirlpools, had carved out huge bowls in the solid granite before being worn away themselves. The fissure I was in had been formed when the river had located a tiny crack and took advantage of it. Pushing relentlessly through, the tiny crack was now a canyon in the making. Given enough time and some more water, the outside portion of the canyon would eventually break away, joining the boulders far below.

But at this moment that didn't seem very likely. The river, always seeking the lowest route, had moved over to another section of rock. The result was a waterfall which now was not quite as high as it used to be, a fact for which I was very grateful. I should have simply waited at the bottom, I joked to myself. Eventually this big monster will be nothing but a babbling brook.

That's the way a lot of life's issues go, don't they? Problems meet resistance, and in the process both the resistance and the problem are worn away. Those big boulders down below the falls are evidence of the water's force pushing against them, but a result that's not so evident is the fact that now the water doesn't have as far to fall. Simple physics will tell you that the lower the drop, the less the force. So in a way, those boulders are not defeated rocks, but rather victorious warriors, having brought the mighty waterfall one step close to babbling brook.

"Resistance is futile," the bad guy says. But that's not true. Resistance is everything. And with every ounce of strength I possess, I intend to keep on resisting until the river gives up.

But the Lord stood at my side and gave me strength, so that through me the message might be fully proclaimed and all the Gentiles might hear it. And I was delivered from the lion's mouth. The Lord will rescue me from every evil attack and will bring me safely to his heavenly kingdom. To him be glory for ever and ever. Amen.
II Timothy 4: 17 – 18

Prayer: My life is constantly meeting challenges which seem to be irresistible. But You remind me, Father, that my resistance has meaning and power. Strengthen me today, I pray, that I might resist and keep on resisting those things which would take me away from You.

Ask yourself: Would resisting evil be easier by yourself, or with a group?

April 6

Over the Top

The fissure I was climbing through was smooth and almost seamless, making it difficult to find a handhold. Several times, I advanced a few feet up, only to come to a section of sheer rock, impossible to climb. Climbing over stones at the bottom of the fissure, I finally reached the place where the two walls were close enough so I could touch either side. By placing my back against one wall, I could push my feet against the other and work my way up.

However, this was impossible while wearing a backpack. The top was only thirty feet or so away, and I had that much rope. Taking it out and tying one end to the backpack, I tried throwing the other end up and out. But I either couldn't throw that far, or if I did, the weight of the hanging rope would pull it back down. Finally I found a fist-sized rock and tied it securely to the end of the rope. Swinging it like a bolo, I was able to toss it up and over the edge, and after a few tries, it stayed. Now I could climb unhindered and pull the backpack up when I reached the top.

Pushing myself up with my back against one wall and my feet against the other, I made slow but steady progress. A couple of times, my legs started cramping and I was afraid they would crumple and send me hurtling back down, but they held. Nearing the top, I started wondering how I would make that final push. I would have to get to a point where I could extend my legs and push myself on over the edge. But there was a crucial point there when my legs would no longer hold me up, and the bulk of my body was still hanging over the edge. Without something to grip with my hands, I'd never be able to make that final move.

"I'll worry about that when I get there," I thought. Well, now I was there, and I was plenty worried. The ends of my toes were pushing against the far wall; any farther and they would have nothing to touch. I reached backward, over my head, searching desperately for something to grip. The top was right there, within my reach, but my fingers could find nothing but wet grass and solid rock.

Suddenly a strong hand clasped around mine. "Give me the other one," a voice called out. There was no time for questions; I extended my left hand behind me and it was immediately gripped by another one. With a mighty pull, I was lifted out of the fissure and released, lying on my back and staring at the sky. From the top of my vision, Andy's face appeared, a huge grin extending from ear to ear.

"I've heard of people coming in by the back door, but you take the cake," he said.

A word aptly spoken is like apples of gold in settings of silver.

Proverbs 25: 11

....

Prayer: Thank you, Father, for sending friends. And thank you for the opportunity to be a friend to someone else today. And thank you most of all because You are my friend for all time.

Ask yourself: Do you have a friend whom you could trust in times of trouble? Is there anyone who would turn to you for help?

April 7

An Old Friend

No sight was ever sweeter than of Andy's face, grinning down at me. My "foundations" trainer back at Rendezvous, he and I had taken an immediate liking to each other. "Andy!" I cried, quickly coming to my feet. "How did you get here?"

"Same way you should have, my friend," he said, the smile never leaving his face. "The trail's right over there. But I can see you have some stories to share with us."

"Do I ever," I said. "But what prompted you to be right *here* just when I needed you?"

"Not a big mystery. I was walking along the river bank, watching the water disappear over the edge. Then I thought, that's funny: if things usually go down over a waterfall, then why is that thing trying to come back up?" He picked up my rock, still held to the end of the rope. "This fellah was fairly shouting, 'Come here! Come here!'"

As we pulled the backpack up together, I said, "Andy, I wanted to thank you for everything you taught me. It seemed, well, a little foolish at the time, but I'm here to say I *wouldn't* be here to say it, if my boots hadn't been laced properly." Andy looked down at my perfectly tied foot gear and if anything, his grin got even bigger. "I'm glad to hear that," he said, as the backpack appeared over the edge. "In fact, I'd like to ask if you'd be willing to teach some of your skills to a group of new comers. They've got a lot to learn, and I think you have a lot to share."

I nodded as I cinched the backpack straps into place. "Sure, I'll be happy to. Will you be there to help me?"

"I'm afraid not," he said, the smile leaving his face for the first time since we met. "I'll be taking over Jonathan's warfare class. We lost Jonathan in a battle a couple of weeks ago. Early pick up."

I was too stunned to speak. Jonathan. The young man with the serious expression and the scar on his face. He had taught me so much about the Evil Man, and there was so much more I wanted to learn from him. "What do you mean, 'battle'?" I finally asked, desperate to know more. "I thought..."

"That this was a simple backpack trip?" he finished my thought before I could express it. "You're discovering what we're all beginning to learn the hard way. There are forces out here that don't like what we're doing. And the closer we get to the goal, the more active they become."

Put on the full armor of God so that you can take your stand against the devil's schemes. For our struggle is not against flesh and blood, but against the rulers, against the authorities, against the powers of this dark world and against the spiritual forces of evil in the heavenly realms.

Ephesians 6: 11 – 12

....

Prayer: Sometimes I forget, Lord, that I am on a battlefield. I know now that the enemy would destroy me if he could, and it is only by your strong arm that I live. But still you call me to fight. Prepare me for battle, for the sake of Your kingdom.

Ask yourself: Does the thought of battle excite you or terrify you?

April 8

An Old Family

Andy and I walked along the riverbank, each in our own world. I still couldn't believe Jonathan was gone, and the implications of that word, "battle," were still sinking in.

"Andy," I began quietly, not sure how to express what I was feeling. "I've had a lot of time on my own back there. The things I saw, and lessons I learned were unforgettable. But I have to say too, it's been lonesome. Many a night, I've wished for a friend to talk to, to listen to. I'm *really* glad to see you again."

"In that case," Andy said, putting a hand on my shoulder, "you're about to be happier than a boy in a bathtub full of bullfrogs. Welcome to Rendezvous!"

My head snapped up, and for the first time I looked beyond Andy to the meadow off in the distance. There were the familiar white tents, the cook fires, the children running from place to place. Small groups were scattered here and there, some praying quietly for each other, some singing, some engaged in lively discussion. "I can't believe I didn't notice this before!" I said, trying to take it all in at once.

"You'd be surprised how many walk right past and never give it a notice," Andy said with a shake. "But you'd have to be totally senseless to miss the smell coming from that mess tent. C'mon, you look like you could use a square meal."

I had not thought about it until just then, but the mention of food brought it all back, and my mouth watered as we made our way to a campfire near the tent with a sign that said, "Eat up." My heart leaped to my throat when I saw a familiar face stirring a summering pot of stew. I wasn't sure I could speak, but managed to get out the words, "Hello Lizzie. Does that wonderful aroma have anything to do with you?"

Gaius, whose hospitality I and the whole church here enjoy, sends you his greetings. Erastus, who is the city's director of public works, and our brother Quartus send you their greetings.

Romans 16: 23 – 24

Prayer: Thank you for your Church, dear Jesus. Thank you for making me a part of it, and for the love we share for each other. May I be all that I should be for my fellow believers, and may their strength and encouragement carry me forward in faith.

Ask yourself: Why do you think people of the church call each other "brother" and "sister"?

April 9

Lizzie

She looked up at once and scanned the area for another face, but then her eyes caught mine. "Well, well, well!" she said, putting the wooden spoon back in the pot and hurrying over to hug me. Her silver hair had fallen in front of her eyes, but I could see there were tears forming. Whether it was the smoke or the moment, I couldn't tell. "I was hoping we'd see you here," she said, taking both my hands in hers. "But I have to admit I was a little concerned. You left before I did, so I expected you'd be here waiting." "I got off the trail," I said, looking down in shame. "It was hard going, and I might still be struggling to get here if Andy hadn't shown up when he did." I wanted to go on, but wasn't sure how to begin. All I could say was, "Charlie...?"

Lizzie let go of my hand and pushed the hair away from her eyes, revealing full-blown tears that campfire smoke had nothing to do with. She smiled reassuringly as she spoke. "He's fine now." I started to blurt out something, but then realized what she was saying. I put an arm around her and we walked away from the fire.

"He talked about the journey; how good it had been and how he was looking forward to seeing it through to the end. He talked about you a lot, too, and from the sound of it you'd think he was personally responsible for how you're turning out!"

"In a lot of ways, he was right," I said. "He taught me so much in so short a time; it was like he *knew* he had to make every minute count."

Lizzie reached into an apron pocket and pulled out a piece of paper, folded carefully. "He wrote you a letter," she said, handing it to me. "He said when I saw you again, I was to give it to you and tell you to go off by yourself and read it."

I thanked Lizzie, gave her a hug, and made my way to a nearby tree, where I sat down and unfolded the letter. All thought of food was put behind me now, and it seemed I was sitting there with Charlie, listening to his words.

The glory of young men is their strength, gray hair the splendor of the old.

Proverbs 20: 29

Prayer: Praise you Father for the old among us. May I learn from them the lessons they have learned from You. May I be a comfort to them, even as they are a joy to me.

Ask yourself: Do you know an elderly person to whom you can be both a friend and a learner?

The Letter

"Dear Friend,

"I hope Lizzie is able to meet up with you again and pass this along. Poor girl, she's not much better off than I am these days. If you do see her and manage to get this letter, give her a little help for me, will you? And make sure she's teaching the younger girls her recipe for that great stew she makes!

"When we parted ways, I have to admit I was not at my best, physically to be sure, but emotionally and spiritually as well. I don't know why young folks seem to think all of us old codgers are just brimming with wisdom, like we've already been there and done that. I guess when you think about it, I *have* been to more places than most, and in the process may have picked up a few pointers. But when it comes to facing what I'm looking at now, I'm still a babe in the woods. I've never been this old before, and I've never died before, so this is all new stuff to me too.

"But I have discovered something, Friend, and I wanted to write this down in the hope that your journey might be a little easier because of it. Like I said, I've never been here before, so I've never needed what I need now. But listen to this: now that I need it, *I've got it.* It's what we've called that "peace that passes all understanding." I sure couldn't explain it, and I won't even try. But believe me when I say, *it's real.* I'm not afraid of growing old and dying, even though today I look at myself and realize I *am* old and I *am* dying. And I'm at peace because of that very fact. God gives you what you need, when you need it, and not before. Maybe that's what faith is all about: taking it as it comes, and not before it gets here.

"Anyway, Friend, let me leave you with the words of another old Irish gentleman. They blessed me, and now I hope they'll bless you:

'May the road rise to meet you,
May the wind be always at your back,
May the sun shine warm upon your face.
And the rains fall soft upon your fields,
And until we meet again,
May God always be with you'"

Now faith is being sure of what we hope for and certain of what we do not see. This is what the ancients were commended for. By faith we understand that the universe was formed at God's command, so that what is seen was not made out of what was visible.

Hebrews 11: 1 – 3

Prayer: Strengthen my faith, Lord, that I may strengthen the faith of others. May my life, and my death, be a testimony to You and Your love.

Ask yourself: What do you worry about?

April 11

A Helping Hand

I folded Charlie's letter and put it carefully in a pocket for safe keeping. Lizzie was back at the fire, talking to Andy and fretting over her famous stew. When I walked up to them, she stood up as straight as her old body would allow, and it was obvious that we both needed a hug.

"We're gonna miss that old coot," she said, holding back a tear.

"Charlie told me to make sure you're not keeping that recipe to yourself," I said, pointing with my chin to the simmering pot which hung over the fire.

"Well, that just shows what he knew," Lizzie said, picking up the wooden spoon and bringing a bit of stew up to the light. "He should have known that there's no secret to it. What makes it good are all the ingredients that each traveler adds to the pot. There's a lot of things in there that, taken by themselves might not be too great. But mix 'em in with a few other contributions from the road and you have the makings for a real feast."

"Well, if that's the case," I said, reaching down to open my backpack, "have I got something for you. Did you guys go through that apple orchard just before the canyon?"

"Oh man, don't remind me," Andy said. "I never wanted to stay anywhere as bad as I did *that* place! And those apples! Unforgettable!"

"Just to make sure you *don't* forget good times..." I stretched out the moment, enjoying the look on Andy's face, then pulled out my sack of dried apples. "Lizzie, would these do anything for that stew of yours?"

"My heavens, yes," she said, putting the spoon down and taking the sack in both hands. That's just the flavor I've been waiting for. You go and get cleaned up now, and I'll have you a real feast when you get back."

It didn't take too long to find the hot showers, and after that the clothes exchange. I didn't have much to leave them, after the storm on the lake had shredded most of what I had packed, but there was plenty to go around.

It was good to be back among family.

For we were all baptized by one Spirit into one body—whether Jews or Greeks, slave or free—and we were all given the one Spirit to drink.

I Corinthians 12: 13

....

Prayer: Lord, I lift up my family to You today: all the brothers and sisters throughout the world and through all time, who share my love for you. Keep us together as a family, so that none of us will ever be lonely, or without support in time of need. Praise You for You church.

Ask yourself: Why do Christians have such a special feeling for one another that unlike any other relationship?

April 12

The Children

Evening was coming on as I settled back around the fire with Andy and Lizzie. As good as her promise, the stew was delicious. The taste of apples was unmistakable, as was the hint of mesquite from the canyon, another spice which I must have missed on my detour, and brook trout from the nearby river.

They shared stories about the path I had missed, and I told them about my trip down the river, across the salt lake and the burning desert. When I got to the part about the children, whose surprise visit and tiny footprints which led me to water, they both looked at each other in quiet reflection.

"The children?" Andy said softly, and Lizzie nodded.

"Without a doubt," she said. "Happened to me once, a longtime ago, but it's something you never forget."

"What do you mean?" I asked. "Who are they, and where did they come from?"

Lizzie stirred the coals of the campfire with a stick, and spoke in a hushed tone. "Some children are set aside for early pickup," she said. "But it's not quite that, either. Most of them are too young to have even begun the trip. Out here is the last place you'd expect to see them, but lots of folks do. And in every case, they're responsible for helping pilgrims like yourself back to the trail."

"Early pickup," I said, trying to take it all in. "Do you mean those kids were about to die?" I thought of Timmy and his grasshopper, and the words choked in my throat.

"Yes," said Andy, looking to see if Lizzie was going to continue. She didn't, so he explained. "You've seen the kids here at Rendezvous. They travel with us, and we learn as much from them as they do from us. But the others are only seen once in awhile, by only a few, and in circumstances like yours. The fact that you saw them means that if they hadn't come around, you probably wouldn't be sitting here with us tonight. You were blessed."

But all I could feel at the moment was a profound sadness for those children, and others like them. Why did they have to die? Could I have done something back there to help them? Timmy's face bore into my memory then, and his big brown eyes, and his last words to me: "I have to go now." Somehow, those words were a comfort.

I tell you the truth, anyone who will not receive the kingdom of God like a little child will never enter it.

Mark 10: 15

....

Prayer: Father, just as you love me and care for me each day, may Your loving mercy go to all the children who suffer. Hold them close, feed them, clothe them and give them safe and happy homes to grow up in. Or, in Your perfect will, call them to be with You so that they will know real joy and peace.

Ask yourself: How has a child helped you to understand something you were struggling with?

April 13

New Comers

The next morning, I went with Andy to the training ground. There, he introduced me to my class for the day. Three men and two women, various ages and all eager to be on their way, greeted me enthusiastically. Two of them, a couple I decided, served as spokesmen for the group. "This is really fantastic," the young man said. "But couldn't we just learn as we go? I mean, you could travel with us and show us things on the way."

I smiled at his enthusiasm, and felt a twinge of envy to see his wife holding his hand and taking in every word he spoke. "There will lots of 'on the trail training', I guarantee you," I said. "You'll be meeting circumstances we can't even anticipate here, and you'll have to learn how to adapt quickly. But first, we need to firm up our foundations, so that all of your new experiences will have a solid base to build on. Today, we're going to learn how to tie our shoes properly."

I expected blank stares, and wasn't surprised to see five uncomprehending faces looking back at me. What I didn't expect was the sound I heard next: a high pitched ripping sound, like someone had just torn a sheet of heavy weight paper. I looked down toward the source of the sound and saw that the man on my left had just tightened the Velcro on his micro-fiber, waterproofed and non skid hiking boots. I followed the line of feet to the right and discovered that all five were wearing similar attire: 21st century equipment for the 21st century pilgrim.

"Okay," I said after a moment, "maybe you'll be able to teach me a few things today." We all laughed, and I went on. "But let me ask you this: what happens to Velcro when it's been through the mud a few times?"

"It loses its sticky," the other lady answered. "And grass builds up in it too."

"And another question," I said, "once I had to use my bootlace for an emergency repair job on my backpack. If all you had was Velcro, how would you make the repair?'

I got five pained expressions at that, so I hurried to add, "I'm not saying that Velcro is bad, and you need to go back and get laces. Let's just learn how to take care of whatever's on our feet, and see how many related uses we can come up with." That brought a flood of discussion, and the rest of the day was spent discovering how to make the most of modern equipment. By evening, I had learned a few things, the group had re-learned some old things, and we all felt better equipped.

May the God of peace, who through the blood of the eternal covenant brought back from the dead our Lord Jesus, that great Shepherd of the sheep, equip you with everything good for doing his will, and may he work in us what is pleasing to him, through Jesus Christ, to whom be glory for ever and ever. Amen.
Hebrews 13: 20 – 21

Prayer: As I look around me today, Father, I can see that You have given me all that I need to do what You have called me to do today. Teach me how to use Your precious gifts for the glory of Your Kingdom. Equip me for whatever comes next, I pray.

Ask yourself: What "tools" do you have today, and how are you expected to use them for God's work?

April 14

Battle Training

Andy asked me to join his warfare training group today, in light of what I had experienced back at the river.

"I don't want to embarrass you, " he told me as we sat in a circle on a hilltop overlooking the camp, "but I think you went through something back there that we all need to hear about."

I spoke of the mountain lion, and the Evil Man, and finally of the creature which caused me to escape into the river and away from the trail. "The Evil Man agreed that he couldn't touch me," I said, "but then came that burned thing, and the Evil Man's threat that I wasn't safe from *him*."

"What do you think the creature would have done to you?" Andy asked.

"I don't know," I said, "and I've thought about that a lot. It's just that he had to be dead, and yet he was acting like he was alive."

"So the real threat in that situation was not fangs, or claws, or a bazooka," Andy grinned. "What won the day was your fear of the unknown, right?"

"Exactly!" I said. "I just imagined what he might have done and... and my imagination won hands down. But wait a minute," I thought of something else. "What about the mountain lion? I don't have to imagine what he would have done. My shoulder is still sore from where he landed on me."

"And where was the mountain lion when you ran away?" Andy coaxed gently.

I breathed a deep sigh. "On the other side of the river, nursing a wound I'd given him with a sharp stick. But... but the Evil Man said that the lion would find a way to get to me!"

"And what kind of track record does the Evil Man have for the truth?" Andy smiled. "But let's stop there. No one is criticizing you for running away. Any of us would probably have done the same thing. But for the sake of future encounters, let's talk about what we need to win the victory: the real truth, and a sharper stick!"

Teach me your way, O LORD, and I will walk in your truth; give me an undivided heart, that I may fear your name. I will praise you, O Lord my God, with all my heart; I will glorify your name forever. For great is your love toward me; you have delivered me from the depths of the grave.

Psalms 86: 11 – 13

Prayer: Defend me today, Lord, from the one who would deceive me. May I walk in Your truth, so that all lies will be revealed for what they are. Teach me to measure all that I hear against the standard of Your unchanging character.

Ask yourself: When was the last time you were lied to? What happened as a result?

April 15

Real Truth

Today I took my "foundations" group up the hill to join with Andy's warrior training class for a day of truth testing. "The best foundation you can get," I reminded them, "is the one that can't be chipped away by deceit."

Andy was only too happy to take up the challenge. "Okay, here's how it works," he told us when we were all together. "I'm going to give you a 'Read it and Weep' list of truths to bring out the next time you're confronted by the Evil Man. He'll try every trick in the book to make you believe his lies. But when he does, just show him your list and say, 'Read it and Weep'! Here goes:

1. "I'm loved by God
2. "I'm forgiven through Jesus' blood
3. "God's Holy Spirit lives in me
4. "Satan has no authority over me
5. When I resist him, Satan has to run
6. I can do anything, by God's power
7. I'm a citizen of God's Kingdom

We all wrote feverishly while Andy spoke. Finally he stopped and said, "That's enough for now, but there's plenty more where those came from. Add to your own list as you explore God's Word."

"What about Jonathan?' I asked when things got quiet. "He knew those truths too, but he died in battle. Did I miss something?"

"Jesus said something that I've thought a lot about," he said. "'Don't be afraid of those who kill the body and after that can do no more. Fear him who, after the killing of the body, has power to throw you into hell.' This tells me that we won't necessarily win every battle on this earth. One of these days a mountain lion or a snake in the grass or some over-toasted foot soldier may get the best of us." Nervous laughter followed that statement, and I shifted uncomfortably. "But never forget this fact," he went on, "You are not the body you live in. The truth of the matter is, you are an eternal soul that will never die. The only thing left for discussion is whether you live with the One who created you, or whether you live forever separated from Him, in that place called Hell.

"Now all of you here have made that decision already, so we don't need to worry about it anymore. What you *do* need to be thinking about, though, is what we're going to learn next: where can I get me a sharper stick?"

To the Jews who had believed him, Jesus said, "If you hold to my teaching, you are really my disciples. Then you will know the truth, and the truth will set you free."
John 8: 31 – 32

....

Prayer: Father, write Your truth on my heart, so that I will never forget it.

Ask yourself: Can anything be stronger than the truth?

April 16

A Sharper Stick

As Andy started talking about physical battles, one of my "foundations" new comers spoke up. "But I thought we weren't supposed to fight," he said. "Aren't we supposed to love everyone, even our enemies?'

"You've been reading ahead," Andy said with a grin. "And you're right: the rule of love is what makes us who we are. From the earliest times, people recognized us because we loved everyone, even the unlovable, even each other. But it's not always easy to decide the best way to love, when we're faced with evil. Do I love my neighbor by letting the Evil Man hurt him, when I have the power to stop it? Do I love my enemy by letting him have his way with me, and thereby making himself stronger to go out and do more evil?

"God gave us a perfect world where decisions like these weren't necessary, but we broke it by sinning. His Son has already paid the price for that sin, and one day soon God's going to set everything right again. But until then, we find ourselves in a world where evil is in constant battle with good.

"We don't honor God by sitting back and letting evil take ground that doesn't belong to him. We're told to run when we can, resist when we must, and fight when there's nothing else to do.

"And when we fight, ladies and gentlemen," Andy said, taking up a sword which lay at his feet, "let's fight like Kingdom citizens, and not like a bunch of groveling victims."

Another of my new comers spoke up. "I hear you, Andy, and I'm ready to get dangerous. But why the swords? I mean, isn't that a little, well, medieval? You know, there's a lot better stuff out there on the market."

This brought a chorus of agreement, and Andy spoke above the clamor. "This sword is a symbol," he said, raising it up for all to see. You can find yourself up against the enemy with nothing more than a rock, or nothing less than a particle beam disintegrator. Each situation calls for specific and unique weapons. But the principle behind them all is the same: am I willing to take this into battle? The skills will come to each of you according to God's grace; the willingness to use those skills must be determined here and now."

"I tell you, my friends, do not be afraid of those who kill the body and after that can do no more. But I will show you whom you should fear: Fear him who, after the killing of the body, has power to throw you into hell. Yes, I tell you, fear him.
Luke 12: 4 – 5

....

Prayer: Father, you have taught me to love my enemy, and You have taught me that I must fight for Your Kingdom. Grant me wisdom to know how to live in this truth. May I never hesitate to strike when You command it, but may my love never be in doubt.

Ask yourself: Would you be willing to fight against evil?

A Heart for Battle

As Andy had said, building skills is one thing; building a willingness to use them is quite another. We spent the morning going through the basics of proper swordsmanship. Defensive maneuvers were followed by offensive tactics. By afternoon, we had paired up and were trying out some of the things we had learned.

Ralph was my partner, a fellow about my age from Andy's class. We both caught on rather quickly, and were soon flying through the routine we had learned. We shouted out the maneuvers together, so that neither of us would miss a move and end up missing a finger, or worse.

"Present! Right sweep! Left sweep! Forward thrust! Overhead! Present!" Stopping for a break, Ralph and I sat under a nearby tree. We talked about our families, and about the decision to make this trek. "That's the problem, you know?" Ralph said, as he tested the edge of his blade with his thumb. "We're both holding back because we're brothers, after all. The last thing I would want to do is hurt you, and so I'm going to keep everything in check."

"Same here," I agreed. "It's like a built-in safety system that overrides all of us here. By definition, we're bound together by love; it's hard to throw that aside and create some kind of 'urge to kill' attitude. If I can't do it in practice, how do I know I could ever do it for real?"

Ralph was quiet a minute, then turned to face me. "The secret, I think, is in learning to distinguish between flesh and spirit. You and I are worried about our flesh, but the controlling factor is the Spirit Who lives in each of us, bringing us together. We could never raise a weapon against God's Spirit, nor would we want to. You've met the Evil Man; so have I. Did you sense anything resembling God's Spirit in him?"

"Not at all," I said with a shudder. "It was like standing next to a refrigerator with the door open."

"Exactly," said Ralph. "And I think that will be true with every enemy we come up against. If the Spirit's there, we'll know it. If not, then no holds barred and no second thoughts."

"I'm with you," I said, getting up to my feet. "C'mon, let's go through a few more routines."

Take the helmet of salvation and the sword of the Spirit, which is the word of God. And pray in the Spirit on all occasions with all kinds of prayers and requests. With this in mind, be alert and always keep on praying for all the saints.
Ephesians 6: 17 – 18

Prayer: Thank you for reminding me today that I am a warrior on a battlefield. May I never be guilty of running from a fight that you want me to engage in. Give me the skills and the heart for battle, so that I might bring honor to Your name.

Ask yourself: Do you know that God's Spirit lives inside every believer? How would that make a difference?

April 18

Lizzie's Story

Charlie had told me in his letter to give Lizzie a hand, and I was looking eagerly for a chance to do that. Finally one afternoon I saw her struggling to carry the big stew pot over to the wash up area. I ran to join her, took the pot out of her hands and said, "Don't tell me the stew is all gone, Lizzie."

"Oh, I've put a little away for re-heating. It's just that we're getting ready to break camp soon, and I thought I'd better get this thing cleaned and packed."

The reminder that Rendezvous was nearly over made me wince, but I offered to help her with all the preparations. She washed spoons while I worked on the big pot. "Lizzie," I said as we worked side by side at the sink," you said the other day that you'd seen the children once. What happened?"

She stopped washing for a minute, as if deciding how to answer, then sighed deeply and told me her story.

"I was young... yes it's true," she said with a glance in my direction. "I was always the 'perfect child'; never gave my parents a moment of worry. No one was surprised when I made the decision to start this journey. Oh, I had the best of intentions but, well, it just didn't turn out like I thought it would. I soon found myself so far away from the trail I didn't figure I'd ever get back to it again. I met a young man, lost like me, and we were drawn to each other, I guess out of common misery. There was... a baby. But there were ways, even back then, of 'taking care' of things. One day I was pregnant, the next day I wasn't. End of story, or so I thought.

"Four years passed. The boy went his way and I went mine. The sad thing was, neither of us went *His* way. Then one afternoon I was struggling through a swamp. I'd been in it for days, and thought I'd die there. Then I came around a cypress tree and there, sitting in the water splashing for all they were worth, were three little girls. They were making leaf boats and then moving them along by slapping the water around them. One of them looked up as I came around the tree, smiled and called out, 'Hi Mom!'"

The infant will play near the hole of the cobra, and the young child put his hand into the viper's nest. They will neither harm nor destroy on all my holy mountain, for the earth will be full of the knowledge of the LORD as the waters cover the sea.

Isaiah 11: 8 – 9

....

Prayer: Thank you Father, for watching over Your children. Remind me today that I am Your child as well. May I never fear what cannot harm me.

Ask yourself: What attitude should you have toward the things which can hurt you?

Lizzie's Story (Part Two)

"I was struck speechless to hear that child call me 'Mom'. I started to protest, then looked again at her face... her eyes. It was impossible, but true: she *was* my child.

'It's... it's you,' I said in a half whisper.

"'Sure,' she said, looking again at the tiny boats floating around her.

"'But,' I began, but didn't know how to say it. 'How can it be you?' I tried to choke back the tears, but there was no stopping them. I cried out the confession I'd been holding inside far too long. 'I *killed* you! I'm a murderer!'

"That sweet child just went on playing with her boats, splashing as if she were in her mother's bathtub on a Saturday night. Then she stopped, looked directly into my eyes and said, 'That's okay.'

"Forgiveness drove me to my knees. I cried and I cried. I kept saying, 'I'm sorry, I'm sorry, I'm sorry' over and over again, until I could neither cry nor speak any more. I looked up again and saw that all three girls had stopped what they were doing, and were watching me intently, as if they were witnesses to something very significant. Then one of the other girls, a year or two older, I think, spoke up for the first time.

"'We're supposed to tell you that you need to go that way,' she said, pointing directly behind her. I looked that way and could see nothing unusual about it. In fact, I would have gone the opposite direction if the choice had been mine. But I was in no position to doubt anything at that moment. I waded through the water a little ways, looked through some vines, and saw it. A trail had been built out of wooden planks, elevated just above the water level of the swamp. I stepped up on it and saw that it ran on as far as I could see. I was to learn that it would lead all the way out of the swamp and set me back on the trail that I had lost so many years before. I was so excited, I cried out. Then I turned back to gather up those poor children and get them, somehow, to safety. But they were gone. I looked and looked, but never saw them again. Years later, I heard about similar stories from other travelers, and it all made sense.

"So there you have it, my young Friend," Lizzie told me as she dried the last spoon and put it away. "All of us here have come to grips with our own past, and been forgiven. But I think I'm the most blessed of all, for having heard it straight from the mouth of the babe: 'That's okay'."

But if we walk in the light, as he is in the light, we have fellowship with one another, and the blood of Jesus, his Son, purifies us from all sin. If we claim to be without sin, we deceive ourselves and the truth is not in us. If we confess our sins, he is faithful and just and will forgive us our sins and purify us from all unrighteousness.
I John 1: 7 – 9

Prayer: Lord, may I know the miracle of forgiveness, as I am forgiven and as I am able to forgive others. If I am harboring any sin, show it to me, then show me how to hand it over for Your cleansing mercy.

Ask yourself: Is there anyone whom you cannot forgive? Have you done anything for which you think you could never be forgiven?

April 20

Attack

The morning was filled with the bustling sounds of activity, as tents were taken down and supplies were packed away. Rendezvous had come to an end, and travelers were already beginning to file out of the camp, moving toward the west.

I was preparing to go as well, but was in no hurry to leave this beautiful place. The brook trout taken from the nearby river had been especially delicious, and I set out to catch just one more for breakfast. With a willow pole, a hook and some fishing line, I looked for a likely place along the river bank, but finally decided to wade out into the center of the wide but shallow stream.

Just as I dropped my hook into the water, something between a scream and a roar split the air, coming from the far side of the river, away from the camp. I looked in that direction and saw a man standing at the water's edge, if indeed he was a man. He was clothed in animal skins, with a metal breastplate and a helmet. In his hand he held a huge sword, which he began swinging over his head as he stepped into the river toward me.

I judged the distance quickly and saw at once that I would not outrun him. In fact, I only had time to raise my fishing pole in self defense before he had reached me. The sword came down on the pole, easily severing it in half, but slowing its progress long enough for me to jump back. The training I had just finished with Andy was still fresh on my mind, and without thinking I thrust the broken pole in my right hand directly at my attacker, catching him in the throat. It was enough to make him stop suddenly, drop the sword and clutch at his throat in shock.

There was no time for hesitation; grabbing the sword, I held it in both hands and executed a forward thrust, connecting just below his breastplate. For just an instant, he seemed to be confused, not knowing whether to clutch his throat or his stomach. But in the next instant all thought gave way and he fell dead, face down in the water.

I still held the sword, and backing away, I soon found myself on the riverbank, now joined by several from the camp who had heard the roar. Suddenly the far shore came alive, as hundreds more like the one I had just killed stepped into the water and began advancing toward us.

The wicked draw the sword and bend the bow to bring down the poor and needy, to slay those whose ways are upright. But their swords will pierce their own hearts, and their bows will be broken.

Psalms 37: 14 – 15

....

Prayer: Thank you for reminding me today that my enemies are Your enemies. You do not fear them, and tell me that I should not be afraid either. Make me bold in the face of the wicked, and let the victory be Yours alone.

Ask yourself: Why do you think the enemies of God have chosen man as their target?

April 21

A Fortress Strong

Someone behind me screamed at the sight of the advancing army of demonic soldiers. There was no discussion about negotiation or the ethics of war. What faced us there on the river was not human, and most certainly was not skilled in the ways of mercy. At that moment, every man, woman and child knew that death had come to our door. Even though we were only seconds away from contact, we had already formed battle lines and were preparing to fight with whatever was in hand. I looked around quickly and saw that only Andy and I had swords. Ralph was holding a hammer and Lizzie clutched a heavy iron skillet in both hands.

The creatures had reached the halfway point across the river, and were drawing back their swords for the final drive to our position, when suddenly they stopped. Rather, I should saw they were stopped by something no one could see but which no one doubted was there.

As if a wall of glass had been erected down the center of the river, every creature found himself smashed against it, the situation made worse by those in the rear, unaware of the barrier and pushing forward. They struck against it in blind rage, using swords, rocks and helmets, but nothing could break it. They tried to climb over; they searched for a way around. A few got too close to the waterfall's edge and were swept over.

We turned away from the cacophony when a voice from behind us called out, "Brothers and sisters! There can be no doubt that we're seeing the Divine protection of God at work. Perhaps our best response at this time is to kneel and give Him thanks."

And so we did. With only an occasional glance back at the river and the frustrated efforts of our enemies, we got to our knees in the meadow and prayed. That act seemed to infuriate the demonic army all the more, and they redoubled their efforts to break through the invisible barrier. But all the while, we prayed and sang, and wondered at this miracle taking place right before our eyes.

Jesus replied, "Blessed are you, Simon son of Jonah, for this was not revealed to you by man, but by my Father in heaven. And I tell you that you are Peter and on this rock I will build my church, and the gates of hell will not overcome it.
Matthew 16: 17 – 18

....

Prayer: Praise You for Your Church, Oh Lord. Praise You for inviting me to be a part of it. Praise You for establishing it on the solid rock that will never fail.

Ask yourself: How has the Church managed to survive 2000 years of persecution, open attack and ignorance from without as well as from within?

April 22

Counter Attack

After awhile, the enemy gave up its rage and simply pressed against the invisible barrier, as if constant pressure might cause it to give way. In between our prayers and songs, we talked about the miracle. Some of the older travelers spoke of seeing similar things happen but for most of us, this was a first.

Ever the pragmatist, Lizzie said, "This is wonderful, but are we supposed to stay here now? They can't get in, but can we get out? And for that matter, what happens if we do? Surely those things out there are not going to just stand back and let us move on."

"Good point, Lizzie," said Andy, coming to his feet. "I think it's time we tried an experiment." Sword in hand, Andy waded out into the river, toward the enemy line, now watching him intently. Now standing face to face with one of the biggest and fiercest looking creatures, he put on his finest grin. The creature went into a rage, howling at the top of his voice and using his sword to beat uselessly on the barrier. Without another word, Andy drew back his sword and thrust it straight forward, through the barrier and into the mid-section of the beast.

His raging came to an immediate stop, an astonished expression came over his face, and he fell backwards. Andy turned back to us and yelled, "There's your answer, Lizzie! Let's send these things on their way!"

A shout rose up all along the riverbank, and we all shot forward as one. Swinging hammers, skillets, sticks and at least two swords, we drove through the water and toward the waiting army. Instinctively, they had all stepped back a pace, which made the effect all the more dramatic, as our makeshift army moved through the barrier as if it didn't exist and started swinging against our tormentors.

A few demons fell, and the rest went into full flight, dropping whatever weapons they held and running for all they were worth back into the surrounding forest.

We waited until evening, to make sure they were not coming back, then settled around the fire and enjoyed Lizzie's re-heated stew one more night.

See, it is I who created the blacksmith who fans the coals into flame and forges a weapon fit for its work. And it is I who have created the destroyer to work havoc; no weapon forged against you will prevail, and you will refute every tongue that accuses you. This is the heritage of the servants of the LORD, and this is their vindication from me," declares the LORD.

Isaiah 54: 16 – 17

....

Prayer: What a great comfort to know that there is no other Creator but You, Oh God. You made all that there is, including all those who call themselves our enemy. You have absolute authority over them and the final word in all they attempt to do. Praise You for Your mercy.

Ask yourself: How do you feel about your enemies, knowing that they too are God's creation?

April 23

Goodbye Again

There were mixed emotions around the camp before sunup this morning, as we prepared again to continue the journey. Some felt we should all travel together for safety, while others suggested we stay in place a few days more, just to make sure our attackers weren't preparing another assault. Andy put that idea to rest by reminding everyone that we had no way of knowing whether the protective barrier was in fact still in place or not. Only the demons had been unable to breach the wall, while none of us had ever been able to sense a thing.

"It seems obvious to me," he told a group discussing the issue around the campfire, "God has every intention of protecting us from them. My feeling is that we are just as safe on the trail as we are here."

I didn't want to remind him about Jonathan and the apparent lack of protection around him, but agreed with him that our call was to move, not to stay still. Whatever we had just experienced was enough to get me to my feet and on the way.

Lizzie was still putting away dishes when I passed by. I gave her a hug and said, "I'm looking forward to your stew at the next Rendezvous."

"Well, you never know about these things," she said, massaging a sore shoulder. "I may just decide I've had enough of these things." Then she gave me a wink and said, "Safe journey, Friend."

I looked around for Andy, but heard from Ralph that he had left while it was still dark, sword in hand. "He felt that since he was so insistent that we move on, he should lead the way," said Ralph.

"What about you, Ralph?" I asked, noticing that his gear still lay about. He was sitting against a tree, cleaning a sword. "You don't seem to be in a hurry to leave."

"Andy and I talked about it, and I agreed to stick around awhile and bring up the rear. Ne sense letting anything pick us off from behind."

I offered to stay and travel with him, but Ralph shook his head. "No, Friend, you have your own journey to think about. We'll be okay, won't we?" He stood to shake my hand, which turned into a hug and a slap on the back. I wished him a safe journey. "Knowing you're back here puts me at ease. Thanks, brother."

For the first time in weeks, I felt the trail under my feet again. It was a good feeling.

I guide you in the way of wisdom and lead you along straight paths. When you walk, your steps will not be hampered; when you run, you will not stumble.
Proverbs 4: 11 – 12

....

Prayer: Thank you for brothers and sisters who stand together against the foe. As we fight the good fight, may we grow closer to You, and in so doing, grow closer to one another.

Ask yourself: What draws old soldiers together?

April 24

False Prophet

The climb out of the valley was a strain, but at the same time invigorating. After so long away from the trail and unsure of my direction, it felt good to move forward with the assurance that I was again headed toward the goal. I passed a few fellow travelers who were moving at a slower pace, but after a smile and a wave was anxious to keep going. Before long, I was once again alone on the trail.

The sounds of the forest came back to my ears. Birds competed with each other like the tuning up sounds of a symphony orchestra. The sound of the waterfall behind me was gradually fading away, drowned out by the wind in the treetops.

But there was another sound in the wind, and I stopped to listen. It was coming from a point higher above me, presumably on the trail. As I kept climbing, the sound became distinguishable as a voice. Closer still, and it took on the aspects of an angry voice, insistent and pleading at the same time.

As the trail gained altitude, the trees thinned out and I was able to see farther ahead, to a place where the trail disappeared over the ridge. A man was standing on a huge rock overlooking the trail and below him a dozen or more travelers had stopped to listen.

A few minutes later, his words became decipherable and my blood ran cold. He was delivering a speech that sounded chillingly familiar.

"How can we hope to protect ourselves unless we band together?" he shouted. "You've seen what they look like. Do you want to see them again someday out there by yourself? Listen to me! They *can* be stopped. That was proven yesterday. All we need to do is build a wall and we'll be safe inside it."

Was I hearing what I thought I heard? Was this man actually suggesting that we try and protect ourselves from the enemy by hiding behind a wall of stone? I looked around to see if the others were as horrified as I was, but instead I saw faces etched in fear. Some were nodding in agreement as the man spoke; others were already walking around the area as if stepping off the dimensions of the fortress to come.

"Join me!" the man was shouting again. "Together we can build a kingdom that no one will overcome. Together we will see a future for our children. *This* is where the journey ends!"

The days will come upon you when your enemies will build an embankment against you and encircle you and hem you in on every side. They will dash you to the ground, you and the children within your walls. They will not leave one stone on another, because you did not recognize the time of God's coming to you."
Luke 19: 43 – 44

Prayer: Surrounded by the threats and intimidation of the evil one, I am often tempted to run for cover. Like so many others, I try to protect myself by my own strength. Forgive me for my lack of faith in You, Father. Guide me through these times of fear and may my salvation be from You alone.

Ask yourself: What have you built up around your life for protection?

April 25

Rebuke

I had a decision to make: either I could keep walking and let these people dig their own graves, or I could try to do something. But what could I do? Already the crowd was preparing to stand behind this man and his folly. Anything I could say would be seen as foolish rebellion.

An idea came to mind, and I took off my backpack, dug through it and brought out the journal I had been carrying. Climbing up beside the man on the rock, I held up the book and shouted, "Listen to the record of Thamakra, warrior of Rock Craig!" The man beside me could not tell if I were an ally or not, and so remained silent. The people listening were more than willing to hear a good story, so I opened it up and began to read:

"How could I forget the day I met my two companions? We were drawn together by a common bond: that irreducible terror of *him* and those who follow his counsel. Our pilgrimage brought us to this high vantage, and we said to ourselves, *this* at last is a place of safety. *He* can never touch us here." I went on, sharing with them excerpts from the journal of the man whose skeleton I had found in the ruins of a fortress back along the trail. The people listened as I told them about the massive walls and the iron-trimmed gate. I described the army which occupied the fortress, and how they came to rule everything as far as could be seen. This was what they wanted to hear, and hoped to build for themselves. Then I turned to the last page of the journal. "It began as a high-pitched scream... The gates were locked and bolted... Surely the walls would hold... The end came so swiftly we never even saw our enemy. The walls were down before the alarm went up. Those massive gates were consumed in an instant by the fires of hell itself."

I closed the journal and held it up for all to see. "This man thought that they could build something which would stand against the Evil One. Yesterday was only a reminder that such thought is folly. Our only hope is in the One who defended us back there, and He tells us that this is not our home. Our home lies beyond these rocks. You can stay here and die fighting a lost cause, or you can move ahead and claim a victory which has already been won." With that, I jumped off the rock, picked up my backpack and set off again. I don't know if anyone followed me or not.

By faith Abraham, when called to go to a place he would later receive as his inheritance, obeyed and went, even though he did not know where he was going. By faith he made his home in the promised land like a stranger in a foreign country; he lived in tents, as did Isaac and Jacob, who were heirs with him of the same promise. For he was looking forward to the city with foundations, whose architect and builder is God.

Hebrews 11: 8 – 10

....

Prayer: "This world is not my home, I'm just passing through; my treasures are laid up somewhere beyond the blue." Remind me of that wonderful truth today, Lord, and keep me on the path to Your kingdom.

Ask yourself: Where is home to you?

April 26

The Ridge

I expected the trail to cross over the ridge I had just left, and lead me down into another valley. Instead, it took a sharp left turn and continued up. The tree line sank below me as the trail gained in elevation, and I felt a cool breeze on my face, hinting of a change in the weather.

To my right the distant forest seemed like an impenetrable carpet of green, dark and foreboding. To the left, the mountain dropped off steeply, ending in a boulder field a mile or more away. As the ridge grew narrower, I imagined what it would be like to slip and fall. Which way would I choose, if I could decide the direction I fell? In some kind of macabre fantasy, I watched myself falling to the left; over the edge, hitting a boulder, sliding across loose rock. Surely I would be dead by then, but my fall would continue. Down a ravine, out onto more boulders, then perhaps coming to rest in a soggy looking area where melting snow had left a perpetual bog. Not too pleasant that way; what if I fell to the right?

The first few hundred yards were steep but grassy. Maybe I would get by with a few abrasions. But I'd be picking up speed, and the forest waited. No way I'd miss those trees. And even if I did, what waited back in the shadows?

What was I thinking, and why these morbid imaginations? I did *not* plan to fall, but still the probability was there, and my mind seemed to take some satisfaction in playing out every possibility.

Is that another way of describing worry? What do I do when I worry? I think about all the things that *might* happen, pick out the least desirable and "flesh them out" in my mind, creating more detail than reality itself.

I remember my father one time telling me that nearly everything we worry about never happens, so I should stop worrying. Hearing that, I concluded that I should worry about *everything* to insure that it wouldn't come true.

But standing on this ridge, with two very unpleasant possibilities to my right and left, I ask myself, what am I accomplishing by imagining the worst? If anything, I'm taking my mind off the trail, where my real safety lies.

Eyes, straight ahead.

Who of you by worrying can add a single hour to his life since you cannot do this very little thing, why do you worry about the rest?
Luke 12: 25 – 26

Prayer: Forgive me when I worry. Your Word tells me that it accomplishes nothing, and in fact it demonstrates a lack of faith in You. Help me face my fears, assured of Your presence and Your ultimate victory over everything that comes my way.

Ask yourself: Can worry ever accomplish anything good?

April 27

Shortcut

The day was moving into late afternoon, and still the ridge continued its steady climb. At one moment I thought I could see it ending at a peak, but arriving there only revealed it to be the lower end of a saddle, with more ahead as far as I could see.

Concerns over a shelter for the night began to express themselves, and while I tried to put them down the way I was ignoring my worry over falling, they persisted. The air was getting cooler by the hour, and with no firewood nearby it looked as though I was facing a cold night.

Topping the upper end of the next saddle, I was able to see a turning in the ridge. It continued upward for a half mile or more, then twisted to the right, actually descending a little. From where I stood, I could look across a basin, *down* toward my trail. And there, at another rocky outcropping, nestled in between two huge boulders, sat a mountain hut. Built out of rock, it had one door, and one window which I could see from this angle, and a chimney, indicating the presence of a fireplace. If it was stocked with wood, I'd be in the lap of luxury by nightfall!

Then a thought occurred to me: I could see the entire trail from here to the hut, and I could see that I would have to climb considerably before winding back down to that point just across from where I stood. As the crow flies, no more than a hundred yards. Down the hill, up the other side, and I'd be there.

With visions of a roaring fire and a roof over my head, I stepped off the trail and started down the hillside. No way I could get lost; my goal was right there in front of me. Going down was easy. The hillside was covered in loose rock, and I slid gently, first on my feet then in a sitting position. This was great, I thought; one step and I'm halfway there. At the bottom of the basin, I started up the other side and realized at once what an error in judgment I had made.

A man who strays from the path of understanding comes to rest in the company of the dead.

Proverbs 21: 16

....

Prayer: How often do I rationalize the decisions I make, saying that "this will make the job easier"? Grant me wisdom, Lord, to do the work You've given me to do, not with the goal of making it easier, but with the desire to bring honor to Your name.

Ask yourself: Is the shortest distance between two points always a straight line?

One Step Forward...

The goal was right there, not more than fifty steps up the hill. Fifty *normal* steps, that is. Because of the loose shale, every step I took resulted in a slide backwards at least as far as my forward progress had been. I tried to dig places to put my feet, but the shale above slid down, filling the holes I kicked out as fast as I could dig them. I recalled a place like this at the beginning of my trip, when I had to traverse across a shale field. It was one of the hardest things I ever had to do, and I was only going *across*, not straight up. Every direction from where I stood now was straight up, except for one, which was straight down.

When would I ever learn to stay on the trail? The last time I got off was because of fear, and the result had been even more fear and suffering than I would have encountered had I stayed and faced it. This time, it was my own foolishness, and a desire to take an easier way. Some shortcut, I thought to myself as I took another step, sliding back to my starting point.

Eventually my kicking and climbing brought me down to a layer of rock which was slightly more stable. After an hour or so I was able to see that I had made some progress. Plenty of challenge remained above me, however, and as it grew dark I resigned myself to spending the night out here, cold and miserable, while my goal sat tantalizingly close, just out of reach.

The night passed, and I struggled. As the sun began to creep over the horizon behind me, I could see that I was nearly there. One more push and I reached the trail, totally exhausted. Dragging my backpack to the hut, I opened the door and saw that it was all I had dreamed it would be: a fireplace with plenty of wood stacked neatly. A bed in one corner, a table and two chairs in another.

Ignoring everything but the bed, I made straight for it, fell into a deep sleep and woke up in the early afternoon. Then over a cup of coffee and a good meal, I sat at the table and caught up on my journal.

Especially the part about shortcuts.

Good and upright is the LORD; therefore he instructs sinners in his ways. He guides the humble in what is right and teaches them his way.
Psalms 25: 8 – 9

Prayer: I know where I want to go, Father, but I don't always know how to get there. Teach me today how to walk on the path You have set before me.

Ask yourself: Where have you learned most of what you know about making decisions?

April 29

A Visitor

By the time I had recovered from my previous night's ordeal, it was late afternoon. From the hut, I could see the trail continuing on up the ridge and out of sight. Perhaps it would be better to stay here tonight, I thought. With a fire burning brightly, I was sitting with my feet to the flames and enjoying the warmth when I heard a sound from outside. Footsteps, shuffling steadily closer, then a crashing of wood being dropped to the ground. The latch slid to one side, and as I stood up, the door opened to reveal a man. At first glance he seemed incredibly old, with white hair and a flowing beard. But the lines around his eyes spoke of strength, and for reasons I couldn't explain, wisdom and warmth.

He came inside, and held out a gnarled hand. "Didn't mean to surprise you," he said with a smile. "Name's Jacob. You can call me Jake."

I shook his hand and was taken aback by the strength of his grip. He sensed my hesitation and continued. "You're the one everybody's been calling 'Friend'; not a bad handle to carry, I'd say."

"You know me?" I gasped. "Were you at the Rendezvous? I'm sorry I didn't see you... I..."

"No, I wasn't there, Friend. I'm not exactly a Traveler like you, although I am under the same Authority." That last word was spoken with such respect, I knew at once Who he was talking about. "I'm what you might call a 'caretaker'," he went on. "I keep the trail in good shape, supply firewood where it's needed, things like that. All in all, it's about the best job someone like me could have been given."

I glanced through the open door and noticed the bundle of wood he had brought with him. Recovering from my shock, I offered him a chair, slipped on my boots and carried the wood inside. As I stacked it carefully by the fireplace I told him how much I appreciated his work. "This hut was a welcome sight," I said, not sure how much to confess. "Spending the night outside at this elevation is not very pleasant."

"I'm sure that's true," he said with a sly smile. "You'd be surprised how many travelers figure they can cut off a little of the trail and end up in a world of misery."

I looked at his face, then into the fire. "So you know?"

He just nodded and smiled again. "Don't feel too bad about it. Just consider it a lesson that no textbook could ever teach."

I had the unmistakable feeling that sitting before me was another source of learning. I built up the fire, sat in the other chair, spoke and listened. The night fell outside, but inside the hut, time stood still.

He who listens to a life-giving rebuke will be at home among the wise.

Proverbs 15: 31

....

Prayer: Lord, please send me people of wisdom, so that I might learn from them. Grant that my ears will be attentive, my heart will be receptive, and my feet will be ready to move according to what I am taught.

Ask yourself How do you feel when someone tells you about a mistake you made?

April 30

Wisdom

We spoke into the night. The thought of food never occurred to me, and apparently neither to the old man who sat across from me in front of the fire. There was so much I wanted to ask, so much to know.

"This wasn't the first time I left the trail," I said quietly. "Yesterday I was just stupid. But before, I was... well I was scared out of my wits."

"The river crossing," the old man nodded and patted my hand reassuringly. "There's not many who would have done it any differently. Like I said, just consider it a lesson you won't soon forget."

"But what lesson did I learn?" I asked, getting to my feet and pacing around the room. "He's still out there and he still scares me. For all I know, I'd probably do the same thing again. I'm just such a coward!"

"You might ask that creature you met back at Rendezvous what he thinks about that," the old man chuckled. "Just imagine the report he's going to have to make." Then the old man mimicked some demon captain's voice: "He killed you with a *fishing rod*? No? Oh I see, a *broken* fishing rod!"

That brought a laugh from us both, and I sat back down. "Just what are those things, Jake?" I asked. "And why do they hate us so much?"

"They hate you because *He* loves you," he said. "If it weren't for you and others like you, they'd be all over this place, destroying it, hurting it just to spite the One who made it. But they can't do that now, see, because you're here, and you're on a mission. They'd love to see you fail, so they could go back to the Creator and say, 'See? They're not worth your trouble!' But here you are, in spite of their threats and all the garbage they try and throw at you. Friend, you're living proof that God knew what He was doing when He made you."

That made me sit up a little straighter.

When I consider your heavens, the work of your fingers, the moon and the stars, which you have set in place, what is man that you are mindful of him, the son of man that you care for him? You made him a little lower than the heavenly beings and crowned him with glory and honor.

Psalms 8: 3 – 5

Prayer: How much You must love me, Father! You have made me and entrusted me with Your creation. You protect me and promised me a place in Your kingdom. Praise You! Praise Your Holy Name!

Ask yourself: Have you considered the fact that you are now only slightly lower than angels, and that some day you will be over them? What do you think that means?

A Glimpse Ahead

"How much farther to the top of the mountain?" I asked as we sat staring into the glowing coals in the fireplace. "What's up there?"

"To answer both your questions with one response: 'I don't know," the old man said. "That trail outside doesn't go to the top. You'll find tomorrow that it skirts around the base and then heads off in another direction. There is a trail going up, which starts on the other side, but not everyone takes it. What's at the top, I suppose depends on who's going up there, and for what reason. If you find yourself climbing it, remember what I'm saying to you now: there's nothing up there or down here that can ever hurt you, at least not in ways that really matter."

I might have been satisfied with that answer, if he had not concluded with that last bit. "So, you're saying I might still get hurt, then? I mean, back there at Rendezvous, I saw a whole army of demons kept at bay by what could only have been God's power. So I started thinking, maybe from here on I'm under some kind of protective shield. Now you're telling me that one day I'll be protected by it, and another day I won't? What kind of game is this, anyway?"

Jake leaned forward, put a hand on my shoulder, and all the fear and anger that had been close to exploding within me suddenly evaporated. His words went straight to my soul. "This is no game, Friend; remember that. When God made this world, it was good. And it's still good. But evil has gotten in, and because of that, you're in real danger. The evil man wants to hurt you, and I won't lie to you: he might succeed. But there's only so much he can do. His power is limited by the One who made him, and that's the same One who made you and me. You belong to God, just like I do, and there's no power in heaven or on earth that can change that fact. When you come to the end of this journey, you'll understand what I'm trying to tell you now, but in the meantime, you just keep trusting God and stay on the trail. You'll be fine. Now, what you need more than anything else is a good night's rest. Get some sleep."

I wanted to follow that thought, but a wave of sleep rolled over me like a warm blanket. I don't even remember getting into bed. But my dreams were sweet, and the night surrounded me with a Presence, assuring me that everything was going to be all right.

> *Rejoice in the Lord always. I will say it again: Rejoice! Let your gentleness be evident to all. The Lord is near. Do not be anxious about anything, but in everything, by prayer and petition, with thanksgiving, present your requests to God. And the peace of God, which transcends all understanding, will guard your hearts and your minds in Christ Jesus.*
>
> Philippians 4: 4 – 7

Prayer: Father, You know that the unknown often frightens me. I face the future with an uncertainty and while Your Word assures me of my eternal salvation, I find no promise of physical protection all day, every day. But I am promised Your peace, and I praise you right now for it. Thank you for being with me, even when the times are uncertain.

Ask yourself: What do you think God's protection means to your daily life?

Fare Well

I was up this morning and ready to go in no time at all. Starting for the front door, I noticed that Jake still stood to one side, watching me but not moving. I looked in his eyes and saw something. What was it? Curiosity? Anticipation?

"Jake," I said, "I haven't really thanked you for all you've done for me. You came just when I needed you, and talking with you has been, well, it's been like being with another friend I knew..."

"Old Charlie," Jake finished my thought. "Yeah, he's a real character, all right. The trail threw him real challenges, but he met them all head on."

A dawning realization caused a wave of emotion to sweep over me like a bolt of electricity. "You... you talk like you know Charlie now. But he's... well, I..."

Jake said nothing, but simply stood looking at me as I struggled to make sense of the thoughts that were racing around my mind. I knew this old man standing in front of me was someone special, but in what way? He spoke as an observer of everything that I had experienced on the trail, even the times when I thought I was all alone. And now he talked about Charlie as if the two of them were the best of friends now. And yet Charlie was dead. Strength left me in a dawning rush, and I fell to my knees, not sure what to do but knowing that I had to do something. Before I could speak, he broke the silence.

"Stand up," he said with a sternness that brought my weakened legs back to life. "I know where you're going with this, and I need to tell you right now, it's the wrong way. You think I'm some kind of superior Being because I know a few things about you and because I talk about your friend in the present tense. But let me tell you something: it's *you* that's turning heads in heaven. From the very beginning, God's been doing some amazing things with the sons of Adam. No one knows for sure exactly how it's going to play out, but everyone knows that you and those like you will be at the center of it all. I'm just a caretaker, nothing more. Whatever you do, don't ever think of me or anyone like me as anything deserving praise. For myself, I would be most pleased if I could shake your hand and wish you God's speed for the rest of your journey.

He held out his hand, and I hesitated for a moment, then reached out and took it in mine. There was a warmth in his hand that filled me with an inexpressible joy. "Thank you," I said, and turned to the door.

Concerning this salvation, the prophets, who spoke of the grace that was to come to you, searched intently and with the greatest care, trying to find out the time and circumstances to which the Spirit of Christ in them was pointing when he predicted the sufferings of Christ and the glories that would follow. It was revealed to them that they were not serving themselves but you, when they spoke of the things that have now been told you by those who have preached the gospel to you by the Holy Spirit sent from heaven. Even angels long to look into these things.
I Peter 1: 10 – 12

....

Prayer: Praise you Father for the heavenly angels who do Your bidding. Watch over them as You watch over me and hasten the day when all the mystery between us will be removed.

Ask yourself: Do you believe in angels? How would you describe one?

May 3

On the Wings of Eagles

There's no adequate way to describe my feelings as I left the hut this morning. I looked back over my shoulder until it was out of sight, but I never saw Jake. The warmth that came from his handshake remained with me, however. It was like a tiny star residing inside me and radiating its energy out to every part of my body. Any doubts I had felt before about the decision to make this journey melted away with every step. I *knew* that I had made the right choice. I knew that I was not alone, and I knew that, somehow, I would make it to the end.

Even the discussion about the evil man and the possibility that he might some day succeed in hurting me had no effect on the joy that carried me through the day. Let them come. I didn't care. All that mattered was that I was a child of God, nothing would ever change that fact, and I was *going* somewhere.

All that day, I continued along the ridge. At times, it would begin a steady climb, but I remembered Jake's words the night before. I was not going to the top of this mountain, at least not today. Sure enough, each climbing section of trail eventually topped out and started back down, or ran parallel along the slope. By late afternoon, it was becoming apparent that I was descending. The trees below were growing closer, and the cool breeze was turning warmer. The ridge finally flattened out into a meadow which ran through lush fields of alpine grass, watered by melting snow just above the trail.

When I finally reached the trees, I saw evidence of past camps. Rocks were set in a circle where a fire had been, and logs had been dragged up close and used as seats. If it was good enough for others, it would be good enough for me, I decided, and took my backpack off for the first time today. I was amazed at the level of energy I still felt. I could have continued on for hours, but common sense told me it was time to stop. After dinner, I sat for a long time with my back propped against a log and staring up at the mountain peak. A full moon illuminated its slopes, but clouds covered the top, and occasionally I could hear distant thunder. I wondered if I would ever climb it, and why.

Tonight I still enjoyed the warmth of Jake's visit, and the assurance I felt. Stirring the coals of the campfire before settling down to sleep, I did something which I had not done in a long time, certainly not on this trip. I sang.

I waited patiently for the LORD; he turned to me and heard my cry. He lifted me out of the slimy pit, out of the mud and mire; he set my feet on a rock and gave me a firm place to stand. ?He put a new song in my mouth, a hymn of praise to our God. Many will see and fear and put their trust in the LORD.

Psalms 40: 1 – 3

....

Prayer: Lord, today I sing to You, and for the wonderful things You have done for Your creation. May all the earth sing to You. May the music of the heavens join in. Praise You God!

Ask yourself: When was the last time you felt like singing? Did you?

May 4

A Forest of Plenty

After a restful night's sleep and a hearty breakfast, I was ready for another day's trek. The glow which had accompanied me all day yesterday was still with me, although it had settled into more of a quiet assurance and less of a burning fire. I was anxious to move ahead, but was more aware of the needs of the day. I had been traveling less than an hour when I came across a thicket of blueberries. If I had seen this yesterday, I might have grabbed a handful and continued on, unwilling to pause even for such a treat. Today, however, I saw this as an opportunity to restock my food supply, just in case the trail ahead was not so abundant.

There were more berries than I could possibly carry, even though I was eating as many as I was sacking away. I remembered my grandmother's blueberry syrup, and wondered if I could make some. Building a small fire, I put a kettle on and filled it with berries. They soon boiled down, and I added more, stirring every few minutes. The longer they cooked, the thicker they became, until what I had was a succulent paste of concentrated blueberry. It smelled wonderful and was quite sweet even without adding sugar as my grandmother had done. I was pretty sure she had added other ingredients as well, but I was happy with my day's work.

Evening had come before I even realized that it was getting late, and I settled in for a night's rest. Digging through my backpack, I found some flour. Mixing some into dough, wrapping it around a stick and holding it over the fire, I managed to produce something resembling a huge biscuit, which in fact was nothing more than a platform for a generous helping of blueberry syrup. Perhaps not the most healthy meal for a pilgrim, but one which left me satisfied with the day's work.

It was a beautiful forest, full of good things. Work was still a requirement: berries had to be picked and prepared, fires had to be built and maintained, but at the end of the day a person could feel something like Adam and Eve must have felt. God had said to them, "There's the garden; here's what needs to be done; go to it." Deep inside, I felt a strange longing, as if this place was a part of my past. Here was the heritage which my ancestors had forsaken, and just as a migrating butterfly returns to a home he's never seen, my soul yearned for the place which God had looked at and called "very good."

The LORD God took the man and put him in the Garden of Eden to work it and take care of it.

Genesis 2: 15

....

Prayer: Thank you, Father, for work. Thank you for giving me a job to do and for the sense of accomplishment when I complete the job. Grant me strength to keep working until You call me home, and may I see the fruits of my labors.

Ask yourself: Is "work" a necessary evil, a punishment or a source of joy? What's the difference?

May 5

A Forest of Giants

The trail today wandered along the edge of a wide valley. Rather than turning down, it seemed to be following the contour of the mountain on my left, but moving more or less level. I was below the tree line, so it was a pleasant walk, interspersed with meadows and groves of aspen and pine trees, and the occasional brook to cross.

I continued through a pine forest which gradually gave way to larger sequoia trees. These monsters of the woods are some of the oldest living things on earth, dating back to the time of Noah. With roots that go deep into the ground and thick bark which can protect against all but the most severe fires, the sequoias are a real lesson in survival. But the thing that grabs my attention is their *size*. Walking through this quiet grove today, I felt like a child among a houseful of adults. The sound of the wind was a distant rustle far up in the tree tops, and what sun was allowed through the canopy had been dispersed into a soft incandescent glow. It occurred to me that a lot of "ancient" things tend to be bigger than their modern counterparts. I remember at the natural history museum seeing fossilized skeletons of bats with four foot wing spans, kangaroos that stood twice as high as a man and crocodiles that could take on Godzilla. Am I mistaken, or is the world getting smaller? Never mind the history books which tell us that our European ancestors stood several inches shorter than we do; research indicates that *their* ancestors were bigger than all of us. I suppose it makes sense, in light of the fact that Adam's curse has brought on a steady breakdown of everything from DNA to society's moral foundations. It's true after all: the "good old days" really *were* better than now, in a lot of ways. I understand that science can even reduce that truth to a formula, contained in something called the Second Law of Thermodynamics, which says in effect that the world is slowing down and breaking down, and that every ounce of energy spent requires more than an ounce of energy to produce. That's why I need to be here, on this journey. Because no amount of painting, repairing and propping will change the fact that our world is falling down. The situation would be hopeless, except for the fact that there is Someone above of this world Who has promised to make it new again. He's promised that I can be a part of it, and more than anything else, I want to know Him. Looking at these trees, I'm reminded of the way things used to be, and of the way things will be again. Someday.

You ought to live holy and godly lives as you look forward to the day of God and speed its coming. That day will bring about the destruction of the heavens by fire, and the elements will melt in the heat. But in keeping with his promise we are looking forward to a new heaven and a new earth, the home of righteousness.
II Peter 3: 11 – 13

Prayer: I see the world around me and I'm reminded both of the brokenness and of the promise that You will restore. Praise You, God, for showing me a glimpse of the world that You called "good".

Ask yourself: Do you think the world is getting better or worse? What examples can you think of?

May 6

History's Record

Evening was approaching, and I began to look for a place to camp for the night. Wanting to be near water, I continued on until the sound of a river caught my ears. Soon the trail reached the place where a medium-sized stream was rushing down the mountain from the left. Before I could begin to worry about getting over, however, the sight of a huge Sequoia tree drew me closer. It was lying on its side, completely across the river with the trail conveniently diverting over and onto the natural bridge.

Crossing it was easy; the log was large enough to accommodate a truck, and equally strong. I stopped halfway over the river to survey this giant of nature. It had stood easily over 200 feet, and from the condition of the bark, seemed to be living when it fell. Reaching the end of the log on the other side of the river, I met a tangle of roots which provided enough steps for getting down onto the ground. It was here that I discovered the probable reason for the tree's collapse, as well as an ideal spot for the night's camp. Inside the maze of roots, I could see a hollowed out area as big as a bedroom, the result of weakened roots which had rotted away. With no anchoring power from the roots, coupled with a gradually eroding riverbank, the tree had finally succumbed to gravity.

I worked my way inside, cleared the area of sticks and rocks, then settled back to look at my home for the night. The progression of decaying roots was clearly visible from my vantage. It had begun at the edge of one side, possibly a disease which had entered through a weak section of bark, then had slowly but surely attacked the entire root system.

I thought about the events which must have led up to this, and the fact that the problem would not have been visible before the tree fell. Furthermore, I would not be able to see it now if I were not inside the source of the problem itself. I wondered if it could have been obvious in the beginning stages. Would a trained eye have been able to say, "That tree has a disease which is going to kill it"? If the tree had been able to think, would it have known itself that destruction was at work in the darkness below?

How many men and women are losing their root systems today? It's always easy in hindsight to look at the fallen wreck of a man and say, "Well of course; he should have seen it coming." But did he? And if he did, was he able to do anything about it, or was the rot so deep and so powerful that he was doomed from the start?

I'm just thankful that there is One who does see deep inside me. And He not only sees, but also reaches in and touches, and heals and reveals and makes things new. With that assurance, I can face tomorrow.

The LORD does not look at the things man looks at. Man looks at the outward appearance, but the LORD looks at the heart.

I Samuel 16: 7

....

Prayer: Lord, it is both a joy and a sorrow to know that You see the innermost parts of my heart. Look and see what is good, and use those things for Your glory. What is shameful, please remove and forgive.

Ask yourself: Who in your life knows you better than anyone else? What kind of relationship do you have?

Not Dead

Before leaving my "tree house" this morning, I decided to fix it up a bit, clearing more dead roots and laying in a supply of wood. Hopefully, the next travelers who came this way would enjoy it as much as I had. As a finishing touch, I picked some flowers which were growing nearby and twisted them into the smaller, green roots along one wall.

Then the thought occurred to me as I tied the flowers into place: these roots are not dry and brittle as I might have expected of a dead tree. Examining some of the others, I found many more which were very much alive. The tree itself was far from dead. Climbing around the outside of the tangle of roots, I found a green twig, standing straight as an arrow and reaching for the sunlight. The sequoia was not about to give up the fight. Looking down the length of the log, and the years and years which had been necessary to accomplish what it did, my eyes returned to the green twig, born of the same root and intent on the same goal. The contrast was almost laughable, and for a moment I was tempted to reach down and yank the audacious thing out of the ground, proof of the impossible task it was facing. But before I could move, my heart was flooded with a wave of compassion for this monument to life.

Things are not always as they seem, I reminded myself. If ever there was an image of defeat and death, it would be this tree, fallen from a great height and now useful only for crossing the river and providing as evening's shelter. And yet, it was not dead at all, not by a long shot. What roots remained had taken the fall in stride and kept churning out whatever it is that roots churn out. Nutrients were still to be gathered from the ground and sent to places where they will be converted into green branches and leaves, which in turn will draw carbon dioxide from the air and feed the system. If I could come back to this place in 500 years or so, I'm sure I would find a strong, healthy sequoia, taking nutrients from the soil and from the rotting wood of its former self.

By contrast, the flowers which I had so carefully picked and tied up this morning are very much dead. They just don't know it yet. And the reason I know is because I have separated them from their roots. They'll be fortunate if another traveler stops by tonight to enjoy their beauty, because by this time tomorrow they will be wilted reminders of what they used to be.

I saw there a sobering picture of myself. Before deciding to make this journey, I was adrift, without roots, without life. But now I have an anchor and a source for the Living Water which I was promised. Even if, as Jake reminded me, the evil man took my life, he could never kill me, because my roots go deep, all the way to my Creator.

But blessed is the man who trusts in the LORD, whose confidence is in him. He will be like a tree planted by the water that sends out its roots by the stream. It does not fear when heat comes; its leaves are always green.

Jeremiah 17: 7 – 8

Prayer: Thank you today for the assurance that my life is rooted in You. I will never be separated from Your watchful care over me, and even though my fragile body may wither and die, Your life still courses through me. Praise You!

Ask yourself: What do you think are the roots which holds a person to God?

May 8

A Stand of Aspen

Leaving my Sequoia home, I set off down the trail, winding through more huge trees before finally leaving the dark forest and moving into a stand of noisy Aspen trees. The Aspen is a fast-growing soft wood with white bark. Because it allows more light through its leaves than the Sequoia groves, the ground is alive with grasses, shrubs and young trees. It has been said that Aspen trees make up the emergency response team of the forest, since they are quick to take root following fire or flood. Walking through this Aspen forest, I began to notice the remains of pine trees, scattered all around. The unusual thing about them was that they were all standing upright. At first, I thought a fire had swept through, burning the pines just enough to kill them without taking them down. But then I saw that all the pine trees had been sheared off about ten feet above the ground, as if a huge pair of hedge clippers had decided to trim everything into a giant hedge. But the shearing had killed the trees, calling for the necessity of the Aspens to come in and hold things down. What had caused such a phenomenon? As I stood contemplating this mystery, my eyes focused on the mountain in the distance, above and beyond where I stood. Pine forests covered the slopes as far up as I could see, except for a strip about 200 feet wide, extending on up into the high country and coming directly down to the place where I was standing. Mystery solved. This was the bottom reaches of an avalanche area, and at some time in the past, the winter snow had reached all the way to here. The point at which the trees had been clipped off was the depth of the snow at the time of the avalanche. I tried to imagine the force and speed of a wall of ice, moving from the slopes high above and racing down over a thin layer of air, destroying everything in its path, including a grove of pine trees whose tops were unfortunate enough to be sticking out above a ten foot base of snow. Of course, it would be foolish to try and blame the pine trees for growing here in the first place. They had no choice in the matter, and the forest did not grieve their passing. Life goes on here, thanks to God's Providence in sending the Aspen response team, and it's only we humans that marvel at such Design. But for myself, I might be held accountable if I decided to stay here and build a home on this spot. All evidence indicates that this is a disaster waiting to happen again. Snow collects on the mountain, gravity pulls it down, and anything in its path is history. There are similar places in life, aren't there? You look around and say, "Uh oh. I think I'd better move on." The tragedy is that many do not move on, but decide to stay in spite of the obvious danger. I guess that's part of the blessing and the curse of being human. I can stay here if I choose, and I can accept the consequences. That's called freedom. That's called real love.

But if serving the LORD seems undesirable to you, then choose for yourselves this day whom you will serve, whether the gods your forefathers served beyond the River, or the gods of the Amorites, in whose land you are living. But as for me and my household, we will serve the LORD.

Joshua 24: 14 – 15

....

Prayer: Lord I thank you for giving me the freedom to choose, for it is from that freedom that I can love and be loved. But I also fear the consequences of my choices. Grant me wisdom to choose what is good, and to reject what is not Your will.

Ask yourself: Can true love be forced upon anyone?

A Deer in the Thicket

Moving deeper into the Aspen, I marveled at the ability of the forest to recover from what had once been a disastrous avalanche. With their ability to shoot up quickly, these trees had brought new homes to a whole new host of forest inhabitants. Mice were scurrying from log to log, and behind them was evidence of foxes and hawks, looking for an easy meal.

Through the tangle, I could see that places had been hollowed out, convenient spots for hiding and sleeping. And there, nestled down in one of the hollows, was a young fawn.

He was not moving a muscle, and I wouldn't have seen him at all if his left ear had not twitched. Perhaps a fly had tickled him, or else he was listening in all directions for sounds of Mother. I moved a little closer to get a better look, but the fawn never moved. His coat was mottled a mixture of brown and gold, and sitting motionless in the thicket he was almost invisible. As I stepped closer, his ears stopped twitching, but his eyes followed me as I moved to the side for a better look.

I'm not a vegetarian, and would never turn down a helping of venison stew if it was offered me. The Bible is explicitly clear in its judgment against cruelty and inhumane treatment of animals, but I find nothing preventing the Sons of Adam from continuing the God-given command to look after, and use responsibly the blessings of His creation. It would have been an easy matter to step closer, grab the fawn and enjoy a tender steak tonight. But I knew I would not do that, even though I was not sure exactly why.

In His wisdom, God has provided a means of protection for every one of His creatures. Some can run fast, others can fight back, and a few can hide extremely well. And in addition, there is something built into creation that says, "Don't harm the young." What is it in us that looks at a baby deer and says "How cute!" For that matter, just about any young creature is endowed with a special blessing of protection from those who might take advantage of its helplessness. Kittens have been raised by dogs, and I once saw a baby duck being cared for by a lion. There are exceptions, of course, but the rule seems to reflect something that finds its origins in the farthest reaches of our existence. Evolution cannot explain it, and science can only describe it. For myself, I can only appreciate my Creator for it. "Mind your Momma, now," I said softly as I turned and headed on down the trail.

The wolf and the lamb shall feed together, the lion shall eat straw like the ox; and dust shall be the serpent's food. They shall not hurt or destroy in all my holy mountain, says the LORD.

Isaiah 65: 25

Prayer: When I look at the young, I am reminded again of Your love and mercy, dear Lord. What a mystery, that You would protect your helpless creatures, and place within our hearts a natural desire to care for them. Remember also that I am Your child.

Ask yourself: Why do you think baby animals are "cute"?

Honey

As the afternoon wore on, I stopped for a break and something to eat. "A big steak would sure be good about now," I smiled to myself, a part of me regretting passing by such as easy feast back there, but still certain that I had made the right choice. A little flour, a little water, a few other ingredients, and I was soon holding a stick wrapped in bread dough over a heap of burning coals. The warm afternoon sun was working its spell on me, and I propped the stick up with a rock so I could lay back and take it in.

Laying there with my eyes closed, I was in a world of half sleep, listening to the sounds of the forest. Some small animal was rustling the grass not far away. A woodpecker was hammering out a staccato off in the distance, and the Aspens were engaged in their non-stop chatter up in the tops of the trees. And underlying it all was a low droning sound which never changed pitch and refused to take a breath. I listened to it for awhile, ignored it, then came back to it. Just there, off to the left, near that big standing pine, long since dead and rotting away. I focused on the pine and noticed a hole in the wood about head height, and there was the source of the droning: bees were coming and going, swarming all around the tree and heading out in all directions. One flew past me and I saw that it was a honey bee. Honey.

I'm not a particularly brave man, and especially when it come to stinging insects, I would rather leave it to the professionals. But sitting here alone, with a loaf of bread starting to send up a heavenly aroma, I found a courage I didn't know I possessed. I'd seen this done on a National Geographic special once, so I knew it was possible. Pulling all the clothing I could find out of my pack, I dressed as if a blizzard were on the way, then fashioned a net out of a thin shirt and held it in place over my head with a hat. With a gloved hand, I took a green stick out of the fire and watched as it smoked profusely.

The bees seemed to sense the threat as I drew near, but the smoke kept most of them at bay. Wasting no time, I stepped up to the tree, reached in and pulled back a huge piece of honeycomb, dripping with honey. Placing it in a cook pot, I beat a hasty retreat, followed by a few angry bees, a couple of which managed to find flesh. It hurt, but success was a great salve. Back at camp, I checked out my bounty. There was nearly a pint of honey trapped in the comb, enough for a real feast, and then some. Even the insects were part of God's provision, I thought as I cleaned out the honey comb and enjoyed a couple of before dinner treats.

My son, eat honey, for it is good, and the drippings of the honeycomb are sweet to your taste. Know that wisdom is such to your soul; if you find it, there will be a future, and your hope will not be cut off.

Proverbs 24: 13 – 14

Prayer: Father, everything You have made is good, and I praise You for Your generous provision. May neither the thorns of the vine nor the stings of the insect keep me from what You have given me. We live under the curse of suffering, but also under the promise of life. In that promise I rejoice today.

Ask yourself: Have you ever gained something which carried with it a cost in pain? How did you feel to receive it?

May 11

A Reunion

With evening, I began cleaning up the mess I had made in gathering and preparing the honey. My gloves were sticky and had to be boiled clean. It seemed every utensil I owned had been used at one time or another and was now covered with drops of honey at precisely the point where I picked it up. I had eaten my fill with the bread, had sweetened my coffee with it, and had made a kind of honey-nut-blueberry dessert. But there was still plenty left, and I was in a quandary as to what to do with it. I didn't seem to have a container which would hold it without leaking, and I didn't think I could eat another bite. Leaving it seemed like such a waste, but...

Off in the darkness, I heard a sound. The night was full of sounds, but this one caught my attention. A twig snapped, and there was the rustle of something which did not seem to be part of the forest. I stood up and moved away from the fire, in order to see better as well as to reduce the ability of being seen. My ears strained to hear more. Whatever it was, it was coming from the direction of the trail, from the way I had come. And it was getting closer.

A clinking sound removed all doubt that this was anything normally heard among the forest and its inhabitants. Whatever it was, it was not animal. That left two conclusions: either man or man*like*, and the thought caused my skin to tingle. Should I try and hide? Should I call out? Glancing over at the brightly burning campfire, I realized that whoever or whatever it was, had known of my presence here for some time now. And he didn't seem to be trying to hide the sound of his approach, which either meant he didn't want to be quiet, or else he knew that he didn't *need* to be quiet. Either of those options could be good news or not, I thought, as I looked around for something which would be used as a weapon. My search stopped as soon as I heard the voice from the darkness, "Hello the camp!"

"Come into the light," I called out, only slightly relieved. "Who is it?"

"The rear guard," Ralph said as he emerged from the shadows, a big grin on his face. "I was hoping it might be you."

Be devoted to one another in brotherly love. Honor one another above yourselves.
Never be lacking in zeal, but keep your spiritual fervor, serving the Lord.

Romans 12: 10 – 11

Prayer: Thank you Father today for the friends who are not with me now. Bless them in their journey, and bring us together again in Your time.

Ask yourself: Do you have a friend whom you rarely get to spend time with, but who remains close to you?

May 12

A Mission

It was good to see Ralph again, and to hear of his journey since we had parted at the last Rendezvous. He had elected to remain behind in case the demon army we had encountered decided to try and attack us from the rear. They had not returned, undoubtedly because they knew we were prepared for them, and because of the Divine protection which had kept them at bay while all the travelers were together. I confessed to being a little uneasy alone on the trail, however, and Ralph agreed.

"Yeah, it's one thing to stand shoulder to shoulder with fellow believers and go against an army of uglies. But out here alone, it's not always so easy to be brave. It's good to see you, Friend, in more ways than one."

"Same here," I smiled. "And boy do I have a treat for you." Holding up the cooking pot still half filled with honey, he took a whiff and threw off his back pack.

"Where did you get that?" he exclaimed.

"Just over there," I said. "Cost me a few stings, but it was worth it, especially now that I can boast about it to someone!"

Ralph demonstrated the admirable ability for biscuit making, and even though I had finished dinner, this was too good to pass up. Finally, over honey-sweetened coffee, we sat back, stirred the coals and enjoy the silence of the evening.

"Not to be critical," I began, half teasing, half serious, "I understood that you were to be the last to leave camp. I took off before several folks, and none of them has passed me. Is there a change in marching order?"

"Some of them decided to stay at the top of the ridge and build a fortress," Ralph said, sadly shaking his head. "I only hope they come to their senses before it's too late." Then he looked at me with a smile. "Some at the ridge were packing up to leave, though, thanks to what you shared with them. That was a great thing you did. It took courage. In fact, that's why I've been walking day and night, passing folks up. I've been trying to catch up with you."

"What?" I asked, incredulous. "What do you mean?'

"I met Jake," he said, knowing that would get my attention. "And I've got a job for you."

But rise and stand upon your feet; for I have appeared to you for this purpose, to appoint you to serve and bear witness to the things in which you have seen me and to those in which I will appear to you, delivering you from the people and from the Gentiles-to whom I send you to open their eyes, that they may turn from darkness to light and from the power of Satan to God, that they may receive forgiveness of sins and a place among those who are sanctified by faith in me.'
Acts 26: 16 – 18

....

Prayer: We look with longing, Father, at the people You have called to serve You. We want to serve as well, to do Your bidding in whatever task You give us. As Isaiah cried out, so do we: "Here am I, send me."

Ask yourself: What would you be willing to do for God? What would you not be willing to do?

A Discerning Heart

"A job?" I repeated. "What could I possibly do? And how does Jake fit in? Do you know what he really is?"

"Slow down!" Ralph laughed. "All things in good time. I met Jake at the hut where you stayed. And yes, I know what he really is. He told me things about my life that no one should know about. But he didn't criticize me for them. He just said that all of that is in the past: forgiven and forgotten. When he said that, I knew which side he was on. The evil man would have used that information against me, for sure."

I nodded in agreement. "He stopped me from treating him like some kind of god. But tell me more about this 'job' thing."

"Jake said that the trail splits a little farther down the way. That's why I had to catch up with you before you got there. He said the correct way is obvious, off to the right. The way to the left is grown over, and blocked, so no one in his right mind would go that way. He told me to take that fork."

"Now wait a minute," I said, sitting up straight. "I'm still recovering from my own tour apart from the trail. If I were you I wouldn't be so anxious to head off in any direction but the correct one."

"I couldn't agree more," Ralph said, "and I told Jake so. He said this was like a rescue mission. A long time ago some travelers went off that way, and now they don't even remember that they were ever *on* a journey. They've built a town, and plan to stay there. I'm supposed to go remind them, and if possible, lead them back to the trail."

"Wow," I said, looking into the embers as if I could see the same thing Ralph was seeing there. "I never expected anything like this. Who are we to try and convince someone to do what we've decided to do?"

"If it was a simple case of rebellion, that would be one thing," said Ralph. "But the fact is, there's more. The enemy has gotten the idea that those are *his* people now, and the land they live on is *his* land. My job is to rekindle the truth, in the hopes that some might come back."

"And where do I fit into this?" I asked, knowing already what I was about to hear.

"I need someone to come along with me," he said. "It may get dangerous. I need someone to fight beside me, if necessary. Jake said to ask you, but to remind you that this is a job *I'm* supposed to do. If you don't want to, that's okay. I'm just asking as a friend. Will you sleep on it and tell me in the morning?"

A friend loves at all times, and a brother is born for adversity.

Proverbs 17: 17

....

Prayer: Lord, it is through adversity that my friends show their truth worth. Thank You for giving me friends who share my good times as well as my challenges. May I be as good a friend to them as they are to me.

Ask yourself: Is it easier to be a friend to someone in need or to someone who has everything?

A Dream

I promised Ralph that I would sleep on his invitation to join him in a "rescue mission" which would take me once again off the trail. This would not be an easy decision to make. I loved Ralph like a brother, and I did not doubt the authenticity of his call. However, I also understood that his call was not necessarily my call. Jake had even said that I could refuse if I wanted to.

Ralph was already sleeping soundly, obviously exhausted from the effort of catching up with me. But there was another reason he slept so readily, and that was the fact that now we were two. What one might miss, the other might hear. While one might be defeated, two might be victorious. As sleep surrounded me, I prayed for wisdom, and was given a dream.

A young child, not more than two years old, was moving down a trail. Sometimes crawling, sometimes toddling, he seemed intent on moving forward, toward a heavy iron door. I knew in my dream that behind that door waited all kinds of horrible things: poisonous snakes, sharp knives, fires... everything that we try and keep young children away from. The door stood open, and I knew at once what the child intended to do: go inside. I made a move to stop him, but for some reason was unable to approach him directly. I shouted, but he didn't seem to hear. The only thing to do was close the door. I raced ahead and gave the door a push, but nothing happened. I pushed harder, but it seemed to weigh a ton. The child kept coming closer and I kept straining harder, but nothing would move it and nothing would stop him. I began to cry out in fear and frustration. Why wouldn't the child listen? Why couldn't I stop him? Why couldn't I close the door? If only I were stronger. If only I had help. The child reached the door, and I watched in horrid fascination as he paused once, then stepped through. From the other side, I heard his screams, matching my own. I cried and I cried, and was still crying when I woke up. Ralph was standing over me, a look of concern on his face.

"Are you okay?" he asked.

I lay there for a moment, relieved that it had only been a dream, but troubled to the core at the message I had just received. "Ralph," I asked at last, "are there children there?"

"It's been several years, so yeah, I imagine there are. Why?"

"Because my questions have been answered. Let's get moving."

Whoever receives one such child in my name receives me; but whoever causes one of these little ones who believe in me to sin, it would be better for him to have a great millstone fastened round his neck and to be drowned in the depth of the sea.
Matthew 18: 5 – 6

....

Prayer: I love Your precious children, Lord, and I want to protect them from all harm. Teach me how to guide them in the way they should go. May I never lead them astray, either by what I do or by what I fail to do.

Ask yourself: Why do you think children are helpless?

Preparing for Invasion

Ralph and I walked together, talking about the task ahead. We reviewed our plans, and considered options.

"All we have to do is give them the word," Ralph said. "We can't force them to come with us. If they come, it will have to be their own choice, just like it was for us."

"But you said that they live under deception," I reminded him. "What if they refuse to come based on a lie? We can't just leave them without knowing that they understand what our message is, can we?"

"No, I suppose not," Ralph said. "In that case, we may have to expose the lie, which means we may have to confront the deceivers themselves."

"And how do we do that?" I asked, becoming more and more despairing. Surely we're not expected to take on a whole demonic kingdom by ourselves!"

"I don't know the answer to that, Friend," Ralph said. "I guess all we can do is go in with our eyes and our hearts open. We'll need to be as prepared as possible. Which reminds me..." he said, stopping and taking his pack off his shoulders. "I have something for you." Opening up the top of the pack, he reached down one side and drew out a sword. I recognized it at once as the one I had taken from the demon in the middle of the river. "This rightfully belongs to you," he said, "and I'll feel better if you're carrying it. I still have the one I got from Andy." He took his own out and compared it to mine. They were about the same size, and the edges sparkled in the sun. He clipped his to his belt and I did the same.

"Let's hope we don't have to use these," I said, trying to hold down the tremor in my voice. "But if we do, you're the one I want watching my back."

We put our backpacks on again and continued down the trail. But now there was a different feel to our step. Before we were moving toward a personal goal: to finish the journey; now we were on a mission. And the lives of others depended upon our success or failure. I felt fear, to be sure, but overriding my fear was a sense of purpose and unity which I had never before experienced. I was glad to be part of something that mattered, something that was true and worthy of all that I had to give it. I smiled at Ralph and knew that he was feeling the same thing. We couldn't wait to get on with it.

And Jesus came and said to them, "All authority in heaven and on earth has been given to me. Go therefore and make disciples of all nations, baptizing them in the name of the Father and of the Son and of the Holy Spirit, teaching them to observe all that I have commanded you; and lo, I am with you always, to the close of the age."
Matthew 28: 18 – 20

Prayer: What a mystery, that You would ask me to do what You could do so much better. What a joy, to be a part of Your mission, used by You. What a promise, that You will be with me always, even until the end of the age.

Ask yourself: Has God ever asked you to do something for His Kingdom? What did you say?

Through the Barrier

Ralph and I slept little the night before. Now as the day wore on, we began to feel the resulting fatigue. Coming to a small stream, we sat heavily on a rock and propped our feet up. "How much farther do you think it is to the split in the trail?" I asked.

"Jake said it wasn't far, and that I would have to hurry to catch you before you passed it," said Ralph. "He did say it was overgrown. I hope we didn't miss it already."

"I've been watching pretty closely," I said. "I don't think we've come to it yet."

"Yeah, I think you're right," he said, sitting up. "I think the trail would be partially visible, anyway." He stood up then, and took a step toward the riverbank. "Like, if the trail is going to split, it should be at a logical place, like the top of a ridge, or... a river crossing."

I sat up and watched him as he took another step toward the bushes that grew along the riverbank. He pulled a few limbs aside, then stepped through and out of sight. "Ralph?" I called out. "Where are you going?"

"To a whole other world," he said, sticking his head back around the shrubs. "This is it! Let's go!" I followed him behind the bushes and saw that a trail was faintly visible, following the riverbank and moving upstream. We walked on for about 500 yards, then the trail abruptly switched back to the left and started up the mountain side. Away from the river now, the undergrowth thinned out and the trail was easier to see. Coming to a level place, we came upon a barricade, built out of boards and wire, stretching across the trail. Nailed to a board was a large sign with red lettering:

"Entry forbidden. Trespassers will be prosecuted."

"Do you suppose that means us?" Ralph asked, feigning ignorance.

To answer his question, I gripped the sign, ripped it loose from the board and threw it into the bushes. "No, "I said, "that's obviously for people who believe everything they read."

We climbed over the barricade, looked around and were a little surprised to find that the land looked no different from that on the other side. Ralph was thinking the same thing, and remarked, "I don't know; I guess I thought it would look somehow *evil*."

"Maybe evil things live here," I reminded him, "but they didn't make this place. I vote we make camp here, then move inland first thing in the morning."

Ralph agreed, and we settled in for the evening. We were both exhausted from lack of sleep as well as from the mental stress of the day, wondering if we would find this place. After a light dinner and coffee, we were both sound asleep.

Even though I walk through the valley of the shadow of death, I fear no evil; for thou art with me; thy rod and thy staff, they comfort me. Thou preparest a table before me in the presence of my enemies; thou anointest my head with oil my cup overflows.
Psalms 23: 4 – 5

....

Prayer: Tonight I sleep in the enemy's camp. He has declared this world to be his, and would through deceit convince me that I am under his authority. Grant me strength, Lord, to stand against his intentions upon me.

Ask yourself: What claim does Satan have on the world? How would you answer him?

Confrontation

Neither of us heard them coming, so sound was our sleep. The first I heard was the quiet laugher of the one standing closest to me. Startled, I threw back the sleeping bag and got to my feet. Ralph did the same, and we stood side by side, faced by three soldiers.

They appeared human, but not quite so. Different from the demonic army which had attacked us at Rendezvous, they still possessed a look and a demeanor which was by now becoming familiar. The one in the center seemed to be in charge, and he spoke up.

"It looks like you boys have come to the wrong side of the fence." He said in a condescending tone. "Are the rest with you, or did they run away when they heard us coming?"

"There are no others," Ralph said, looking straight into the eyes of the leader. "We are the only ones."

That brought another laugh from one of the others, and a knowing glance toward the leader. "So what happens now?" I asked. "Are we under arrest?"

At that, both soldiers broke into uproarious laughter, until the leader held out his hand to calm then down. "We don't waste our time with boys like you," he said, taking a step backward. "Kill them."

The soldiers drew their swords and picked out their victim. Ralph and I jumped backwards at the same time, grabbing the swords we had laid out the night before alongside out sleeping bags. When they saw we were armed, the soldiers hesitated. The leader took a long look at my sword, then said, "I don't believe that belongs to you. Where did you get it?"

"From the one who tried to kill me with it," I said. "He doesn't need it anymore."

That brought a cry of rage from both the soldiers, and they came at us together. The attack was a classic overhand charge, just like Andy had taught us, and the only one the demon army seemed to have known. Ralph and I both responded as we had been taught, deflecting the blow then returning with a forward thrust to the midsection. Both swords found their mark, and within seconds both soldiers lay dead on the ground.

The leader was too stunned to move at first, then as we advanced toward him, he turned and ran a few paces, stopped and shouted over his shoulder, "You haven't seen the last of me!" then ran on, out of sight into the woods.

We both stood there shaking, looking down at what we had done, then looking up to see if there would be more. Finally Ralph spoke, "I suggest we pack up and move before our hero finds more soldiers."

Finally, be strong in the Lord and in the strength of his might. Put on the whole armor of God, that you may be able to stand against the wiles of the devil.
Ephesians 6: 10 – 11

....

Prayer: Lord, I want to be a pacifist, but Your Word tells me to be a warrior. When I must fight, then give me the skill and the courage to bring honor to Your Kingdom.

Ask yourself: How do you feel when the Bible says you are to prepare for battle?

At the Well

Following Ralph's advice, we hurriedly packed up our camp and headed on into the trees. Stopping after a few minutes, we discussed the next move.

"Let's move on," I suggested, "avoiding the trail as much as possible, until we come to a settlement. Maybe we can find someone to talk to before the alarm goes up."

We kept moving uphill, skirted around what seemed to be a military barracks, then followed a well-worn path that led up a valley to the right. As the day moved on with no further sign of pursuit, we began to relax a little. "Maybe the soldiers are stationed mostly around the borders," I said, "to try and catch people as they sneak in."

"Or as they try and sneak out," said Ralph.

After another hour of walking, we could see a cloud of smoke hanging over the trees just ahead. "Looks like a settlement," Ralph said.

A small stream had been flowing to our right, and up ahead we could see a water wheel, turning slowly. The wheel was connected to a small house where there seemed to be a mill of some kind. Several people were gathered around it, some carrying sacks of grain inside, some just standing around talking. They didn't seem to pose any kind of threat, so Ralph and I walked up and got a drink.

The reaction was more suspicion than anything else. Some moved farther away from us while others stared intently, as if to read our thoughts. Ralph and I drank slowly, not sure what to do next, when a little girl of about eight or nine approached us.

"Who are you?" she asked as only the innocence of a child could ask. Ralph spoke.

"My name is Ralph," he said. "And this is my friend. What's your name?"

"Nicki," she answered immediately. "Actually it's Marsha Nicole, but that's too hard to say, and besides I like Nicki better. What are you doing here?"

"We've come to tell you some really good news," said Ralph. "In fact, we want to tell everyone. Is your mother or father around?"

Before Nicki could answer, an older girl stepped up and took her by the upper arm. "She's not supposed to be talking to strangers," she said. "C'mon, Nicki."

They started walking away, and I called out after them, "Please tell your parents we're here. We want them to know something very important." From behind me, a woman's voice spoke softly.

"I'm Nicki's mother," she said, "and you shouldn't be here."

"If the world hates you, know that it has hated me before it hated you. If you were of the world, the world would love its own; but because you are not of the world, but I chose you out of the world, therefore the world hates you."
John 15: 18 – 19

....

Prayer: Dear Jesus, I know You told us that people would hate us because they hate You, but it's still difficult to bear. I want to be accepted, but the message You've told me to share is not very acceptable. Give me courage, and help me to endure the world's critics.

Ask yourself: Have you ever been ridiculed because of something you said? How did it feel?

Hope

I turned to look at the woman, hoping to find an ally, but instead was brought face to face with an expression of pure hatred. "I don't know what you think you're doing here, mister, but if you'll take my advice you'll keep right on moving. We don't want your kind around here putting ideas into our children's heads."

"'My kind', I said, completely caught off guard. "How do you know what 'kind' I am? My friend and I just want to tell you about the One who made all this, and about the journey He's offered us. We know that you've been deceived into thinking that this is all there is, but..."

"You know *nothing!*" she spat out. "Now for the last time, get out of here, both of you, or I'm going to call for the authorities."

Ralph put his hand on my shoulder, a silent signal. I looked around to see that the other people had gathered behind the woman and seemed to be in agreement with what she was saying. This harmless gathering of townsfolk was about to erupt into an angry mob. I looked at Ralph, and he mouthed the words, "Let's go."

Around the corner and out of sight of the mill, we could finally breathe a little easier. Ralph spoke first. "Well, I knew it would be difficult, but somehow I expected the soldiers to be the worst part. We can't very well take our swords to women and children, can we?"

"No," I agreed. "This may be a bigger job than we counted on."

From behind, we heard the pounding of feet, and instinctively reached for our swords as we turned together. I relaxed a little to see that it was a boy, perhaps a teenager. Running up to us, he panted out the words, "Follow me!" and took off into the bushes beside the trail. There was no time for discussion, so we followed him, running through thickets, jumping over logs and streams until finally coming to a stop deep in the forest.

The boy looked all around, then whispered, "My father wants to talk to you, but you can't let anyone see you. Wait here until it gets dark, then I'll come back and take you to our house." Then he ran away, back in the direction we had come from.

"What do you think?" I asked Ralph. "It could be a trap."

"Could be," Ralph agreed. "But it's the only things we've got so far. I say we wait."

"Do not think that I have come to bring peace on earth; I have not come to bring peace, but a sword. For I have come to set a man against his father, and a daughter against her mother, and a daughter-in-law against her mother-in-law; and a man's foes will be those of his own household."

Matthew 10: 34 – 36

....

Prayer: Lord I pray for those whose faith in You has placed them in jeopardy within their own homes. Surround them with Your Spirit, I pray. Protect them, and according to Your will may all in their household come to know You.

Ask yourself: Do all of your family members share the same faith? What problems have arisen?

May 20

A Secret Meeting

The longer we waited, the more nervous we became, imagining all kinds of scenarios involving demonic soldiers and angry townspeople carrying pitchforks. It was now completely dark, and we realized that we couldn't run if we wanted to, since we could barely see our hands in front of our faces.

From somewhere in the distance, we heard the cracking of twigs and instinctively put our hands on our swords. The sound grew closer, then stopped. A soft whistle, followed by "Are you there?"

"We're here," Ralph whispered, and the boy stepped closer.

"Follow me," he said, "and don't talk."

We started off behind the dark form that was our guide, but rather than head back toward the road, he led us deeper into the woods. We tripped and stumbled for a half hour or more, then stopped when we ran up against the boy. Off in the distance, I could see light coming through windows. "Be especially quiet now," he whispered. We left the woods and started across a field, moving silently toward the buildings. One house showed no lights at all, and I thought it at least would be empty and thus safe. But to my surprise, the boy led us directly to that one, around to a small door at the back and inside.

Once inside with the door closed, I heard the sound of a match being struck, and a candle was lit. By the faint light, I could see the boy who had led us here, a man standing nervously by the table, and back near the wall, a woman with her arms around two girls. "My name is William," he said in an almost normal tone of voice. "My son, Nathan." Then pointing with a toss of his head, "My wife and daughters. I hope you understand what a risk I'm taking, doing this. The word is that you've already killed two men."

"Soldiers," I nodded. "They were trying to kill us."

He was silent. Nathan moved over to the kitchen and sat on a stool. The wife and daughters did not move. "I have heard stories," he began. "Of people coming from a place we know nothing of. They urged us to go with them."

"We are such people," Ralph said, leaning into the candlelight. "If you will allow me, I will answer all your questions and tell you of this One I serve. But what of the others like us," Ralph said, speaking to everyone in the room. "Did anyone go with them when they left?"

"They did not leave," William said softly. "They all died."

O Jerusalem, Jerusalem, killing the prophets and stoning those who are sent to you! How often would I have gathered your children together as a hen gathers her brood under her wings, and you would not! Behold, your house is forsaken and desolate.
Matthew 23: 37 – 38

Prayer: Lord I know You will not forget those whose blood was shed for the cause of Your Kingdom. Remember them and hasten the day when there is no more persecution, no fear and no death.

Ask yourself: What is a "martyr"? Are there martyrs today?

May 21

A Seed is Sown

Ralph and I both sat speechless for what seemed like several minutes. At first we thought we had misunderstood what William had said, but then looking at his face realized the seriousness of this conversation.

"As I said," Ralph began again. "if you will let me, I will answer all your questions about the One who made everything, and Who has sent us here to urge you to return to Him."

"Don't you get what my father's saying?" Nathan stood up and came into the room where we sat. "People like you have come here before, and they all died! We're trying to save your lives. I know these woods blindfolded. If we get started now, I can lead you out of the area by daylight. After that, you're on your own. By staying here, you're putting us all in danger. Leave. Please."

Ralph looked at me and I nodded. We both stood up. "We made the choice to come here, knowing and accepting the danger to ourselves. But we have no wish to put you at risk. Thank you for what you've done already. If you'll just tell us which way to go, Nathan, we'll leave now. You stay here with your family."

There was an audible sigh of relief in the room as we turned to leave by the back door. But before we could get away from the table, the smaller of the two girls spoke up from across the room. "Couldn't they tell us a story first, Daddy?"

It was a voice I had heard before. Straining to see through the candle lit gloom, I looked toward the back wall where the little girl was standing, still clutched tightly by her mother. It was the child from the mill who had approached us. I looked to the older girl, and saw that it was the big sister who had led her away. I smiled at them and started to say something, but the mother's voice put an end to all conversation. "These men don't have time to stay, Nicki. They have to go."

Both the words and the voice were all too familiar. It was the woman from the mill, who had warned us to leave.

Now this I affirm and testify in the Lord, that you must no longer live as the Gentiles do, in the futility of their minds; they are darkened in their understanding, alienated from the life of God because of the ignorance that is in them, due to their hardness of heart;

Ephesians 4: 17 – 18

Prayer: Lord I know that no man comes to You unless You call him. So I pray that You would call. Melt the hearts of those hardened by sin. Bring them into Your loving presence and let them feel the joy of being accepted.

Ask yourself: Have you known anyone who will simply not listen to reason, in spite of evidence which goes against what they are saying? Why do you think they do that?

From the Mouths of Babes

The woman's voice carried both fear and anger, one undoubtedly a product of the other. "If you want to get yourself killed doing some big quest, that's up to you. But when you bring it into my home, then it's up to *me*. And I will not let you destroy my family. I told you this afternoon, and I'll tell you again: if you don't get out of our lives *right now* I'm going to see that you're caught and killed. Do you understand me?"

Ralph spoke with a gentleness that I had never heard from him before. "Yes, I understand you," he said quietly. "I understand that you love your family, and that's a wonderful thing. I had a family once, a long time ago. Two sons, a daughter, and a beautiful wife who was devoted to me. We decided together to follow the One who made us, and we started out on a journey which would take us to Him. But an evil man came and offered me something which I thought I needed: guaranteed protection for us all. I believed him, and I did what he told me to do, in the firm conviction that I was doing the right thing. But he was a deceiver. What I thought was a safe haven in a time of storm was actually a narrow precipice. They all fell, one by one. I tried to get to them, to pull them back to safety, but it was too late. That same evil man has deceived a whole village into believing that where they live is the most secure place in the world. But he's wrong. It's another precipice and it will take every man, woman and child to their deaths. Dear lady, you are to be commended for your love. Now I pray that you will receive an equal measure of wisdom, for the sake of your children. For the sake of this village."

As he spoke, I stood with my mouth agape. I had never heard the story of Ralph's family, and my heart went out to him. Looking over at the mother, I could see that she was listening as well. Her face remained impassive, but in the corner of one eye I saw a single tear emerge and find its way down her cheek. Little Nicki looked up at her mother, uncertain of what to say, but choosing to say nothing except to hold her all the more tightly. Finally, the mother fell to her knees, embracing Nicki and her sister and crying out, "My precious babies. What am I to do? What am I to do?"

In two quick steps, William was at his wife's side, holding and comforting her. Nathan stayed where he was in the kitchen doorway, but he looked at me and smiled. Finally William spoke. "We've known for years that we were being lied to, but we were too afraid to do anything about it. We thought we could keep quiet and keep out of trouble." He looked into his wife's eyes as he went on. "As of tonight, we're through being quiet.. No matter what happens, we're going to speak out, and speak the truth." Then he looked at Ralph and me "But I don't know what the truth is. Can you teach me?"

Why is my language not clear to you? Because you are unable to hear what I say.
John 8: 43

....

Prayer: In a world full of lies and deceit, dear Father, show me Your truth. May I not fall into the snares my enemy has set for me, but may I walk upright, confident that Your way is the one true way.

Ask yourself: What is the difference between "correct" and "true"?

May 23

Willing Ears

For the rest of the night, we sat around the kitchen table and opened up a whole new world to a willing family. At first, I told children's stories from the Bible which Nicki could understand and enjoy. I was surprised to find however that the whole family listened with rapt attention. As the evening grew late, Nicki begin to drift off to sleep, and her sister carried her upstairs to bed.

Ralph took up the lessons from there, explaining in clear but powerful images the truth of God's Word. He told of Eden, and of the world called "very good". He explained the need for freedom, if love is to be genuine, and the simple means whereby that freedom could be demonstrated: "Eat not of that tree." When they heard of man's rebellion, the family was incensed, then shamed as they realized that they too were guilty. They rejoiced at the love of God; then they were horrified to learn of man's treatment of the His Son. But with the resurrection and the promise of His return, they were assured again that this was indeed the truth that they had been waiting to hear.

As the sky in the east was beginning to turn a shade of grey, William said, "We *will* leave this place and return to the path which has been too long forgotten. But I cannot leave until every other person in this town knows what I know." Looking at us, William said, "You my friends must go on without us, but rest assured that we will see you again. You have done what you were sent to do. Now please, go with God."

I stood up, but noticed that Ralph had not moved. When everyone noticed him, he said, "I failed one family. I will not fail another. With your permission and by God's grace, I would like to stay on with you. I will help you accomplish what has to be done, defend you if necessary, and then we will all leave together."

I started to protest, but one look in Ralph's eyes told me that this was not the time to argue. From the top of the stairs, Nicki's sleepy voice called out, "Mommy, where's Deidre?" Mother looked up at Nicki, then over to her husband, who shook his head.

"She took Nicki to bed. I don't remember her coming back down, do you?"

A wave of realization fell over Nathan's face. "She wasn't here all night. She's gone to the authorities!"

"That's impossible!" William began. "She..." but then he stopped and motioned for us all to be quiet. Stepping over to the window, he pulled the curtain back a fraction and saw on the road outside a platoon of soldiers. They had just arrived and were getting their orders from the officer standing to one side: the same officer we had encountered back at the barrier.

Lord, they have killed your prophets and torn down your altars; I am the only one left, and they are trying to kill me.

Romans 11: 3

....

Prayer: Lord forgive those who in their zeal for You have brought suffering to Your Church. Protect those whom they would harm, and lead them to Your truth. For the glory of Your name and the honor of Your Kingdom.

Ask yourself: What do you think of "religious fanatics"?

Escape

Moving swiftly, William went to the closet by the front door and pulled out a coil of rope. "There's no time to talk," he said. "We must go out the back way before the soldiers get there. I will take you to a place where you can elude them."

Ralph started to say something, but William raised a finger as if to silence him and moved on to the back door. We followed him out and ran for the trees. Once inside the cover of the forest, William turned right and moved swiftly. I was beginning to think that Nathan was not exaggerating when he said that he knew these woods blindfolded, especially if he had learned from his father. After about thirty minutes, the woods broke out into a clearing, but ended abruptly at a cliff, dropping about a hundred feet straight down. Tying the rope to a nearby tree, William spoke swiftly and without looking up. "When you reach the bottom of this cliff, I will toss the rope down, preventing them from following you anytime soon. Move straight downhill until you reach a river, then turn to the right. After about six hours, you will find the trail you left. I've known it was there for years, but chose to ignore it. A mistake I will not make again." He stood up at last, looked at me and smiled. "Go with God, Friend. I will see you again."

From the edge of the clearing there came a shout as a soldier spotted us. He drew his sword and moved forward, carefully this time. He must have heard what happened to the last two who attacked us. Ralph pulled his sword and turned to face him. "This one's mine, Friend. You go first. I'll be along."

There was no time to argue. I grabbed the rope and swung over the edge. A fleeting thought passed through my mind, reminding me that I didn't have my backpack, but it couldn't be helped. The sooner I got down, the sooner Ralph could join me. It seemed like I descended forever, but eventually my feet struck the bottom and I shouted up, "I'm down! Let's go!"

I could hear the sounds of metal striking metal, and voices: lots of voices. Men were shouting, and there was an occasional scream of pain. I started to climb back up the rope, but then Ralph's face appeared over the edge. He was smiling as his sword flashed through the air, severing the rope. The broken end fell, landing in a neat coil at my feet. The sounds of battle continued up above, but I could see nothing. Gradually the sounds got quieter.

One thing was certain: I was alone. Choking back tears, I turned downhill and began to move away from the sounds above.

He said, "I have been very jealous for the LORD, the God of hosts; for the people of Israel have forsaken thy covenant, thrown down thy altars, and slain thy prophets with the sword; and I, even I only, am left; and they seek my life, to take it away."
I Kings 19: 10

....

Prayer: Father, sometime I feel deserted by everyone, including You. I know it's not true, but I can't deny the feeling. Forgive me for my lack of faith, and show me how to overcome.

Ask yourself: Have you ever felt completely deserted? What happened?

May 25

Back to the Trail

William had led me correctly. After a short descent, I came to a steam, just as he said there would be. I turned right, and worked my way through the undergrowth, stopping several times to listen, but heard no sounds of pursuit.

Neither were there any sounds of Ralph. Why had he cut the rope, leaving him stranded at the top of the cliff? He had accomplished what he had been commanded to do. He had shared the message of the Creator, and at least one family was now committed. Or at least I hoped so. From the sounds of fighting I heard as I made my escape, it was quite possible that the entire family, and Ralph, were now dead. Early afternoon came, and I saw a faint trail on the hillside up to my right. It gradually descended until I was able to step once again onto a genuine path. I realized that I had been here before. This was part of the side trail Ralph and I had gone up... was it only two days before?

Continuing down along the river, it eventually opened up at the crossing, joining the main trail. I sat down to rest, and think about my next move. Should I go back the way Ralph and I had gone, and try to rescue him? No, I decided, if he was still alive, then I had no doubt that he would refuse rescue. If he was dead, then there was no point in going back anyway. Neither would going back for the sake of the townspeople accomplish anything. Both Ralph and Jake had made it clear that this was Ralph's mission. I was going along only as a friend and support. No, I must go on, and leave things in God's hands. If He were to call me back, I would gladly go, but one thing I was beginning to learn on this trek was the fact that doing the right thing for the wrong reasons was just as bad as doing the wrong thing for the right reasons.

I stood up to leave, but was overcome by dizziness. Sitting back down, I realized that I had not eaten in nearly two days. With no backpack, food was going to be a challenge now, and I looked around to see what I might find. There was no sign of berries anywhere, and no honey bees either. There were fish in the stream, but how could I catch them? Using my sword, I cut an armload of sticks, took them to the shallow river crossing, and found a place where the current funneled into a narrow channel. There I placed the stick upright into the mud in a "V" shape, with the open end pointing upstream. A few more baffles, and I had devised a crude fish trap. Later, I should be able to catch or spear whatever had found its way into the trap.

I lay down on the grass by the river, said another silent prayer for Ralph, William and the others, and was soon fast asleep.

The LORD is my shepherd, I shall not want; he makes me lie down in green pastures. He leads me beside still waters; he restores my soul. He leads me in paths of righteousness for his name's sake.

Psalms 23: 1 – 3

Prayer: Lord teach me when to fight, and when to rest. Show me, not just the best way to go, but the way which is in keeping with Your will for me. May I be obedient to You above all.

Ask yourself: Have you ever been told to do something which at the moment did not seem best, but in retrospect turned out to be the wisest choice?

Rejoicing in the Morning

The combination of hunger and exhaustion had taken its toll on me, and what I thought would be a short nap turned out to be a night's rest. I awoke to the sun's warmth on my face, the sound of a fly buzzing nearby, and the laughter of children off in the distance. Children? I sat up and listened again. There were voices coming from the woods near the river: adult voices, children's voices. They were coming nearer, and I stood up, totally confused at this new sensation and uncertain what to do. I didn't have long to wait. The bushes along the side path parted, and I found myself face to face with William and Ralph, walking together and sharing a story of some kind. They both stopped when they saw me, shocked at first, then breaking into broad smiles as they came and hugged me. "Friend!" cried Ralph, "I was hoping I would meet up with you, but had no idea it would be this soon. We're planning to stop here for breakfast. Sit down and tell me about your adventures."

"*My* adventures?" I could hardly get the words out. "I thought you..." I looked over at William. "I thought all of you were dead!"

"Bit of an exaggeration," said Ralph, guiding me to a spot along the river and out of the way, as townspeople began filing out of the trail and setting to the task of building a fire. The children had already made their way to the river crossing, and were looking excitedly at my fish trap. "Sorry about leaving you stranded at the bottom of the cliff," he went on. "There was no time to explain, and well, William and I had our hands pretty full."

"But the sounds of fighting," I started. "Surely you were outnumbered."

"At first, yes," said Ralph. "William and I stood back to back, me with a sword and he with nothing more than a stick. We each took a soldier down, then I noticed that the rest were distracted by something behind them. As it turns out, the whole town had gotten word of the battle, and come to *our* rescue."

"These are good folks," William said, pointing to the bustle of activity. "They always have been. They were just confused and afraid. Once you two came in, it was like the blinders came off and everything made sense again."

"Daddy!" It was Nicki's voice. She was wading out of the river, holding a huge salmon in both arms as it struggled to get free. "Daddy, look what I found. Can we eat it?"

And immediately something like scales fell from his eyes and he regained his sight. Then he rose and was baptized, and took food and was strengthened.

Acts 9: 18 – 19

....

Prayer: Lord, I pray for those who are still blind. The enemy of this world has hidden the light from them, and they struggle in darkness. Please restore their sight, and their joy.

Ask yourself: Close your eyes and try to walk around. Now put your fingers in your ears so that you can't hear. How is the problem multiplied?

May 27

Fellowship

Besides Rendezvous, I don't know when I've had a better time. Ralph and William introduced me to the rest of the village men, and we worked together preparing the group for travel. The women were a constant source of chatter as they laid out dishes and tended the fire. I caught a glimpse of William's wife, and she seemed a different woman now that she was freed of her fear. She saw me and smiled, and I saw in her face a look which said "forgive me". I nodded and smiled back, and she turned back to the ladies. Nicki's salmon, taken from my fish trap, was a welcome addition to breakfast plans, and before long several more were added to the pot.

William and I were watching the children as they played in the water when I had the impression that someone was standing behind me. I turned, and there was Deidre, Nicki's older sister. She was looking down at the ground, and I could see that she had been crying. William put an arm around her shoulders and gave her a hug. "Deidre here is cut out of the same cloth as her mother," he said with a smile. "She loves her family, and would give her life for any one of us. And, as we saw last night, would have given *your* life as well."

"I'm so sorry," she sobbed. "It's just that, I didn't understand. I wanted to protect Nicki, and the rest of the family. When I came back to the house, Mother told me what you had said, and as she spoke I felt this warm glow filling me with... I don't know..."

"Joy?" I fished the thought for her, and she nodded vigorously. "That's what the truth usually does. It takes away your fear and distrust, and helps you to see what really beautiful, both inside and out. Welcome to the family, Deidre."

She let go of her father and gave me a hug, her tears of joy running down my shirt. I looked up to see Nathan standing behind her, a huge smile on his face. "You've got a great sister, here, Nathan," I said. "Take good care of her."

Nathan said nothing, but put an arm on Deidre's shoulder, shook my hand, and led her down by the river where they sat and talked. I expected they had a lot to talk about.

"One more thing," Ralph said, joining us from the pile of supplies which were being sorted and distributed. I know the Bible says we're to carry one another's burdens, but I really think you should take this one yourself." And with that, he laid my backpack down in front of me.

For if any one thinks he is something, when he is nothing, he deceives himself. But let each one test his own work, and then his reason to boast will be in himself alone and not in his neighbor. For each man will have to bear his own load.

Galatians 6: 2 – 5

....

Prayer: Thank you for brothers and sisters in the faith. Thank you for the opportunity serve them and for the works of service they do for me. Strengthen our bond, and may we in that strength serve You better.

Ask yourself: How are Christian brothers and sisters like the ideal family relationship?

Preparing to March

Ralph and talked together after breakfast and decided that the group needed to have a little basic training. I called them together and said, "And now folks, if you will be so kind to give me your attention, I'm going to teach you all how to tie your shoes."

That brought a laugh, then a few mumbled comments as they realized that I was serious. "Given the proper foundation," I went on, "even the most unruly burden can be quickly and easily moved from point 'A' to point 'B'. On the other hand, the best equipped army in the world, tripping over its shoe laces, is destined for trouble."

And so we sat, and tied, and re-tied, and checked our progress with each other. By early afternoon, I felt that they had the basics, and in the process had learned an important lesson in foundations. These people had suffered years of separation, suspicion and pain, all because the enemy had chipped away at their foundation of truth.

I was helping Nicki double knot her laces when Ralph and William came up to me. "Friend," Ralph said, "I can't thank you enough for all you've done for me, and for these folks. You didn't have to do it, but your willingness was a real inspiration to me."

"No more than you would have done, had it been the other way around," I said, shaking his hand. "So what do you think? Are they ready to travel?"

"That's why we're here," said Ralph. "William and I have been talking, and we feel that everyone needs more of the basics. You know what it's like out there. They'll be meeting challenges and hardships that will try and get them to return to the way it was."

William spoke up. "I've asked Ralph if he would stay here with us a few days, teaching us more of the basics. We all want to learn, and I can see that he's eager to teach. It's a combination too great to pass up!"

"Friend," said Ralph, "it's time you were getting back to your own journey. God wants me here with these people for awhile longer. But I think you've done your part now. Take the point. We'll see you at Rendezvous."

I knew that he was right, even though it saddened me to think of leaving all my new friends and family here. I nodded, shook their hands and got my gear in order. Nicki saw that I was leaving and came to give me a hug. "Can I call you Uncle Friend?" she asked, looking up with those huge blue eyes.

"Of course you can," I said. "And tell the other children to do the same. I'll see you all soon!" As the whole townsfolk waved and shouted goodbyes, I waded over the river and started up the far bank.

A new commandment I give to you, that you love one another; even as I have loved you, that you also love one another. By this all men will know that you are my disciples, if you have love for one another.

John 13: 34 – 35

Prayer: May my love for Your precious children be matched by the love You have for me, Dear Father. May the world look to us in wonder, as we demonstrate what Your Son Jesus demonstrated and taught us. Bind us together by Your love.

Ask yourself: Which is the stronger bond: love or hatred? Which has a future?

"Here Am I"

I didn't expect to travel far today, since I had gotten such a late start. However, the trail opened up onto a wide and pleasant meadow, and by evening I had put several miles between myself and the river crossing. A lone tree in the middle of a grassy plain made an ideal campsite for the night. A gentle breeze had blown the clouds away and the stars were brilliant as I laid back and re-lived the events of the past few days.

I would not have believed it possible that a situation so hopeless could have been resolved so quickly, all because of a little girl's desire to hear a story. Granted, other people and situations had been orchestrated and prepared by God. But what a wonder, I thought, that He would use the least likely of all the available resources to accomplish the most unbelievable. But then, that's often the way God works, isn't it? Little David against Goliath, Little Bethlehem against a world fallen into sin. Oh, to be a chosen part of some eternal plan!

I was humbled as I thought about the small part I had played, and couldn't help but feel a touch of envy for Ralph, and the fact that he had been chosen to accomplish what he did. I was "allowed" to go, but made to understand that I was under no obligation to stay.

Was this part of my training, I wondered? Was I given this opportunity in order to prepare me for the day when I would get my own assignment? I looked at my life and immediately thought, no, I could never take on a challenge like that. I was no great warrior. I had no particular speaking skills, and certainly was not one of the "brave" ones. There must be plenty of folks out there who could do the work better than I ever could. Why should I expect to be used? Maybe I'll always be placed into the role of observer.

But then I thought, go back to the Bible and look again. It's *never* the strong or the brave or the smart that God chooses to do his bidding. It's people like me, nominal at lots of things, but exceptional at none. That way, when the job is finished, no one can honestly stand up and say, "Look what I did!" because in their hearts of hearts, they'll know they did nothing but obey.

I think Isaiah must have felt this way, as he heard in a dream the God of the heavens outlining a huge task to be done and asking the rhetorical question, "Whom shall I send?".

Here am I Lord; here am I.

We are fools for Christ, but you are so wise in Christ! We are weak, but you are strong! You are honored, we are dishonored!

I Corinthians 4: 10

....

Prayer: Lord, I know that I will never be worthy of Your calling, but I pray for a willing heart. Use me for the glory of Your kingdom. May I bring honor to Your Holy Name.

Ask yourself: Have you ever wanted to be chosen for a part in a play, or a spot on a team, or a job to do? What did you do?

Sand in my Shoes

The terrain didn't change much today: still rolling hills and wide meadows separated by stands of Aspen and Pine trees. However, the trail itself was changing subtly, I noticed. Instead of the hard packed or rocky surface I had become used to, it was getting softer. Low areas especially seemed to be collection spots for a fine white sand, making for a beautiful picture but a less than ideal surface for walking. In addition, the sand was finding its way into my eyes, my mouth, and worst of all, into my boots.

It wasn't too noticeable at first, but as the miles went by I became more and more aware of this tiny distraction. Slowly but surely, it found it way to bottoms of my feet and the spaces between my toes, where it served as a microscopic abrasive with every step I took. I stopped several times, took off boots and socks and tried to shake out the miniature intruders, but there was no way of getting rid of them completely.

What started as a minor distraction soon developed into a full-fledged hazard to forward progress. The irritations became blisters, the blisters broke, and my feet complained with every step.

I stopped earlier than I had intended and made camp for the night, anxious to free my feet from their torture chambers and into the open air. Sitting around the fire tonight, with my sore feet begging for mercy, I thought about the power of a grain of sand, given the right environment in which to work. Almost too small to see with the naked eye, its sharp edges and small size enable it to reach and destroy the most inaccessible places imaginable.

Not unlike sin, I thought. Sometimes the smallest things can produce the most damage, given the freedom to work. An unkind word, a casual glance that becomes an obsession, anything allowed a place in my heart has the ability to work it's power. Rubbing my aching feet again, I thought, let's just hope it's the right kind of power.

Then, after desire has conceived, it gives birth to sin; and sin, when it is full-grown, gives birth to death.

James 1: 15

....

Prayer: Lord, You know how weak I can be, even when I might try to deny it. Please protect me from the smallest sin which will in time take over my life. May I learn to listen to You when You warn me about them.

Ask yourself: Do you think there is such a thing as a "little sin"?

May 31

The Ocean

In the quiet before dawn, I could just sense the sound. It was more like a vibration, coming at regular intervals. I thought at first a tree had fallen somewhere off in the distance, but when the sound kept repeating every few seconds, I knew that it was something else. By the time daylight had come, the sound was no longer noticeable, although a scent in the air gave me a clue to what I had heard. A definite smell of salt told me there was an ocean nearby.

Throughout the morning, the ocean smell continued to grow stronger, and the wind shifted to the west, coming at me head on. The sand in the trail grew deeper, and once I saw a sea gull fly by, it's brilliant white feathers standing out in sharp contrast to the blue sky.

The Aspen trees gave way to a low-growing pine, their branches twisted and gnarled, evidence of the relentless wind in the area. Finally, the land began to rise into a series of sand dunes, with pampas grass fighting a losing battle to hold them in place. The trail disappeared altogether, but it was obvious that there was only one logical way to go, between two particularly large hills. Breaking out at the highest point between them, I at last was able to see what I knew was waiting: an ocean extending as far as the eye could see. To the right was a rocky cliff, with boulders lying along the beach and into the surf. Wondering if the trail might go that way, my question was answered as soon as I looked to the left. A series of wooden poles, about ten feet high and approximately 500 yards apart, had been placed along the beach at what I thought must be the high tide line. They had to be my trail markers.

I took my back pack off and sat down where I had stopped, gazing at this majestic sight. As each wave broke on the beach, the ground beneath me shook, a reminder of what I had sensed early this morning. Far off in the distance, clouds raced along the horizon, carrying with them their own weather patterns which I would never experience. Crabs played tag with the birds at the water's edge, each one intent on the subject of food: either eating it or not becoming it. The sand which had been such a misery for me the last couple of days now rewarded me with a bed fit for a king. I determined that I would make camp here for the night.

The seas have lifted up, O LORD, the seas have lifted up their voice; the seas have lifted up their pounding waves. Mightier than the thunder of the great waters, mightier than the breakers of the sea— the LORD on high is mighty.

Psalms 93: 3 – 4

....

Prayer: When I see the ocean, I am reminded of Your power, Oh God. Thank you for such a magnificent display! Show me each day a portion of Your handiwork, that I may praise you and stand in awe.

Ask yourself: What is it about the ocean that impresses you?

June 1

Holding Back the Ocean

My camp had been at the very place where I had first come to a stop yesterday: the slightly protected "saddle" between two large sand dunes with a view of the ocean to die for. I was lulled through the night by the sound of the crashing waves and off shore breeze, and the sound of seagulls scouring the shoreline served as my alarm clock.

Rising and walking down onto the beach, I decided to test the water's chill, venturing about knee deep into the pounding surf. Standing there with the constant onslaught of approaching waves, I remembered the words of a Sudanese Christian, having seen the ocean for the first time. "The ocean is an angry thing," he said. "It's always trying to come up onto the land. But it cannot. How wonderful a God, that He would choose the sand to hold it back."

I bent down and scooped out a handful of sand and let it run through my fingers. How amazing indeed. That Sudanese Christian didn't know much about water, having been raised in the desert, but he knew about sand. With its unique properties and ability to either hold together or flow like water make it the perfect choice for defining the ocean's boundaries. I chuckled to myself as I looked up and down the broad beach. Sometimes I feel like one of those grains of sand. Not much different from anything else around me, subject to the first gust of wind that blows me away.

And yet... the God of the universe had placed me here along with countless more like me. And He commands us, "Stand and hold!" And we do just that. The ocean cannot overrun the land, because its boundaries have been set. And those boundaries are enforced by an army of tiny servants, by whose cooperation and unity the task is done.

I have no doubt that God could accomplish whatever He wants by a spoken word, or even by His will alone. And yet... He has chosen me to accomplish something. And knowing that I could never do it by myself, He has placed me into a community of fellow believers who stand and hold back the gates of hell itself. That's pretty amazing.

This far you may come and no farther; here is where your proud waves halt.

Job 38: 11

....

Prayer: Thank you God for making me part of a community. Thank you for work to do which could not be done alone. Thank you for the power that I can experience as a part of your creation.

Ask yourself: How does the image of a grain of sand sound to you? Does it make you feel special or "one of a crowd"?

June 2

Breaking Waves

I decided to use the day to do some laundry in a nearby stream, re-pack my gear and soak up some sun. The beach was like a bit of paradise, and it was hard not to imagine that I was just outside the door of some upscale resort in the South Pacific. After a full morning of hard work followed by a lunch of boiled mussels gathered from the nearby rocks, I lay back against what I now considered "my" sand dune and tried again to take in the full grandeur of the ocean.

The waves had a certain pattern about them, I soon discovered. Ten to fifteen medium waves would be followed by a larger than normal breaker, then the routine would settle back into the ten-fifteen normal range. I'm not an oceanographer, so I couldn't begin to explain why that was, but it was interesting to observe. I also wondered about the shape and flow of each wave, something about which any surfer worth his boardies would be able to tell me. I remember reading somewhere that waves travel with the same intensity throughout the ocean, but that as they approach the beach they begin to build up in height, a result of the shallower water underneath. As the moving force encounters the rising sea bed, water is pushed upwards until it's visible as a wave. After a certain height, gravity takes over and the wave "breaks" over itself in a display of white foam and swirling currents.

There's a lesson there, I thought. Forces move through our lives all the time, but if our faith and emotions are deep enough, they pass right through, sometimes even undetected. When things get shallow though, watch out; that constant force will push something to the surface, higher and higher until finally it has to break. When a couple's trust and love for each other is deep and dependable, everyday temptations to be unfaithful can move right through without a second glance. Distrust and hurt feelings can make a relationship grow shallow, though, and outside forces can then build things to the breaking point in no time.

Pity the person who gets caught in a breaker.

But you, man of God, flee from all this, and pursue righteousness, godliness, faith, love, endurance and gentleness. Fight the good fight of the faith. Take hold of the eternal life to which you were called when you made your good confession in the presence of many witnesses.

I Timothy 6: 11 – 12

Prayer: Lord I need a deeper faith that will carry me through the difficult times of life. Strengthen my grip on You, and never let me go.

Ask yourself: How can you have a deeper faith?

June 3

Unending Beach

With my gear clean and packed, my aching feet improved by the fresh air and salt water, I set out this morning with a spring in my step, in spite of the soft sand which tended to slow me down. The rhythm of the waves seemed to urge me on... and on... and on. After a few hours of hiking, I began wishing for something to break the monotony. And yet as far as I could see, there was nothing but unbroken beach and sand, interrupted only by the regular trail markers assuring me that I was still on the right track.

With nothing else to look for, I started anticipating the markers themselves, Five hundred yards to go, four hundred, three hundred, two hundred, one hundred... there it was. Much like the last one, I realized. Oh well, five hundred yards until the next one.

Life is not always full of change and challenge. Sometimes, like this stretch of beach, it can get pretty uneventful. That doesn't mean it's unpleasant: I still enjoy the ocean and the sky. But let's face it, as humans we thrive on challenge. The hills make us stronger. The unexpected makes us smarter. The worst of all possible scenarios would have to be the one with no contrast with which to provide life's tapestry. During times like that, such as this incredibly long and unchanging stretch of beach, then the emptiness itself must be my focus and goal for the moment. Those who study "ikebana", the Japanese art of flower arranging, tell us that the space between the flowers is just as important as the flowers themselves, since they give the background upon which the beauty rests. Without that emptiness, the fullness has no meaning.

I know that my life will not always be what it is today, but today will be part of the definition of tomorrow, and for that I can be thankful. Each mile of smooth and level journey sets the stage for what comes next. I look ahead with anticipation.

In the beginning God created the heavens and the earth. Now the earth was formless and empty, darkness was over the surface of the deep, and the Spirit of God was hovering over the waters.

Genesis 1: 1 – 2

....

Prayer: Thank you Father for life's seemingly "uneventful" times. I'm reminded that it was in the void of nothingness that You created all things. I know that You are present, even when to my eyes there seems to be nothing. Praise You Father, for being there.

Ask yourself: When have you been bored lately? Looking back on the time, was it the circumstance itself or your own emotional situation that resulted in the feeling?

June 4

Something to Focus On

One of the toughest decisions I've had to make on this trip was where to stop and sleep last night. The problem arose from the fact that there was *nothing* to which I could attain and thereby celebrate by making camp. As it turned out, I laid out my sleeping bag at the base of a trail marker, since it was at least something which broke the monotony of the beach.

Venturing a little ways back into the sand dunes which formed my left side back drop, I found enough drift word to build a small fire and cook a meal. Sleep didn't come as easily as I thought it would, since even though I was tired from the long day's hike, I had no sense of accomplishment. Not surprisingly, I found it difficult to get started this morning, since there was no goal looming ahead.

I walked on through the morning hours, counting trail markers and timing waves, hoping that today would bring some change in terrain. By late afternoon, it came. Far off in the distance, I could just make out a dark shape on the beach. For the next hour, I could only speculate as to what it may be, still unable to discern its true shape and size. My pace picked up as I grew nearer, and I decided not to stop for an afternoon break as I usually did, but pushed on.

Finally, I was able to determine that what I was looking at was a piece of driftwood. Huge, to be sure, probably a whole tree. But nothing more than that. Thinking about it was enough to occupy the rest of my afternoon, however, and I imagined scenarios which would have resulted in the giant landing up on this particular beach. By the time I finally arrived, I had concluded that it was a Sequoia, much like the ones I had passed through a few days ago. Except for missing most of its small limbs, it was completely intact, including the root system, an indication that it had not been cut down. Probably some flood had taken it down and pushed it down a river into the ocean. It could have floated for years, I suppose, before the currents brought it here.

There was no question of moving on. This was my camp for the night. I picked a spot next to the tree, out of the wind, and settled in. Funny I thought; in any other circumstance such a sight would not have caused me more than a few minute's contemplation. But because of the absolute lack of any thing else along this beach, this piece of driftwood has occupied my entire afternoon, and now is the center point of my evening's entertainment.

Let your eyes look straight ahead, fix your gaze directly before you. Make level paths for your feet and take only ways that are firm.

Proverbs 4: 25 – 26

Prayer: Lord, thank you for giving my eyes something to focus on. May I always see those things worthy of the attention.

Ask yourself: What do you do when you're bored?

June 5

A New Horizon

Yesterday morning I didn't much want to get started because of the absence of anything of interest. At first today, I hesitated to leave camp because the only thing of interest was the driftwood log beside which I had slept. After a long and contemplative breakfast, sheltered behind the once-majestic Sequoia, I packed slowly, then examined my find again. The tide was out, so I was able to walk completely around the tree without getting my feet wet.

From the roots, I was able to climb up onto the log, which even on its side still rested higher than my head. Standing a scant two meters than I stood down on the sand, I could imagine that the wind blew stronger, the sky looked more distinct than from down below. Turning slowly, I gazed out on the ocean and to the clouds drifting in the distance. Looking back in the direction from which I had come, I saw only unbroken beach, with an occasional footprint marking my passing. The sand dunes to my left still stood too high to see over. Time to survey the day's march ahead. Much like yesterday's, I saw with a trace of disappointment. Straight beach, white sand, blue water.

At the end of the horizon, I thought I could make out a faint shape, and that stirred something in me. Straining to see, I shielding my eyes from the sun and squinted. Yes, there was definitely a shape of something, probably a land mass of some kind. I remembered from science class that a person looking across a featureless plain on the earth could only see about five kilometers. Standing up on something like this log would increase that distance, but not by much. Before noon, I decided, I could be at that place I'm looking at. What it was I still wasn't sure, but I knew one thing: it was different from the place I now stood. Leaping down from the log, I quickly cinched up my back pack and started off, a goal now firmly fixed. From the level of the beach the distant mass was no longer visible, but I knew it was there and my steps lengthened with a purpose I had not felt for awhile.

So we fix our eyes not on what is seen, but on what is unseen. For what is seen is temporary, but what is unseen is eternal.

II Corinthians 4: 18

Prayer: Father, the goal we seek is not always visible, but sometimes you allow us the wonderful blessing of standing on a higher plain and catching a glimpse of what lies ahead. Thank you for such visions, and for the excitement they bring.

Ask yourself: Do you have a life goal? Can you see it?

June 6

A Lava Flow

As the morning progressed toward noon, the distant shape ahead gradually rose from below the horizon and with each passing hour became more distinct. It was definitely a land mass, and it intersected the beach. I could see no evidence of vegetation. If anything, it seemed to be solid rock, judging from the consistent brown hue it cast.

I drew closer and a mountain appeared to my left which gave me a clue. It had the unmistakable shape of a volcano, its cone-shaped peak evidence of an eruption sometime in the distant past. Now I could see that the brown mass ahead of me was an ancient lava flow, extending from the volcano's summit all the way down to the ocean. In fact, there seemed to be a layering of the lava, as one molten river had run over the cooled pathway below it. What stood before me now was a huge ridge of shiny rock, cutting across the beach and extending five hundred meters or more out into the water. Reaching the surf, it had fanned out in all directions, seeking the lowest direction of travel, until the water's cooling effect had managed to solidify the molten rock and bring everything to a standstill.

Dropping my back pack to the ground, I looked for a way to climb the slippery surface of the rock. Hardened bubbles provided hand and foot holds, and I managed to reach the top of the ridge, taking care to avoid the razor sharp edges where the wind had thrown the lava up just before it hardened. I stood at the base of this ancient riverbed and looked up at the volcano's peak, several miles away. What an awesome sight that must have been, to see a flaming wall of rock make its way to the ocean, turning the surf into a monstrous cloud of steam rising into the stratosphere. Only the ocean could have put a stop to its forward progress.

Four days ago, I had been impressed at the sand's ability to hold back the ocean. Now I'm equally awestruck at the ocean's ability to hold back the land. The immovable object head to head with the unstoppable force: a battle of the Titians if there ever was one. And yet everything is held together by the spoken Word, and man moves and lives from one to the other, driven by the Divine challenge: have dominion over My creation.

God blessed them and said to them, "Be fruitful and increase in number; fill the earth and subdue it. Rule over the fish of the sea and the birds of the air and over every living creature that moves on the ground."

Genesis 1: 28

....

Prayer: I'm struck today by the implications of Your command, Father: to rule over Your creation. You know my weakness; but You know also my strength, and we both know that it comes from You. Help me to be faithful to Your Holy calling.

Ask yourself: What does it mean to "have dominion" over the earth (King James version)?

Tidal Pools

I spent the rest of the daylight yesterday climbing around on my lava flow, exploring crevices and admiring the patterns made by successive layers of molten rock. In the evening, I camped next to the wall and built a fire in a depression made by a bursting bubble of lava. As the glowing coals reflected off the smooth surfaces, I tried to imagine what it looked like as it made its way from the volcano's mouth to the ocean's edge. My sleep was filled with dreams of fire and steam.

This morning I awoke to find the tide out, and more of the hardened lava visible. Walking out as far as I could go, I discovered that indentations in the flow had created pockets of water left by the receding tide. Looking closer, I could see fish and crabs trapped in these pools, unable to escape until the tide brought the ocean back to them.

Retrieving a saucepan from my pack, I set out to see what the morning fish market had to offer for my breakfast. A veritable feast awaited, and I had to pick and choose from a wide variety, finally settling on a nice perch and some shrimp. Roasted over hot coals, it was a meal to be remembered.

I was thankful for the tidal pools which made the morning's catch possible, since I would never have managed to snag such delicacies with the limited fishing equipment I had on hand. Too bad for the poor creatures left behind by the receding tide, I mused, but a windfall for me. I wonder at what point they realized they were trapped? One moment they're darting in and around rocks, looking for food, dodging predators. Gradually perhaps, they would sense that their choices for thoroughfare were diminishing, until there was nowhere left to swim except within the tiny confines of the pool. For some, this would mean certain death, as the pool emptied of water and leaving them stranded. For others, it would mean a long wait until the tide returned and once again opened up its access for them. Or else it would mean becoming easy prey for a not-so-adept predator as myself.

Are there tidal pools in our lives, I wondered? Do we get so preoccupied with living that we fail to notice when our options are disappearing? We've all experienced the feeling of being trapped by circumstance; I pray for the wisdom to see the trap closing before it's too late.

We have escaped like a bird out of the fowler's snare; the snare has been broken, and we have escaped. Our help is in the name of the LORD, the Maker of heaven and earth.

Psalms 124: 7 – 8

Prayer: Grant me eyes to see the snare, Dear Lord, and wisdom to know when to step back.

Ask yourself: What things are closing in around you today?

A Distant Whale

It was with some reluctance that I packed up camp and continued on my journey today. Straining my eyes from the top of the lava ridge, I could see nothing but straight and unbroken beach ahead. Some kind of souvenir was in order, and I looked around the beach until I found a small piece of lava rock. It was full of holes left by molten bubbles so hopefully it wouldn't weigh me down too much.

The morning passed quickly, since as I walked I continued to think about the lava flow and the incredible power which had made it. More than that, I was reminded again of the awesome strength of the ocean, which today seemed gentle and inviting. The waves were not more than one or two feet, lapping quietly up onto the shoreline.

If the ocean had not been so calm, I might not have noticed the waterspout, about 500 yards out to my right. Seeing it from the corner of my eye, I thought at first it was spray blown by the wind off a wave, but in the absence of either wind or wave, the sight caught my attention. I stopped and waited and a few seconds later was rewarded with another view, slightly farther ahead. This time I could tell that it was a whale surfacing to breathe.

Even from this distance, the sight was inspiring. He was at least twenty feet long and moved through the water like a nuclear sub. Once he breached and slapped a monstrous tail on the water. Because of the distance, the sound took a couple of seconds to reach me, but when it did, it was like seismic shock which I could feel in the sand under my feet.

I thought of Jonah and his encounter with the "large fish" appointed to swallow him and keep him for awhile. Seeing this leviathan prowling the shoreline caused a shudder to run through me as I contemplated that night on a storm tossed boat: the terrified sailors, the casting of lots, Jonah's confession, the sea weed infested water and the dark shape of his fate coming toward him.

I hope I can always remain obedient to God without the necessity of such object lessons.

Then they took Jonah and threw him overboard, and the raging sea grew calm. At this the men greatly feared the LORD, and they offered a sacrifice to the LORD and made vows to him. But the LORD provided a great fish to swallow Jonah, and Jonah was inside the fish three days and three nights.

Jonah 1: 15 – 17

Prayer: Father, I want to obey you in all things, but you know my weaknesses. Send me whatever I need to learn how to walk according to your will, even if it's something like Jonah had to experience. But please, be merciful.

Ask yourself: What would you be willing to endure for the sake of learning more about your relationship to God?

June 9

Close Encounter

I camped on the beach last night, and in the quiet of the evening, I could hear the whale offshore swimming back and forth, breaching and slapping the water. Was he alone? I wondered. Where was he going? I had heard that single males did sometimes cover huge territories in search of food before rejoining their pod. But if this were the case, I thought that he would have moved on, rather than stay in the vicinity. I suppose the fishing must good in the area, and he's in no hurry.

Still, there was a whisper in the back of my mind that he somehow knew of my presence and was choosing to stay nearby. I quickly shook that off, however, because it made no sense whatsoever. I had nothing he wanted, and had no intention of going out to meet him for closer communion. I know that some people have a special affinity for the animals of the sea, as if they were some kind of prehistoric ancestor, but to me they were something to be admired, feared or eaten. That big fellow fit the first category, and I planned to keep it that way.

The next morning I didn't see him at first and was surprised to feel a little lonely. Before noon, however, I heard a familiar "slap" of water and turned to see him as he dove again. He was a little closer to the shore, I suppose following a school of fish. The barnacles on his sides stood out like scales on a dragon, and the sound of his breathing was thrilling and disconcerting at the same time.

Isn't that the way it is? We love to see the awesome and the powerful, but from a safe distance. King Kong is fine on the big screen, but keep him out of the theater. Maybe that's why so many people prefer to think of God as a distant amusement: an interesting topic of conversation, but keep Him out of my heart. Come to think of it, if I didn't know Him the way I've come to on this journey, I'd probably feel the same way. It's like the Narnian described Aslan in the classic C. S. Lewis series, "Safe? Of *course* He's not safe. He's a lion! But He's king."

And so I shudder to think of being any closer to the whale offshore, while a part of me wishes I could touch him. I wonder if it would be safe?

Can you pull in the leviathan with a fishhook or tie down his tongue with a rope?
Can you put a cord through his nose or pierce his jaw with a hook?

Job 41: 1 – 2

....

Prayer: Lord, teach me what it means to fear You. Show me Your awesome might while holding me in your merciful arms. Calm the fears in my heart. Cast out the fears in my soul.

Ask yourself: Should a person be afraid of God?

June 10

Run Aground

The whale stayed just off shore again last night. I didn't hear him for long periods of time, and assumed he was sleeping (when *do* whales sleep?); or else perhaps it was I who was sleeping. But then I would hear a deep throated *whoosh* as he surfaced and blew up a huge column of water. I dreamed about Pinocchio and little Geppetto huddling inside the belly of the huge whale, the sounds of the waves and the splashing nearby adding a touch a realism. I awoke just before daylight, realizing that the sounds had become closer, and more intense. In the starlight, I could just make out the white wave tops offshore. The tide had gone out, and my sleeping bag was at least fifty yards from the water's edge.

But right there, at the point where the water reached the beach, a huge dark form was splashing wildly, struggling to move but not going anywhere. I came to my feet and looked closer: it was the whale, and I could see at least two thirds of his body above the water. Apparently, he had come in too close and was now stranded by the receding tide. With timid steps, I eased toward the beast until I stood less than ten feet away. It was like standing next to a Mack truck, only worse, because this monster could see me. He tried to respond by moving his massive tail, but it only served to splash the water around us both.

What could I do? This is the kind of thing that makes the 6:00 news, and is usually followed by an army of Greenpeace volunteers who organize the proper machinery to rescue the brute. I didn't even have a shovel.

I hate to see any living thing suffer, and watching the whale struggle was tearing me apart. I tried to think of anything which would help, and finally decided that all I could do at the moment was offer comfort. I slowly closed the gap between us, still not certain of how much he was able to move, nor how much damage he might do to me, intentional or otherwise. I drew up next to one eye, which was watching me intently, and held out my hand.

"Hey big fellow," I said softly. "Looks like you've gotten yourself into a mess here." The sound of my voice seemed to calm him, and he stopped struggling. I laid my hand on his side, and felt the flesh tremble in response. The skin was dry already, a condition I've heard can be quickly fatal. I used both hands to splash water over him, then stopped again to speak quietly. "So what do we do now?" I asked.

Can you pull in the leviathan with a fishhook or tie down his tongue with a rope? Can you put a cord through his nose or pierce his jaw with a hook? Will he keep begging you for mercy? Will he speak to you with gentle words? Will he make an agreement with you for you to take him as your slave for life?

Job 41: 1 – 4

....

Prayer: Father, the giants of the sea are Your creation, and I stand in awe before them. And yet I know that You have made me responsible for them as well. Show me how to manage things bigger than I.

Ask yourself: Does the size of a creature determine its authority, or the command of its Creator?

June 11

Unexpected Help

The sky grew light, and I could see the futility of the situation. The whale was stuck in three feet of water and there was no way I could possibly move him. I splashed water over him with my hands, thinking that might help. Then when the sun came up and the air grew warmer, I went to my backpack and dug out a pot. Using it as a ladle, I kept walking around him, pouring water and trying desperately to think of a better idea.

By noon, the whale was struggling less, and I was afraid he was about to die. I bailed furiously, kicked at the sand beneath him and kept speaking words of assurance which I didn't feel. Finally I stepped back up to the shore line, dropped the pot on the sand and sat down in total fatigue. "I'm sorry big fellow," I said more to myself than to him, "I don't think I can do anything else for you."

Sitting there watching that magnificent beast, I felt a lump come to my throat and realized I was fighting back tears. Why was I so upset over an animal, especially one with less personality than a fencepost? Is this feeling of responsibility part of God's original command to "rule over the beasts of the earth"? Whatever the reason, I was feeling as if I were a pretty poor ruler, forced to watch as one of my subjects suffers and dies. I put my head down on my knees and cried out in desperation, "What else can I do?"

I closed my eyes and sat there for a long while, unable to think rationally. Opening them again, I saw the whale struggling and felt a wave of despair. The midday sun was burning us both.

Suddenly I felt cooler, and thought that the sun had gone behind a cloud. But the shadow was only over me. Someone had stepped up behind me and placed a hand on my shoulder. I turned and saw the silhouette of a man framed in front of the sun. I squinted for a better look, but opened my eyes wide when he spoke.

"Dad?"

The father of a righteous man has great joy; he who has a wise son delights in him. May your father and mother be glad; may she who gave you birth rejoice!
Proverbs 23: 24 – 25

....

Prayer: Lord, bless our children, wherever they are, whatever their age. Guide them in their choices so that they will be safe and will become all that You have created them to be.

Ask yourself: Can you remember the first important decision you made without the help of your parents?

June 12

Rescue

I was speechless for a millisecond, then jumped to my feet and hugged my son. The tears could not be held back, but I managed to choke out the words, "I've missed you so much. You look fantastic! How are you?"

He tried to be cool, but I knew that he was glad to see me as well. "I've missed you too, Dad. I'm fine. I can't believe I found you here."

"So what *are* you doing here?" I asked, guessing the answer, but praying that I was right.

"It's just that, well, I thought about everything you said, and I decided to check it out for myself. I did, and, well, you were right... about everything. Anyway, I started a couple of days ago, and when I hit the beach I saw the humpback. Then I saw you."

"Humpback? Is that what that is?"

"Yeah," he answered, "and he's in a lot of trouble. How long has he been there?" Even as he spoke, he was moving out toward the animal. Approaching it slowly, he spoke quietly, moving around and occasionally reaching out to give it a gentle pat. "He's already got a sunburn started," he said after a moment. "We need to keep him moisturized. Towels, sleeping bags, shirts, anything that will retain water. He just might make it if we get right to it. The tide's coming in, so he has a chance."

I was seeing my son in a way I'd never seen him before. Confident, efficient, a real leader. "How did you learn all this?" I asked as we sorted through our backpacks for wetting cloth.

"You thought I spent all that time at the beach just to look at the girls?" he said with a shy grin, then went on. "We need to cover as much of his body as possible. But don't cover the blowhole or put water down it. He'll drown if we do. Keep the fins clear, because they help carry off body heat, like an elephant's ear."

We worked through the day, covering "Monstro", as we'd named him, after the famous whale in the story of Pinocchio. Toward evening, my son said, "Let's get our stuff off his back. We don't want him leaving with any souvenirs." We had just removed the last shirt when the whale gave a huge shudder, rolled to one side and began to move. We pushed together, and when a big wave swept in, Monstro was afloat. He seemed disoriented at first, but eventually he got turned in the right direction and headed out to sea. By now, it was too dark to make out more than a dim shape, but the sound of his splashing and slapping was enough to convince us that he was okay.

Blessed is the man who fears the LORD, who finds great delight in his commands.
His children will be mighty in the land; the generation of the upright will be blessed.
Psalms 112: 1 – 2

....

Prayer: Lord, bless those who are sons and those who have sons. May they share the image of God in their works and actions. May they reflect the model You gave us through Your Son, Jesus Christ.

Ask yourself: Why do you think God is presented as a Father and Jesus as His Son?

June 13

Catching Up

Sleep was out of the question last night. For one thing, every piece of cloth we owned, including our sleeping bags was soaked. But more importantly, we had so much to talk about. I asked him about his decision to make this journey, and what kinds of things he had experienced already. Finally I broached the subject that had been eating at me.

"What about Mom and your sister?" I asked. "How did they react to your decision?"

"Sis follows Mom's lead. Mom is... well... she's confused. She wants to believe all this, but it's just such a radical move. More than anything, she wants the family to be together. But this decision of yours, and now my decision, I think has really scared her."

My heart ached to hear of her distress. More than anything, I longed for her and my daughter to see things the way I saw them, and to understand that this decision was something I could not and would not ignore, even if it meant losing everything that I had held dear in this life. My son was beginning to understand that now, and the thought kept me sane. We prayed together for our family: that they would see the truth for themselves and come join us.

"But you know, Son," I said as we gazed quietly into the fire, "this is a decision that every individual has to make alone. I couldn't decide for you, as much as I might have wanted to. And we can't decide for them. All we can do is remain faithful to what we're being shown, and pray for them every day."

"Yeah, I know," he said, not looking up. "But it was your prayers that led me here. That's about the best thing a father could do for his kid. Thanks."

And we pray this in order that you may live a life worthy of the Lord and may please him in every way: bearing fruit in every good work, growing in the knowledge of God.

Colossians 1: 10

....

Prayer: Sometimes all we can do is pray for our families, so that's what I want to do right now, Father. Bless them. Protect them. Save them. May we be united in and by Your love for us.

Ask yourself: Do you feel a loyalty for your family? How does that compare with your loyalty toward God?

True Strength

Having my son thank me for praying for him was the best gift I could have ever gotten. If only he knew the hours I had spent on my knees during this journey, praying for him and the rest of the family.

"But you know, Son," I said as we watched our sleeping bags dry in the fresh morning air, "I didn't know about praying when you were growing up. I look back on those days and, well, it tears my heart out to think of what I *might* have done for you and your sister. I hope you'll forgive me."

He smiled, looked out over the ocean, and spoke. "God used you back then, too, Dad. Before you even knew Him. You were teaching me about Him when you hadn't even learned the lessons yourself. One thing I've picked up right away on this trip is a new understanding of where real strength comes from. I saw that strength in you, even as a kid.

"I'm not talking about the guts and glory kind of strength. I figured that out pretty quick. I almost had you up in the Incredible Hulk category until I realized that anybody with a good jack can pick up a car like you did. But there were other things. Remember that time when Mom was real sick and in the hospital? I didn't know how serious it was, but Sis and I both could tell from looking at you that it was bad. But what really amazed me during that whole thing was how strong you were. You took care of us, even when you were worried about her. You kept the home together: mowed the lawn, paid the bills, got us off to school, and gave Mom all the love and support she needed, when she needed it. Even as a kid, I said to myself, '*That's* the kind of Dad I want to be when I grow up.'

"So when you made this big decision and blew us all out of the water, none of us knew what to make of it. But something deep inside me said, 'Trust him; he's your father, he knows what he's doing.'"

I write to you, fathers, because you have known him who is from the beginning. I write to you, young men, because you have overcome the evil one. I write to you, dear children, because you have known the Father. I write to you, fathers, because you have known him who is from the beginning. I write to you, young men, because you are strong, and the word of God lives in you, and you have overcome the evil one.

I John 2: 13 – 14

Prayer: Just as You have been a faithful Father to me, Lord, may I be faithful to those who look up to me. Use me to teach them, even when I do not understand the lessons themselves. Keep me strong for their sakes.

Ask yourself: Have you ever modeled something to a child without being aware of it?

Modeling by Intent

Our gear was dry, and we laid everything out carefully in preparation for packing. My son was a willing student as I instructed him on the fine art of filling a backpack. Looking over my own "essentials", his eyes fell on the sword which had once belonged to a demon from hell, now mine by right of battle.

"Whoa Dad," he said, partly in admiration, but sprinkled with a touch of uncertainty. "What's with the Konan the Barbarian blade? Where'd you get it?"

"There's some things we need to talk about, Son," I said after a deep breath. "This trip we're on is not always safe, and you may find yourself up against some pretty scary situations. I've had to learn to use this, and now I have to teach you."

He stared at the blade in shock, then his eyes met mine. "I don't understand," he said. "Do you mean you actually kill people with that thing?"

"Not people," I answered quickly. But there are forces out here who will do anything in their power to keep you from finishing this trip. The thing that tried to use this sword on me was some kind of demon warrior. The second time I had to kill, the thing looked a little more human, but there was no mistaking it for flesh and blood."

"Now you're scaring me, Dad," he said, unconsciously taking a step backward. "Are you telling me that you've used that thing to kill, not once but twice? And you think I'm going to do the same?"

"With all my heart, I hope not," I said, moving closer and putting an arm around his trembling shoulders. "But if it comes to it, then I want you to be as prepared as I can make you. We can start with some simple defensive maneuvers, and move on from there if you're ready."

I looked around the beach until I found a stick which could be fashioned into a mock sword. After some basic handling instructions, I showed him how to use the stick to fend off an overhand blow, the most common type of attack. Finally we sat down in the sand, our gear still spread out in preparation for packing. We could take up the journey tomorrow. This was too important.

"You've got a good eye," I complemented him. "You'll be dancing circles around me before you know it." He was silent, and I knew he was still trying to process this new information. "These things have always been around us, you know," I said quietly. "They haven't been a problem until now because we were no threat. Because of your decision, you've become their worst nightmare. Remember that, and don't be afraid."

Train a child in the way he should go, and when he is old he will not turn from it.
Proverbs 22: 6

....

Prayer: Lord, it's an awesome realization, to know that people we love make decisions based upon what we teach them. They may be blessed; they may be hurt, but either way it falls on us. Make me a better parent, Lord, and a better friend and a better mentor.

Ask yourself: What part of your personality would you like to see your child copy?

16 June

Led By a Child

The gear was packed and we were ready to hit the trail, but I suggested we relax a bit first. My son dug a Frisbee out of his backpack and tossed it to me. I threw it back, and he caught it deftly, flung it back to me from behind his back and ran down the beach. It was good to see the old self-confident smile back. We threw it back and forth, trying different styles. He tried a high, lofting toss which caught a cross wind and ended up about 30 yards out in the surf. I ran to get it, but hesitated when my son called out, "No! Let it go, Dad!" I ran on, thinking that he just didn't want me getting wet. The water was only about waist deep when I reached the floating Frisbee; I grabbed it and held it aloft in victory just as a wave caught me across the shoulders and swept me off my feet. Before I could react, I heard a deep sucking sound as the receding wave carried me straight out.

Thank you, Lord, for letting me see my son before taking me to be with You, I prayed. At least we .. No! As a wave lifted me up, I could see him in the distance, swimming for all he was worth, out to where I struggled. "Go back, son! Go back!"

But he came on, never changing pace, never taking his eyes off me, until finally he drew to a stop just out of my reach. "Dad," he said, "do you have enough strength left to swim?"

"Why did you come out here, son?" I asked. "Now we're both in trouble, and..."

"No we're not," he cut me off. "It's just a rip. I've done this lots of times. You just can't swim straight back, that's all." Looking right and left, he finally said, "Okay, let's go off in this direction. If you need help, I'll come around behind and pull you. Ready?"

His confidence took me by surprise, and I found myself submitting to his authority. This was his element, after all. He seemed to know what he was doing, which was more than I could say for myself. We started off slowly, and I could see that we were moving parallel to the beach, still being carried out, but making progress across the rip. After a few minutes, I felt a change in the direction of the water's pull, and realized that the waves were now carrying us back in. After what seemed a lifetime, we lay sprawled on the sand, moaning and laughing at the same time.

"You saved my life, you know?"

He just smiled, obviously embarrassed, and mumbled something before laying back and finding a passing cloud to focus his attention on.

It is not only the old who are wise, not only the aged who understand what is right.
Job 32: 9

....

Prayer: Father, Your Word says that we will be led by children, but I confess that I don't understand that, not completely. However, You do give us glimpses from time to time of the wisdom and strength within those younger than we. May we not close our minds because of preconceptions, and may we be led, however You choose, to the gates of Heaven.

Ask yourself: Do you feel uncomfortable when someone younger than you is placed in a position of authority over you? Why or why not?

June 17

The End of the Beach

After an hour or so, we were ready to resume our trek, our clothes sufficiently dry and my pride sufficiently restored. The beach was changing shape, now, gradually narrowing and interspersed with rocky sections. In the distance, we could see what appeared to be a dark cliff, rising above where the beach apparently came to an end.

By late afternoon, we stood at the cliff's base, it's rocky ledges smoothed by centuries of wind and water. The trail seemed to continue around the cliff, out of sight and just next to the water's edge. A wooden sign stood anchored in rock and spelled out the warning: "Consult tide schedule before proceeding. Move ahead only at lowest level".

Below that announcement a chart had been fastened to the wooden board, giving the times and measures of each day's rise and fall, complete to the end of the month.

"It looks like the next low tide will be at 4:00 tomorrow morning. What do you say we make an early camp here tonight, then set out just before daybreak?"

My son agreed, and we took advantage of the enforced stop to repack gear, do a little laundry and prepare an assorted seafood platter, made up of everything we could glean from the receding tidal pools nearby.

"There's one thing I'm wondering about," my son said as he cracked open a mussel shell. "If whoever put that sign up is really concerned for our safety, then why didn't they warn you about the danger of jumping into a rip tide? That could have killed you just as easily as being caught out on the rocks. I mean, do they really care what happens to you or not?"

"Believe me, they care," I answered. "I've seen enough to have no doubt about that. When it comes to how they care, I probably have as many questions as you do. One thing I'm beginning to see, though, is that God's concern is expressed in more ways than we could ever imagine. It's not always a sign post; sometimes it's a change in the weather, or feeling in the heart, or a loving son who yells out, 'Hey Dad! Let it go!'"

He smiled at that, and we drifted back into silence, each of us thinking back to all the times when our lives were directed, more often than not without our being aware of it.

Trust in the LORD with all your heart and lean not on your own understanding; in all your ways acknowledge him, and he will make your paths straight.
Proverbs 3: 5 – 6

Prayer: Lord, how are You leading me today? What people, which things, what events are shaping my decisions and keeping me on the path toward You? Please give me eyes to see, hears to hear, and a heart to follow.

Ask yourself: How have people and events affected your life recently? What is happening around you today?

June 18

The Narrow Path

The moon was still shining brightly when I opened my eyes and looked out over the water. Everything seemed so calm, it was hard to remember that I was lying next to the ocean. In the faint light, I could see that the shoreline was far out beyond the rocks. Low tide. The eastern sky was beginning to lose a few stars, and a single bird was crying in the distance as we shouldered our backpacks and started onto the trail again. The rocky cliff was close enough to touch on the left side, while I had a sense of openness on the right. The ocean seemed far away and almost a thing of memory. With the coming light, I was reminded, however, that the ocean was still with us. Dampened rocks above our heads served as reminders that we were in a tidal area. The splashing of fish and crabs in small pools around our feet promised that the ocean would return, hopefully after we had passed. The sun made its way over the horizon, and now we could see what appeared to be the end of the cliff face, with nothing but open water lying beyond. But when we arrived there, we could see that the trail took a sharp turn to the left, into a long narrow inlet. The cliff still rose majestically over our heads, and the trail still clung to its sides, with broken rock and tidal pools off to the right. Far off to the right, I could see the sheer cliffs on the other side of the inlet. There was no indication of a trail, however, and we both wondered where we were being taken. Rounding another bend in the cliff, that question was answered. Ahead of us rose a sheer wall of rock, climbing three hundred meters or more into the sky. And there on the cliff face, our trail was clearly discernible, zig zagging five or six times before breaking out onto the top. Any question of continuing around the shoreline was immediately put to rest as we stood awestruck at the sight of the rocky cliffs on the other side of the inlet. The only way out was up. After a brief stop for breakfast, we were ready for the ascent. I took the lead, and we leaned into our shoulder straps, picking our way carefully and avoiding unnecessary conversation. Stopping at the first switchback in the trail, I heard for the first time that morning the sound of waves breaking on rocks. I looked back along the way we had come and realized that the tide was moving back in. In places it was already splashing onto the trail itself. I took a quick glance up and thought to myself, this is not a trail I would have chosen, if I had the choice. It's steep and rocky, and I still admit to a fear of heights. But looking back down at the way we had come, and the rising tide, I had to whisper a brief prayer of thanks. Some ways are definitely better than others.

Whoever loves his brother lives in the light, and there is nothing in him to make him stumble.

I John 2: 10

Prayer: I don't always like the paths I have to walk; I confess that, Lord. Some days, I wish I could go back to greener pastures and better days. But today is what You've given me, and by faith I will walk it. And one day, I know, I will look back on this trail and thank you with all my heart for Your loving care. Until then, Father, guide my feet.

Ask yourself: Do you think that a Christian is entitled to a life free of difficulty and danger? Why or why not?

June 19

Death on the Trail

By the time the sun had made its way to the top of the sky, we had made our way to the top of the cliff. The trail broke out onto a grassy hilltop overlooking the inlet below and continued toward a forested area off in the distance. We took off our gear and sat with our legs dangling over the cliff, congratulating one another on a successful climb. From this altitude, it was easy to see that the tide was returning quickly. From the open sea, it hit the narrow inlet and picked up speed rapidly, moving in a succession of awe-inspiring waves toward the waiting rocks along the trail's edge. Suddenly my son leapt to his feet, pointed below and shouted, "Dad! I see someone!" I had to strain my eyes, but finally I could see him too. He was about halfway between the point where the trail turned into the inlet and where the climb up the cliff face began. He was running, and his desperation was evident as we watched him throw off his backpack and race all the faster. A wave caught him and nearly swept him off the trail, but he clung to a rock and was soon on his feet again. From our viewpoint, we could see that he was doomed to lose. Huge waves were building at the inlet's entrance, crashing along the sides of the cliff and growing with ferocity as they neared the wall at the end. He was too far away to make out details of his face, but my son and I both shared the terror he must have felt. For him, there was no escape, no hope, and yet he ran as if there were. For a moment, we even dared to think he might make it. The wall was less than fifty yards away, but from our position above, we could tell that even reaching the wall would not help him, since a wave at least two stories in height was almost on him. We looked straight down to see him reach the first switchback when the monster wave took him. There was a crash of foam, a faint shudder beneath our feet, then the sound of water striking the cliff. The tide churned for a few moments, as if uncertain of where to go next, then began its retreat to the sea, only to be met by the next wave. We watched for several minutes, but never saw the man again. Whether he was pulled out to open water by the undercurrents, or simply dashed incessantly against the rocks was a moot point: he was gone. I put an arm over my son's shoulders, and felt him trembling. He was obviously trying to maintain control of his emotions, but was losing the battle. " Why?" he finally blurted.

I wasn't sure who that question was supposed to be for. I wasn't sure, myself, for that matter. I mumbled something about "he should have..." and "we have to..." but I knew I wasn't helping my son deal with what we had just seen. Finally we both just lay back on the grass and tried to find some peace.

Are not two sparrows sold for a penny? Yet not one of them will fall to the ground apart from the will of your Father.

Matthew 10: 29

Prayer: Father, Your Word tells me that You know when even a sparrow falls to the ground. How does it break Your heart to see your people suffer and die? How do You bear it? How can I bear it? Lord, grant me strength that comes from Your heart. Help me to know that all things are in Your hands, and that all things will be made right.

Ask yourself: Have you or someone close to you been involved in a disaster of some kind? How did it affect you?

Making Sense of the Senseless

We must have laid there for an hour or more, saying nothing. The sun was at an angle in the sky, reminding me that we had to prepare for evening. I finally sat up, reached out to take my son's hand, and spoke softly.

"That man broke a rule. Whether he intended to or not, he ignored a clear warning and moved forward when he should have sat and waited. He paid for it with his life."

"But why did he have to die for it?" my son said, sitting up and looking out over the ocean. "There's a lot worse things people do, and nothing like that ever happens to them."

"There was a wise king once who made the same comment," I said, remembering Solomon. "He said that it seems the wicked never get punished, while the righteous always suffer. He finally concluded that we live in a world broken by sin, and because of that people are going to get hurt and die, regardless of what they do. But he also discovered that God sees everything that happens, and one day, He will set everything right. We have to believe that, Son. Because if we don't, then nothing makes sense, ever."

I don't know if he accepted that explanation or not, but at last he was able to stand up with me. We put our backpacks on and continued down the trail. Nothing else would have made sense.

In this meaningless life of mine I have seen both of these: a righteous man perishing in his righteousness, and a wicked man living long in his wickedness.
Ecclesiastes 7: 15

....

Prayer: Like Solomon, I too agonize over what looks like injustice in the world. I cry out for answers, even as I realize that YOU are the answer. Keep my eyes fixed on You, Lord, and help me though the times of confusion. Hasten the day when I will "know even as I am known."

Ask yourself: Does the fact that you are disturbed by the appearance of injustice help you understand that justice does in fact exist?

June 21

Into Darkness

We walked on, toward the line of trees in the distance. I was thinking that it would be better to camp in a sheltered area away from the sound of the ocean. But as we moved into the forest, I began having second thoughts. My heart was as dark as the trail, and my feet stumbled as often as my troubled thoughts. I was desperate to try and find some answers to what we had seen, and not only for the sake of my son, who was still trembling as he walked in silence. We came into a clearing, and I suggested we stop and build a fire. He responded by taking off his backpack and sitting heavily on the ground. I decided not to coax him into helping with the work of making camp, but later thought that might have been a mistake, since I found my own emotions distracted by the challenge of physical labor. Before long, a fire had lit up the clearing. "Son," I said at last. "You need to get your pack opened up. Supper will be ready soon, and whether you feel like eating or not, we need the strength." I brought over the pot of soup and filled his cup, watching to see if he would eat. The cup came to his lips occasionally, but he never swallowed. "We have to get through this, Son," I said at last. "That was an awful thing to have to see today, but it's not the worst there is out there. If we can't get deal with this, it'll be that much harder to deal with the next thing."

"'Next thing'?" he blurted out, looking directly at me for the first time today. "Who says there's going to be a next thing? I don't like this trip anymore, Dad. I don't like what happened today, and I sure don't like whoever could have stopped it and didn't! I want to go home."

"Think about what you're saying, Son. Can you honestly say that nothing like this ever happened back home? God's not responsible because a man chose to ignore the rules. People suffer and die every day, because people break the rules: rules that were set up to help them live. This trip is not to blame for all the hurt out there." I stopped for a minute, looking at the dying coals of the campfire. "This trip, " I went on, "is the only way that you or I will ever make sense of things. It's okay to tell me how you feel. But please... please don't do anything you'll regret later. At least sleep on it tonight, and we'll talk more tomorrow, okay?" He nodded and pulled out his sleeping bag. I drew up closer to the fire and prayed. How can I help him, Lord? From deeper in the woods, I heard a sound; too far away to make out distinctly, but close enough to cause a cold chill to run up my back. Perhaps the answer would be as painful as the question.

When a scourge brings sudden death, he mocks the despair of the innocent. When a land falls into the hands of the wicked, he blindfolds its judges. If it is not he, then who is it?

Job 9: 23 – 24

....

Prayer: Come to me in midst of my despair, Lord. Teach me Your ways, and comfort me with Your presence. Forgive me when I doubt Your love and mercy. Teach me how to walk by faith, and not by the sight of the world around me.

Ask yourself: Why do you question "senseless injustice" if you do not believe deep in your heart that there is a "Justice Giver" who will hear your cry?

From Out of the Darkened Heart

A rumble of thunder woke me from troubled dreams. I looked around to see that the fire was completely out. I turned to my son, and saw that he was sitting up, staring into the black coals of the campfire. "Been awake long?" I asked, anxious to see if he was doing any better. His answer sent a chill over me.

"Never slept."

I came out of my sleeping bag and went to him, wrapping both arms around him. "Son," I pleaded, "we've got to work through this. I... I heard something last night, and I was reminded of something a good friend told me not long ago. He said that the enemy likes to come at us when we're down. He knows he could never defeat us out in the open, so he waits until we fall. He's a coward, but he can be deadly. That's why you have to let me help you. C'mon, let's get our things together." I gently pulled until he came to his feet. There was danger here, I knew that. I had heard it last night: a familiar sound I had hoped I would never hear again. I had surprised him once, wounded him a second time, and escaped a third. But the words of the evil man came back to me like the sound of a dying animal: "He will find a way, you know." I jumped at the sound of thunder, looked up through the trees and saw that the sky which a moment before had been gray was now churning with black clouds. Even as I looked, a cold drop of rainwater struck one eye.

"We have to move, Son," I said, taking him by the arm. A few moments later, the rain began in earnest, soaking us through before we could even think of stopping to find shelter. But shelter was not what I sought. I wanted only escape: escape from this dark place, from the unknown, and worse yet, escape from what I knew without a doubt was out there, waiting. We came to a stream which was flowing across the trail, taking with it the remnants of the trail itself and washing them away, deeper into the forest. I paused only a second, took a leap for a rock on the other side of the stream, missed and fell flat on my face. I used the running water to wash the mud from my eyes, looked back to see my son. He was looking across the stream, toward me, but beyond me, farther up the trail. His face was a mixture of fatigue and fear, incomprehension and dawning realization. I turned back to look in the direction he was facing. At first, I could see nothing, but kept straining, certain that something was there. The next flash of lightning confirmed my worst fear. There in the trail, half hidden by the undergrowth stood the evil man, a malicious sneer on his lips. Off to his right, hidden by the trees, came the sound of a lion.

As a shepherd looks after his scattered flock when he is with them, so will I look after my sheep. I will rescue them from all the places where they were scattered on a day of clouds and darkness.

Ezekiel 34: 12

....

Prayer: I don't know why I must walk through dark places, Lord, but I praise You for Your light. Guide my footsteps when I cannot see the way. Warm my heart when all about me is cold. Bring me through the gloom, into the sunshine again.

Ask yourself: How does fear affect your decision making?

June 23

Draw Swords

At the sight of the evil man, the last vestige of bravery washed away from me like the riverbank, as it eroded into the growing flood. I leaped to my feet and backed away until I stood beside my son. Coming in contact with him jerked my senses back to reality. We had to do something. "This way!" I shouted, pulling him into the undergrowth. We stumbled together through the bushes, not sure and uncaring where we were going, as long as it was away from him.

A cedar tree blocked our progress, its thick branches bending all the way to the ground and providing a solid wall of green. I moved a few branches aside, and discovered that the area around the base of the tree was relatively clear, even dry. We got out of our packs and sat facing out. I dug through mine until I found the sword. Pulling it out, I asked, "You have a knife, don't you?" He nodded, and I said, "Get it." He obeyed, and spoke up for the second time this morning. "Who... what was that, Dad?"

"He's known as the 'evil man'", I said, trying to peer out beyond the branches. "But listen to me, Son. He can't touch you. You belong to God, and he has no authority over you. You have to believe that, no matter what he says."

"Then why the sword?" he asked, still fumbling for his knife. "Why can't we just walk past him and get out of this place?"

I took a breath and thought a moment before speaking. "Because there's a lion with him. He's a part of this world, and he does what the evil man says. But he can be hurt. I've hurt him myself. And I've fooled him, and I've gone places where he couldn't go. We just have to be brave. God will give us what we need, when we need it."

And with every ounce of my being, I hoped that I was right.

He trains my hands for battle; my arms can bend a bow of bronze.

Psalms 18: 34

....

Prayer: Lord, You tell us that the real battle is against the spiritual world, and yet we are faced every day with flesh and blood enemies who want to destroy us. Keep my heart on You, and my hand on my sword. May I be brave when I need to be, strong when I must. And keep me, dear Father, in Your loving care.

Ask yourself: What is the difference between physical and spiritual warfare. How are they related?

June 24

Waiting for Battle

This must be the worst part. I dreaded the prospect of seeing the evil man and his lion, but waiting here, shivering in the cold and letting my imagination run wild was infinitely worse. When would he come? How would I respond? Would I win? Could I?

Looking over at the face of my son, I saw that I was not alone in my thoughts, except for one crucial thing: he had never encountered the enemy before. He had never tasted victory, had never seen a demon flee in terror. I reached out and laid a hand on the trembling arm which held the knife.

"Did I ever tell you about how I got this sword?" I asked.

"I think you tried to, the other day, but I didn't want to hear about it. That seems like a long time ago. So tell me, Dad: How did you get that sword?"

"I'm glad you asked, Son," I said with a smile. There was life coming back into those eyes. Even here, or perhaps especially here, in the midst of such fear and misery, we were both discovering something we didn't know we had: real strength.

"Now a demon, he's plenty strong, but between you and me, he's a little thick between the ears. Like that day when a bunch of them decided to come at us. This one big ugly thing comes toward me, but get this: ten feet away he's already broadcasting what he plans to do. He's got his sword... this sword... up over his head, and he's running at me as if to say, 'Now just stand perfectly still, 'cause I'm plannin to take this here sword and plant it right on top of your head.' Now, all I have on me is a fishing rod, so I hold it up in front of me like this, that demon comes down on it with his sword, and, well, now I have two fishing rods, one in each hand, and they're kinda pointy on the ends, where the sword cut them. It didn't take me long to figure out that they'd make a lot better weapon than a fishing rod, so I just, well..."

Looking at his face as I spoke, I could see hope return to my son's eyes. And in turn, I began to feel that hope for myself. We are God's children, after all. We have skills, and strength, and the power of God Himself on our side. And we have a promise: this battle is not even ours. It belongs to the One Who made us, and set us on this journey in the first place. Win or lose, live or die, the outcome is in His Hands, and either way, we come out the victors.

I finished the story with perhaps a little embellishment, promising to myself that I would confess and apologize later. Right now we have a job to do. And we will be faithful.

He ransoms me unharmed from the battle waged against me, even though many oppose me.

Psalms 55: 18

Prayer: Remind me of the battles You have won, Oh Lord. Tell me again how the enemy of this world flees before Your awesome might. Fill me with the confidence that can only come to those who belong to You. And may I use that confidence to serve You.

Ask yourself: Have you ever fought in a battle (wartime, sports, work place)? How did you feel beforehand? How did your attitudes change as the battle progressed?

A Calculated Retreat

We sat for what seemed like hours in the shelter of the cedar tree. The rain continued, and occasionally a drop would find its way down the back of my neck. There was no indication that the evil man or the lion were even nearby, but I knew they would be. In spite of the hope I was harboring that maybe, just maybe, they had lost us and gone away, I knew in my heart that they were somewhere close, waiting.

And with that knowledge came a growing realization: they will never attack us here. Not while we're prepared and waiting. They've never fought that way before, and they're not about to start now. The enemy's strength is in deception and fear, not in face to face confrontation.

The sky was growing dark, and I had no desire to face a night huddled under this tree, waiting for a foe who would not come until my guard was down. Suddenly, I knew what I had to do. Handing the sword to my son, I said, "Give me your knife." He did, and I explained. "As long as he thinks we're ready and waiting, he'll never come. He'll just stay out there and wait for us to panic, or go to sleep. So we have to make him think we've done just that: panic.

"I'm going to make a break for it. I'll run like I'm scared to death, back down the trail. If I'm not mistaken, that lion will be right after me. He's got to think that I'm scared and defenseless. That's why I need your knife, to hide under my sleeve. If he attacks me like I think he will, I'll do what I can with this. I'm hoping you'll be along to finish the job with that," I said, pointing to the sword.

He started to protest, but I didn't want to give him a chance. "Stay quiet and watch. If nothing happens, I'll come back." And with that, I broke out of the shelter and started running.

O Sovereign LORD, my strong deliverer, who shields my head in the day of battle— do not grant the wicked their desires, O LORD; do not let their plans succeed, or they will become proud.

Psalms 140: 7 – 8

Prayer: Thank you, Father, for your promise to be with us in battle. May the battles we face be at the time of Your choosing, and not that of the enemy's. May I face my foe unafraid, certain in the knowledge that You will be victorious. Use me, I pray, for Your Name's sake.

Ask yourself: If the enemy's power is in deception, do you think it would be possible to deceive him?

June 26

Confronting the Lion

It's not difficult to act terrified when you are, in fact, terrified. I couldn't feel my feet as they struck the ground, leaving me with the impression that I was flying. But if I was flying, then it was terrifyingly slow, as I raced past trees, rocks and bushes, knowing that the lion was in all probability behind one of them, getting ready to pounce on me as I went past.

If that thought was not frightening enough, then the other most assuredly was: that is, that the lion, seeing my attempt at deception would leave me and go instead for my son. Alone, untrained for battle, questioning the wisdom of a father who would desert him at such a time.

I began having second thoughts about this plan, and unconsciously slowed down, in preparation for returning to the tree where my son waited. I glanced over my shoulder just as the lion appeared from behind a tree and leapt. I only had time to raise my arms in self defense when he struck, knocking me onto my back. The air left my lungs, and I was uncertain whether to try and take a breath or do something about the sharp teeth headed for my throat. I chose the latter, striking him with an elbow and reaching for the knife hidden up my sleeve. Somewhere in the process, I must have found my breath, since a primal scream seemed to be escaping my lips. I kicked. I gouged. I made feeble attempts with the knife to find a weak spot. But the lion was all sinew and muscle, and I accomplished little more than enraging the beast, with the result that I was being torn to tatters by his claws.

We rolled together, then I was on my back, with his full weight against my chest. I was still stabbing at him with my right hand, but noticed that the knife was no longer there, having been flung aside during the scuffle. His claws held me securely, and it was only a matter of moments before his teeth found a jugular vein, ending my life once and for all.

"Lord," I cried, "take care of my son!" And then, as if in answer to my prayer, I was given a vision of my son, tall and strong, holding a gleaming sword over his head, a look of battle-hardened determination in his eyes. So this was his future. A real warrior. Thank you Father for that image. Now I can die in peace. I relaxed my grip on the lion's throat, and as I did, the vision came down with the sword, striking him just behind the ears. For a second time, the wind left my lungs, as the full weight of the cat crashed down on my chest, bringing with it a sweet darkness.

Praise be to the LORD my Rock, who trains my hands for war, my fingers for battle.

Psalms 144: 1

....

Prayer: Thank you for help in battle. By Your strength, may I fight well, know victory, or according to Your will, may I die well. My life is in Your Hands.

Ask yourself: Would you rather be victorious in a battle which was not yours to fight, or be defeated as an obedient warrior of the true King?

June 27

Return from the Shadows

The crackling sound of a fire nearby called into my darkness. When I could ignore it no longer, I opened my eyes to see flames dancing not an arm's length away. I was aware of their warmth, and looking down the length of my body could see steam rising from my sodden clothes. Raising my head to see what else I could discover, I was riveted back to the ground by an electric bolt of pain which began at my feet and exited somewhere near the top of my head. An involuntary cry erupted from my mouth and in the next instant my son's face was next to mine.

"Don't move, Dad. You've been hurt. I've tried to bandage what I can, but I'm not very good at this."

"How... long... " I struggled with the question, but he finished it for me.

"The lion attacked you last night. It's now early evening the next day, so about twenty four hours ago."

The lion. It was coming back to me. "You... I saw you..."

He grinned, which sent a surge of strength through me. "Yeah, just call me Konan. I thought I was going to have to take your fingers along with his head, until you finally let go. That was some fight you put up."

His grin faded, and I knew that there was still a problem. "You say I'm pretty cut up, though, huh?"

I could see a tear forming in the corner of one eye as he spoke. "His claws caught you all over, and I think he got his mouth on one arm. There was a lot of blood. Dad? I don't know what to do."

"You've done fine, Son," I said, trying to sound stronger than I felt. "No father could be prouder." I tried to think clearly, examine every alternative. Finally the only solution possible came to me.

"I haven't told you about Rendezvous, have I?" His expression answered my question, and I went on. "It's a place where fellow travelers come together. It's been awhile since the last one, so we should be getting close to the next one. What you need to do, Son, is leave me here. Travel as light as you can. Find the next Rendezvous, and send help back." I tried to move, grimaced, then said, "I'll be waiting right here."

"No, Dad! I can't leave you here alone. You're hurt. That... evil man..."

"...can't touch me," I reminded him. "And you took care of the lion. Don't worry, Son. I'll be fine. You just be careful on the trail, okay?"

That is why, for Christ's sake, I delight in weaknesses, in insults, in hardships, in persecutions, in difficulties. For when I am weak, then I am strong.
II Corinthians 12: 10

....

Prayer: Father, in my weakness, I can know Your strength. How awesome, that You would show me that strength in the words and actions of a loved one. Give me a chance to do that for another I pray.

Ask yourself: Have you ever had to depend totally upon someone else for your care? What did you feel?

June 28

The Longest Night

The fire burned brightly for awhile, and the makeshift camp still held the fresh memory and scent of my son. Eventually, though, the evening chill set in. I tried to use the firewood sparingly, but the darkness was just too unbearable. By midnight, the last ember was fading, and the night seemed to close in from all sides. I pulled my sleeping bag around me for warmth, but the cold was not caused entirely by the weather.

A twig snapped nearby, and for a moment I thought perhaps my son had returned. When the silence continued, I called out, "Is there anyone there? " The only sound came from a rustle of wind in the trees, so I closed my eyes, trying to shut out a growing imagination. I felt feverish, and whether from my wounds or simple fatigue, I was finding it increasingly difficult to stay alert. I must have slept, because when I opened my eyes again, the wind had shifted, and the campfire was glowing as a fresh breeze swept over the coals. I pulled a handful of grass and threw it over the embers. It smoldered for a moment, then burst into flame, quickly illuminating the area around me before settling back into darkness. The flash of light was enough, though; not six feet away from me stood the evil man, staring directly at me.

I tried to jump up, found it impossible, started to cry out but caught myself. Finally I was able to whisper, "What do you want?"

"Hurt ourselves, have we?" he said with a smile totally lacking in humor. "Looks bad. You may even die."

He was probably right, I decided, and the realization gave me the courage to speak up. "Too bad about your pet kitty. He really should have stuck to rabbits and field mice."

Even in the darkness, I could feel the seething hatred. And yet it struck me as odd that he still did not move toward me as he obviously wanted to. What I had been taught must be true: he can't touch me. "I'm sure you must have some other people to torment. Why don't you move on and let me get some rest?"

"Mark my words..."

"No! You mark *mine.* I *order* you in the Name of the One who made me, who bought me and who sent me on this journey: be gone!"

I don't know what happened after that. The energy I had spent was all I had to give. I fell back, semi-conscious, and drifted into a fitful sleep. Sometime later, I woke and looked around, but saw that I was alone. Had I dreamed all that? Were my wounds giving me hallucinations?

Perhaps, but I don't think so.

Submit yourselves, then, to God. Resist the devil, and he will flee from you.
James 4: 7

....

Prayer: It's easy to talk about resisting the devil, Lord, but the reality of it still scares me. Give me strength when I need it, I pray.

Ask yourself: What is it about the Name of Jesus that gives a person authority over demons?

June 29

Delirium

I've heard it said that a person facing a near death experience will see his life pass before him. If that's true, then my life began on January first. Lying there, beside a cold campfire with a raging fever and a torn body falling into a state of shock, I was led through a dream world, back through my journey. I remembered that first day, and the squeak of new leather. I could feel the straps of my backpack as they settled into flesh which had grown soft and yielding. My boots were stiff back then, and poorly tied. How my feet would suffer the next day!

Charlie came to visit me, and we talked a long time about friends, and history. It was good to lie there and listen to his stories, some of which I had never heard before. Lizzie joined in some time later, and offered me some of her famous stew. "Not right now," I said with a smile. "I think I'm dying."

"Oh nonsense," she laughed. "There's a lot more yet you'll have to discover." Her face turned serious and she moved close to my ear. "Some of the things yet to come will not be pleasant, Friend. Not like today. But listen to me: you'll make it through. And won't we have some stories to share then!"

My son was standing behind her, not saying anything. Odd that he wouldn't join into the conversation. But he was smiling, so I knew he was okay. His sword was resting on the ground, point down, and he was leaning on it in a casual sort of way. As if he were finished with it. What a warrior he turned out to be, I thought. I'm so proud of him.

Occasionally my mind would drift awake and I would look around the camp. Sometimes it was light. Sometimes it was dark. Every time I started to move, the shooting pain would remind me that I was in a bad way, and I would let the dream time come again.

All in all, it was the best day of my life.

I will lie down and sleep in peace, for you alone, O LORD, make me dwell in safety.

Psalms 4: 8

....

Prayer: Praise You, Father, because You come to me even when I am far away. Your Presence and comfort are my life, my joy. Please never leave me.

Ask yourself: Have you ever had a dream so vivid that it seemed to be real? What were the circumstances?

June 30

Reunion

"Now Lizzie, you know that any good stew needs dill weed to make it perfect!"

"Don't you start telling me my business, Charlie. I've been making this stew since before you came around, and I haven't heard any complaints yet!"

"I'm not complaining; I'm just tryin' to share a little of my wisdom with you, that's all."

"Well, if you want to share some wisdom, why don't you go help that poor young man. Can't you see he's hurt?"

"You're right, of course." Charlie bent down low and whispered in my ear, "Still needs dill weed."

Another voice broke in over Charlie's. "Let's get him onto his side. Gently now. That's good. Now hold him steady while I get this bandage off. Nurse, open up that bag and set up a drip. We need to get some fluids going right away."

"Is he going to be all right?" Charlie asked. "He sure looks pale."

"He's lost a lot of blood, and infection has taken over some of these wounds. Let's just do our best and see what happens."

My dream world was starting to fade, and in its place there were shafts of light, and noise, and pain. I tried to cry out, but only managed a moan.

"Friend! Can you hear me? Open your eyes. Can you squeeze my hand?" None of the words I was hearing made sense. I did manage to squeeze something, which resulted in a yell of delight from somewhere, hurting my ears. I determined not to do that again.

Little by little, the world started coming into focus. I could see a man I recognized from Rendezvous. I think he was a doctor. There was Nurse What's-Her-Name, and she was sticking my arm with a needle. Behind her stood... Charlie?

No, it was my son. But he sure looked like Charlie. He heals the brokenhearted and binds up their wounds. He determines the number of the stars and calls them each by name.

Psalms 147: 3 – 4

....

Prayer: How sweet to know the healing power of our God! How wonderful when in His grace that power comes through the ministry of a friend. Use me to heal just as I have been healed.

Ask yourself: Would you be willing to care for a friend who needs you desperately? How about an enemy?

July 1

Back from the Brink

The sounds of easy conversation and gentle laughter nudged me awake. My first image was of a sky full of stars. There was a sensation of warmth running along my left side, and I turned my head to see a campfire nearby. A coffeepot hung suspended over the flames. "Coffee?" I mumbled weakly.

"Well, I guess we see what's really important to him, after all." Ralph's voice came from beyond the fire, and as he stood up to move toward me, I felt a surge of joy.

"Ralph! How did you get here? It's good to see you again."

"Likewise, Friend. As to the question of how I got here, your son found me and told me what happened. He's a fine man, that boy.

"My son!" It was coming back to me now. "How..."

"I'm here, Dad." A voice from somewhere off to the right. "Rendezvous was just a day's hike away, like you said." That brought an exaggerated "humph!" from somewhere in the darkness, along with a mumbled "...sure took *me* more than a day."

Then a man I recognized as one of the Rendezvous doctors was bending close and looking at my eyes with a tiny flashlight. "You took quite a beating," he said. "Then along with infection and dehydration, it was pretty touch and go. You still have a lot of recovering to do, but I'd say you're going to be back on your feet again soon. The nurse and I are going to change your bandages now, and then we'll want you to get some rest before we start moving tomorrow."

A lady came into view. One look at the pencil hanging precariously in her graying hair told me it was the one I met the first time I came to Rendezvous last February, referring to her as "Nurse We" . My memory was confirmed when she said, "We need to turn over so our bandages can be removed. Shall we?" I started to make a joke, but instead said simply, "Thank you for coming."

O LORD my God, I called to you for help and you healed me. O LORD, you brought me up from the grave ; you spared me from going down into the pit.
Psalms 30: 2 – 3

···

Prayer: Once in a while, Father, You show us our mortality, and remind us that our lives on this earth are limited. Thank you for providing along with that revelation the assurance that death will only serve to bring us closer to You. Thank you for healing, but thank you too for the perfect healing that will someday bring me into Your kingdom.

Ask yourself: How can death be called a "perfect healing"?

Take Up Thy Bed

Early the next morning, the camp was buzzing with activity. The doctor and Nurse "We" were checking bandages, adjusting IV drips and speaking assurances. A man I didn't recognize and my son were cutting poles and fashioning a stretcher. Ralph had just finished feeding me breakfast and was holding a cup of coffee to my lips.

"Sorry you had to leave Rendezvous to come get me," I said. "You must be pretty busy. The last time I saw you, you were leading a town full of people up the trail."

"Hey, those guys are doing great," he said. "The man and his family who took care of us? They've taken over teaching and training responsibility for the whole group. I meet with them once in awhile to help iron out details. That just leaves me with the battle training class. Hearing you and your son had been going to head to head with the evil man and the lion together, I figured this might give them all some hands on experience. I brought the whole class with me." He winked. "If there's nothing to fight, then I guess they can take turns carrying your stretcher."

"It's *true*, Ralph," I said in a whisper. "He really *can't* touch us. He stood right there like his feet had been nailed to the ground! Then when I told him to leave... well, I'm not sure exactly what happened, but when I looked around later, he was gone.

"That's good to hear, Friend," Ralph said. "I'd like you to share all this with my class, when you're able. Of course, those scars tell us something else as well. Even if the evil man can't touch us, others he controls *can*. And that's where a good sword comes in handy. Your son has been pretty quiet about the whole thing. He's still trying to process it, but judging from the lion's body I found when I got here, I think we can be sure he'll do the right thing when he has to.

"Hey Dad," my son was carrying a crude stretcher over to where I lay. "I need to measure this to see if you fit. How are you feeling?"

"Like I'm the most blessed man in the world," I smiled.

Perfume and incense bring joy to the heart, and the pleasantness of one's friend springs from his earnest counsel.

Proverbs 27: 9

....

Prayer: Praise you Father, for friends who share my faith, my fears and my hope. May I be as much a blessing to them as they are to me.

Ask yourself: How is the help from a friend different from the help of a professional?

July 3

He Ain't Heavy

I had always imagined that being carried on a stretcher would be a pretty easy way to go. But between the IV tube jerking with every step and the wounds on my back screaming for attention, it was sheer torture. I dared not complain, though, because one look at the faces of those who carried me said that they were not enjoying it any more than I was. There were eight men, plus the doctor and nurse. It was decided that the medical team would be excused from stretcher duty, since they had to keep an eye on my condition, as well as carry all the extra medicine and bandages. All of our gear was combined into four backpacks, so that the four men who took places on the stretcher did not have to carry anything else. We traveled in thirty minute shifts, stopping for a brief rest and a drink; then everyone would rotate one position. That way, everyone had a place at the stretcher for two hours, then two hours carrying a backpack, then back to the stretcher.

"This reminds of David Livingstone," I said. "His faithful servants carried his body all the way out of darkest Africa so that he could buried back in Scotland."

"I remember," said Ralph as he renewed his grip on the stretcher. "But I also seem to recall that they left his heart and liver buried under a tree. How about it? Got anything you can give up to make for a lighter load?"

"Only my pride," I confessed. "As heavy a burden as it's been on me, somehow I don't think it would affect your job."

"Don't be so sure about that," Ralph puffed. "I'm trying to imagine how hard this job would be if you were ordering me to do it, like I was some kind of hired hand. Just knowing that, if the situation was reversed, you'd be right here for me makes it light work." He stumbled, caught himself, then added, "Well, relatively speaking, anyway!"

A man's pride brings him low, but a man of lowly spirit gains honor.
Proverbs 29: 23

....

Prayer: Lord, keep me from false pride. Show me my own heart, and the motivations which rule my life. Help me control the things which bring me low.

Ask yourself: Do you find it easier to help a person who does not expect or demand help from you? Why?

July 4

Pride

It was a quiet camp tonight, as everyone went about the business of fire, food and taking care of sore muscles. Even Nurse "We" was not very talkative as she changed my bandages and saw that my medicines were taken properly. Only a few moments later, I noticed that she had already gotten into her sleeping bag.

Ralph brought two cups of coffee and sat beside me as we listened to the stillness settling in. "You know what?" he said finally. "You said this morning that you've had to lose your pride, being carried around and treated like a baby. But I think all of us have discovered a little pride in ourselves that we didn't know we had. Take that guy over there," he pointed with his cup to a young man cutting firewood for the evening. "He handles a sword better than anyone I've ever known. Problem is, he knows he's good, and wants to make sure you know it as well. Today, though, he's had trouble pulling his weight on the stretcher duty. Not as physically strong as he thought he was. We all love the Doc, but well, it's no secret that he's smarter than any five of us put together. He doesn't want to admit it, but he tends to hold that over us sometimes. Today, brains just couldn't compete with brawn, and it's been fun to watch him trying to be 'one of the guys'. I just want to thank you, Friend, for helping us all deal with our pride today."

"What about you, Ralph?" I asked. "What pride issue has come up for you today?"

He stared into the fire a long time, then said, "The fact that your son killed the lion, and not me. I'm the battle teacher here. People are supposed to look up to me. It's just... well, I wish it had been me."

"And how has today helped you deal with this?"

Ralph ran a hand along my stretcher. I noticed blisters between his thumb and forefinger. "There's four handles on this thing," he said. "Not one is more or less important than the other three. Only by every person sharing exactly one fourth of the load can we move forward. It doesn't matter how smart you are, how strong you are, how many places you've been. One handle, one fourth. That's it. I think this whole journey is a lot like this stretcher. From where we are, we can't see the big picture and we somehow get the idea that what we're doing is more important than what someone else is doing. But God says, 'Wait right there. All I'm giving you is this part of the load. No more, no less. Can you handle it?'" He gave the stretcher a pat, then said, "Thanks for the load!"

> *Each one should test his own actions. Then he can take pride in himself, without comparing himself to somebody else, for each one should carry his own load.*
>
> Galatians 6: 4

....

Prayer: Forgive me, Lord for my foolish pride. Help me not to compare myself to others, but to take hold of what You've given me to carry.

Ask yourself: What is a source of pride in your life?

July 5

Homecoming

Camp was broken before daylight this morning, everyone spurred on by the possibility that we might make Rendezvous before having to stop again for the night. It was a painful beginning for all, as sore muscles complained at the prospect of another day like yesterday. By midmorning, however, the sun had warmed all the aches and pains, and soon I began to hear the sounds of laughter again: friends sharing the day with each other.

We stopped for lunch beside a small stream. Ralph took off his shirt, and with great screams and shouts set out to wash off the grime from the morning's march. "Great idea," I said. "But as soon as we get back, I want a long, hot shower."

"Guess again," said the Doc. "With those bandages, all you can hope for is a lukewarm sponge bath. By the way, can I have your water allotment, since you won't be needing it?"

Humor. I chuckled to myself. The Doc is learning.

After some discussion, it was decided to send two of the men on ahead to alert the people at Rendezvous of our coming. "Funny," I said to Ralph as he lifted one corner of my stretcher and moved forward. "Less than five months ago, I didn't even know about Rendezvous. Now it seems like home."

"That's because it *is* home," he said. "At least, the only home that will last. The brothers and sisters we have there will be with us for all eternity. All the more reason to learn how to get along with them!" he laughed.

The sun had disappeared behind the mountain, and a cool breeze was starting to chill my feverish skin. My stretcher bearers hadn't seemed to notice it, however, and I could see trickles of sweat running down the arms which bore me along. Some were insisting that we were close, and picked up the pace, while others started suggesting that we stop again for the night. Finally, we stopped to hold a conference. Everyone had an opinion, and the noise level kept rising until Nurse "We", who had been standing quietly at the back of the group spoke up.

"Quiet everyone!" she called out. Amazingly, everyone heard and obeyed, and suddenly we were surround by silence. Almost.

"What's that?" someone asked.

"It's music," she answered. "They're singing us a song, so we can find our way home in the dark."

Speak to one another with psalms, hymns and spiritual songs. Sing and make music in your heart to the Lord, always giving thanks to God the Father for everything, in the name of our Lord Jesus Christ.
Ephesians 5: 19 – 20

....

Prayer: Let my song be lifted up to Heaven, O Lord. May I sing with the saints and the angels the praises which are due You. Listen to our singing, Father, and may Your heart be glad.

Ask yourself: Is your faith worth singing about?

July 6

Reunion

Night was well and truly settled around us by the time we could see the first campfires of Rendezvous, but the music had sustained us for miles. Drifting across the valleys, the sound of hundreds of men, women and children singing praises guided us like a beacon. There was no more talk of stopping for the night, no more complaints of sore muscles and blisters. There was no more idle talk, because everyone wanted to hear the heavenly sounds coming to us from up ahead.

When we finally broke into the clearing, a shout rose up from the people who had been singing together for hours. They cheered us on, took over for the stretcher bearers and led the way to the hospital tent. I was carried inside and immediately handed over to another doctor whom I had never met, along with a team of nurses and orderlies, dressed in their finest scrubs and waiting anxiously to tend to my wounds.

"Get me some light over here!" someone shouted. "Oh yeah, that will need stitches."

"How's his BP? Check that IV line. I think he'll be needing some more plasma."

"Friend, can you hear me? Listen, we need to do a little patching on you, and I think it would be best if you just slept through it. Is that all right with you?"

I nodded weakly, and they continued their work of prepping. Amidst all the no nonsense activity, my son's face appeared, trying unsuccessfully to hide a worried expression. "Dad?" he called out. "You're going to be okay. I'll be right outside."

"You go hit that hot shower, grab something to eat and rest for while." Why was I slurring my words? "I'm in good hands. See you in the morning."

A nurse with a surgical mask over her face found her way next to my ear and spoke softly. "Now, if you wouldn't mind, we'd like to count backwards from ten. Can we do that?"

"Why of course, Nurse We." Her eyebrows came up into a silent question. "Ten, nine... eight.... seven..... ssssss."

Heal the sick, raise the dead, cleanse those who have leprosy, drive out demons. Freely you have received, freely give.

Matthew 10: 8

....

Prayer: Though I am wounded, You will sustain me. My pain would be unbearable, except for the healing power that comes from You through friends like these. Praise You for Your wonderful mercy and kindness.

Ask yourself: Is being hurt worth the joy of knowing the loving care of friends?

July 7

Recovery

My senses were assaulted by the smell of hot canvas and medicine. I looked up to see the sun beating down on the ceiling of a white tent. That explains the canvas, but what about the medicine? Oh yes; I'm in the hospital. I reached over to scratch my right arm and discovered that it was connected by a clear plastic tube to a bottle of something hanging on a hook. With my left hand, I began exploring my surroundings. My chest was covered in thick bandages. My left arm was wrapped in some kind of plaster. I tried to move my legs, but could not. Either they were strapped down, or I was too weak.

Moving my arm farther to the left, I came in contact with something metallic. It slid off the table it was resting on and raised such a clatter that a nurse came rushing in. "Oh! It looks like you're awake. Here, let me get your arm back over here where it belongs."

Feeling like a child who had been caught doing something inappropriate, I asked, "Am I still in one piece?"

"There we are," she said, giving my arm a gentle pat while giving me a message in no uncertain terms that I was not to move it again. "I'll just see if the doctor's available to see you now."

Why do nurses never tell you how you are? She left quietly, and soon the doctor who had first seen me on the trail came in with a big smile. I felt better already. "Thank you," he said without preamble. I gave him a questioning look, and he went on. "The last couple of days were some of the best times of my life. I've always been a good doctor, but it seems like I never had a chance to be a real friend to anyone. Out there, I wasn't just 'Doctor Artinian'; I was Robert. Out there, Robert discovered some of the finer points of life: like how to split firewood, how to roll a sleeping bag, and well, how to sit with a bunch of guys and talk. I've got you to thank for the experience."

"Robert?" I asked.

"Yes?"

"Would you be a real friend right now and tell me how I am?"

A cheerful look brings joy to the heart, and good news gives health to the bones.
Proverbs 15: 30

....

Prayer: May I always be the bearer of good news. And may I never forget the greatest news of all: that by Your Son, Jesus Christ, we are saved.

Ask yourself: What good news do you have to share with someone today?

July 8

Lizzie's Visit

It was a busy morning, not like what I thought hospital life would be. First there were medications to take, then bandages to change. I was just finishing a cup of coffee when Lizzie peeked through the curtain. "Are you receiving visitors?" she asked.

"Lizzie! It's so good to see you. I've been thinking about you a lot the past few days."

She straightened up the sheets on my bed, gave the room an appraising look, then said, "Well, they seem to be taking good care of you. We were all a little concerned when you came in last night; you looked so pale. The boys said you were hurt pretty bad."

"I suppose I was. But you know what Lizzie? It was some of the best times I've ever had, lying semi-conscious and dreaming. I saw you, and Charlie. He told me things I'd never heard before, and..."

"Wait just a minute," Lizzie put a hand gently on my arm. "I want you to start from the beginning and tell me everything. You see, I've kind of become the camp story teller around here, and folks are going to want every detail."

"Okay," I began. "It all started when my son and I saw a man die. It was..."

"Take me there," she interrupted. "A good story teller doesn't just report the facts; she brings the listeners to the story. Describe the day for me." She closed her eyes and waited.

"Let me see," I closed my eyes as well, recalling that morning. "It was still dark. The ocean was calm. The tide was way out, and that brought the smell of seaweed up to our campsite. We packed in silence, not knowing what lay ahead, but anxious to see..."

I talked on and on for most of the morning, surprised at the details that came back so vividly. When the nurse brought lunch in, I looked at Lizzie and said, "I'm sorry, the time just slipped away. You must have better things to do."

"Oh no," she said. "This is what I do, nowadays. I listen to stories, and then I tell them. You're giving my life meaning. Thank you."

Remember to extol his work, which men have praised in song.

Job 36: 24

....

Prayer: Father today I remember the stories I was told in years gone by: stories of You and Your mighty work. Praise You, O Lord for keeping those stories in my mind. May I tell the next generation, so that they too will know the joy of remembrance.

Ask yourself: What stories were you told as a child? Do you still remember them, and the lessons they taught?

July 9

A Son's Love

By the second day in the camp hospital, I was able to sit up in bed, no small feat for someone who had been flat on his back for so long. It was a dizzying experience, and I was beginning to wonder if I would ever fully recover.

I was attempting some kind of strengthening exercise when my son stepped through the curtain. He looked as if he had just come from a workout, and I noticed that my sword was still fastened at his waist. "Hi Dad," he said softly, as if afraid of waking me. "What are you doing?"

"Come in, Son," I practically shouted. "I've missed you. Looks like you're staying busy, though."

"Yeah, Dad, this place is so cool. I started to come in yesterday, but I saw that Lizzie was visiting, so I thought I shouldn't disturb her. You should listen to some of her stories, Dad! She's really awesome."

"So, are you learning how to use that thing any better?" I asked, pointing at the sword.

"Ralph let me into his class. I wanted to ask you if I could keep using it for awhile. He's teaching me so many neat things, Dad. But... what I really wanted to say was that, well, you were right. You know, I was kind of shocked when you told me that you'd killed things. I said to myself then that *I* would never do anything like that. But, like you said, there are just some things that need killing..."

"I told you that sword was mine by right of battle. It's only fitting that the same privilege be offered to you, Son. You saved my life, no doubt about it. I want you to keep the sword, and learn to use it well."

I wasn't sure, but I think I saw a small tear in the corner of his eye. He looked away a moment, as if embarrassed, then looked back at me and said, "I love you, Dad."

My eyes had tears enough for the both of us.

Sons are a heritage from the LORD, children a reward from him. Like arrows in the hands of a warrior are sons born in one's youth. Blessed is the man whose quiver is full of them. They will not be put to shame when they contend with their enemies in the gate.

Psalms 127: 3 – 5

Prayer: Through the stories we tell, the gifts we leave, and the living of our lives, we train up the next generation. Help me Lord to be faithful to the task You've given me.

Ask yourself: What is the most significant gift ever given you by an adult?

Baby Steps

I took my first steps today since the attack. It was quite an achievement, considering the fact that the last time I was on my feet, I was running for my life, and probably could have set a new record for the 100 yard dash. Running was the last thing on my mind today, though. This time the greatest challenge was simply to stay upright, and if that succeeded to place one foot in front of the other.

With the help of nurses, I walked to the doorway of the tent, and enjoyed a glimpse of the outdoors. Rendezvous was going in full swing, with classes scattered here and there, Bible studies, prayer meetings, sewing groups, play groups, just about anything that might interest a person. Up on the hill, I could see my son, going through sword drills with Ralph, while down by the main campfire Lizzie was surrounded by about twenty children who seemed to be listening to a story.

I wished with all my heart that I could be out there among them, rather than standing here with each hand being held by a nurse, wishing the world would stop spinning. As my eyes drifted to the treetops over the campsite, I saw what looked like a huge eagle, circling with the air currents, no doubt watching the ground intently for some unsuspecting morsel.

I was reminded of Isaiah's words about "soaring", and "running" and "walking" . That verse had always puzzled me somewhat, because the order seemed to be reversed. It seemed to me that "walking" should come first, followed by "running", and then if I can pick up enough speed, perhaps to "soar". But standing here today, expending every ounce of strength I had just to stay upright, I thought, that's it, isn't it? One day's accomplishments don't necessarily lead to the next. Each day's strength is sufficient for that day. Perhaps tomorrow I will walk; the next day I may even run. But today, I have the strength to stand here and look out on a beautiful world. And for today, that's enough.

...but those who hope in the LORD will renew their strength. They will soar on wings like eagles; they will run and not grow weary, they will walk and not be faint.

Isaiah 40: 31

....

Prayer: Lord, I confess that I always seem to want just a little more than what I have. If I can walk, then I want to run. If I can run, I want to fly. Forgive me for the ambition which fails to recognize what I have today, and be grateful for it. Thank you for today's blessing.

Ask yourself: Do you think ambition is a good thing, because it leads you to improve, or is it a bad thing because it blinds you to what you have today?

July 11

An Unexpected Visitor

The morning had gone well; wounds were steadily healing and strength was coming back. By afternoon I was ready for some well deserved rest, and had just settled back in my bed when I heard a faint cough. I looked around, and saw a man standing just inside the door. He kept glancing outside, as if he was afraid of being spotted.

"Hello," I said. "Can I help you with something?"

"Why do you say that?" he asked, taking a step farther into the room.

"What? About 'helping', you mean?"

"Exactly. Why should you want to help me?"

"Why shouldn't I? We're all part of this Rendezvous, aren't we?"

I hesitated, then asked, "You *are* a pilgrim, aren't you?" "Yes," he answered quickly. Much too quickly, I thought. "It's just that, well, I'm not used to people going out of their way to... help anyone."

"That's one of the things that make this group so special," I said. "We're bound by love. I wouldn't be here today if the folks here hadn't gone out of their way to rescue me. I'm surprised you..." I stopped when I saw tears welling up in his eyes. Finally he fell to his knees on the floor and wept openly. "I'm so sorry I'm so sorry I'm so sorry," he said over and over. "Please forgive me."

"Forgive...? For what? What are you talking about?"

"I... I was there. I saw you, lying by the fire. I heard you calling out. But I was afraid. I ran away."

For I am about to fall, and my pain is ever with me. I confess my iniquity; I am troubled by my sin.

Psalms 38: 17 – 18

....

Prayer: It hurts when You show me my sin, Father. But if that's the only way I can know the joy of forgiveness, then show me more. Let me see myself for who I really am. Then touch me with Your healing hand and make me whole again.

Ask yourself: Have you ever had to confess to something for which you were ashamed? How did you feel before? How did you feel after?

July 12

Confession

"You... you were *there?*" I asked, incredulous.

The young man on the floor gained control of his sobbing long enough to answer, "You were alone. The fire had gone out. I tried to slip past unnoticed, but I must have stepped on a twig. You called out. You called for help."

I remembered the moment, and I remembered the fear I had felt, hearing sounds in the darkness, hurt and alone. I couldn't think of anything to say. All I could feel was a growing anger, that this wretched human being would have seen my condition and refused to stop and help. Finally, I thought of a question. "Why were you traveling at night, anyway?"

The young man was still on the floor, but at the question he stood and moved to one corner of the room. "It's... safer that way. I get uncomfortable around people, and people don't seem to care much for me either. I usually move at night, then find a place off the trail during the day to sleep and stay out of sight."

I thought of my own pilgrimage, and the goal that lay before me. "But where are you going?" I asked. "Why make this trip at all, if you don't want to see people?"

He shrugged his shoulders and said, "I don't know. I guess there was nothing else to do. Where I lived was pretty rough, and I didn't want to stay there. I kept seeing all these people... people like you, who seemed to be going somewhere. I thought I'd follow along, maybe find something better."

"Something... You really have no idea what all this is about, do you?"

He seemed to miss the point, and went back to his own misery. "I *know* I should have done something back there. I feel terrible about it. Believe me, the last thing I wanted to do was come into this camp and face all these people. But I had to find you, and tell you what I did. And I have to ask you: can you forgive me?",

I lay there for a long time, pondering the question, unsure of my answer. *Could I forgive him?*

> *Then Peter came to Jesus and asked, "Lord, how many times shall I forgive my brother when he sins against me? Up to seven times? Jesus answered, "I tell you, not seven times, but seventy-seven times.*
>
> Matthew 18: 21 – 22

....

Prayer: Father, You tell us to forgive those who have wronged us, but it's not always an easy thing to do. Remind me of the terrible wrongs I have committed against You, and of the forgiveness which is mine. Then help me to do the right thing.

Ask yourself: Is there anyone in your life whom you feel does not deserve forgiveness?

July 13

The Important Question

Could I forgive this man? He saw my suffering, and he kept going. At that moment, still unable to stand alone without help, with every part of my body in pain, I felt as though I had every reason to hate him. How could I possibly forgive him? I put off my answer to him by asking another question. "Why is it important that I forgive you? You obviously don't care much for people, and go out of your way to avoid them. Why then don't you just keep going your own way? Until you told me what you did, no one even suspected you had done anything wrong." I closed my eyes as if going to sleep. In actual fact, I knew that I could never sleep until I had worked through my own feelings.

"To tell you the truth, I don't know why this is so important, but believe me when I say that nothing has ever affected me like this before. I haven't exactly been a model citizen." He gave a short 'humph!', then said, "Who am I kidding? They don't come any worse than me. I lie. I steal. I cheat. I'll do anything and everything, just because I can. It doesn't bother me; at least it never did, before you. Now it feels like there's a concrete block lying across my shoulders. Nothing will make it go away. But *something* keeps telling me that coming to you will help."

As the young man spoke, a nagging thought found its way into my mind. With painful certainty, I knew what he was talking about. I knew, because I had once felt the same way. "I think I know what that something is," I said at last. "And it's not a thing; He's a *Someone*. And if that's the case, then I have no choice. Like it or not, I have to forgive you."

He looked confused, started to smile, then the confusion returned. "So... does that mean you forgive me?"

"Yes. Yes it does. I forgive you, because *He* forgave me. We're not all that different, you and me. I don't know much about the world you came from, but I know that we both have the same heart problem. Sometimes we get reminded of that problem; and sometimes," I smiled at last, "the reminders can get painful." I offered him a bandaged hand to shake, and for an awkward moment, we tried to connect. It's a guy thing. Finally, we both relaxed and were able to laugh at our discomfort. Funny thing: forgiveness. It can turn enemies to friends, and friends to brothers.

For if you forgive men when they sin against you, your heavenly Father will also forgive you. But if you do not forgive men their sins, your Father will not forgive your sins.

Matthew 6: 14 – 15

....

Prayer: It's humbling to realize that I am just as much in need of forgiveness as anyone else, but I confess that it's frightening to understand that my own forgiveness is dependent upon my willingness to forgive others. Enable me, Father. Please.

Ask yourself: Does knowing that you need God's forgiveness help you offer it to others?

July 14

A New Pilgrim

His name was Hank, he told me, and the more we talked the more I liked this young man. In spite of his rough edges, he had an obvious desire to learn, and while I wasn't much of a teacher, he soaked up every word like a sponge.

I wasn't surprised to hear that he had never encountered the evil man, the lion or a single demon on the trail. "You weren't a threat," I explained. "If anything, you aided and abetted the enemy without knowing it. Remember, sin is often something you *don't* do that you should, rather than something you *do* that you shouldn't. Like passing me by, for example." He looked to the floor in shame, but I added, "Hey, remember that issue has been dealt with and forgiven. Don't let anyone – even me – put it back on you."

"Man," he said with a grin that went from ear to ear. "I've got a lot to learn. I hope you don't mind if I stay here for hours."

"I don't mind," I said. "In fact it's an honor to be able to do whatever I can for you. The problem is, I'm pretty new at this myself. What you need is to talk to someone with more experience, who can get you off on the right track toward real maturity. Listen, did you notice the main campfire when you came in?" He nodded, and I went on. "You should find an older lady there by the name of Lizzie. She cooks a great stew, and from what I hear has become quite an accomplished story teller as well. I want you to find her, tell her everything you just told me, then do whatever she tells you."

Hank gave a look of worry at that, but finally took a deep breath and said, "Okay, I guess if I'm going to start a whole new journey today, then I need to get hooked up with a whole new set of friends. I'll do it!"

He left the room, and I whispered a prayer for him. He's got a lot of history to live down, I thought. It might be tough on him farther down the trail. The enemy's going to bear down on him, hard. "Give him strength, Lord," I prayed. "Send him friends and fellow warriors who will carry him through the tough times."

I tell you that in the same way there will be more rejoicing in heaven over one sinner who repents than over ninety-nine righteous persons who do not need to repent.

Luke 15: 7

....

Prayer: Lord, May I know the joy of seeing with my own eyes as a new believer comes to faith. Let me sing with the angels and bear him up on his journey.

Ask yourself: Have you ever seen the look of comprehension come into a person's eyes, and watched as that person prays to receive Christ? How did you feel?

July 15

Stepping Outside

Doctor Artinian came in early today. "So, Friend," he began, "are you ready for a little journey today?"

"I am so ready," I said, throwing the sheets off. "Where are we going?"

"Well, if you're up to it, I'm thinking we might make it all the way to the main campfire."

"Just there?" I asked. "That's not more than thirty steps away. I was thinking more of a hike up to the top of the hill and back."

He just smiled, looked over the top of his bifocals, and said, "Let's see."

I was feeling great. I figured I'd sail past the campfire, wave at the folks on my way to the hilltop, then maybe stop for awhile on the way back, just to be sociable. Then I stood up. The world spun circles around my head, and my knees felt like they were made of modeling clay. Then there was the pain. Every place where the lion had bitten or scratched shouted back at me to be left alone. By the time I reached the doorway leading outside, I was about ready to give it up and turn back for the bed. Then Doctor Artinian pulled the tent flap away, and I felt as though I'd been given a double dose of adrenalin. The whole camp had turn out for the event. Lining a straight pathway, carefully cleared of rocks and twigs, they stood expectantly on both sides, children down front or else hoisted on the shoulders of adults. Waiting by the campfire, I could see Hank, Ralph, Lizzie and my son, smiling brightly. As soon as I took one step outside, a cheer went up. I took another step, and heard shouts of "All right, Friend! You can do it! C'mon!"

No Olympic marathon runner has ever been more supported. Step by faltering step, I covered the distance in record time: at least it was a personal best for me today. When I finally arrived at the campfire, I was offered a chair that someone had brought from the hospital tent and a bowl of Lizzie's stew. Finally, everyone made their way back to whatever activities they were involved in for the day, except for a group of children, Hank and my son, who settled comfortably around the fire. Lizzie stood at one end of the circle, and spoke up in a voice that carried the strength of a tribal warrior.

"Thank you all for coming this morning," she began. In a little while, I'm going to ask our bandaged brother to share a few words with us. But first, I want to tell you a story." Every eye was on her, and there was not a movement in the crowd as she looked off in the distance and began. "It was still dark when they awoke. The tide was out, so the smell of seaweed was especially strong in the air..."

Just as each of us has one body with many members, and these members do not all have the same function, so in Christ we who are many form one body, and each member belongs to all the others.

Romans 12: 4 – 5

Prayer: How precious are the hours spent in fellowship with brothers and sisters in Christ! Praise You, Lord, for the wonderful gift of family, through Your Holy Church.

Ask yourself: How do stories and families go together?

July 16

New Friends

Lizzie arranged the wood on the campfire as the last of the children left to play. Hank and my son straightened up the area, then came back to sit next to me. "That was quite a story you told, Lizzie, " I said. "It's hard to believe my son and I were the main characters in it. I guess when you're in the middle of something it's hard to see the significance."

"Most things in life are like that, Friend," Lizzie said. "It's only by looking back and putting the pieces together that we can start to see the tapestry we're making. That's why I want to be the best storyteller I can be; to help folks see the important things that are happening all around them."

"Dad, Hank and I want to go join that 'Foundations' class today. I hear they teach some great basics."

"Don't let him kid you," Hank broke in. "What he hears is that the class is full of beautiful babes!"

"By all means, go check it out, whatever your motivations. They taught me some lessons I've used nearly every day since." They got up to leave, and I added, "Oh, and guys? Are your boot laces tied?" They both looked down, glanced at each other, then gave a 'gotcha!' laugh as they headed toward the meeting place.

"They think I'm kidding," I said to Lizzie as we watched them go. "Unbelievable, isn't it, that those two wouldn't have had two words to say to each other if they'd met on the trail last week. But looking at them now, you'd think they had been best friends for years."

"I remember the song," Lizzie said, "'Friends are friends forever, if the Lord's the Lord of them'. It's like I was saying about the tapestry: stepping back and seeing the history of an experience or a relationship is what gives it real meaning. And knowing that a friendship is eternal brings us closer, sooner."

I thought of Charlie as she spoke, and the incredible friendship we enjoyed which only lasted a matter of weeks. And there was Lizzie. I caught her eye as she stirred the pot of stew and said, "Friends forever." She smiled.

A man of many companions may come to ruin, but there is a friend who sticks closer than a brother.

Proverbs 18: 24

....

Prayer: I'm reminded today, Lord, that the friends I have in Christ will be with me for all eternity in Your kingdom. Thank you for adding a whole new dimension to the term, "lifelong companions".

Ask yourself: Have you shared the truth of eternal friendship with your own friends?

July 17

Scars

The doctor removed my bandages today, and after a careful examination decided that most of them would not have to be replaced. "That arm is still pretty nasty," he said, "but the scratches are healing nicely. I think we can let them enjoy some fresh air now." He watched as I felt carefully over the ridges tracing furrows over my upper body, then added, "Of course, those scars will remain, I'm afraid. There's not much I can do about them."

"Well, I won't be entering any beauty contests, that's for sure. But you know what, Doc? I kind of like them." He raised an eyebrow, and I went on. "Someone said that scars are tattoos with more interesting stories. And I guess these things will give me enough to talk about for a lifetime."

He thought about that for a moment, then said, "Yeah, I guess you're right. By the way, have you seen this baby?" He pointed to a four inch scar running along the top of his left hand. "I got that during a surgical procedure I was performing. It was quite a case, really. The guy was suffering from a rather rare form of... well, it's a big medical term, but anyway, I had just begun my incision when he had a spasm, striking my hand with his shoulder. Well, I can tell you that..."

I listened for the next thirty minutes as the Doc told me the history of his scar, and I thought to myself, this is what the tapestry is made of, isn't it? We all have experiences along the way, and in the process we often have scars to show for them. And what better way to make the history come alive than through the recounting of our scars.

I remembered Jacob and his memorable night of wrestling with an angel. It was a time I'm sure *he* never forgot, and I'm sure he spent many hours telling the story of how he got his limp. "It really happened!" he would have insisted. "And here's the scar to prove it!"

What a sad thing, I thought, to complete the journey of a lifetime totally unscathed and with nothing to tell. "Great story, Doc," I said when he had finished. "Have you got any more?"

So Jacob called the place Peniel, saying, "It is because I saw God face to face, and yet my life was spared." The sun rose above him as he passed Peniel, and he was limping because of his hip.

Genesis 32: 30 – 31

Prayer: As I consider my body, I can see scars and remember events which resulted in them. Thank you for these memories, and for the things which I have learned through the experience. May my scars be a beacon to others of Your love and care.

Ask yourself: What scars do you have? Have you told their stories to others?

July 18

A Fellow Patient

I was awakened early this morning by the sounds of crying in the next room. It sounded like a child, and he was obviously in pain. I started to pull myself out of bed and see if I could help, but then I heard the soothing sounds of the doctor and the nurse as they ministered to him. It finally grew quiet, and a short while later, Nurse "We" came into my room with breakfast. "Sorry we're a little late this morning," she said. We've been quite busy."

"I thought I heard a child crying," I said. "I hope it's nothing serious."

"No, we were just playing in a tree and fell out. Looks like we have a broken collar bone, but it will mend nicely, I'm sure. I hope you won't mind having a fellow patient with you today." After he had been properly set up with a cast, my new room mate was wheeled in and placed in a bed next to mine. He was still whimpering, and from the look on his face, I could tell that he wanted to be anywhere but here.

"Hi there," I said after the nurse had left. "Does it hurt a lot?"

"Yes." He said, obviously trying to be brave, but losing the battle.

"I've never had a broken collar bone," I said. "You'll have to tell me all about it when you can."

"I hate it," he said with as much anger in his voice as he could muster. "Dad and I were going to go fishing this afternoon. Now I can't go anywhere."

"Where's your dad now?" I asked, wondering why he hadn't been in to see his son.

"He's out with the firewood crew. He doesn't even know about this yet."

"And what about Mom?" I hesitated to ask.

"She died. When I was a baby." We talked for another hour or more, until I could see that the medicine he'd been given was making him drowsy. As he drifted off to sleep, I thought about my new friend, and marveled at the fact that even though we had so little in common, we were already "brothers in pain." In the months to come, that term would be recalled in situations I could never have foreseen.

Not only so, but we also rejoice in our sufferings, because we know that suffering produces perseverance; perseverance, character; and character, hope.

Romans 5: 3 – 4

....

Prayer: Lord, You know that I will try to avoid pain at all costs. And yet I recognize that some of my most significant friendships have come about because of shared pain. So while I continue to ask for protection from hurt, please use the suffering I must endure for the tapestry of life.

Ask yourself: How has pain and suffering enhanced your relationships with your friends?

July 19

A Father's Pain

The boy's father came in just after lunchtime. We had improvised a couple of fishing poles from tongue depressors and tape, and were trying our hand at casting off the end of our beds. Between his broken collar bone and my mangled arm we weren't having much success.

"Jason!" the father said as he practically ran into the room. "I just found out about your accident. How are you feeling, son?"

"Better," he conceded. "My friend and I are fishing for crocodiles."

"It looks like your friend caught one already," he said as he looked over my scars. Then he remembered. "Hey, you're the one who tackled the lion, right? My son and I just came into camp yesterday, but everyone's talking about you."

I started to answer, but his attention turned quickly back to his son. "Are you sure you're okay, Jason? I'm really sorry I wasn't here." He sat on the edge of the bed and held his son's hand as he spoke. I noticed that his other hand had moved unconsciously up to his own shoulder as if feeling the pain himself. He stayed through most of the afternoon, only leaving when the nurse insisted that we both needed rest. As he backed out the doorway, blowing Jason a kiss as he left, I couldn't help but see that here was a father who truly hurt for his son. The pain in his eyes spoke volumes.

What a wonder, that a parent can be so tuned with their children's feelings that they can actually suffer with the same intensity. What a wonder, that God has given us this model in the life of His own Son, Jesus Christ.

He himself bore our sins in his body on the tree, so that we might die to sins and live for righteousness; by his wounds you have been healed.

I Peter 2: 24

....

Prayer: As a parent suffers for his child, so You Father have suffered for me. How precious a gift, that we might know a glimpse of this love through our own experiences as parents and as children. Praise You Lord.

Ask yourself: Have you ever known someone who actually suffered physical pain at the sight of their injured or sick child?

Nurse "We"

Jason left the hospital today, bundled in the strong arms of his father. They thanked me for our new found friendship and promised to come back and visit. After they left, I felt a tinge of self-pity, wishing that it was I who was leaving with a loved one. Nurse "We" came in awhile later to clean up his bed. As I watched the professional way she accomplished each task, I was impressed with her ability to serve day after day, ministering to people in pain.

"I need to ask you a question," I said at last.

"Yes? What is it?"

"What's your real name?"

She looked uncomfortable, and turned back to her bed making as she answered. "Everyone just calls me 'Nurse;' which I suppose is sufficient."

"Well, not exactly," I confessed. "Actually, a few of us refer to you as 'Nurse We'" She straightened up at that and gave me a quizzical look. "Shall we think about that for awhile?" I said with a smile. Her face remained blank for a few moments, and then my meaning became clear.

She went back to fluffing a pillow, then said, "My name has never seemed that important. I am what I *do*, and what I do is care for people."

"But what would happen if suddenly you couldn't be a nurse anymore? Where would your identity be?"

"I can't imagine that ever happening," she said. But I could tell that the possibility was running through her mind.

"You see people here everyday who have encountered what they didn't expect. Jason thought he was going fishing with his father, but ended up spending the day with me. Now, I may be prying too much into your personal business, but I'm beginning to learn that we're all family here. It's becoming more and more clear to me lately, that what we *are* is not necessarily what we *do*. We do all kinds of things, but they can change. What doesn't change is what we *are*, and in our case, we're children of a loving God. And just like the stars in the sky, He knows each of us and calls us by name, not by job description. Anyway, forgive me if I was too personal. I was just wondering."

She went on about her work in silence, and for awhile I thought I had really offended her. But then she started out the door, paused, turned to face me and said, "It's Jennifer."

The watchman opens the gate for him, and the sheep listen to his voice. He calls his own sheep by name and leads them out.

John 10: 3

Prayer: Praise You Father, for You know my name! Call to me today, and help me to hear You, and obey.

Ask yourself: What's so important about having a name?

July 21

Growing

Hank and my son came to see me today, grinning from ear to ear. As if on cue, they stepped up to the side of the bed and propped one foot each up on top of the sheets for my inspection. What I saw were two well-oiled boots, perfectly laced.

"Hey congratulations!" I said. "It looks like you've passed your Foundations class with flying colors. I can honestly say I've never seen two more beautiful boots."

"That class was *great*, Dad. We learned all about packing our gear, selecting a campsite, building a fire..."

"And get this," Hank interrupted: "we even know the difference between magnetic north and true north!"

"That's a good thing to know," I said. "Even a small difference in direction can *make a huge difference in destination...*" I didn't have to finish the last part of the maxim, since the two boys joined in and said it with me.

"Speaking of destinations," my son continued, "the class is planning to head over to a lake nearby and try out our skills." This brought a burst of barely suppressed laughter from Hank, until my son confessed. "Well, it's not exactly the whole class. It's Patricia and Heather. We were just kind of thinking it might be nice to go have a picnic there; maybe do some fishing, you know."

"Go ahead, boys," I said. Just be back before dark. And be gentlemen."

Watching them bound out the door, slapping one another on the back and talking excitedly about the day ahead, I had to marvel at the process I was observing. Both of them had already faced a world of challenges without sufficient training, and the result had been a time of misery for both of them. Now they were finally getting the training they needed, and I found myself praying that they would never need it. If only we could remain as children. But then I remembered that the world, broken as it is, will always be a place of danger, and no respecter of age. Much better then, to face it with all the maturity and strength I can find.

I gave you milk, not solid food, for you were not yet ready for it. Indeed, you are still not ready.

I Corinthians 3: 2

Prayer: Dear God, I confess that I am still a child in this world. There is so much to learn, so much I should know and be prepared for. Guide me today through the paths You have for me: paths that will teach me and lead me to wisdom. For Your Name's sake, I pray.

Ask yourself: When did you last feet immature?

July 22

Discharged

Doctor Artinian came in today with great news: my wounds were healed sufficiently enough that I could leave the hospital. "I still want to see you every couple of days for awhile," he cautioned. "The infection seems to be all cleared up, but it could come back. And you've had some serious ligament damage to that left arm. We need to make sure your physical therapy stays on track."

Even though I was only moving across the clearing to the main sleeping tent, this felt like a major shift. My gear had already been packed up and transferred over. I had a supply of medicine in one hand, and a cane in the other. Give me a week, I thought to myself, and I won't need either.

Nurse Jennifer offered to help me out, but I insisted on trying it alone. "Thank you, Jennifer," I said. "You're the best nurse a guy could have." She fiddled with the pencil still stuck precariously in her graying head of hair and said, "Thank *you*, Friend. I'll remember what you said."

The walk across the clearing was not quite as dramatic as the first time, when I had been cheered on by the entire camp. I had been outside on a few occasions since then, and people had gotten used to seeing me hobble back and forth. For me, however, it was the most exciting thing that had happened in a long while. I reached the doorway leading into the sleeping tent out of breath from the exertion, leaned on a tent pole and looked inside. Everyone had left for the day, involved in various activities, but it was easy to see where my bed was located. Close to the door, easy to reach, and surrounded by flowers, it was a welcome sight indeed.

I sat down gingerly on top of my sleeping bag, which had been laid out with great care. I wondered who had gone to so much trouble for me. My question was answered the next moment, as a small head peered around the doorway. "Is it okay?" he asked.

"Jason! You mean the bed? It's wonderful! Did you do all this by yourself?"

He came inside, one arm in a sling. "Well, I had some help from my dad. Oh, and I'm supposed to ask if you'd come to dinner tonight. We're having fish!"

Praise the LORD, O my soul; all my inmost being, praise his holy name. Praise the LORD, O my soul, and forget not all his benefits— who forgives all your sins and heals all your diseases, who redeems your life from the pit and crowns you with love and compassion, who satisfies your desires with good things so that your youth is renewed like the eagle's.

Psalms 103: 1 – 5

....

Prayer: Lord, in times of sickness, it seems like I will never be whole again; but praise You for Your mercy and power! You take what is sick and make it well; You take what is injured and make it whole again. Praise you Oh God.

Ask yourself: Can you recall an illness or an injury for which there is no evidence left?

Fish Dinner

Jason came to lead me to where he and his father were camped, down near the river. It was a pretty far walk, but having him to lean on made it easier. Even with a broken collar bone, he was able to offer me his good side from time to time. As we approached the camp, the smell of fish baking over hot coals was enough to spur me on with an extra boost of energy. Jason's dad was arranging the fire as we arrived, and he stood up to greet me.

"Welcome to our home away from home," he said with a smile. "I need to apologize for not talking with you much the other day at the hospital. It's just that I was worried about Jason, and well, anyway, my name's Stewart."

"No apologies necessary," I said. "I'm a father myself. I think I have an idea of what you were going through. Hey Jason," I called out, "did you catch these fish?"

"Yep," he said, coming back from the river where he had been washing up. Then he corrected himself, "Well, some of them. My dad caught some, too." We talked about bait, and fishing gear, and the best places in the area. Finally, the fish was served up with great fanfare.

The camp grew dark as we enjoyed a cup of coffee. I said, "Jason tells me that his mother died when he was a baby."

"It was just this last year," Stewart said quietly. "I think he's trying to deal with his grief by making it sound like a long time ago. Actually, it's because of the grief that Jason and I are on this trip. She had tried all of her life to get me to read her Bible. I kept putting it off. Then she got sick. One day, just before she died, she said, 'Stewart, I want to see you again. *Please* read it.' I sat down that night and opened it up. I never had a chance to tell her that it changed my life. I hope I get the chance, someday."

I leaned over and placed a hand on his shoulder. "You will, Stewart. I guarantee it."

Jabez cried out to the God of Israel, "Oh, that you would bless me and enlarge my territory! Let your hand be with me, and keep me from harm so that I will be free from pain." And God granted his request.

I Chronicles 4: 10

....

Prayer: I grieve over those who have gone before, and I pray that in Your mercy, we will be re-united again at Your feet. I pray for those loved ones who have not yet accepted Your offering of salvation. Rescue them, I pray, before it's too late.

Ask yourself: What are you doing to make sure your loved ones will be re-united in God's kingdom?

July 24

The Living Loved One

Stewart was visibly relieved when I encouraged him that he would see his wife again in God's kingdom. "That's the only thing that keeps me going," he said at last. "That, and seeing Jason's face each morning." We sat in silence awhile, then he spoke up. "I've met your son, but I haven't come across your wife. Is she around?"

The question re-opened a wound in my heart. "She's still at home," I answered. "And a daughter, too. They just couldn't understand my decision. I pray for them every day. My son joined me a few weeks ago, so I know there's hope. It tears my heart out, though, to look at all I've learned on this trip, and to have such a joy on one hand, but then realize they're still at home, confused. I just wish... I wish there was some way I could let them see things through my eyes, just for one day. I know they'd come around. They're good people, both of them. They just... don't know."

Stewart thought awhile, then said, "I don't think God will condemn a person for not knowing. From all the things I've studied, I believe He's just, and loving. I believe He does everything short of Divine force to make sure every one of His creation understands what the offer is. If people refuse it, it's because they honestly want no part of Him. From what you've told me, I believe your wife and daughter will come to Him, once they realize Who He really is. Until then, we'll just pray for them, okay?"

And we did.

For since the creation of the world God's invisible qualities—his eternal power and divine nature—have been clearly seen, being understood from what has been made, so that men are without excuse.

Romans 1: 20

Prayer: Lord I know we are without excuse; You have shown us Your glory and love through the things You have made. May that reality be burned into the hearts of my loved ones today. May they find no rest until they rest in You.

Ask yourself: Why do you suppose that every culture in the world has a system of worship?

Exercise

The rest of the bandages were removed from my arms, and I could see that I had a lot of work to do. The muscles which had gone unused for a month now had been reduced to almost half their original size. I had never gone in much for weight lifting, but I could tell right away that what strength I might have had a few weeks ago was now a thing of the past. As if that were not bad enough, the ligament damage had affected my range of motion, so that now it was extremely difficult or impossible to do things which I had taken for granted, like raising a sword over my head, or scratching my back. The doctor was encouraging, however. "Keep up the physical therapy," he said when I complained. "The miraculous thing about muscles is that they never lose the ability to develop."

"Oh yeah?" I asked. "Then why don't we ever see any 80 year old body builders?"

"Actually there are a few around," he said, then added, "and I dare say any of them could beat you in a bench press today. But what usually happens are unrelated disease or injury that cause our senior community to lose physical strength. Whatever it happens to be, don't blame the muscles."

I set to work on small tasks, like stretching. Then I found some smooth stones in the river and tried lifting them in repetitive patterns. At first, I had to go back to the river for smaller rocks, but eventually was able to increase the weight.

As I crawled into bed tonight, my newly awakened muscles screaming for mercy, I thought about what the Doc had said. Muscles never lose the ability to develop. All they need is exercise. One thing I'm learning on this trip is the fact that the world is full of "truth models". Everywhere I look, I see spiritual truth demonstrated, whether it be in the miracle of a flower, the mystery of a shell, or the awesome power of a single atom. The truth of my situation today is this: whatever I stop using, be it good or bad, is going to diminish in importance. That's worth thinking about.

Everyone who competes in the games goes into strict training. They do it to get a crown that will not last; but we do it to get a crown that will last forever.

I Corinthians 9: 25

Prayer: Lord show my today what I need to develop, and what I need to put away. Help me train those things which need strengthening, and deny those things which are doing me harm.

Ask yourself: What in your life needs to be stronger? What needs to be eliminated?

July 26

The Man of God

I was going through my physical therapy routines this morning when a lone figure came into view, coming down the trail into the valley. As he got closer, the first thing that struck me was his lack of gear. He had only a small backpack, and it looked as though it wasn't carrying much. Even from a distance, I could see that he was a man with a purpose. His stride was long, and his head was held high. He seemed to know where he was going, and that impression made me want to speak to him. As if reading my mind, he looked my way as he approached. A smile broke onto his face and he called out from a distance, "Good morning to you! Are you part of this company?"

"I suppose I am," I replied. "People call me 'Friend'."

"Then 'Friend' it shall be. From the looks of you, however, I would guess that not everyone has been so inclined." My shirt was off while I was exercising, and I reached for it. "No, don't be ashamed of those scars, Friend. They look to be that of a lion, and I'm wondering if the carcass I came across the day before yesterday had anything to do with these?"

"My son killed it," I explained. "It was traveling with... do you know anything about the evil man?"

He smiled and laid a hand on my shoulder. A kind of strength seemed to flow through his arms. "The evil man and I have been adversaries for many years now. I've devoted my life to helping pilgrims like you stand up against his wickedness. Tell me, Friend, who could I speak to about staying for awhile here at Rendezvous?"

And how can they preach unless they are sent? As it is written, "How beautiful are the feet of those who bring good news!"

Romans 10: 15

....

Prayer: Thank you Father for calling men and women to the work of ministry. Strengthen them for the task before them. Protect them from the evil one, and use their efforts for the glory of Your kingdom.

Ask yourself: Has a minister ever been of any help to you?

A Holy Calling

I took the newcomer down to meet with Lizzie at the main campfire. She looked up from her stew, saw us and cried out, "Pastor McAllan! It's so good to see you again!"

"I guess I don't have to introduce you then," I said, watching as they greeted one another like long lost relatives.

"Oh no," said Lizzie. "Pastor McAllan has been in and out of our lives for a long time. But we don't get to see you nearly as often as we'd like. Where have you been, Pastor?"

"Mostly around the mountain," he said. Then his voice grew softer. "There's a lot of people hurting up there, Lizzie. It just breaks your heart. I stayed for as long as I could, but well, it seemed that now I should be down here among you folks for awhile." He rubbed his hands together as he looked into Lizzie's stew pot. "My, my; don't tell me that's your famous Rendezvous stew."

"Pull up a seat and sit a spell," said Lizzie as she reached for an empty bowl. "We'll get you settled after you've had a chance to catch your breath."

"I notice you're not carrying much," I said. "Did you lose your gear along the way?"

"Let me answer that one," said Lizzie as the newcomer took a bite of the stew. "Pastor McAllan is a man of God. He spends his life moving along this trail, helping folks where he can, rescuing some of us when we lose our way. In return, we make sure that he has all he needs. We share our food with him, and our bedding and anything else that we can do. It's a hard calling he's taken on; it's the least we can do to help make it as easy as we can."

Pastor McAllan reached into the small backpack that now rested between his feet. "This is the only burden I carry, Friend." He pulled out a large book that I immediately recognized as a well worn Bible. "But you know, it's surprisingly light."

For the Scripture says, "'Do not muzzle the ox while it is treading out the grain', and 'The worker deserves his wages.'"

I Timothy 5: 18

....

Prayer: Today I lift up the name of a pastor I know. Bless him, Father. Encourage him through this day, and may he know that he has been under your watch care. Give him all he needs, and more.

Ask yourself: What do you think the Bible verse above means when it says not to "muzzle the ox who treads the grain"?

More About the Mountain

As I watched Pastor McAllan eat, I thought about what he had told Lizzie about being "around the mountain." Could he be talking about the same one I had seen my second day out on the trail?

"Pastor," I began. "You talked about a mountain. I came around one awhile back. I had thought that the trail would go over it, but someone told me that it's only for a few..."

"Would that have been Jacob?" he asked. When he saw my face beaming, he continued, "Jake and I have met on a couple of occasions, just when I needed him most. You're a blessed man to have seen him."

"But I don't understand about the mountain," I said. "If the trail is there, why doesn't everyone travel it?"

"Because that path is by invitation only. Not everyone is called to travel it. It can change a person's life forever. It can take your life."

"Have you been up the mountain?" I asked.

"Once, when I was young. It was the most wonderful, most terrible experience I've ever had. I was called to this ministry while I stood at the top. I'd like to tell you more about it, but we need to get to know one another better before I can do that. And speaking of getting to know one another: Lizzie, tell me about the camp. Who's here that I don't know?"

So the discussion about the mountain had ended, and I was left wanting to know more. But at the same time, I had begun to feel a little uneasy about it. What did he mean by "the most terrible experience"?

Jesus replied, "Not everyone can accept this word, but only those to whom it has been given."

Matthew 19: 11

....

Prayer: Lord, I know that we all have a path which is set before us. May I be faithful in following the one You have given me. May I not be judgmental or envious of the way others have gone, but instead may I rejoice in my own journey.

Ask yourself: Do you believe the Christian life should be difficult and challenging in order to be genuine?

July 29

An Impromptu Gathering

Word quickly spread that Pastor McAllan was in camp. First by twos and threes, then whole groups would come to see him, remaining in the area while he spoke with each one. I was amazed at his ability to remember names and faces.

"Hello David! How's the knee? It's good to see your sister over there. Is she getting on okay? Ralph! Look at you, leading a battle class. Yeah I heard about Jonathan; we're gonna miss him." He kept moving around the crowd, greeting old friends, introducing himself to new ones. When he came close to where my son and Hank were standing, he stopped and everyone grew silent. "Your name is…"

"Hank," the young man answered. "I remember you. You came through my camp one night. I tried to talk to you, but you kept going."

"And when you got up the next morning, you were missing some food. I'm sorry, Pastor. I was so stupid. I hope I can make it up to you."

"Just seeing you here is reward enough. Judging from your face, I'd say you've made some pretty important discoveries here, haven't you?"

"I'm a new person, that's for sure. Let me introduce you to someone. Pastor, this is my friend, the lion slayer!"

From that point, the conversation took a whole new turn. But I had heard enough to know that this was truly a man of God. I wanted to be just like him.

"You are the light of the world. A city on a hill cannot be hidden.

Matthew 5: 14

....

Prayer: It's scary, to think that people watch me, and make life decisions based upon what they see in me. Lord May I always be a reflection of Your Son. May those who see me look beyond my weakness and see only Your strength.

Ask yourself: Who do you think has observed you in the past week? Do you think they will make any decisions based on what they saw in you?

July 30

Tent Meeting

Pastor McAllan was finally led off to a place where he could rest, but I knew it wouldn't be for long. I noticed people carrying boxes of supplies out of the storage tent while others carried in chairs to set up. Soon the faint sound of music was drifting out of the tent, as an impromptu team of singers started preparing. I asked Lizzie what I could do, and was immediately set to the task of improvising some kind of lighting. In the meantime, she put the word out around the camp that a potluck dinner was scheduled for the evening. Everyone was to bring whatever they could to a central table near the main campfire. As the afternoon wore on, I watched as the table began to groan under the weight of hams, chickens, vegetables, salads and pies.

The sun was setting as the camp began to gather. Children came dressed in their finest, and the women somehow seemed transformed. How did they manage to look so stunning? Even the men combed their hair for the occasion. From somewhere in the middle of the gathering crowd, Pastor McAllan appeared, obviously standing on something. "Brothers and sisters!" he called out. "It's so good to see you here tonight. I pray that we will all leave this place knowing that we've been in His Presence."

An "Amen" or two was heard, the pastor led us in a prayer of thanksgiving, and thoughts turned to food and fellowship. Everyone was eating, talking, laughing and being family together. Finally, the crowd began to make their way into the tent, finding seats wherever they could, or standing along the back. The music team broke into a song and soon everyone was standing and singing together. Some of the older children had moved to the front where they see better, and I noticed that they were dancing in front of the raised platform, a look of sheer joy on their faces.

How could I have missed this for so many years, I thought. Where else can a person find such unconditional love and pure joy? If this is a glimpse of what Heaven is going to be like, bring it on!

> *Then I heard every creature in heaven and on earth and under the earth and on the sea, and all that is in them, singing: "To him who sits on the throne and to the Lamb be praise and honor and glory and power, for ever and ever!"*
>
> Revelation 5: 13

Prayer: Lead us as we worship together, Lord. Show us what is good, and appropriate and pleasing to You. May our music, our fellowship and all that we do in Your Name bring honor and glory to You. In Jesus' Name.

Ask yourself: What do you think is the main goal of worship?

Testimony Time

We sang for what must have been a long time, but no one took notice. The joy of celebration and worship was evident all around us, and there wasn't a single complaint to be heard. Eventually, the music moved from noisy and loud to soft and meditative. My heart also was carried from the heights of praise to still, sweet moments of thanksgiving. No one was surprised when a young lady stepped to the platform and spoke up.

"Before I came on this trip, my life was headed nowhere. Days came and went. Friends came and went. Finally, I looked back over my life and said to myself, 'Just where have you been, and where do you think you'll end up?"

She sat down, and Hank stepped up. "I knew where I was headed," he said softly. "And I thought it was a place I wanted to go. All my friends were going there, and that seemed to make it right. But then one night I saw myself for who I really was: a selfish, uncaring thief. I could have helped someone, a few weeks ago, but I didn't. Jesus broke through my heart that night, and I knew at once that I didn't want to be that way; not anymore. But the problem was, I didn't know what to do about it. I finally had to... to..." Hank tried to finish, but his emotions took over and left him crying uncontrollably. I slipped to the front, stepped up beside him and put my arm around him.

"What he had to do," I said, "was what each and every one of us has had to do: to strip away all the stuff we put around ourselves and come clean with God. Hank has done that, I'm proud to call him my brother."

He smiled at me, gave me a hug, and everyone in the tent broke into applause. The applause led to another song, and we stepped off the platform to where my son was waiting. Hank looked at both of us and said, "Thanks, guys."

My son gave him a slap on the back and said, "Right; now let's thank the One Who made it all possible." We turned back to the front and joined in the singing. Thank You, God.

But in your hearts set apart Christ as Lord. Always be prepared to give an answer to everyone who asks you to give the reason for the hope that you have. But do this with gentleness and respect.

I Peter 3: 15

....

Prayer: It is only by Your forgiveness, Father, that I can know what being in a real Christian family is all about. Thank you because You forgave me. Thank you that I can forgive those who have wronged me. Thank you that we can worship You together as brothers and sisters.

Ask yourself: Is there anyone in your life that needs your forgiveness?

August 1

The Pastor Speaks

When things got quiet again, Pastor McAllan stepped to the front. He looked around the gathering, at all the expectant faces. Finally, he spoke:

"It always moves my very soul, to be at a place like this and realize that I'm only an observer. God is at work in our midst tonight. He's working in your heart, and He's working in mine. And I can see His face just now, as He brings forgiveness into a young life. Then he turns and rekindles a love that's grown cold in someone's heart. He reaches across and heals someone who's been suffering for a long time. His eyes meet mine as I wait to see what he's going to do next, and I see a gleam in his eyes: an excitement that is there because He knows every heart He touches tonight, and He loves each one. And then He says to me, "Watch this.""

"There's power in this room tonight," the Pastor went on, his voice filled with awe. "The enemy knows nothing of this kind of power. He got a taste of it a short while ago when some of his subjects tried to break into this camp." That brought some hearty "Amens" and a few chuckles of laughter. The Pastor said, "I wish I'd been here to see it. That power is still here, brothers and sisters. This church is God's church, and the Bible says that the gates of Hell itself will not stand against it. Do you see what it's saying there? Did you think that the enemy is going to take down Hell's gate and come try to break in here, using it as a battering ram? No! This tells us that it's the *Church* which is going to do the battering. We're going to move forward, right into the land which the enemy has claimed, and we're going to re-claim it for God. And the devil is going to back away. Why? Because he's already been defeated at Calvary, and he knows it!"

The message went on, but I was inspired already. The pastor's words of encouragement and power had found a place deep in my heart. I was more convinced than ever that God was calling me into His service. I didn't know what that service might be, but right then it didn't matter. All I wanted was to stand up and say like Isaiah, "Here am I! Send me!"

Then I heard the voice of the Lord saying, "Whom shall I send? And who will go for us?" And I said, "Here am I. Send me!"

Isaiah 6: 8

....

Prayer: I'm reminded today, Father, that you are not an absentee landlord. You did not just create the world and then step away to see what happens. You are here now, working in lives all around me. Work in my own life, I pray. Call me to Your side. Use me for Your glory.

Ask yourself: What kinds of things might God call you to do?

Confirmation

The service went on into the night. After Pastor McAllan finished speaking, we sang some more, then there was a time when people would come to the front and pray for specific things. Some prayed for family, some for healing, some for courage. For me, it was all of the above. My heart was bleeding for my wife and daughter, who had never known what my son and I were experiencing tonight. As I knelt, I was painfully aware of my wounds, which were healing slowly. I asked God to touch them and make me whole again physically. But most of all, I asked for courage. I was more convinced than ever of God's call for me to minister in His Name. I looked back on my journey to this point, and the most fulfilling, satisfying moments had been when I was sharing my faith with someone along the way. Is that a valid reason to enter into a full time ministry? I wasn't sure, but I intended to find out.

I waited until Pastor McAllan was finished praying with a young lady nearby, then stepped up to him. "Pastor," I said, "I believe God may be calling me into full time service for Him. How can I be certain that it's really Him, and not just my own desire?"

He looked deep into my eyes, then said, "One way is to share your thoughts with fellow pilgrims, like you're doing now. If God is indeed calling you, then He will make that evident to those around you. We talk about people like these here tonight as being part of the Body of Christ. That means that no one stands alone. We support each other; we hurt for each other; we rejoice with each other. And in times of decision, we confirm each other." He paused a moment, then put his arm around my shoulder and led me to a secluded part of the tent. "When I first saw you this morning, God spoke to me. I wasn't sure exactly what He was saying, but I knew that it concerned you. I'm still not sure, but I will promise you this: I will pray about it tonight, and as soon as I have a Word from Him, I'll share it with you."

We prayed together, and I made my way back to my bed for what remained of the night. But sleep was far from coming. What was God saying to me? Was I to serve Him like Pastor McAllan was doing? My sleep was uncertain, but exciting.

Before I formed you in the womb I knew you, before you were born I set you apart; I appointed you as a prophet to the nations.

Jeremiah 1: 5

....

Prayer: Surround me with the people of Your Church, oh Lord. May they encourage me and reprove me when I need it. May I be for them what they are for me.

Ask yourself: Where would you go if you had an important decision to make?

August 3

Sharing the Decision

I thought it would be hard to get out of bed this morning, but my excitement drove me up and out with the first light. Apparently, I wasn't the only one blessed by the meeting last night: Lizzie, Hank and my son were already sitting around the campfire, coffee in hand, speaking in low tones.

"Couldn't sleep either?" I asked as I made my way to the empty cups.

"Dad," my son started, "last night was just... incredible! I've never enjoyed anything so much in my life. And as we were singing, I felt... no, I *knew* God was right there with us. It was like, all those doubts I used to have just melted away."

Hank picked where my son left off. "If you had told me a month ago that I'd be standing before a crowd of people and crying like a baby, I probably would have knifed you as a liar. But somehow, last night, it was okay. It's like I was really honest for the first time in my life. By the way, thanks for coming to my rescue!"

"Don't mention it," I smiled over my coffee cup. "In fact, I want you guys to hear something that I haven't told anyone except Pastor McAllan." All three unconsciously leaned toward me in anticipation. "I think God may be calling me into full time ministry." A chorus of "All right!" and "Way to go!" broke the stillness of the camp. Then Lizzie spoke up.

"I never doubted it from the first time I ever saw you," she said. It's easy to see the pastor's heart in you. That's why Charlie was so drawn to you. He knew that God had something very special in store for you. I never said anything, because something like this has to come from God, and not from people. But now that you've shared this with us, let me say I'm very happy. And I pray that God will use you in mighty ways."

We sat around the fire for another hour or so, while the rest of the camp came to life. Here was the affirmation I had been hoping for: my son, his friend and my mentor all in agreement that God was calling me into special service. Now if I only knew what it was...

But you, keep your head in all situations, endure hardship, do the work of an evangelist, discharge all the duties of your ministry.

II Timothy 4: 5

....

Prayer: Thank you for this great mystery: that You have chosen us for the work of Your Kingdom.

Ask yourself: What "works of service" can you think of which would bring glory to God's Kingdom?

A Word From God

Breakfast was finished, and everyone was going to their respective duties for the day. I had decided to get straight to work on my physical therapy. Was it my imagination, or had the wounds on my arm improved dramatically overnight?

"Good morning, Friend," Pastor McAllan greeted me as he came up to the campfire.

"Pastor! It's good to see you. Thanks again for a wonderful experience last night."

Pastor McAllan poured himself a cup of coffee as he spoke. "You know, I promised you last night that I would tell you if I had a word from God about your decision." I stopped what I was doing and straightened up. "I'd like to take a walk with you, if you have time."

We left our gear around the fire, and with a cup of coffee each walked out of the camp and into a meadow nearby. The morning was crisp and peaceful, but my heart was racing in anticipation. "So tell me, Pastor, what do you think about my decision to go into full time ministry?"

Pastor McAllan took a long sip of coffee, then turned to me. "The decision is the right one; no doubt about that. God is going to use you in mighty ways." He paused, and looked out over the meadow. "You know, to be used by God is the greatest privilege a man or a woman can receive. It's like no other calling in the world. But I have to be honest with you: it's not always pleasant. We have no guarantee that our lives will be trouble free and painless. On the contrary, a person who serves God openly is often the first to fall when the battles come."

"Are you trying to say that God showed you something else about me last night?"

"Not exactly, Friend. I'm not like a prophet who can see into the future. It's just that, as I was praying for you, I sensed God telling me to prepare you for more suffering."

I gave a nervous laugh and said, "What could be worse than being mauled by a lion?"

Pastor McAllan stood silent for a moment, then said, "Let's pray together, shall we?"

For it has been granted to you on behalf of Christ not only to believe on him, but also to suffer for him, since you are going through the same struggle you saw I had, and now hear that I still have.

Philippians 1: 29 – 30

....

Prayer: Father, I look back over the history of Your Church and see so many who have suffered and died for their faith. I can't say honestly that I want to join them, but I do ask for strength to endure whatever I must. For Your kingdom's glory.

Ask yourself: Are there things worth dying for?

August 5

Commitment

As Pastor McAllan and I prayed together in the middle of the meadow, my thoughts were conflicted. On the one hand, I felt a wonderful joy at knowing that my decision to go into full time ministry had been confirmed. At the same time, though, I was troubled by the pastor's warning that I was to prepare for more suffering. Was this a definite prediction of things to come, or simply a way to get my guard up and so that I could avoid coming problems? Was the suffering he spoke of a direct result of my decision to enter the ministry? And if it was, then did I have the option to change my mind: ignore the calling and thereby avoid the suffering?

I tried to imagine worst case scenarios. Let's say another of those big demons from hell comes at me with a sword. Only this time I'm defenseless. Would I be willing to stand there and take whatever he gives me if it meant that I would honor God by doing so? That sounded like a tough one, but then I started considering the alternative. The demon comes at me. I say, "Hey, I'm not the guy you're looking for. I'm just minding my own business." He stops and goes away. I'm left unhurt, but with a lifetime of regret that I denied God. Which form of suffering is worse?

It was really no contest in the end. I knew that I could not and would not step back from what I knew God wanted me to do. If He chooses to send me into battle with a toothpick, then so be it. I'm His man.

Pastor McAllan and I finished praying and started back into camp. I felt good about the morning. My decision had been made, confirmed, and now I was dedicated to seeing it through. It was a great moment.

The moment quickly passed when Hank came running out to meet us on the meadow. He was breathing hard, and looked frightened. He stood in front of us for a moment, then said, "It's your son."

> *Do not be afraid of what you are about to suffer. I tell you, the devil will put some of you in prison to test you, and you will suffer persecution for ten days. Be faithful, even to the point of death, and I will give you the crown of life.*
> Revelation 2: 10

....

Prayer: How much do I love you, Lord? The question tortures me sometimes, when I think that there may be a place where my love is shown to be wanting. But I rest in the comfort that there is no such place in You. Praise You for Your perfect love.

Ask yourself: Which is more difficult: to suffer personally or to watch a loved one suffer?

Real Fear

Pastor McAllan and I ran back to the camp, looking for my son. It wasn't hard to find him, since a large crowd had gathered around the hospital tent. I pushed my way inside and was met by a nurse. "The doctor's with him now. He's collapsed. Please wait here; as soon as we know anything, we'll be right out."

The pastor and I sat together, his arm around my shoulder. "Take courage, Friend. God is with him. And with you."

We waited for what seemed like an eternity, but was probably less than an hour. Finally, Dr. Artinian came out to meet us. Before I could say anything, he started talking. "Your son had a mild seizure. He's okay now. You can go in and speak with him. I still don't know what caused it, however. We'll have to do more tests."

I didn't wait for more, but rushed past the doctor into the room where my son lay. It was the same bed that had recently been my home. "Son," I said, putting a hand on his forehead. "How are you feeling?"

"Like a truck ran over me. What happened? The last thing I remember, I was going through some sword drills with Hank. Then... I was here. Did something hit me?"

"The doc said you had a seizure. They're running tests now, but you'll be okay." I cringed at that, wondering if I had just told my son a lie. He seemed to relax a bit.

"That's cool," he said, closing his eyes. "I'm just really tired right now. I think I'll sleep awhile."

"You do that, son. You do that." I stroked his hair a few more moments, then turned to see the doctor again. He was waiting outside the door. I could tell he had dealt with anxious parents before, and was ready with the answers to questions I hadn't been able to put into words yet.

"Seizures like this can be caused by any number of things. I've got blood samples testing now. Let's not jump to conclusions until we know more. We'll take good care of him. In the meantime, you get all the rest you can."

I thanked him and found my way outside, but his last words troubled me: why should *I* be getting all the rest I can?

However, if you suffer as a Christian, do not be ashamed, but praise God that you bear that name. For it is time for judgment to begin with the family of God; and if it begins with us, what will the outcome be for those who do not obey the gospel of God?
I Peter 4: 16 – 17

....

Prayer: Suffering comes in many different forms, but You understand that, Father. You are the Suffering Servant, and You understand my pain. Please touch me and heal me, but more importantly, heal those I love.

Ask yourself: What can you do for someone who is grieving over a loved one?

Shock

They say victims of trauma often go into a state of shock, a condition which is very unpredictable and potentially dangerous. I was the classic case as I stepped out of the hospital tent. I honestly didn't know what to do. I remembered my physical therapy gear, which I had left by the campfire. "Got to get my stuff together," I mumbled to no one. "I think my arm's definitely better this morning. Exercise. Plenty of exercise. Has anyone seen my stuff?"

Pastor McAllan had not taken his hand off my shoulder since leaving the hospital. He now gave me a squeeze and said softly, "Let's sit down for awhile. We need to talk about this."

"What's to talk about?" I asked. "My son is sick. He'll get better. The doc said so. I need to... to... what do I need to do?"

"The first thing is to make sure your son has all he needs. Let's go to his tent and gather a few things. After he sleeps awhile, he'll probably want to clean up, change clothes. He may be in the hospital awhile, so I suggest we pack up all his gear and store it some place. The next thing we need to do is make sure you have everything you need. Lizzie is going to take care of your meals for awhile, so you won't have to worry about that. The best thing you can do for him right now is keep yourself healthy. So after you do all the things I just mentioned, I think you need to get on with your physical therapy, like you said. And you're right, your arm does look better this morning."

I'm better. He's worse. Good news. Bad news. How am I supposed to feel?

"I the LORD do not change. So you, O descendants of Jacob, are not destroyed.
Malachi 3: 6

....

Prayer: Lord, some days it's hard to identify how things are going. My emotions are thrown about and I'm left unable to do anything effectively. Be with me in times of shock, I pray. May Your unchanging love and power surround me even when I'm not aware of it.

Ask yourself: Have you ever been in a situation where someone else had to make your decisions for you?

Anger

I followed Pastor McAllan around, numb and unable to understand exactly what we were doing. Sorting through my son's clothes, picking out something for him to wear and packing his gear away, I felt a twinge of guilt. Why was I going through his personal things? This was wrong.

We left his tent and returned to the campfire. Lizzie said something about lunch, but I didn't understand, and didn't respond. The pastor picked up my exercise gear and led me back out to the meadow. "You'll have to show me your routine," he said. "I'll see if I can help you stretch a little more range of motion into that shoulder. Come to think of it, I could use something like this myself. The old body's not what it used to be."

I picked up a weight and started lifting like the doc had taught me. In a few moments, though, a muscle cramp shot through my arm. The sensation was enough to bring me out of my morose, and I turned to look at the pastor. "Why am I doing this?" I asked suddenly. "The last thing I remember, you and I were standing here talking about my call into the ministry. The next thing I know, my son's lying in the hospital suffering from who knows what. Is there a connection here? You *knew* about this, didn't you? You saw this coming. I'll bet you could have stopped it, if you'd wanted to. Did you think I wouldn't go along if I'd known what was coming? What kind of God would play games with a helpless child like that?" I glared at Pastor McAllan with an all-new image of him. "What kind of man would stand by and watch? Who are you, really? I think..."

I wanted to go on: to lash out at the first thing I could. Pastor McAllan was standing there, so he would do. But as I watched his face, looking for any sight of complicity which I could attack, all I could see was compassion and sadness. He wasn't enjoying this any more than I was. I stood there, breathing heavily, looking for words that wouldn't come. Finally, I fell to my knees and cried. I was vaguely aware that he was on his knees beside me, and I think he was crying too.

But now you must rid yourselves of all such things as these: anger, rage, malice, slander, and filthy language from your lips.

Colossians 3: 8

Prayer: As Your Son suffered with us, so we must suffer with those closest to us. Give me strength to suffer, Lord: strength to stand beside someone who is suffering and to share that pain. And in the sharing, may we both know Your comfort.

Ask yourself: Why do think it helps to have a shoulder to cry on?

Denial

By afternoon, I had cried all I could: at least for the moment. I told Pastor McAllan he could go on about his business, and after awhile he left to visit others in the camp. I stayed in the meadow, partly because I didn't want to talk to anyone else just now, and partly because I needed to work through this thing. What exactly had happened, after all? My son had a seizure; he's in the hospital now, resting comfortably. Lots of things cause seizures, most of them not even serious. Why was I so worried?

The more I thought about it, the more I realized that I was being silly. Look at the facts, I reminded myself. My wounds were healing nicely, and after a few more rounds of physical therapy exercises, it was undeniable: since last night's prayer for physical healing, my arm was dramatically improved. Coincidence? I didn't think so. If God is taking care of my maladies, which He obviously is, then he'll take care of my son. This will all turn out to be nothing. Nothing at all. "So sorry," Dr Artinian will say. "Seems we've made a mistake. It wasn't really a seizure after all. Just lost his footing on the loose rocks. He's fine."

"That's okay," I'll say. "Mistakes happen. Don't worry about it. Come join us for dinner."

It was well past lunchtime. I picked up my gear and headed back for camp. Lizzie will have something for me; I think I heard someone say that she would be feeding me for awhile. What a deal, I grinned to myself. Meals provided, and there's not even anything wrong!

Lizzie handed me a bowl of stew as I approached the fire, her eyes asking a thousand questions. "I'm okay," I assured her. "Everything's okay. We'll be fine."

Listen to my instruction and be wise; do not ignore it. Blessed is the man who listens to me, watching daily at my doors,

Proverbs 8: 33 – 34

Prayer: Father, teach me the difference between sinful worry and constructive concern. Help me to recognize the problems which face me, and deal with them as I should. May I not ignore situations out of denial, but rather, accept them for what they are.

Ask yourself: What's the difference between "worry" and "concern"?

August 10

Waiting Again

I didn't sleep much last night, and when I awoke I was more exhausted than when I went to bed. This is ridiculous, I thought to myself. I'm ruining my health over nothing. In a day or two, this will all be over. I'll have to apologize to people for the things I've said. My physical therapy program will be shot, and I'll have to start all over. I was reaching for a shirt when that thought went through my mind, and I stopped in mid stretch. My arm was fully extended, something I had not been able to do since before the lion's attack. Furthermore, there was no pain, anywhere. A quick self-examination revealed that my scars were still in place, and I confess to a certain relief at that discovery. I was rather proud of my scars. But in every other way, I was healed. Completely.

I stood up from my bed and was not surprised to find that there was no dizziness whatsoever. A jog around the camp would have to confirm it, but I strongly suspected that my strength had returned as well. I bounded out of the tent and made my way to the campfire. I gave Lizzie a quick kiss on the cheek and accepted the breakfast she had prepared for me. "You really don't need to do this anymore, Lizzie," I said, then shared with her the amazing discovery of my healing.

"Oh that's wonderful," she said. "Now let's pray for the same healing mercy for your son."

I agreed, but was taken aback at her response. By now I had convinced myself that my son was not even sick. Surely, he doesn't need healing. Dr. Artinian had promised some test results by tomorrow, and by then this whole nightmare would be behind us. All we have to do today is wait.

I was reminded of a time not so long ago. I was standing on the trail, watching as a bush fire threatened me. Every part of my being wanted to run the other direction, but God told me to wait. It was the hardest thing I'd ever had to do up to that time. But it paid off. I survived. Then why do I dread the thought of waiting again?

"They are dismayed and have no more to say; words have failed them. Must I wait, now that they are silent, now that they stand there with no reply?"
Job 32: 15 – 16

....

Prayer: Lord, of all the things I'm called upon to do, one of the most difficult is the command to wait. Teach me how, I pray. Grant me patience and faith, and if it's Your will... soon?

Ask yourself: When was the last time you had to wait for something? How did you feel while you were waiting?

August 11

Test Results

I tried to be nonchalant this morning, but there was an urgency in my step as I made my way to the hospital tent. Dr Artinian had sent word that the results of the blood tests were in, and he wanted to see me. Why hadn't he just sent word that everything was okay? I'd have to talk to him about his professionalism as a doctor.

Entering the tent, the nurse showed me to a small room in the back which served as his office. He was sitting at a desk, looking over some papers. "Sit down, Friend," he said. "I have some reports to show you."

My patience left by the nearest exit and I blurted out, "I don't *want* to sit down, Doc. Just tell me my son is okay and let us get out of here."

"I can't do that," he said, a sombre look on his face that I'd never seen before. "The fact is, your son is a very sick young man. He has a condition which is quite rare, but unmistakable in its diagnosis. I could give you the name, but it would mean nothing to you."

"What are you saying? That we need to leave this trip and get him into treatment? I'll do whatever's necessary. Just give me some referrals and..."

"That of course is your prerogative as his father. I would certainly recommend that you seek another opinion. But I can tell you now, with 100% certainty that my diagnosis is correct, as well as the outlook."

I felt as though a bucket of ice water had been poured over me, and was working its way to every part of my body as I sat there. "What do you mean, 'outlook'?"

"This condition, I'm afraid, is always fatal. There is no treatment which is even recommended. The best I can do is keep him comfortable and relatively pain free. Mercifully, it usually moves very fast, and except for occasional seizures and lack of motor control, he will feel no particular discomfort."

"My son..." I tried to speak. "I need to..."

"I've already told him," Dr. Artinian said. "He's old enough. He deserves to know."

Show me, O LORD, my life's end and the number of my days; let me know how fleeting is my life.

Psalms 39: 4

....

Prayer: I cannot deny that we live in a fallen world, Father. And I know that pain and suffering and death are a part of our lot. But I pray for peace: the kind You promised, that the world does not understand. By that peace may I live and work and minister.

Ask yourself: If you could see into the future, would you want to?

August 12

My Son's Response

I walked into the room where my son lay. He eyes were open and he was staring at the ceiling. A tear had left its track down the side of his face. When he saw me, he called out "Hi Dad," and let me hold him.

"Son," I began. "We're not going to accept this. Not for a moment. Look at my arm!" I showed him how I could move it freely. "God has healed me completely. It must be a sign that He's going to heal you too. We just have to..."

"That's not what the sign is for," he said, interrupting me. "Dad, I had a dream last night. At least I *think* it was a dream. But it was so real. There was a man here in this room. An old fellow with a smile that just seemed to make everything all right. He said his name was Jacob, but that I could call him Jake."

The ice water sensation returned, and I felt like I might collapse onto the floor. Instead I sat down on the nearest chair and said, "I do know Jake, and he's no ordinary man. What did he tell you?"

"First, he told me not to be afraid; that he was sent by God, and that God loved me more than I'll ever know. I can't explain it, but I believed him, Dad. I still do."

"What else did he say?" I prompted.

"Jake said that God was going to heal your arm and restore your strength. In fact, he said that you would be even stronger than before. He said that you would need to be strong, especially now."

My voice cracked with emotion, but I managed to utter the word, "Why?"

"Jake said; let me see if I can remember this exactly. He said, 'Tell your Dad, remember that mountain? You're invited.'"

Then God said, "Take your son, your only son, Isaac, whom you love, and go to the region of Moriah. Sacrifice him there as a burnt offering on one of the mountains I will tell you about."

Genesis 22: 2

Prayer: Lord, I do want to serve You in any way I can. Even if it means going to the highest mountain or the deepest sea. But right now, I don't think I would have the strength to do that. If You do call me to go, and I pray You will, please give me the strength I need, when I need it. Thank You Father.

Ask yourself: Have you ever done something especially difficult, and afterwards wondered how you found the strength to do it?

August 13

Sharing the Burden

I stayed with my son for another hour or so. We talked about the journey we'd experienced together, and the things he was learning now at Rendezvous. We talked about his mother and sister, and how we would get word of these developments to them. When all else had been exhausted, we talked about the mountain. I told him about seeing it when I first began this trip, and wishing I could stand at the summit. Then I described my meeting with Jake, and his explanation that the trail up the mountain wasn't for everybody.

"But what does it mean, Dad?" he asked. "Is that where a person goes to get healed?"

"I honestly don't know, Son," I said. "But I think that's a pretty good possibility." Even as I said the words, I knew they weren't true. But what was I supposed to do? Tell my son that he was going to climb a mountain so he could die? No, as long as hope remained, I would hope for the best. And the best is what I would present to my son. Let him live or die in that hope.

When I came outside, I noticed a small group standing around the campfire, obviously waiting for me to join them. As soon as I reached them, they were all around me. Hugs, words of encouragement, meaningful looks: they were doing all they knew how to do. We sat down together and I made the announcement: "My son and I are leaving tomorrow. We'll be climbing the mountain."

A few gasps and whispered words floated around the fire, then Hank spoke up, as if for the group. "Then we'll all go with you. We can help carry things, and, be there for you." A few murmured their agreement, but most were silent, knowing the truth of the situation.

"I wish you could go, Hank." I looked around me, "I wish you could all come along. But the mountain is not for everyone; only those God calls are to set foot on it. As near as I can understand, my son and I will be going alone."

"But we will be with you." It was Liz's voice. "Every day, we'll be praying for the two of you. And by God's grace, we will be with you in His Spirit, just as you will be with us."

May the God who gives endurance and encouragement give you a spirit of unity among yourselves as you follow Christ Jesus, so that with one heart and mouth you may glorify the God and Father of our Lord Jesus Christ.

Romans 15: 5 – 6

....

Prayer: Thank you that today I can pray for loved ones anywhere in the world, and know for certain that You are with them, just as You are with me now. Keep us together by Your Spirit.

Ask yourself: If God lives in two people's hearts, then how could they ever be separated from one another?

August 14

A New Journey

It was still dark, but I knew it was morning. The camp was silent, but from all around me I could hear the sounds of waking: hushed conversations, a fire being built, the occasional rattle of dishes. No one would be staying in bed this morning. I rose up, against my will, and finished packing my belongings. If ever there was a day when I did not want to see the sunrise, this was it. How could I leave this place of peace and joy and take my son away to a mountaintop in order to watch him die? As I dressed, I prayed, "Lord, just take me home now. Take us both. Please don't make me face this future."

But my prayer was not answered, and I stepped out of the tent to see my son already waiting by the fire. Lizzie had given him something to eat, and Hank was talking softly. I joined them and said, "Looks like we'll get an early start today." No one said anything.

The sky was turning a dark shade of blue when my son spoke up. "Guess we'd better be going, huh?"

"Yeah, I guess so. How do you feel?"

"Great," he said. "It's hard to believe I'm even sick."

The lump in my throat threatened to choke the life out of me. I couldn't think of anything to say, so gave him a pat on the shoulder instead. By now the entire camp had turned out, waiting silently for our departure. Pastor McAllan went to my son, spoke a few words of encouragement, then turned to me. "If God allows, I'll meet you somewhere up there," he said. "Until then, don't forget how much He loves you both. Even when it doesn't seem like it. Stay on the trail, no matter what, and come back to us as soon as you possibly can. We'll be praying for you every day."

I thanked him, gave my son a nod, and we turned to leave. As we moved into the shadow of the woods, a song drifted up from the meadow behind us. "Til we meet, til we meet, God be with you til we meet again."

I can do everything through him who gives me strength.

Philippians 4: 13

....

Prayer: Lord, I don't always understand why I have to walk down certain roads, but I thank You and Praise You for going with me. Thank you for the strength of fellow believers and the guiding Hand of Your Holy Spirit.

Ask yourself: Think of a time when you did something you desperately did not want to do. What gave you the strength to do it?

August 15

Backtracking

It wasn't until we started walking this morning that I realized how far we would have to go back down the trail, in what I would have thought was the "wrong" direction. The dark woods, the ocean, past the detour leading to the village where Ralph and I had our adventure, the Sequoia forest and finally, the fork in the trail which leads to the mountain. That represented *weeks* of travel. If Dr. Artinian was correct, we didn't have that much time.

We both had strength to spare, however, and we seemed to be covering ground quickly. I was especially amazed at my own stamina, until I remembered that this was promised by Jake, along with the healing of my wounds. How could I doubt the goodness of God, in the light of such miraculous healing? The last time I came over this trail, it was on a stretcher, borne by four men. Now my son and I fairly flew over the ridges and valleys which had been such a physical challenge before.

By evening, we had arrived at the site of the lion's attack, and decided to make camp for the night. Not much was left of the carcass: just a few scattered bones and some pieces of skin. I found the skull and after some working at it managed to extract the four largest teeth. Even with my arm completely healed, I still felt a tingling sensation when I thought about those teeth sinking into my flesh.

"These belong to you," I said, handing the teeth over to my son. "Keep them as a reminder. You met the enemy, and he is yours. You did it before; you'll do it again."

He smiled, but had nothing to say. Instead, he pulled out his pocket knife, and with a tiny awl began drilling a hole in the first tooth.

For I am already being poured out like a drink offering, and the time has come for my departure. I have fought the good fight, I have finished the race, I have kept the faith.

II Timothy 4: 6 – 7

....

Prayer: Father, thank You for memory, and the fact that I can recall days gone by, when I stood to up the enemy and he fled. May the memories of past victories, as well as past defeats strengthen me for the challenges of today.

Ask yourself: Do you carry any reminders of experiences in the past? How do you feel when you look at them?

A New Trail

The next morning, we were up and finishing our coffee by the time the sun was creeping over the horizon. We were ready to go, but wanted the moment to last. The memories of this place were so powerful.

"That night when I stood here," my son reflected, "I was so scared. The lion, that *thing* from the other side: what scared me the most, I think, was the whole *unknown*. What were those things, and what could they do to me? Then the next time I was here, I was scared again, but in a different way. You were hurt, and I didn't know what was going to happen. And now here I am a third time; and I'm scared again. And it's different kind of fear, but it still goes back to that unknown factor. What's going to happen?"

"I wish I knew, Son. I wish I knew." I threw the rest of my coffee into the fire and stood up. "But if it helps, remember this: God knows it all, and He's the one Who sent us here. In the meantime, maybe it helps to go back to places and events we know, and learn from them."

As I spoke, I was looking over the campsite one last time, savouring the memories, looking for hope. Gazing beyond the scattered bones nearby, a glint of sunlight caught my eye as it reflected off something shiny. I stepped closer for a better look, moved some bushes aside, and found myself standing in front of a trail marker I had not seen before. It seemed to be made of bronze, and was set solidly in the ground. There were no words written on it, but the meaning was crystal clear: a picture of a mountain was engraved on the front of the marker, and beside it was an arrow pointing beyond. Looking closely in that direction, a faint trail was obvious.

My son came to stand beside me, noticed the marker, and said, "It looks like we head into the unknown today."

When times are good, be happy; but when times are bad, consider: God has made the one as well as the other. Therefore, a man cannot discover anything about his future.

Ecclesiastes 7: 14

Prayer: In all honesty, Lord, I don't want to see into the future. I would rather face each day with You at my side, fully prepared by Your mercy for what comes. Only assure me of this: that You will never leave me nor forsake me.

Ask yourself: Would you want to know what will happen tomorrow?

August 17

Into the Unknown

I thought my son's words all day as we walked. The root of his fear, it seemed, was the unknown. And, I admitted to myself, the same was true for me. As a child, I used to be terrified of getting injections from the doctor. "Will it hurt?" I would cry to my mother. Wisely, she never promised that it would be a painless experience; only that it would not be as bad as I was anticipating. And it was true. Many years and countless injections later, I can now roll up my sleeve without the slightest dread, knowing I've been there before.

But what now? I've never faced a situation like this before. Receiving my son's diagnosis was bad enough; now we have the added terror of moving along a trail which is unknown to both of us. I have a foreboding sense about it, that it will somehow be unlike anything I've ever experienced. I remember with a shudder Pastor McAllan' description of his own journey to the mountaintop: the most wonderful, and the most terrible thing he's ever done.

The trail itself does not look terribly unique. There are trees surrounding us, an occasional stream to cross, the sounds of birds. But all through the day I know that we are gradually climbing. There are ups and downs in the path, but it's more up than down. Perhaps it's only my imagination, but the air already seems cooler, in anticipation of the mountain's own weather patterns.

In the midst of the unknown, I cling to the familiar. The backpack which has been a part of my journey since the beginning. My son, my own flesh and blood, the child who I raised from infancy to the strong young man I see beside me now.

And somehow, they comfort me.

I am laid low in the dust; preserve my life according to your word. I recounted my ways and you answered me; teach me your decrees.

Psalms 119: 25 – 26

....

Prayer: Lord, when I must travel into unknown places, and I begin to fear, comfort me with the familiar. Show me that I am still Your child and walking where You would have me walk. Guard my steps and light my way.

Ask yourself: What calms your fears when you are facing the unknown?

August 18

First Glimpse

The trail began a series of switchbacks, and I knew we were climbing at a rapid rate. I was surprised at my own stamina, but looking back at my son, it was obvious that his strength was failing. "We'll stop at the next ridge and make camp for the night," I promised, to which he gave a silent nod of the head. An hour later, the trail made a final turn and topped out on a ridge. The ground leveled out somewhat, and there were several places big enough to set a tent. But the thing which demanded out total attention was the sight of the mountain.

The ridge on which we stood was a major spine leading all the way to the summit. One more day of walking, and we would reach timberline, and from there on, only the mountain itself would stand between us and the goal. As the setting sun turned the high country into a brilliant shade of gold, we strained to see details of the trail to come. I could make out more switchbacks, and possibly an area which would require some rock climbing. Toward the top, a layer of clouds had settled in, obscuring any view.

"Looks easy enough," I said, then turned to see my son sitting on a log and sorting through his backpack. Eventually he pulled out a bag filled with medicine, located a pill and took it with a drink of water from his canteen. "What's that for?" I asked quietly.

"The Doc said to take it for pain." He saw my dark expression and added, "It's not that bad; I just need to stay on top of it."

I wondered if it would help the agony I was feeling.

If I say, 'I will forget my complaint, I will change my expression, and smile,' I still dread all my sufferings, for I know you will not hold me innocent.

Job 9: 27 – 28

Prayer: Sometimes, Lord, I confess that I feel like Job must have felt: accused and convicted. Your Word tells me that I am forgiven, but my daily path shows me trials which I must yet suffer. Comfort me, I pray.

Ask yourself: How should a Christian behave in the face of suffering?

A Tough Question

The trail continued along the ridgeline today, sometimes descending into small canyons, sometimes breaking out onto awe-inspiring vistas. But the progress was always up, as evidenced by the trees around us. They were now smaller than those below us, and more twisted. These trees near timberline were mute expression of life's determination to survive, even in the harshest of conditions.

My thoughts were mixed as we sat on a dead log and gazed beyond it to the summit above. The conversation which followed brought my fears into focus. "Dad, you know the story of Abraham and Isaac?"

I did, but wasn't sure I wanted to think about it. "Sure," I said tentatively. "Why do you ask?"

"Well, you know Abraham was supposed to take his son to a mountaintop and sacrifice him to God. On the way up, the kid says, 'Here's the wood for the fire, but where's the lamb for the sacrifice?' Abraham turns to his son and says, 'God will provide a lamb.' My question is, was Abraham lying to his son when he said that, or did he really believe that God was going to come through at the last minute?"

My insides tied themselves into a knot and I looked away. Did my son know the despair I felt, in spite of my assurances that everything was going to be all right? Finally I answered, truthfully, "I don't know, Son. I'd like to think that Abraham was hoping all the way up the mountain that something would come through for him."

"That's what I think, too," he said. We were quiet for a long time, then he turned back to me. "Dad? Let's keep hoping, okay?"

Be strong and take heart, all you who hope in the LORD.

Psalms 31: 24

Prayer: Teach me the difference between blind hope and steadfast faith, Dear Lord. May I rest in You and in Your promises.

Ask yourself: What is the difference between faith and hope?

Faith and Hope

I went to sleep last night thinking about the conversation with my son. I had agreed with him that we would continue to hope for the best, but how was that different from placing our faith in a certain outcome? The discussion had been about Abraham, a man known for his remarkable faith. By faith, he left his home and lived in tents, confident of God's promise to give him land and children. By faith, he showed his willingness to slay his own son, even if by doing so would make the promise seemingly impossible. But in every case, Abraham was not just hoping that God would come through on His promises: he knew it, and so was able to go to such drastic lengths.

I can be assured of the same promise today: that is, that God will lead me through this life and all the way to His kingdom. To that extent, I guess I can say that I can make this journey, even to the mountaintop, by faith. But as to the details of whether or not a lion will hurt me, or whether I will lose my way from time to time, or whether my son will be rescued at the last moment, faith can only answer the general questions. After that, hope must give me a hand. I hope there are no thorns in my path, but if there are, I hope I can avoid them; but if I don't, I hope for a speedy recovery. Whatever happens to my hopes, I can still rest assured that at the end of the day, I will rest with God. And that's faith.

All these people were still living by faith when they died. They did not receive the things promised; they only saw them and welcomed them from a distance. And they admitted that they were aliens and strangers on earth. People who say such things show that they are looking for a country of their own.

Hebrews 11: 13 – 14

Prayer: Lord, teach me to walk by faith, and to not lose sight of my goal. Consider my hopes, and in Your perfect will, grant my heart's desires. When that is not to be, then grant me faith to accept what I must endure.

Ask yourself: If you do not get what you ask God for, is your faith affected?

Timberline

By early afternoon, we had come to the last stand of trees. They were small and hard, bent into a permanent slant, away from the prevailing winds. With the increasing altitude, I was beginning to find my breath shorter and more difficult. One look at my son and I knew we had to stop for the night. His face was pale and twisted with pain. He was gasping for every breath and seemed to be fighting to stay on his feet. I lifted his pack off his shoulders, and got him as comfortable as I could. Soon, a fire was blazing and a pot of Lizzie's stew was simmering. I could close my eyes and imagine that we were back at Rendezvous. My son brought me back to reality, however.

"I guess tomorrow night we'll have do without the fire, since we're leaving the trees behind."

"Nonsense," I said, with bit more confidence than I intended. "I'll carry a load of firewood from here. I suggest we leave everything but the bare essentials here. We just need sleeping bags and some food. We can pick them up on the way back."

He looked hard in my face, almost said something, then turned back to the fire. I was glad. "The great thing about this wood," I said, anxious to change the subject, "the trees grow so slowly that the wood is compact and hard. A single stick will burn all night. It's not like that soft aspen from down in the valley. It'll put on two inches in a single year, but it burns like paper. One look at the flame and poof! It's all gone."

"Do I hear a sermon coming, Dad?"

I laughed at that and said, "Well, let's see... this hard timberline wood is tough because it's weathered some hard times. The wind and lack of moisture made it strong: a real survivor. The aspens, well, they've had it easy. Plenty of topsoil, constant supply of water, shelter from the storms. They look good on the outside, but there's no substance. Me? I want to be like this old fellow," I said, pointing to the tree which bent over our heads.

"You are, Dad," He smiled. "You are."

Make a tree good and its fruit will be good, or make a tree bad and its fruit will be bad, for a tree is recognized by its fruit.

Matthew 12: 33

....

Prayer: Even as I pray for strength, Father, I know that it must come at a price. May I be willing to do what is necessary in order to become strong and fit for Your kingdom. Protect me from the temptation to trade ease for weakness.

Ask yourself: Are you willing to earn your strength?

August 22

The Lamb of Anger

Neither of us slept last night. Pain, worry, the cold and the wind teamed together to make us miserable. The sky had grown light enough that I could now see my son writhing next to the fire, long since gone out. I watched him as long as I could, then got up to face the day. A deep resentment had worked its way into my heart overnight, and I was looking for a way to express it. Why did I have to be here? Why was my son suffering? He had barely started on the journey; it seemed only right that he should have a chance to experience more of life before it's taken from him. As I gathered wood for the fire, I found myself yanking on the dry branches and hoping they would break, not so that I would gain a piece of firewood, but so that I might experience the feeling of hurting something.

I came to a small tree which seemed dead, and rather than break off branches, I kicked at the tree itself, as if it were something, or someone, I could hold responsible. It cracked, so I kicked again, and again. I took hold of it and pulled back with all my might, and without warning, it came free of the ground, sending me backwards. I lay there with my eyes squeezed shut, ignoring the pain from a bruised shoulder and fighting back tears.

A voice spoke up from just behind me. "Hurts, doesn't it?"

I turned quickly and looked back. Standing not three feet from me was a lamb.

And he was speaking.

In your anger do not sin: Do not let the sun go down while you are still angry, and do not give the devil a foothold.

Ephesians 4: 26 – 27

Prayer: Forgive me when I am angry, Father. Teach me how to control those emotions which harm myself and others. Grant me patience and understanding sufficient to bring honor to Your Name in every situation.

Ask yourself: Have you ever been "blinded" by anger? What did you do?

August 23

The Lamb Speaks

My shock at hearing words coming from an animal was short-lived. After all, this was a journey I had never experienced before. This mountain, in particular, seemed to hold more mystery than I could fathom. I decided rather than look for an explanation, I would instead seek to learn who this creature was, and why he was speaking to me.

"Are you a messenger from God?" I asked. At the moment, that was the only possibility that made sense.

"Why do you ask? Are you hoping for some message of comfort?"

"I... well, I was hoping that there might be some help to be found on this mountain."

"God has no intention of helping you," the lamb spoke through clenched teeth. "He just wants to see you make a fool of yourself. He likes watching you squirm. He likes seeing your son hurt. He thinks you can't touch him, up there on his big throne, but he's wrong. You *can* touch him. Your anger can reach all the way to the heavens. There is no part of the universe which cannot feel the wrath of an angry man."

I was speechless. To hear an animal talk was one thing; but to hear him say such venomous words against God left me powerless to respond. I tried to turn away: to rebuke him for his blasphemy and leave his presence. But something in his tirade rang in my ears: "You *can* touch him," he had said. In my heart, I know that much is true. God desires fellowship. I have the freedom to give or withhold fellowship, so I have the ability to affect a desire that God Himself feels. He is all-powerful: I know that. He doesn't *need* me, but I believe that he *wants* me. Yes, I thought, I can touch God. But right now I'm angry at Him. I might as well be honest.

The lamb seemed to read my mind. "That's right! Give honest expression to your anger. Don't hold it inside. Shout to God how you feel about him. Tell him what a sorry ruler he is. Do you want to hurt something? Go ahead; hurt me."

In your anger do not sin; when you are on your beds, search your hearts and be silent. Offer right sacrifices and trust in the LORD.

Psalms 4: 4 – 5

Prayer: I know there are expressions which are appropriate and those which are not, Father. The problem is, I cannot always choose the right expressions for each occasion. Grant me self control and wisdom, so that together they will lead me to honor You in all things.

Ask yourself: Is it ever right to hurt someone out of anger?

Lashing Out

For a moment my anger was averted by the lamb's offer. Hurt him? But the object of my anger was *God*, not him. What good would it do to attack someone else? It seemed the best I could hope for would be to stand before the heavens and shake my fist at God. But as I stood there, fist raised to the sky, I realized what a ridiculous sight that was. "Fists are not made for waving," I thought to myself. "They're made for hitting."

I turned back quickly and saw the lamb still standing there, looking at me with an evil smile. Had he actually moved closer? I looked back at my fist, still tightly clenched, then at the lamb, who at that moment was the embodiment of everything I hated: my frustration, my impotence, my fear. I swung. The lamb did not flinch, but stood still as I connected with his jaw. The blow sent him reeling backward two or three steps, and for a moment his eyes rolled back until I thought I had knocked him unconscious. But then he straightened up and looked directly into my eyes. I could see a tiny drop of blood on his mouth. "That's right," he said. "You'll show him. Do it again!"

I closed my eyes as a primal scream rose up in my throat. I drew back for another swing, but just as I was about to unleash my anger a second time, a voice spoke inside my heart. "Don't. You're only hurting yourself."

But I know where you stay and when you come and go and how you rage against me. Because you rage against me and your insolence has reached my ears, I will put my hook in your nose and my bit in your mouth, and I will make you return by the way you came.

II Kings 19: 29 – 28

....

Prayer: As if I don't have enough enemies around me, Lord, all too often I hurt myself by my own actions. Teach me to overcome my foolish ways, I pray, and to live according to Your will for me.

Ask yourself: When was the last time you hurt yourself because you lost your temper?

Seeing Through the Rage

The voice in my heart puzzled me for a moment. It was a familiar voice, but unexpected. The anger inside me had tried to drown out the voice, but I had heard it, loud and clear. I stopped, my right hand drawn back and frozen. The lamb sensed my hesitation and stepped closer.

"You can't quit now!" he screamed. "You're just beginning to accomplish something. He hates you, don't you see? He hates you and wants you to hate him!"

That last statement was foolish enough to make me hesitate again. A vague sensation of pain found its way into my senses. I brought down the fist I had poised to strike with, and noticed a gash across two knuckles. Blood seeped into the palm of my hand, carrying with it a tiny strand of wool. I looked back at the lamb and saw that he was showing real indications of fear. "What are you doing?" he shouted. "Don't stop! Don't stop!"

I looked closer at the lamb's mouth, where the drop of blood was beginning to dry. The blood was mine, not his. I had merely struck his teeth. He could not be hurt, I realized. The more I struck him, the more grievous my own wounds would become.

"Dad?" I turned to see my son, a look of incomprehension on his face. Rushing to his side, I wrapped my arms around him and wept.

"I'm okay," I said at last. "I was just angry. That *thing* back there almost convinced me to do something we'd both regret. But it's over now. I'm okay."

"Dad? What thing are you talking about?"

We turned together and looked behind me, but saw nothing. At first, I thought I was losing my mind, but then an aching hand drew my attention back to the gash across my knuckles. Whether the lamb of anger was real or not, the scars most certainly were.

Nations are in uproar, kingdoms fall; he lifts his voice, the earth melts.

Psalms 46: 6

Prayer: Man's anger is nothing next to Your holy wrath, Oh God. Remind me the next time I start to lose control that vengeance belongs to You and You alone.

Ask yourself: Does it help to control your anger, knowing that ultimately all wrongs will be made right?

August 26

The Lamb of Denial

We continued climbing today, leaving behind the trees, the streams and nearly everything else of beauty. Rocks littered the mountainside as if hurled there by forces intent on the destruction of every thing and everyone who dared approach. We climbed in silence as we worked our way through the rubble. As we passed one particularly large boulder, we both stopped suddenly at the sound of a voice.

"Where are you going?"

It was another lamb, standing in the shelter of the boulder and watching us with sly curiosity. The question was repeated, so I gave the only answer I could think of. "To the top of the mountain."

"Why?"

"Because I was told to... *we* were told to. I must reach the summit, and..."

"And what? Watch him die?" the lamb questioned, his chin pointing at my son. I couldn't answer. My son was watching me intently. Finally, I simply looked down at the ground.

"Do you want to do this horrible thing?" the lamb asked.

The question was absurd. "No! Of course not. I don't want to be here, and I don't want to go there. I just want to go back. If only, I mean, if I just had..."

"A lamb?"

"Yes."

"I'm a lamb. Why look any farther?"

"Do you mean, you would be willing to..."

"I said so, didn't I? You don't have to be here in the first place, you know. I'm really amazed you've come this far, considering."

Abraham answered, "God himself will provide the lamb for the burnt offering, my son." And the two of them went on together.

Genesis 22: 8

....

Prayer: Lord, when I face difficult situations, I always hope that, somehow, the coming trials will not be necessary. But help me to distinguish between Your salvation and the enemy's compromise.

Ask yourself: Do you think the enemy would like you to give up the pursuit of a God-given goal?

Substitute

My hands were shaking with excitement born of hope. Was this the miracle of the mountain? This lamb, as a substitute for my son's life, just like Abraham and Isaac. I stole a glance at the lamb, who was standing casually within easy grasp. "But... don't we still have to go to the top of the mountain?" I asked. "That was the understanding, and..."

"Why would you do such a thing?" said the lamb, looking back and forth between my son and me.

"'Why'? Well, because He said so, and because we have to, don't we?"

The lamb took on an angry stance, and I was afraid he might run away. "You keep saying '*He* said so'; why do you always do what *He* says?"

"But I thought..."

"Never mind," the lamb continued. "The fact is, you don't want to be here. You don't want to go there. You want a substitute. Here I am. Go home."

I was still confused. "But surely I can't just, well, go home. Shouldn't we go to the top with you?"

"Who says I'm going to the top?"

"But I thought you just agreed to be the substitute for my son. That means..."

"I *know* what it means, and I'm telling you for the last time, if you want me to take care of things, turn around and go home."

"But if you don't go, then there won't be a substitute. Then He will.."

"There you go, talking about *Him* again. Look, what do you think would happen if you simply refused?"

The question was unthinkable; and yet I found myself thinking about it. The lamb seemed to sneer as he spoke again. "That's the problem with your kind. You never consider alternatives. Think about it: He told you to do something, but He never mentioned any options, did He? How do you know there aren't any? And maybe better ones at that.

Obey me, and I will be your God and you will be my people. Walk in all the ways I command you, that it may go well with you.

Jeremiah 7: 23

....

Prayer: All too often, Lord, I exchange simple obedience for foolish questions. Protect me from those who would lead me astray, and help me to be strong in the face of temptation.

Ask yourself: Do you think God gives alternatives to His will?

August 28

The Choice

"I'll tell you one last time," the lamb repeated, as I stood with my son, considering what was being offered. "Forget this whole thing. Turn around and go back down. It won't be nearly as hard as you think."

A "sacrificial lamb" stood in front of us, an alternative to the command we both received: to proceed to the summit. It seemed too good to be true, and perhaps it was. The lamb did not necessarily promise to go in our place; he only said that he would "take care of things." More than life itself, I wanted to turn and leave this mountain. But what would happen to my son if we did?

My uncertainty left me speechless, until finally my son spoke up. "I don't know, Dad," he said giving the lamb a careful appraisal. "He's not nearly as good looking as I am. I don't think I want him taking my place anywhere. Why don't we just have him for dinner?" He drew out the sword that hung on his belt and took a step forward. Suddenly, all the confidence and criticisms fell away from the lamb and he jumped back in fear.

"No! Wait! You fools!" He fell over himself as he backed up, scrambled over the loose rock then backed up some more. "You'll regret this," he said as he turned to run.

"I regret it already," my son said. I turned to him and he went on. "I'm sorry I wasn't fast enough to catch him. You didn't believe him, did you, Dad?"

"No, of course not," I answered quickly. "Still, it was a great idea."

A rumble of thunder echoed up from the valley below as we made our way steadily on, up the trail.

I have chosen the way of truth; I have set my heart on your laws. I hold fast to your statutes, O LORD; do not let me be put to shame.

Psalms 119: 30 – 31

....

Prayer: Sometimes I hesitate to declare my obedience to You, Father. Thank you for sending people who will restore my zeal.

Ask yourself: When was the last time you were required to take a stand for what you believe?

The Scapegoat

The sound of thunder grew closer, and we could see clouds beginning to build in the valley below us. I started to worry about being on an exposed mountain in a storm, but then remembered that any hope of life and death had long since left me. If anything, I would have welcomed a quick and merciful end to this torture.

The clouds overtook us, and a fine mist of rain began to envelop us. The trail grew slippery and more difficult to negotiate. More than once during the day, we would stumble and fall, then lie still, grateful for the chance to rest, and grateful even more for delaying what waited at the top.

Working our way around an outcropping of rock, we stopped for another moment to take advantage of the comparatively level section of ground. Leaning back against the stone, we gazed upward along the trail. There, not fifty steps away, stood a goat. At least, it appeared to be a goat, although it was so scrawny and matted, it seemed to be barely alive. As we walked up to the miserable creature, I could see tiny horns curving around its head, stopping just before coming in contact with its eyes. It was shivering, and as we approached, it looked at us with eyes that spoke of despair and death. And yet the eyes caught mine and bore through to my soul. I tried to look away, but could not.

From experience and from his eyes, I knew without a doubt that this creature also could speak. I didn't want to, but found myself saying, "What brings you to this miserable place?"

Even as I asked the question, I wasn't sure if I was referring to the mountain or the animal's condition. He made it easy for me. "Nothing has brought me here, just as nothing has brought you here. We are victims, you and I: victims of false hope in Something... which is really nothing." He hesitated, then his eyes turned to my son and added, "All three of us."

What I feared has come upon me; what I dreaded has happened to me. I have no peace, no quietness; I have no rest, but only turmoil."

Job 3: 25 – 26

....

Prayer: Be near me, Lord, when I feel like a victim. Remind me, as You reminded Job, that You are my God. Comfort me when I cry to You.

Ask yourself: Have you ever felt like a victim?

Victim of Chance?

The miserable creature shivering before us seemed to make no sense. At the same time, the suggestion that he might know something of my suffering made me angry. "What do you mean by calling me a 'victim'?" I demanded. "We've been brought here for a purpose: one which I detest, but one which I must obey. How dare you call our ordeal 'nothing'!"

"Call it what you will," the goat said in a rasp. "But in the end, we are nothing more than the sum total of a string of random figures. Chance has brought me here, and chance has brought you here. If you're trying to find a pattern, a reason, then you're more of a fool that I thought you were."

Even in my fatigue, I managed to stand a little straighter. "Who are *you* to be talking about chance?" I asked. "I suppose chance has decreed that you stand here like this. Or did you just wake up one morning and find yourself here, looking like a decaying bag of bones? Are you trying tell me you had no voice in what has happened to you?"

"Oh, I had plenty of voice, all right." For the first time, the goat raised his head, and I felt a chill which made me clutch at my collar. "I bleated like there was no tomorrow when the shepherd grabbed me and the one next to me by the scruff of our necks. And for all we knew, there *would* be no tomorrow. As it turned out for the other goat, his fears were well founded. Right there, before my eyes, they lifted him up to an altar and cut his throat. He cried out for as long as he could, but of course that was not for long." He gave me a malicious smile, and I realized that my hand was resting on my own throat. I dropped it to my side and started to speak, but he continued. "Chance was in force from the very beginning. If only I had been at the other end of the feeding trough. If only my head had been lowered when the shepherd passed, perhaps I would have been spared this act of fate."

Such is the fate God allots the wicked, the heritage appointed for them by God.
Job 20: 29

....

Prayer: Father God, I know that eternity is laid before Your feet. For You, the future holds neither mystery nor question. But how do I fit into Your plan? Have you laid before me a path from which I cannot stray, or have You given me choices, and consequences for them? Grant me wisdom, I pray.

Ask yourself: Do you believe that a person's fate cannot be changed?

Act of Fate?

I felt as though my legs were about to give way beneath me. My breath was coming in short gasps. I wanted to deny the words of this pitiful creature who stood in my way: to stand up to him and challenge his accusations. But instead, I staggered, trying to find solid ground beneath my feet. My son reached out and I took his hand. Together we stood up and faced the creature who had attacked so cruelly all that had brought us this far. If I too am the property of a Shepherd, as this goat was, then can He rightfully kill my son? Could He cast us out into the wilderness, to die in despair? I looked back at the goat, and saw that he had now lost that first image of abject misery. Now he seemed to be barely containing a violent rage. The tiny horns which before pointed to hollow, dark eyes now seemed to threaten anyone who would dare come close. Those were not the eyes of one who feels victimized by chance. There was a hatred there; and hatred must have an object. In spite of what he told me about the futility of life, his eyes betrayed a fire which sought to lash out and destroy. It was a feeling that I could share. Just like the goat, I needed something tangible to despise.

Before rational thought could take over, I rushed to the goat, grabbed one horn and twisted him to the ground. Reaching back and taking the sword my son was holding, I placed the point just above the jugular vein in his neck. Bending low, I whispered into his ear, "Since you have no hope of altering your fate, then I'm sure you won't complain when I take you to the mountaintop with me. My son needs a substitute, and it's going to be you! I would rather present a living sacrifice at the altar, but I'll do what I must to deliver your carcass."

The goat's eyes, which reflected first, emptiness, then hatred, were now filled with pure terror. "No!" he cried. "It isn't supposed to be like this! No! Stop!"

Aaron shall bring the goat whose lot falls to the LORD and sacrifice it for a sin offering. But the goat chosen by lot as the scapegoat shall be presented alive before the LORD to be used for making atonement by sending it into the desert as a scapegoat.

Leviticus 16: 9 – 10

Prayer: Lord of Heaven and Earth: You are my God. All that befalls me is in Your Hands. May I rest in the promise that You love me and care for me as a perfect Father. May I always be Your obedient child.

Ask yourself: Does the suggestion of fate excuse you from making a bad decision?

September 1

The Scapegoat Confesses

I held the goat firmly to the ground, the sword pressed against his throat. "What do you mean, 'It wasn't *supposed* to be like this,'" I demanded. Are you now telling me that there is some purpose after all to our misery?"

He hesitated until I pushed the sword closer, then he screamed out, "It wasn't me! I was told to meet you. I was told you'd give up the journey. All you needed was a little case of despair. It's not my fault," he whimpered. "Please let me go!"

The miserable creature was almost at the end of his strength. Just another fraction of pressure and I could end his pitiful bleating. But as I watched his eyes, now rolled back in horror, I understood that this defective object would never suffice as a substitute. Standing up, I resisted the urge to kick him away. Instead I turned my back on him and said, "Get out of here. Tell your master you've failed. Let him decide what your *fate* will be."

At first the goat was silent, and for a moment I thought he was gone. But when I turned around, I saw him standing there, looking first at me and then at the gathering darkness around us. He seemed to be weighing his alternatives. Then with a sigh, he began to move backwards. His steps were slow and careful at first, as if he was still uncertain as to where he should go. But then I took a step toward him and he jumped with a start, clambering down the mountainside. I was surprised to see such speed and agility in one who seemed so wretched. In another moment he was gone.

The adrenaline left me as well, and I collapsed to the ground. I had almost believed him. I came close to falling into a pit from which there could be no rescue, for in its depths there is no hope of a shepherd.

After awhile, my son laid a hand on my shoulder and said, "Let's go Dad. At least we have a place to go *to*."

Let us fix our eyes on Jesus, the author and perfecter of our faith, who for the joy set before him endured the cross, scorning its shame, and sat down at the right hand of the throne of God.

Hebrews 12: 2

....

Prayer: Lord, in a world which so often seems to be without purpose or direction, praise You for Your Son! In Him, I have my reason for living and a standard by which to measure my growth. May I keep my eyes fixed on Him, every day.

Ask yourself: What would life be like with no goals?

September 2

The Lamb of Trade

Long before we reached him, we could hear his bleating. At first the sound was like the distant noise from a marketplace, then as we drew closer I could start to distinguish words. Finally a kind of sing song chant lifted up above the clamor.

Oh who will buy, who will buy?
Take it home and give it a try;
The cost is not much, a pittance indeed,
Look in your purse: you'll find what you need

There was no one else around, except for a single lamb, standing alone. Though he sang of wares, there were none in evidence. Curious, I drew closer. He didn't seem to notice me but continued his chant.

Who will buy, who will buy?
I have treasures untold
Just reach into your purse
And I will consider it sold.

"What are you selling?" I finally asked as he paused for breath. The lamb turned to look at me, then gazed beyond to where my son was standing. "You don't know?" he asked, still looking past me. "You of all people should know the answer to that." There was an expression of deep sadness on his face. But it soon changed, as he looked into my eyes and broke into a kind of all-knowing, shared-secret smile. I looked away quickly and cleared my throat.

"Well, yes. I suppose I do know what you're selling. And I'm interested; I really am. I don't care about the cost. I just want... it."

"Yes, you do," he smiles. "I can see that. And why not? What could be more precious than a man's own flesh and blood: what price too dear?"

Say to Tyre, situated at the gateway to the sea, merchant of peoples on many coasts, 'This is what the Sovereign LORD says: "You say, O Tyre, "I am perfect in beauty."

Ezekiel 27: 3

....

Prayer: Lord, it's one thing to fear for my own well-being, but it's quite another to consider those I love. How could I refuse to act when they are being threatened? Teach me to trust You, Father, not only with my own life, with the lives of those closest to me.

Ask yourself: Consider the heroes of fiction: is it a strength or a weakness that they always give in to the villain when an innocent person is threatened?

The Transaction

"As I said, I don't care about the cost," I told the lamb. "Just tell me what it is, and I'll get it, somehow."

"A wise man," the lamb announced to the rocks lying about. "A wise man who knows what he wants and will stop at nothing to get it. Truly a wise man. Tell me, wise sir, what have you brought?"

"Only myself, and what few possessions I have in my backpack. And my son, but..."

"No, we mustn't consider *that* commodity, eh? After all, he's the object of our transaction." The lamb was silent for several moments, considering me as one might consider a middle-aged horse on the auction block. His face clouded over, and I thought I read disappointment in his face."

"If more is required, perhaps I can..."

"Oh have no doubt about that," the lamb cut me off. "More will definitely be required. I had no idea you were so... deficient. But never mind, there are ways to achieve what one truly desires, eh?"

"Yes, yes of course," I said, not entirely sure of myself. "Could we please go over the terms of the contract? Just so there's no mistake?"

"Oh the agreement is simple enough," he said with a faint air of flippancy. "My life for the life of your son. A fairly easy concept to grasp, when you think about it. At any rate, I will fulfill my part of the bargain, but I must have some assurance that you will honor *yours*."

"But you haven't told me what the price will be," I said. "How can I agree to terms when I don't know yet what they are?"

"But you've already said that price is no object." The lamb's condemning tone made me draw back a step. "And I've said that the requirements will not be impossible, only that they will be more than you now possess. I think it's time we concluded this transaction, unless of course you're anxious to meet *Him*."

"My feelings, exactly." My son stepped up next to me. "Let's forget any deals with my father. I'd like to do business with you directly." With that, he tossed something down at the lamb's feet. I looked, and saw that it was a necklace, made of four lion's teeth on a string.

Let not my heart be drawn to what is evil, to take part in wicked deeds with men who are evil doers; let me not eat of their delicacies.

Psalms 141: 4

Prayer: The offerings of this world can be so glamorous and inviting that I often forget their source. Forgive me, Lord, when I am tempted to deal with the enemy. Remind me that my allegiance is to You alone.

Ask yourself: Have you ever bought something on the street which made you feel suspicious about the seller?

September 4

Offer Withdrawn

The lamb kept looking from the string of lion's teeth to my son, as comprehension soaked in. Finally, he took a step backwards and said quietly, "I think our business here is finished." He kept backing up until finally he turned and ran, glancing occasionally over his shoulder with an expression somewhere between surprise and fear.

"Why did you do that, Son," I asked, as a wave of disappointment swept over me. "Don't you see what he was offering?"

"Don't *you* see, Dad? He wasn't about to do anything for me. My life is not in his hands, and he knows it. He had his sights on *you*, to try and make you enter into a bargain of some sort. That way, whatever happened, he would come back and demand something of you that you shouldn't be giving."

I picked up the lion's teeth and fought back a lump in my throat. "You're right, I suppose. It's just that, there's nothing I wouldn't do for you. I thought if there was any hope at all, I owe it to you as a father to..."

"No Dad. You don't owe me that. As a father, you've brought me into this world, you took care of me when I couldn't take care of myself, and you taught me right from wrong. But we both know now who our *real* Father is. And anything which takes us away from our commitment to Him is wrong, even if it involves our commitment to each other. Right?"

I held the string of teeth in my hand, rubbing over each one with my thumb. Then I handed them to my son and said, "Tell me, how is it that you've gotten smarter than your own Dad?"

He smiled, put his arm around my shoulder and said, "I don't know; I guess it's in the genes!"

I will walk among you and be your God, and you will be my people.

Leviticus 26: 12

....

Prayer: Father, let me declare to You again today that I am yours, completely. May there be no desire, no fear, no ambition that comes between us. May I come to understand that my own family is a gift from You, and that no matter how much I love them, You are still to have first place in my life.

Ask yourself: Would God ever make you choose between Himself and one you love? How would you choose?

September 5

The Magician's Lamb

Darkness fell over the trail, but my son and I decided to press on. Sleep was out of the question, now, and with the increasing altitude, cold was becoming a real problem. I pulled my collar up closer, but it did nothing to prevent the icy sensation from finding the inmost reaches of my heart. We stopped for a moment to blow into our hands and slap at our arms to try and restore circulation. I looked around me; the mountain seemed dark and deathly silent. Why is it that darkness and death seem to go hand in hand? Is that why dead people are supposed to have their eyes closed? And by the same token, if a dead person has his eyes open, there's something unnatural about it: even frightening. Standing there in the darkness, shivering not just from the cold, I felt as if I were already in the presence of Death itself. Was I anticipating what lay ahead, or had Death already begun to surround us, its icy fingers gripping our throats as we struggled for each breath?

Moving around, stamping my feet, trying to generate even a tiny bit of heat, I gradually became aware that the atmosphere surrounding us had begun to change. I could even imagine that there was a certain warmth in the air. No, not so much *warm* as perceptibly not as cold as before. Either way, I turned in the direction of the change. My senses were fine-tuned: listening, feeling. There it was again, a definite presence, not as cold as the surroundings, carried by the wind and wrapping itself around me. I stepped off the trail and moved around a large boulder which was blocking what little view I could make out in the darkness.

There was a lamb, facing away from me. He seemed to be gazing intently toward something at his feet. I moved closer for a better view. The object looked like a piece of coal, or something similar. It was black, about the size of a large grapefruit, and while there no glow about it, still it seemed to be radiating some kind of heat. The lamb had his head down, the end of his nose touching the mysterious object. I wondered if he knew I was standing behind him. Just then, he spoke.

"There is power in this place. Mortal man cannot know the width and breadth of it; but with guidance, he may discover its depth."

Let no one be found among you who sacrifices his son or daughter in the fire, who practices divination or sorcery, interprets omens, engages in witchcraft, or casts spells, or who is a medium or spiritist or who consults the dead.

Deuteronomy 18: 10 – 11

....

Prayer: Lord, I acknowledge that You alone hold all power. Yet there are those who would try to imitate it. Protect me from their false practices, and grant me wisdom when faced with them.

Ask yourself: Have you ever been involved in "magic"?

The Token

The lamb's words seemed to be meaningless, but somehow I felt that they were *supposed* to be, as if the saying of them was more important than the words themselves. For the moment, however, I only wanted to get a closer look at the black object which held the lamb's attention. "What is it?" I asked in a whisper, as if it might disappear if I approached too suddenly.

"The question of the ages," the lamb said in a trancelike voice. "Standing at the portals of knowledge, man can only wonder what lies beyond. Will he ever know the answer to the riddle?" For the first time, he looked up at me. "Will you?"

"I want to know," I answered, as a stirring of hope pushed me forward. I wanted desperately to reach out and touch the black object, to feel its warmth and test its weight. Something inside me was warning me to back away, but the desire to *know* was too great to resist. I pushed caution aside and said to the lamb, "I want to know. If there is power, then I want to have it. Can you help me?"

The lamb seemed to be deep in thought, staring off into the darkness. Or was he looking at something? I strained my eyes in the same direction, but could see nothing. Finally, the lamb turned back to face me. "Yes, I can help you," he said. "I see that you have a heart to seek what was forbidden. You are a warrior, and will not be prevented from winning what is rightfully yours. Pick up the token."

Without asking, I already knew what he was talking about. The black object seemed to be warmer as I stared at it. There was still no glow; not even a trace of light was escaping from it. But there *was* heat. And where there's heat, there is power, I thought to myself. Power to warm the body. Power to control. Power to heal.

I reached out slowly with both hands. From the corner of my eye, I noticed the lamb. He was not looking at the object which so riveted my attention; he was looking at me. I hesitated. Just what did he expect to happen when I touched it?

Blessed is the man who does not walk in the counsel of the wicked or stand in the way of sinners or sit in the seat of mockers.

Psalms 1: 1

....

Prayer: Father, You have warned us repeatedly of the dangers of following those who would try to imitate Your powers. But the temptation can be strong, when they promise such wonderful dreams. Protect me from their enticements. May my strength be only in You.

Ask yourself: What do you think is significant about magical charms and tokens? Do they hold power in themselves?

The Token Revealed

"Why do you wait, Mortal One?" the lamb asked, noticing that I had taken my eyes off the black object and was now looking at him. "The key to your quest lies within your grasp. It is yours. Take it."

I moved a step closer, presumably to place my feet in a better position, but actually to gain a moment to think. Was this after all the object of my search, or was it yet another trap? Maybe I should grab the lamb instead, I thought. Maybe *he's* the real source of power. With difficulty, I took my eyes off the object and for a second time looked at the lamb. Noticing my hesitation, his expression changed. Where before he seemed to hold the wisdom of the ages, now I could see real fear in his eyes. "What are you doing?" he demanded, his voice cracking. "Are you mad? Take the token! Take the token!"

"What is the token?" I asked. "What will I have to pay to take it?"

"Those are the questions of a *fool*," he sneered. "Do you think such an opportunity comes to every mortal, and more than once in a lifetime? This is your chance. Think of what *He* will do to your son."

I had heard that before: behind us, another lamb had spoken in contempt of *Him*. Why were they so concerned? Was it really us they wanted to help, or were they simply plotting against *Him*?

The lamb could see that my mind was backing away, and he was thrown into a rage. "Mortal!" he screamed. "You have no more right to *real* power than does your son. Now *both* of you will live to regret your mistakes. Taste the bile of fear. Let it lie in your throat, until your miserable lives are choked out of existence."

With a sudden movement, the lamb lunged at me, pushing me off balance. Instinctively, I threw out my left hand to meet ground, and it landed on the black object. The pain of a thousand burning needles pierced through my palm and shot upward until my entire arm was in agony. "Oh God! It hurts!"

My prayer was heard.

All men will hate you because of me, but he who stands firm to the end will be saved.
Matthew 10: 22

....

Prayer: I am reminded, Lord, that while the enemy of this world may hate me, I know that he first hated You. I stand under his threat because I represent Your most precious creation. As your representative, may I bear his blows and wait on You, my salvation.

Ask yourself: Have you ever had unkind feelings toward someone simply because they were related to someone you didn't like?

Advocate

My involuntary cry of pain was not meant to be directed at Anyone in particular, but it was heard. The lamb, which had been standing over me with a vicious grin on its face suddenly froze. For an eternity which was probably not more than a few seconds, the world was silent. Then from beyond the boulder behind us there came an ear shattering roar. Whether it was animal, human or something altogether different, I couldn't tell. The lamb lifted its head to look behind and above me. An expression of sheer terror fell over him like a net, and he began backing away.

"No!" he cried. "I've done nothing wrong! *He* made me! It was *him*! Let me go!"

I struggled up onto one elbow and turned my head in the direction of the boulder, an unspoken terror filling my own heart at what I might see. But what I saw was absolutely nothing: at least nothing I could perceive. I looked back at the lamb, but he was still staring up at the space over the boulder, all the while screaming out his innocence. Then he turned and ran, leaping over a ravine and disappearing in a matter of seconds.

I rose to my feet and looked back again, but there was nothing I could see. I rubbed my injured hand and was surprised to discover that it no longer hurt. My son was kneeling near the spot where we had first seen the lamb. He turned to me and said, "Ashes. Nothing but ashes." There, where the mysterious black orb had rested was a pile of ash, without a trace of warmth in them. My son blew on them and they were gone, spread into the darkness. There was nothing else to keep us there, so we returned to the trail and continued upward.

Keep on, then, with your magic spells and with your many sorceries, which you have labored at since childhood. Perhaps you will succeed; perhaps you will cause terror.

Isaiah 47: 12

Prayer: Lord forgive me when I stray into the darkness, searching for what I don't have. Bring me back into Your precious light, and help me understand again that I have all I need in You.

Ask yourself: What "tokens of wisdom" are offered to the world today?

A Fire in the Darkness

We moved quickly at first, wanting to get as far as possible from the spot where the Magician's lamb had tempted us. Cold and hunger finally forced us to stop, and I suggested we build a fire with the last of the wood I was carrying. A few moments later, and we were huddled close to the crackling flames watching a pan of stew heating. "Now that's *real* warmth," my son said, rubbing his hands together and holding them out to the fire. "I think what we just experienced back there was *relevant warmth*."

"What do you mean by that?" I asked, stirring the stew.

"Well, take the ocean for example. You know how I liked to surf, all year round?"

"Of course," I mused. "You were crazy about it, even in the middle of winter."

"But you see, Dad, the water felt warm, even in the winter. It's not that it actually was warm, but compared to the air outside, it felt that way. I don't think that 'orb' thing the lamb had was capable of producing a bit of heat, but by making it *less cold*, it seemed that way to us."

"Okay," I said, seeing where he was going with this. "It's like when a bully at school steals your lunch, but leaves you your shoes, you want to thank him for his kindness. But the bottom line is, he's still stolen your lunch."

"Right," he said. "So I'm thinking about that evil man and the things that work for him. When you think about it, they don't have the power to give us a single thing; everything comes from God, right?" I nodded in agreement, and he went on. "So all they do is offer to torment us a little less, and we get the idea that they're doing something great for us. It's all in the packaging. He took his cup and poured some hot stew into it. I watched the steam rise from the pan and saw that this was a great revelation. The enemy was the master of imitation, and we had nearly fallen prey. I helped myself to the stew, enjoyed its warmth and said, "Thank you, Lord, for the real thing."

You belong to your father, the devil, and you want to carry out your father's desire.
He was a murderer from the beginning, not holding to the truth, for there is no
truth in him. When he lies, he speaks his native language, for he is a liar and the
father of lies.

John 8: 44

Prayer: Show me what is real today, Oh God. Grant that I may see through the enemy's deceits and recognize when I am being led up a way I should not go. Thank you for you bountiful blessings, all sufficient.

Ask yourself: What examples can you think of which illustrate the enemy's attempts to deceive?

The Demon Lamb

The top of the mountain was getting closer. Even in the darkness, the sensation of height was surrounding us. I began to think about stepping off the trail and falling into an abyss. I knew it was there, just out of sight. I wouldn't fall on purpose of course; still, the thought of being down there rather than up here was powerful and enticing.

It was getting harder to breathe, but I didn't think it was because of the altitude, and I knew it was not fatigue. Death waited just above us, and a part of me had already begun to die. Anger no longer lived, nor did denial. Any hope of finding a magical formula, or a scapegoat or a successful trade had died during the ascent. There was nothing left inside the shell of my body but the remnants of a broken heart kept alive by short gasping breaths, and a vague sense of resolve to carry out what was begun. I wasn't looking for lambs anymore; I knew there would be none. All that was left was the act itself: an act so reprehensible I couldn't bear to think about it, much less talk about it with my son. So we both walked on, side by side but each in our own worlds which we shared with no man.

As if it wasn't dark enough already, the clouds which had been hovering below now rose to envelop us in a thick, wet blanket, closing out not only the last remnants of light but also any distant sounds. Finally, the silence was complete, the darkness total. The only sound was that of our breathing, shallow and rapid, but strangely in cadence with one another. The sound was somehow comforting, and while it stirred no hope from within my shattered heart, still it offered an unspoken message which if given words might sound like, "It's all right. It's all right. It's all right."

There was a break in the rhythm. Something was out of step. I tried to adjust my pace to match that of my son's, but it didn't help. It was still there: a discordant sound. A wave of nausea swept over me as I began to understand that the sound was neither from me nor from my son. There was a third source.

They worshiped their idols, which became a snare to them. They sacrificed their sons and their daughters to demons.

Psalms 106: 36 – 37

....

Prayer: Father, Your Word tells me that we are not alone on this earth, but that an army of dark forces surrounds us. Thank you for the spiritual blindness which mercifully hides their activity. Grant that I may see of them what You want me to see. Give me courage to face them or flee from them, as You lead.

Ask yourself: Do you believe that there is a world of spirits around us which we cannot see?

The Demon Speaks

My son and I both came to a stop. He must have heard it too, that third source from somewhere nearby. For more than a minute, we both held our breaths, all of our senses tuned to detect the slightest intrusion. There it was, off to the left. A breathing sound, but not regular, as if it was trying to hold its breath as well, but not succeeding. I strained to see, but the darkness hid all traces of the Third Source, all but the irregular breathing.

"Who is it?" I trembled at last. The breathing stopped and remained silent for a long time. Then it began again. I tried to muster a confidence I didn't feel and raised my voice. "I command you in the Name of the One Who sent me here, speak up!"

With that, two catlike eyes suddenly became visible. They had evidently been closed before. The Source was less than six feet away, and from the eyes I judged it to be slightly taller than myself.

"You command me to speak? Very well. But you won't like what I have to say."

"I'll be the judge of that," I said, involuntarily stepping back away from the eyes. "Who are you, and what are you doing here?"

"I am the one you warn others against, and I am here to watch a killing."

The eyes closed for a moment, and fear swept over me like a cold wind. Where was he? Had he moved? I was just about to run in panic when the eyes opened again and I could see that he was in the same place as before. "What do you mean, 'warn against'? I don't even know you. How could I warn others against you?"

"Oh you know me all right. I've never been too far away. At times you've even invited me a little closer. But most of the time we simply enjoy a mutually contemptible relationship. That is, until you went dabbling in forbidden areas, speaking out about things you know nothing about. But all that is in the past now. You will bother us no more."

The Spirit clearly says that in later times some will abandon the faith and follow deceiving spirits and things taught by demons.

Timothy 4: 1

....

Prayer: Lord, my heart hurts when I confess that I have often invited the enemy closer by the things I have said and done. Please forgive me. Grant that I may see the folly of my actions before I fall victim to my own sin. Show me how to live in a dark world.

Ask yourself: How could a Christian invite the devil to a closer relationship?

September 12

Accusations

"Why do you I say I will "bother you no more"? I asked the creature before me. I hoped that my voice carried more conviction than I felt. I was terrified, but all the while testing the ground around my feet for a stone large enough to use as a weapon.

"Don't you know why you've been thrust up on this lovely mountain? It's because of *me*!" he shouted; then as if thinking better of it, lowered his voice to a hoarse whisper. "*I* am responsible for your being here, and you are at fault. You dared to tread upon me, and now you will pay with the life of your son."

"No!" I screamed, but my voice couldn't hide the question.

"Yes," he whispered back. "*You* are at fault. And when you go back down this mountain *alone*, remember this: I can strike whenever and wherever I please. Back away, or we will meet here again."

In spite of the chill in the air, I felt a flush come to my face and beads of sweat along my forehead. Was this the lamb I had been looking for? Not some innocent animal which I could lay on an altar in place of my son, but a creature of power with whom I could negotiate? The top of the mountain was so near; if there was ever to be a rescue, it had to here, and now. What if I could overpower him, kill him, and take his wretched body to the top? Would that result in any kind of mercy from *Him*?

I thought about my chances; he was obviously larger than me, and I suspected that he was somehow able to see in the darkness better than I could. I knew that he must possess abilities far beyond mine, since he knew so much about me. But still, he had eyes, a voice, and he *breathed*. He was no more than a creature.

And what had I become during this journey but a creature myself, devoid of any hopes, dreams, love of life? All I wanted was to see my son live. If I died trying to accomplish that, then I would die satisfied. Before me stood the embodiment of all that was evil. He was right: I *had* warned others about him. Now I would rid the world of him, throw his carcass at the feet of God and say "*Now* release my son from the curse!"

Do not be afraid of those who kill the body, but cannot kill the soul. Rather, be afraid of the One who can destroy both soul and body in hell.

Matthew 10: 28

Prayer: Father, in my passion to hate those who hate You, may I not lose sight of who I am: a sinner forgiven by the blood of Your Son Jesus. Guide me when I am confronted by the enemy, and help me fight or flee, as You will it.

Ask yourself: Do you think Christians are called to battle the demonic powers of this world?

Conflict

My right foot found a stone in the darkness. I judged it to be not much bigger than an orange, but it would have to do. In one motion, I bent down, swept the stone into one hand and leapt toward the eyes which glared down at me. But instead of finding his flesh, I struck what seemed like a solid wall of rock. I fell back, the weapon flying from my hand. Blood was gushing from my head, and the world seemed to be spinning. Above me, the eyes opened wider than before and a voice rang out in triumph: "You see what your pitiful attempts on me are worth. Human! You are weak, and I curse you for your weakness. *I* would have smashed your miserable body out of existence long ago, but *He* decided to keep you. The fool! Doesn't He see what a worthless mass of clay you are? Now, *human*, you will see what power *I* have! This is what I was cast out of heaven for, and this is how I deal with those *He* would save."

I closed my eyes, expecting at any moment to feel sharp talons wrenching my heart out. For all the brokenness, in spite of the dead hopes and dreams I had cherished, still there remained within me a spark of desire. I wanted to live.

"God!" I cried out. "Save me!"

My eyes were still closed, but suddenly the world was bright. No covering could shut out the light which poured in from all directions. I opened my eyes and found that the night had turned to day in an instant. Directly overhead, there was an object, brighter than the sun, too dazzling to look at but too awesome to ignore. The trail was clearly visible below me, and I could see every stop I had made along the way. The lambs which had confronted me were all there too, in plain sight, but like me they were cringing from the light.

Rising directly in front of me was a cliff, its rock face smooth as glass, except for a tiny ledge about six feet off the ground. And there, perched in terror, was the creature I had feared. He was about the size of a small rabbit, his catlike eyes disproportionately large for his body. He was trembling, looking up at the light, then burying his head in his tiny paws.

You believe there is one God. Good! Even the demons believe that – and shudder.

James 2: 19

....

Prayer: In the light of Your Presence, my enemies can be seen for who they really are. May Your light shine through me every day, so that my path will not be darkened, and my feet will not stumble. You alone are the light of the world.

Ask yourself: Why is it that the scariest movies don't show you the monster until the end?

September 14

God Speaks

Seeing this tiny creature that only moments before had filled me with such fear, I was overwhelmed with both relief and blind rage. Looking around me, I saw the stone which had fallen from my hand. Grabbing it up, I moved toward the creature. "So this is the 'awesome power of the night'," I sneered. "*You* are the one who would kill my son? Take a look around you, *creature*, because it's going to be your last!"

I raised my hand to strike the miserable object before me, but before I could do so, a wave of paralysis swept over me. The stone fell from my hand, and my arm dropped uselessly to my side. In a moment of panic, I looked back to the creature on the ledge, but he was still trembling, taking no notice of me whatsoever.

From the light above me, a voice rang out and buried itself in my very soul. "It is not yours to destroy what I have created. His fate is in My Hands, and I will deal with him as I see fit; just as I will deal with you."

After that, the world fell silent. No other words were necessary. All that needed to be said had been said. The light, which had been so impossibly bright, now grew smaller, moving up to the top of the mountain. The demon might not have moved from the ledge; I didn't know, and didn't care anymore. My son may have been with me as I turned to move up the trail, or he might have gone on ahead. All I knew was that the Light waited at the top, and that was where I wanted to be.

In the beginning was the Word, and the Word was with God, and the Word was God. He was with God in the beginning. Through him all things were made; without him nothing was made that has been made. In him was life, and that life was the light of men. The light shines in the darkness, but the darkness has not understood it.

John 1: 1 – 5

Prayer: By Your precious Light, Oh God, help me to see the world around me as it really is. May the sin which has hidden in darkness be brought into the open, and may my life, which sometimes seeks the shadows, be always and only before You.

Ask yourself: What dark things chip at the joy in your life? How could they be brought to the light?

September 15

The Summit

The journey up the mountain had been emotionally and physically exhausting. In desperation, I had searched the path for a lamb which would serve as a substitute for the fate which awaited my son. Anger and Denial were my constant companions, but pitiful comfort. The lamb of Trade couldn't begin to pay the price my son's life demanded, nor could the Scapegoat take his place. The Magician's lamb and his brother Demon had taken their toll on my emotions until I stood at last at the top of the mountain, broken and dejected.

My legs gave way and I collapsed to my knees, hands clasped together in an effort to keep from sprawling face down in the dirt. The light I had followed during the last part of the climb had now disappeared, and I was left wondering if I had ever seen it at all. In its place, was a world of shadows and images, which any other time would have caused me to fear for my safety. But I was beyond fear now. Death, even violent and painful death, would be welcomed as a dear friend.

A few paces away, a stone table. For some reason, I was not surprised to see my son's body lying on it. The rough hewn edges of the stone seemed to threaten any who might try to come near. I wanted to step forward: to take my son in my arms, to hold him like I never held him in life, to whisper in his ears the words I never spoke when I had the chance. But the cold, gray stone warned me away, and I remained where I was, on my knees and struggling to hold onto consciousness.

Looking beyond the stone, I could see another stone behind it, slightly higher than the one in front. And another one beyond that. What I thought was a table was in fact only the first of a series of steps leading higher still. Peering through the darkness, which I realized was growing lighter, I could see the real altar beyond the top most step.

It was already occupied.

I wept and wept because no one was found who was worthy to open the scroll or look inside... Then I saw a lamb, looking as if it had been slain, standing in the center of the throne.

Revelation 5: 4, 6

....

Prayer: Praise You, Father, for the Lamb's image, which You gave John. Praise You for the blood of Your Son Jesus, which washes away my sin and enables me to approach Your throne.

Ask yourself: Why was it necessary for Jesus to die?

The Lamb of Lambs

The Lamb of Lambs stood on the top most step. I could see at once that He was different from the others I had encountered on the trail below. I was amazed that I had been so easily deceived by them. They had been nothing at all like what stood above me now.

I raised my hands in total surrender. I tried to speak, but the words caught in my throat, as I realized that the Lamb was bleeding. I watched in horror as blood began to spill over the stone steps and run down toward where my son lay. As it reached the bottom step, it collected in pools around his body, tiny rivulets converging and outlining his cold form, setting him apart from his surroundings. Then the blood began to cover him, until he was completely enveloped.

By this time, I was so far removed from the reality of what I was seeing, that any ideas of intervention would have been unthinkable. I knew that my only role in what was unfolding was that of observer. Small wonder then, when I saw my son's eyes open and watched unmoving as he stood to his feet. He paused only a moment, then began climbing the steps. He stopped at the last step and turned back in my direction. The face was his: no doubt about that. But it was not the face of a child anymore. It was a handsome, grown man with the expression of one who had become all he had been created to be. His eyes met mine for a moment, and I saw there a depth of love that I had never seen there before. It was a love devoid of all pretense, all selfish motives, all fear. There was a twinkle in his eyes that I had seen only on a few occasions during his childhood.

Watching him standing there, I felt I had to speak: to tell him of my joy for him and how proud he had made me. But before I could open my mouth, he turned back toward the top step and continued on. When he came to the place where the Lamb stood, I was suddenly blinded by a light so bright that I was thrown face down, the force of its rays holding me immobile. When at last I was able to look up, he was gone.

Precious in the sight of the LORD is the death of his saints. O LORD, truly I am your servant; I am your servant, the son of your maidservant; you have freed me from my chains.

Psalms 115: 15 – 16

Prayer: Father You have told me that the death of Your children is nothing more than a coming home, to be with You in Your kingdom. Thank you for that assurance, and for knowing that You wait beyond the Mystery. Prepare me for my time of homecoming, that I may die well, a testimony of Your love and mercy.

Ask yourself: How do you think a baby feels about being born? How does that compare with the death of a Christian?

September 17

The Lamb Speaks

My son was no longer in view, but the Lamb remained, standing motionless and looking directly at me. When I thought I could no longer bear it, He spoke.

"Do not be dismayed," He said. "Your son is with me, and in the Father's time you will also come up these steps. I am the Lamb you sought for. I am the way to life."

I could not look away, even if I had wanted to. All that I could see, all that I ever wanted to see, was this glorious Presence before me. No other sensation found its way into my thoughts. Whether it was day or night, hot or cold, whether I was hungry or thirsty: these were not even a remote part of my consciousness. I would have dismissed them if they had found a way into my thoughts. All I knew, all I wanted to know, was that I was in the Presence of God, and I wanted the moment to last forever. Mercifully, clouds began to move in and cover the mountain top. The image of the Lamb became fuzzy, then disappeared altogether. I started to weep, and tried to move closer, to regain the image, but my body would not move. Instead, an overwhelming desire to sleep came over me. I fought it, desperately trying to keep the moment, but it was impossible to resist. Before I knew what was happening, I lay face down where I had fallen, and gave in to the darkness.

Do not hide your face from me, do not turn your servant away in anger; you have been my helper. Do not reject me or forsake me, O God my Savior.

Psalms 27: 9

....

Prayer: As much as I desire to see You face to face, Dear Lord, I know that such a thing would make me unfit to remain in this world. In Your mercy, You hide Your Presence from me and bid me do Your will until I am at last called home. Keep me faithful until that day.

Ask yourself: What do you think would happen if God revealed himself to you today?

Alone

There was no way of knowing how long I had been asleep. The sun was high overhead, but had my last conscious thoughts taken place at night or in the daytime? Those thoughts... yes! That image of the Lamb. My son. I came to my feet and looked around. I seemed to be standing on a mountaintop, but it was unlike any I could recall. There were rocks scattered about, and patches of snow in their shadows. The vistas below me spread out in all directions as far as I could see, but nothing looked familiar.

A table. There had been a stone table... and my son. I looked around the area but found only more rocks and snow. Had I dreamed everything? Was I suffering from some sort of delusional episode? But if that were the case, how had I arrived at this desolate peak, and where in fact was my son? Perhaps he was still alive, after all, Perhaps the nightmare had begun long ago, and was finally over. Perhaps...

A glint of metal caught my eye, off to the left. I walked over to it and saw that it was a sword: my sword. The one I had given my son. When I reached down to pick it up, I noticed something else lying beside it. A necklace, made of four teeth, strung together. Lion's teeth. Whatever else may have happened, this at least was certain: my son was gone, and the only thought which could find its way into my mind was, how will I ever get down from this mountain alone?

The king covered his face and cried aloud, "O my son Absalom! O Absalom, my son, my son!"

II Samuel 19: 4

....

Prayer: Father, You have led me to the mountaintops, and into the valleys as well. It is only by Your grace that I move from one to the other. But there are times, in the midst of trial and grief, when I forget that You are with me. Hold me close then, Lord. Speak to me, I pray.

Ask yourself: Why do you think grief is such a powerful force in a person's life?

Numb

In the midst of grief, one cannot expect to think or act rationally. But why was I grieving? I had been in the presence of the Lamb of God! My son was now with Him, and I was promised that the day would come when I too would join Him. Such revelations should have filled me with joy. Instead, I had awoken to the reality of a lonely mountaintop and a dead child. In spite of the wonderful blessing which had been mine, I could not deny my grief, and the grief overtook me.

I sat where I had fallen, next to the sword and the string of lion's teeth. I mourned for my son, I mourned for myself and I mourned for the journey which so occupied my life these past several months. How could I possibly go on, now that my life was shattered? What difference would it make if I lived or died here on this mountain? I gazed at the sword lying at my feet and a mirthless laugh escaped my lips. So what if I slay a thousand demons from hell, or ten thousand lions who attack me? Death will win in the end. I could not fight it, not anymore. What use were friendships, or sunsets, or Lizzie's stew? If there were no more meaning to life than this, why should I concern myself with it?

I remained unmoving: unthinking for the most part, except when such thoughts of futility tortured me. In an unconscious attempt at self-preservation, I drove all thought from my mind, until all that was left were the involuntary motions of heartbeat and breath. I would have stopped those if I could, but such an action would have required more than I was prepared to give. So instead, I sat. The sun moved across the sky and finally settled below the horizon. The wind blew the clouds away, and stars filled the night sky, but I cannot remember looking at them. All was emptiness.

Are not my few days almost over? Turn away from me so I can have a moment's joy before I go to the place of no return, to the land of gloom and deep shadow, to the land of deepest night, of deep shadow and disorder, where even the light is like darkness."

Job 10: 20 – 22

Prayer: Father, I can remember times in my life when grief took away my joy, my hope, my desire to live. Praise You that the time was short-lived. Thank you for staying with me through the dark times. Remind me again when those times return that You will never leave me nor forsake me.

Ask yourself: What can you do to help a person who is grieving?

Morning

In spite of our grief, our bodies will eventually demand attention. Hunger, cold and sickness may be ignored for a time, but the body will continue to provide the requirements for survival. And when those requirements are not met, the mind is often jolted into awareness.

That time came for me just before dawn. The temperature had dropped below freezing and I remained where I had fallen to my knees the previous morning. Lack of circulation, together with bitter cold, caused my muscles to cramp and shiver. Lack of nourishment and the need for food was making itself known through an aching stomach. Had I been able to ignore the symptoms awhile longer, my body would have started shutting down, going into shock and eventually the sweet relief of death. But there remained a spark of life, and it would not be disregarded. As a wave of dizziness swept over me, my senses were stabbed. For the first time, I was aware that I was freezing to death. I tried to stand up, but my legs refused to cooperate. Slapping myself to restore circulation, I accepted the self-inflicted pain with a measure of relief. At least the pain was something I understood.

I dug through my back pack for a sweater and came across some dried fruit. It wasn't much, but it brought me back to my senses. I couldn't stay here forever; I knew that. Where I would go, and how I would get there I neither knew nor cared. Just move, I told myself.

Finally finding my legs, I got to my feet. As if in a dream, I put the sword and the necklace in my backpack, closed it up and put it on. Which way? It was still dark, but the sun would soon appear. I started down the mountain by the nearest slope. If there was a trail, I couldn't see it, and didn't care. Just move.

But your dead will live; their bodies will rise. You who dwell in the dust, wake up and shout for joy. Your dew is like the dew of the morning; the earth will give birth to her dead.

Isaiah 26: 19

Prayer: **Thank you Lord, for building into me the will to live. Even when my emotions try to ignore the basic needs of the body, there is still a power at work within me to survive. And when the crisis has passed, I'm able to recover because of that will. Praise You, for I am fearfully and wonderfully made!**

Ask yourself: **Have you ever had to attend to a physical need, even when your emotions demanded full attention?**

September 21

Into the Valley

By the time the sun was up, I had reached timberline. The descent had been straight and uneventful, my progress unhampered by trees, rocks, or any semblance of a trail. I simply went down, by the easiest route available. Now that I was entering a forested area, I had to start making decisions: should I go to the left or to the right of the next tree? Still, there was no overall plan guiding me, so each obstacle was passed according to the path of least resistance.

If there was anything driving me, it was a desire to be as far away from the mountain as possible. In spite of the evidence of God Himself back at the summit, my mind had been shattered by the realities of grief. My son was dead. My life had no purpose, no joy, no hope of recovery. On the mountain, I had been met by a succession of creatures, all of whom wanted to hurt me and my son. Yet they all failed: all but the last One. I knew it was irrational, but the only thought I could process was the fact that the only lamb capable of taking life and leaving me a broken shell of a man was the Lamb at the summit.

I remembered something C.S. Lewis had written in the midst of his own grief. "It was not so much that I came to disbelieve in God, but rather to begin to believe terrible things about Him." I had no doubt that God had met us on the mountain. I knew with certainty that He held absolute power and authority. But with that knowledge was the simple fact: my son was dead, and while God could have spared him, He chose not to.

And so I stumbled down the mountainside, not sure of my destination but determined to leave this place of darkness and pain. Perhaps tomorrow I would be able to put into words what my heart was crying to express, but not today. Today I would simply move away.

Oh, my anguish, my anguish! I writhe in pain. Oh, the agony of my heart! My heart pounds within me, I cannot keep silent.

Jeremiah 4: 19

....

Prayer: Father, You know my heart perfectly, and there is no thought I could ever hope to hide from You. You know then the unspoken fear, and doubt, and yes, even anger I feel when grief takes over. Forgive me when I let these thoughts grow into sinful rebellion. As I share them openly and honestly with You, grant that I may either understand Your ways, or else that I may accept them by faith.

Ask yourself: Do you think it is a sin to be angry with God?

September 22

Blame

Deep into the forest, my progress had become slower and less certain. The trees were thicker now, and more difficult to go around. Finally, I pulled out my sword and used it as a machete, hacking away at the undergrowth. Fatigue turned to anger, and each blow was accompanied by a curse. What was I doing here? Why had He led me all this way, just to leave me like this? I didn't ask to come on this journey, and I didn't call my son along. Why did he have to die? God could have prevented it. He could have easily stepped in and... The next swing of the sword glanced off a limb and came around to strike my left arm.

I threw the sword down and with another curse gripped the wound with my right hand. Closer inspection revealed that it wasn't serious; just a minor cut. I tore off a piece of my shirt and using it as a bandage held it tightly until the bleeding stopped. Tying it in place, I thought about what I had done. What was of more concern than the wound itself was the realization that my anger had been a direct factor. Had I so soon forgotten the encounter with the lamb on the mountain? Lashing out would only result in self-affliction.

Then what was I to do? If expressions of anger would not remove this agony in my heart, then I would have to separate myself from the source of the rage. God would have to go.

He says to himself, "God has forgotten; he covers his face and never sees." Arise, LORD! Lift up your hand, O God. Do not forget the helpless.

Psalms 10: 11 - 12

Prayer: How it must grieve Your heart, O Lord, when we in our foolishness determine to reject You. We cannot find a reason for our suffering, and so we try to place the blame on You. Forgive us for our ignorance and please be merciful. Teach us the measure of our faith, and help us use it to draw near to You.

Ask yourself: How often have you lashed out in anger to someone you love, only to regret it later?

September 23

A Hollow Heart

Deciding to remove God from my heart proved to be a bigger challenge than I expected it to be. How could I separate and discard something which had made itself a vital part of my very being? Since the day I had entered into this relationship, God had come into my life and made me a totally different person. I no longer enjoyed the company of friends I had known for years. My speech, my attitudes, my ethics were different than they were before. My own family had come to see me as a stranger in my own house: not a bad person by any means, but a person who lived by a different set of values. All of these changes I attributed to the Presence of God in my life.

Now I no longer wanted that Presence. It was because of Him that I was suffering so. He was to blame, if not directly for the death of my son, then for His failure to heal him. I started by expressing these feelings to God. "I don't like what You've done," I cried. "I want no more part of this journey. I want to go back to the way it was." But even as I shouted my declarations, I knew He was still there. I could not remove Him as I would a sliver from my thumb. He had entered my heart, just as He had promised, and had every intention of staying there.

If I couldn't remove Him, then I would ignore Him, I decided. If the heart is His dwelling place, then I will never go there. Let Him remain. I would live my life, heartless. If joy comes from the heart, then I would never seek it. Kindness, forgiveness, passion and hope, all would be denied if that was what it took to be rid of Him.

I sat back and explored this new commitment. It would take strength and dedication to live by this creed, I realized. But already I could feel my despair slipping away. Grieving is for those with a heart to grieve. I would have none, and I would survive.

...God has said, "Never will I leave you; never will I forsake you."
Hebrews 13: 5b

....

Prayer: Praise You God for Your faithfulness, even when we are unfaithful. Praise You for Your promise that You will never leave us nor forsake us. Forgive my rebellious wanderings, and bring me back to Your side.

Ask yourself: Can a person live without a heart to love?

September 24

The First Test

After concluding that I would deny every longing in my heart, I set out to live by my decision. When feelings of remorse and grief began to rise, I shouted back in defiance, "No! Those are the emotions of a fool! I will not let myself be ruled by them." I hacked at the undergrowth as if it were a mortal enemy. When evening came, I built a fire and stacked on the wood, laughing as the flames leapt to the sky. I imagined that it was my heart, burning away all that had been me. "Call me 'Friend' no more," I said to the inferno. "I will be friend to no man. My life is mine alone. I will never share it, lest I lose again something precious."

By morning, the fire in my camp and the fire in my soul had burned themselves out. I lay exhausted, trying to sleep but to no avail. Without peace there was no comfort; without comfort, no rest. Finally I rose and began to walk. There was still no purpose, no direction, so my feet led me further downhill, away from the mountain. I walked all day, and as evening approached I stood on a hillside, overlooking a wide valley below. Campfires dotted the meadow, and the sound of singing met my ears. It was Rendezvous.

I could imagine Lizzie over by the largest fire, stirring her stew and telling her stories. The clank of metal striking metal told me that someone was still engaged in sword practice. Ralph teaching some newcomer. A hunger rose up from my heart, and my body was already leaning toward the camp, when I remembered my resolve. They would never understand my decision. They would try to bring me back, to rekindle the fire which had gone out in my heart. And the agony would return. I turned away from the meadow and continued around the mountainside, skirting the camp and moving on. Soon the sounds of Rendezvous were lost to the night. I was truly alone.

Let us not give up meeting together, as some are in the habit of doing, but let us encourage one another—and all the more as you see the Day approaching.

Hebrews 10: 25

....

Prayer: Father, why must joy and pain dwell in the same place in my heart? How can I live with emotions which are so volatile and impossible to control? All I can do is give my heart to You, Dear Father. In Your love and mercy, take what You will and leave me only what You want me to have.

Ask yourself: Do you agree that anger and joy are closely connected emotions?

September 25

The Swamp

I stumbled for hours in the darkness. Now that the decision was made to bypass the Rendezvous camp, I wanted to get as far away as possible, lest someone discover me while gathering wood. The trail was somewhere off to the left, so I bore to the right, moving into the forest and downhill, away from the meadow. The stars provided enough light to make out the shapes of trees ahead, but did little to guide my feet. I tripped and fell repeatedly, but kept moving forward. I was driven either by fear of being found or by the emptiness in my heart; I didn't know which, but knew only that I must deny the pain and fatigue that threatened to overtake me.

I judged it to be about midnight when I could go no farther. The ground was becoming steadily softer, with patches of water I would step into, soaking my feet. Once more I fell head long, but instead of getting up, I remained where I had landed, covering my head with a sweater and closing my eyes to the night.

The next I knew, it was daylight, and I was lying with my feet in a muddy pool of water. The backpack was still in place on my shoulders, no doubt providing a small degree of warmth during the night. My hands and arms were covered with mosquito bites, and from the sounds around me there were plenty more waiting their turn.

I slipped out of the pack and stood up to look around. The woods were still dark and thick, but instead of the evergreens which had been so common along the trail, I now found myself in a cypress forest. Roots rose up out of the water as if standing on tip toes. Where I had slept was the largest dry spot of land in sight: everything else was a swamp.

When they are diminished and brought low through oppression, trouble, and sorrow, he pours contempt upon princes and makes them wander in trackless wastes; but he raises up the needy out of affliction, and makes their families like flocks.

Psalm 107: 37 – 41

....

Prayer: Lord, all too often, the valleys I walk in are of my own choosing. Forgive me when I rebel and leave the way You have put before me. Lead me back to the plain that is higher than I. Bring me to Your loving Presence again.

Ask yourself: Look back over difficult times in your life: how often could those times have been prevented by your own choices?

September 26

Settling In

"Let's see them find me *here*," I said to myself, gazing in all directions and seeing nothing but cypress swamp. This was perfect: my place of solitude. No one would be passing by to ask my name or my destination. No one would care that I had made my home in this forsaken place. I could live here with my empty heart, neither knowing nor caring what might be happening in the rest of the world. This would be my world for as long as... how long? I wondered briefly. Would there come a time when I might choose to leave this place? Perhaps, perhaps not. But if I did, it would be my decision. No one else would determine my path: not anymore. I would be master of my fate, ruler of this, my world.

I would need shelter. By gathering dead limbs and vines, I was able to put together a rough lean-to. It wasn't much, but I didn't need much. I desired neither comfort nor joy. I wanted only to live alone, unhindered by the expectations of others, responsible to no one: not even *Him*.

The efforts of building my camp had left me weak, and I lay down in my new home. Gaps in the roof gave me glimpses of blue sky, evidence that the sun was shining somewhere. I would have to patch that soon. Reminders of normal life outside this swamp only served to threaten my resolve to stay in this dismal place. I wanted to be here, in spite of what I could see beyond the treetops. I would not return to the land of the living; not now, not ever. Living meant pain and fear, disappointment and heartache. I would devote what was left of my miserable life to seeking nothingness, for it was only there, I felt, that I could survive.

The words of the Teacher son of David, king in Jerusalem: "Meaningless! Meaningless!" says the Teacher. "Utterly meaningless! Everything is meaningless."
Ecclesiastes 1: 1 – 2

....

Prayer: Lord, even the Teacher of Ecclesiastes suffered the despair of emptiness. Yet, as You brought him to wisdom and understanding, so bring me to that place of peace, where I rest in Your purpose and plan.

Ask yourself: How important is it to see purpose in life?

Food

I made it through the day, mostly by sleeping or by staring aimlessly into the darkness of the surrounding swamp. Whenever I did rise, dizziness would force me back down, where I would remain. By the next morning, I understood what my problem was: I needed food. Such a realization filled me with disgust. I had devoted my new life here to the denial of everything which might suggest a return to normal. I had determined to never again seek joy, or friendship or anything which might suggest comfort. I was proud of my crude shelter, and of the roots which dug into my back when I lay down.

But then I was angry at the sense of pride I felt. Was that not a source of joy as well: to accomplish something and to make use of that accomplishment? Some things, I concluded, had to be done for the sake of survival, but I would try my best to keep those to a minimum. Then came the hunger pangs. Besides the bit of dried fruit on the mountaintop, I had eaten nothing for at least two days, and my body was complaining.

Rummaging through my backpack turned up nothing but a few condiments such as oil, flour and salt. I would have to live off the land, I decided. The only living things I had seen during the day had been a few snakes and some kind of swamp rat, about the size of a rabbit. I pushed back the revulsion and reminded myself that I *wanted* to be miserable. This would be perfect. The rats were plentiful, and not accustomed to being hunted. I found that by chasing them into the water they could then be caught quite easily. It wasn't long before I had three carcasses roasting over the campfire.

Trying to avoid comparisons to Lizzie's stew, I tore off pieces of meat and ate in silence. This was perfect, I thought. If this frail body of mine is going to demand to be fed, then I'll feed it. "How do you like rat?" I said aloud, then laughed at my joke. "Keep complaining, and I'll find you some snake!"

I despise my life; I would not live forever. Let me alone; my days have no meaning.

Job 7: 16

....

Prayer: I know that You desire joy, and not misery for my life. Teach me how to face my trials, not with a sense of hopelessness, but in the knowledge that You have something better for me. Teach me today how to live.

Ask yourself: Do you think that God enjoys watching His children suffer? If not, then why would He allow it?

September 28

Passing Predator

The sound of splashing nearby woke me this morning. I raised up on one elbow and peered out of my lean-to. There at the edge of the water, just a few paces away, lay an alligator. He had found the rat entrails I had dumped the night before and was making them his breakfast. "Something for everybody," I thought to myself. As low as I had gone in deciding what I would eat, there was a lower level yet, and the alligator was more than willing to take up where I had left off.

I crawled out of the lean-to and stood up. The alligator froze, as if in doing so he would disappear from view. His eyes moved, almost imperceptibly, as he checked me out. Nope, too big, he decided, backing away into deeper water and moving on into the swamp.

It's as simple as that, then. Whether you eat or get eaten is just a matter of size and strength. There's nothing special about a man beyond an opposable thumb and a brain which can figure out how to use it. Another day, a careless step, and I could just as easily be that alligator's lunch, in the same way that he could be mine if he came any closer.

Why should I think for a moment that I'm any different from the rest the creatures which crawl over the earth? Remember your science textbooks? My ancestors were the size of a mouse, hiding from the dinosaurs for millions of years until a meteorite finally leveled the playing field. A few lucky breaks, a few chance discoveries, and here I stand, the pinnacle of nature, lord of the universe. That is, until the universe hits back and I return to the slime from which I came.

There. That wasn't so difficult, was it, I thought as I built up the campfire for another round of roasted rat. Take *Him* out of the picture, and everything falls right into place. Everything is chance, pure and simple. There's no need to look any farther for explanations. If only...

God made the wild animals according to their kinds, the livestock according to their kinds, and all the creatures that move along the ground according to their kinds. And God saw that it was good.

Genesis 1: 25

....

Prayer: Today when I look outside, Lord, show me the miracle of Your creation. Help me to see Your Divine Hand at work, and tell me again how You made all this, so that I might look in wonder and worship You.

Ask yourself: How could it possibly comfort a person to conclude that all life is simply a matter of chance, with no Creator? Is it because the prospect of facing that Creator is so much worse?

Fever

My sleep was troubled, if indeed I slept at all. Visions of alligators feasting on rats and looking sideways at me all the while. Snakes wrapping themselves around my feet, keeping me from walking, or moving at all. The stars spinning impossibly as I tried to get away from shapeless images that wanted to hurt me.

When I opened my eyes, the sky was still spinning. Beads of sweat lay on my forehead and I was shaking uncontrollably. I was lying with my feet sticking out of the shelter, a steady rain falling and soaking me from the knees down. Maybe I should have boiled the swamp water before drinking it.

I had to do something; even in my delirium I knew that. But what could I do? I tried to pull back into the shelter, but only succeeded in kicking off the sleeping bag, leaving my feet more exposed than before. The effort left me exhausted, and I must have slept, because when I looked out again, it was dark. Wasn't it just morning a few moments ago? It was still raining.

I was no longer sweating, but now my body felt hot and dry. I was thirsty. A steady dripping sound caught my attention, and I looked to the left to see a trickle of water falling next to my head. Thank goodness I didn't patch the gaps in the roof like I had wanted to. With an effort that seemed to take hours, I moved over until the water was trickling onto my head. By stretching my neck up, I could get a little into my mouth, and that seemed to help. Reaching into my pocket for a handkerchief, I soaked it in the water laid it over my forehead, and rolled back away from the stream.

If I had been seeking misery, then this was it. My joints ached from the fever, my body cried out for food, and my sleeping bag, soaked with rain from the outside and with sweat from the inside, clung to me like a corpse. Congratulations, I thought to myself. You're killing yourself.

If I am wicked, woe to me! If I am righteous, I cannot lift up my head, for I am filled with disgrace and look upon my affliction.

Job 10: 15

Prayer: In times of sickness, I realize, Father how dependent I am on You for my strength and health. Praise You when I am well! Praise You when I am sick, for it is through affliction that I come to depend upon You more.

Ask yourself: Have you ever been so sick that you could not care for yourself? What did you do?

Fire

Another night was quickly settling in, and I had gone through several cycles of fever followed by chills. The rain had stopped, but everything was dripping, including the roof of my shelter. Hypothermia was a very real possibility, and I decided that I needed a fire. There was wood stacked nearby, but it was soaked and unlikely to burn without some encouragement.

Crawling around the fireplace, I gathered wood and set it in place. I still had a few matches, and got them out. But there had to be something dry to set underneath it to get the wood going. But what? Digging through my backpack, I found some paper. Pulling it out, I started to tear it into pieces for the fire, then looked to see what it was. It was my journal.

I hesitated, then ripped out the first page and started to stuff it under the wood. The words caught my eye, and I stopped to read in the dim light. "There's a smell of waterproofed canvas in the air. The journey has begun," I read. Turning the page over, I saw the last part of that first day's entry. "Now, with the scents and sounds of newness all around me, I lean into the straps and push ahead. No need to look back anymore."

But that's exactly what I was doing, wasn't it? Looking back. Remembering a time of new hope and discovery. Recalling the challenges of the past. It had not always been easy, back then. But I had gotten through the day and took comfort in looking back on it. And now what was I doing? Lying cold, soaked and dying of fever alone in a swamp, and why? Because I was still looking back, to a time when my world fell apart.

So that was the question, wasn't it? Do I look back or do I forget the past? Do I let yesterday's joy and sadness determine where I go today? It was a question I couldn't answer: at least not in my present condition. Maybe I did need to get rid of the past, starting with this journal. I shoved the page under the wood and struck a match. Holding it close to the paper, more words were brought to the light: "...now last year is last year. Past. Forgiven Forgotten." Something in those three words caused me to hesitate. I blew out the match and thought about it.

Remember the days of old; consider the generations long past. Ask your father and he will tell you, your elders, and they will explain to you.

Deuteronomy 32: 7

Prayer: Father protect me from my looking backward. When I remember past mistakes and sorrows, remind me of my future in Your kingdom. Help me to learn from my past, but not to be judged by it.

Ask yourself: Are traditions important in your life? Is that a good thing?

October 1

In the Firelight

Lying in a wet sleeping bag on a cold, wet evening, suffering from a fever-induced haze, there's nothing like a blazing fire to draw a person's attention. The heat worked its way to my body's core, removing moisture as it went. I was still sick, but the fire, started thanks to a generous helping of cooking oil, encouraging me to heat some water and make a poor man's soup out of oil, salt and whatever scraps of meat I could uncover. It was probably the foulest thing I had ever tasted, but the warmth and nourishment were slowly restoring me.

In the light of the fire, I read through the pages of my journal. I was reminded again of the trail which I had rejected: the dangers, the joys, and the things which make up any journey. I thought of Charlie's wisdom, Jonathan's bravery, Ralph's humor. Did I really want to put all of that behind me, never to experience it again?

If only I could select those things that brought me joy and leave the painful things behind: the lion, the evil man, the desert, my son. Would I really reject the despair that I had known with my son, knowing that in doing so I would also be rejecting the joy I had with him? Why must every experience in life be a two-sided coin? Laughter and tears, thirst and refreshment, fear and victory; it seemed that one could not be had without the other. My solution had been to deny it all and empty my heart of any emotion which might hurt me. But where was I now? Was this the natural result of trying to live a life devoid of all perception?

I could try to deny it all I wanted, but at the end of the day, I was sick, hungry, cold... and lonely. The fever seemed to be on the rise again. I lay back with my eyes closed, and just before drifting back to sleep whispered a single word, "Lord..."

There is a time for everything, and a season for every activity under heaven: a time to be born and a time to die, a time to plant and a time to uproot, a time to kill and a time to heal, a time to tear down and a time to build.

Ecclesiastes 3: 1 – 3

....

Prayer: Father teach me to take the bitter things in life along with the sweet, in the knowledge that it is only through all of those things that I become all You have created me to me. Comfort me in times of pain, and in Your mercy, spare me, heal me.

Ask yourself: What would your life had been like if you had never known a day of suffering?

October 2

Answered Prayer

With a simple prayer on my lips as I slipped back into a fever-induced sleep, one truth burned itself into my heart: the simplest prayer is often the most profound. Darkness closed around me, but in the next instant I was transported back to the mountaintop. When I realized where my dream was taking me, I fought back, wanting desperately to get away from there and the agony I had left behind. "No! No!" I cried to the darkness. "Not there!"

A shaft of light lit up the summit and burned straight through to my soul. A Voice which by now was no stranger to me spoke from the light. "Do you call me 'Lord'?"

" I... Y... yes, Lord. I must."

"Why?"

"Be...because, I do not belong to myself. I belong to You."

"Why?" "Because... You bought me, with the blood of Your Son."

"Then why do you try to live as though you belonged to yourself?"

The words cut to the marrow, and I had no answer to give. Instead, I fell on my face, speechless. He spoke again. "Did you think that you would make a better Master than I am?"

"No! I mean... yes, I did. But I was wrong. Please forgive me... forgive me..."

I was back at my camp. It was daylight, and a single ray of sunshine would have been shining directly into my eyes, except that it was being blocked by the figure of a man standing in front of my lean-to, leaving him as a silhouette.

"Are you... are... are you Jesus?" I asked the figure.

"No son, but it looks to me like you've met Him."

Why do you call me, 'Lord, Lord,' and do not do what I say? I will show you what he is like who comes to me and hears my words and puts them into practice.

Luke 6: 46 – 47

....

Prayer: Teach me, Lord, the cost of discipleship. Help me to know that the road to maturity does not come without a price. And be merciful when I stumble.

Ask yourself: What does it mean to "belong" to God?

October 3

Found Again

Pastor McAllan knelt down and laid a hand on my forehead. "You seem to have picked up a bug somewhere. Let me get this fire going, then we'll see what I can find in my bag."

"Pastor," I started. I couldn't have been more surprised if it *had* been Jesus. "How did you find me?"

"I started back to the mountain to see if I could help you down, but on the way, well, God spoke to me and told me to come in this direction." He laughed, then went on. "Boy, talk about your step of faith! I kept thinking, 'No way am I going to find anything down here but a mess of trouble!'" He sniffed, and I shuddered to think about what I smelled like. "But I have to say," he said, "I really like what you've done with the place. Do you mind if I burn it?"

"Pastor," I tried to find words, "I didn't want to come back. I'm not sure if I even want to now. It's just.. just.." I broke into sobs and tried to cover my face in the wet sleeping bag. Pastor McAllan put a hand on the back of my head and just sat there, saying nothing. After awhile, I was able to find a part of my voice. "It just hurts so bad!"

"I know," he said. "Let's take it one step at a time. First of all, we need to get you clean and dry. Then I'll cook up something from the kitchen. *My* kitchen, not yours," he said with a grimace, looking at the pile of bones I had left near the fire. "Then we can talk."

I must have fallen back to sleep; the rest of the day was like being in a warm fog, unable to move. It would have been a frightening experience except for the occasional sound of Pastor McAllan as he worked around the camp. He was whistling: hymns, I think. No other sound could have been more precious.

The moon will shine like the sun, and the sunlight will be seven times brighter, like the light of seven full days, when the LORD binds up the bruises of his people and heals the wounds he inflicted.

Isaiah 30: 26

....

Prayer: Praise You, Oh God, because You come to me when I am hurting. Praise for the faithful servants You send. Bless them, even as You are blessing me.

Ask yourself: How would you feel if God sent you to a dirty place to do a despicable job?

Strength Returning

The ray of sun in my eyes woke me. This time, Pastor McAllan was not there to block its light. He was squatted down at the fire, stirring something in a pot. "I must have dozed off," I said feebly.

"You got that right," he laughed. "The last time you spoke to me was yesterday morning!"

I sat up, felt the world spin a couple of times, then laid back down. "Yesterday... but how is that possible? You were getting ready to build the fire back up, and.."

"Which I did," he said. "Then I cooked up some soup. Managed to get a couple of mouthfuls in you before you were completely out of it. I got you into some dry clothes, then put you in my sleeping bag while yours dried out over the fire. You spent a pretty restless night, but the fever seems to have broken. How about some more soup now?"

I was stunned. How could so much have happened without my knowing about it? "Pastor, I... I don't know what to say. I..."

"The only thing you need to say right now is 'yes' to my offer of soup. You can tell me later how delicious it is. We'll talk later, as much or as little as you want to. But first let's get your body back in shape."

The soup *was* delicious, and when I asked him what kind it was, he said, "Catfish. Lots of them in the swamp. You just have to have the right equipment to catch them." He smiled, and added, "I won't even ask you how you caught the rats."

By late afternoon, I was strong enough to stand and walk around. The camp was immaculate. My crude shelter had been strengthened with extra poles and waterproofed with a small tarp strung over the top. A generous supply of wood lay neatly stacked by the fire, and a separate pit had been dug and filled with hot coals, over which several large catfish fillets were being grilled. I was surprised to discover that the smell was wonderfully inviting. A wave of guilt swept over me as I sat down beside Pastor McAllan.

"You shouldn't have come for me," I said. "I saw Rendezvous, but I circled around it and came down here. I didn't want to see anyone... even you. It would have been better to leave me here."

The son said to him, 'Father, I have sinned against heaven and against you. I am no longer worthy to be called your son." But the father said to his servants, 'Quick! Bring the best robe and put it on him. Put a ring on his finger and sandals on his feet. Bring the fattened calf and kill it. Let's have a feast and celebrate."

Luke15: 21 – 23

....

Prayer: Lord, You teach us that we must first confess our sins before we receive forgiveness. Show me my sin, I pray, and show me how, and to whom, to confess them.

Ask yourself: Why do you think it is important to confess wrongdoing?

October 5

The Pastor's Story

"Believe it or not, I once felt the same way as you do now," Pastor McAllan said as he made a pot of coffee. "I didn't want to see anyone, especially friends or family, and I sure didn't want them to come looking for me."

"Was that the time you went to the mountaintop?" I asked. He nodded silently, poured the coffee into two cups, then continued.

"I was a young minister; very sure of myself, and my walk with the Lord. I gathered a group of fellow travelers around me, and decided that I would lead them along the trail. Not that I had been that way before; it's just that I figured my spiritual maturity would make me just the kind of man those folks would need to follow." He took a sip of coffee and stared into the flames for a few moments.

"And they did," he continued. "They saw my confidence and put their trust in me. Whenever we'd stop at Rendezvous, we wouldn't even mix with the others. I figured I could teach my flock all they needed to know, so we'd have our own classes, separate from the rest.

"Late one afternoon, a couple of pilgrims came running into the camp, all excited. They said they'd seen a band of demon warriors moving along the ridge about a mile back. Were they headed our way, I asked, and was told, no, they were moving slowly in the other direction.

"This was my chance to really make my mark as spiritual leader. I told my group, 'Let's go! We'll show those things what the army of God can do. They'll know better than to come so close in the future.' One of the leaders from the Rendezvous camp urged us not to go. This wasn't our fight. Of course, I called him a coward, and we set out to demonstrate our faithfulness. There were twenty men with me, more than twice the number of demon warriors, I was told. It would be an easy victory, and a real feather in my cap.

Pastor McAllan looked up at me from his coffee sup and said, "Have you ever had one of those 'still, small voice' messages in the back of your head? I heard it loud and clear: 'don't go'."

Pride goes before destruction, a haughty spirit before a fall.

Proverbs 16: 18

....

Prayer: Lord, my pride is all too clear to You, Who know me perfectly. Forgive me when I think too much of myself and not enough about You.

Ask yourself: Does it encourage you or disillusion you when a man of God whom you respected confesses to sin?

The Pastor's Fall

I remained motionless and silent as Pastor McAllan told me of his youth and his passion for being a spiritual leader. I couldn't imagine him as being so confident and self-seeking: not when I saw him as he was now. I didn't like where this story was going.

"We set out from camp at a slow jog," he said. "I told my men to conserve their strength for the fight. But they were all as eager as I was, and it was difficult to keep from running. When we finally reached the ridge where the demon warriors had been spotted, we were all out of breath and talking excitedly."

"Where did they go?" someone asked.

"Let's check that grove of trees over there," another suggested. "It looks like a good place to camp."

"I wanted to lead out, but I was still breathing too hard. Before I could say anything, they had taken off for the grove. When I was ready, I pulled my sword and ran to catch up. Before I'd gone ten steps, I was stopped in my tracks by a blood-curdling scream, followed by a roar that was definitely not human. What followed was a massacre. Had my men been surprised and ambushed? Were they outnumbered? I'll never know the answers to those questions.

"I ran for my life, back to the Rendezvous camp. I didn't stop until I was inside one of the tents, hiding under a crate of supplies. My sword was no longer with me; I don't know when I lost it. A group of men from camp formed up and ran out to see what had happened. When they came back a few hours later, our worst fears were confirmed: my men had been killed, every one of them. The demon warriors had moved on, taking anything of value they could carry.

"I didn't come out of the supply tent for two days. People brought me food and water, but I was afraid, ashamed and at a complete loss as to what I should do. Finally, three men from the camp came in and said, 'We've gotten a word from God. You're supposed to go to the mountain's summit.'"

Better to be lowly in spirit and among the oppressed than to share plunder with the proud. Whoever gives heed to instruction prospers, and blessed is he who trusts in the LORD.

Proverbs 16: 19 – 20

Prayer: Father, when You must deal with the pride in my heart, be merciful, I pray. Teach me how to recover when my heart has been shattered.

Ask yourself: Why is it difficult to face the world when your pride has been exposed?

October 7

The Pastor's Ascent

The night was getting late, but neither of us had any thought of sleep. Pastor McAllan' story had to be told; I had to hear it.

"The men had said that I was to climb the mountain. It was a direct command from God. I knew they were right, because I had sensed the same message the day before, but was ignoring it, hoping I'd been mistaken.

"Of course, I assumed that I was going to the mountain in order to be crushed. In my vanity, I had been responsible for the deaths of twenty faithful pilgrims. I deserved to die, slowly and painfully. I didn't know what waited at the mountaintop, but I knew this much: I would not be coming back down.

"Or would I? I met some creatures on the way up that I suspect you may know. Talking to others since then, I've figured out that they're the same ones every time, but they show themselves in different forms, with different names and different propositions. But the goal is the same: to try and get the climber to back away, to disobey a direct order from God. If they can succeed at that, then the enemy has a wedge he can use to drive into your heart, to try and separate you from God's Spirit who lives there."

My own heart constricted at those words, when I realized that what the lambs had failed to do with me, I had determined in my own mind to accomplish on my own. Pastor McAllan was talking, but I had to pull myself away from my own thoughts to hear him.

"One creature dogged me all the way to the top, calling me a coward and a fool. I didn't even try and drive him away, because I figured he was telling the truth. Once in awhile, another creature would join him and insist that I was adding to my stupidity by climbing the mountain. 'Why do you think *He* wants you up there?'" he yelled at me. "'He's going to laugh at you, then humiliate you in front of those you had killed, then He's going watch you die. Do you want that? Turn around. Do the first smart thing you've ever done, you idiot.'

"I almost did what he told me to do," Pastor McAllan said. "The only thing that kept me going was the fact that I believed him. And I truly wanted to suffer like he said I would."

Therefore, since we have been justified through faith, we have peace with God through our Lord Jesus Christ, through whom we have gained access by faith into this grace in which we now stand. And we rejoice in the hope of the glory of God. Not only so but we also rejoice in our sufferings, because we know that suffering produces perseverance.
Romans 5: 1 – 3

....

Prayer: Remind me today, Lord, that You have paid the price for my sin. My suffering produces perseverance as Scripture promises, but it is not for the purpose of paying a debt that You have already paid.

Ask yourself: Do you sometimes feel like "paying" for your sin, even though you know it has been forgiven? Why?

October 8

The Pastor's Encounter

"The first time you asked me about the mountain, I told you it was the most terrible and the most wonderful thing that had ever happened to me," Pastor McAllan told me as he put another log on the fire. "What I've just told you was the most terrible; now let me tell you about the most wonderful.

"I got to the top, and the place was covered with clouds. I could see nothing, but in my imagination I heard everything: my accusers, my Judge, my executioner. I fell down on my face and waited for the worst. The next thing I knew, there was someone standing next to me. I looked up and saw what I thought was an old man. He reached down and took my hand. I stood up, and he said, 'Name's Jacob; you can call me Jake.'"

My head shot up at the name, and I started to ask, but Pastor McAllan answered, "That's right: the same one you met back on the ridge. I asked him who he was, and what he was doing there. He said, 'Sometimes a man needs someone to stand with.'

"When he finished saying that, the clouds rolled away in an instant, and I was face to face with a bright light. I couldn't bear to look at it, and turned my head to see Jake, a big smile on his face, looking straight up. A Voice seemed to come from within me, but I knew it had its source in the Light.

"'Do not be afraid,' the Voice said. 'You are in the Presence of the Lamb.'

"Even in my terror, I knew that I was hearing words of truth. Jake was holding onto my arm, lest I fall again, and the Voice was the most beautiful sound I had ever heard. I wanted to speak, but found it impossible. The Voice spoke again, 'I know your heart, and I know the agony you suffer. But I have forgiven you, and no one can condemn you. Return and be a leader for My children.'

The light faded away, and I would have died in despair at its going, except that Jake remained. 'He will always live in your heart,' Jake assured me. 'And I'll be close by. You just do what He told you.' Then he was gone, too. But I was left with a sense of forgiveness and peace I never would have thought possible. The people back at Rendezvous saw it in my face, and they loved me all the more for it. It's been forty years now, and it still seems as though it was yesterday. I was given a new life, a new hope, and a new calling.

Here is a trustworthy saying that deserves full acceptance: Christ Jesus came into the world to save sinners—of whom I am the worst. But for that very reason I was shown mercy so that in me, the worst of sinners, Christ Jesus might display his unlimited patience as an example for those who would believe on him and receive eternal life.
I Timothy 1: 15 – 16

....

Prayer: Oh the healing power of forgiveness! Thank you Father for showing me daily both the depth of my sin and the power of Your love. May I remember today how far I have fallen, and with that memory may I know the heights to which You have lifted me.

Ask yourself: Have you accepted completely the fact of your own forgiveness?

October 9

Time to Move

We went to bed after Pastor McAllan had finished his story. I lay watching the fire for a long time, my thoughts conflicted. I had no doubt that he told the truth; so many of his experiences on the mountain compared with my own.

But there was a crucial difference, and I didn't know how to express it to him. In Pastor McAllan' case, he had to deal with a terrible mistake for which he needed forgiveness. He received it, and his life was changed forever. But in my case, it seemed like I was the victim, and as unbelievable as it sounded, God was the one needing forgiveness. He was the one who killed my son. Or, if I thought of it as simply another disease for which there is no cure, then why didn't He heal my son? Surely, to be able to save and yet refuse to do so is as bad as carrying out the act itself. There's even a legal term for it: culpability. My son was dead, and God was culpable. Until I could come to grips with that, I was not ready to go back.

Tomorrow, I would present this problem to Pastor McAllan. If he had no explanation I could accept, then I would thank him for his help and tell him that I would be staying behind. I could not, I would not be part of a group who left this issue unanswered. If God was big enough to do what I had already seen with my own eyes, then He was big enough to deal with this.

I might incur His wrath for asking, I thought to myself, but I could not face a lifetime of doubting either the power or the loving nature of God. One or the other seemed lacking here, and I had to know which.

What would tomorrow bring? I desperately hoped for answers, but was terrified at what I might learn. I tried to pray, but there was still a barrier between us: one that I had set there myself.

Oh Lord, You deceived me, and I was deceived; You overpowered me and prevailed.
Jeremiah 20: 7a

....

Prayer: Father, I know in my heart that You are perfect in all your ways, but I confess that I do not understand Your ways, and as a result am sometimes troubled. The ignorance in my heart says I should forgive You when I suffer, even though Your Word teaches me that You have done nothing wrong. Help me to have the right attitude.

Ask yourself: Does it seem unthinkable to forgive God? Have you ever felt that you should do just that?

October 10

Morning's Answers

I slept the night through. The fever seemed to have run its course, and my body was definitely stronger than yesterday. But still, I awoke troubled, and after a few moments remembered why. Pastor McAllan was already up and building the fire. He noticed I was awake and said, "Good morning! Ready to get out of this swamp today?"

"No," I said quietly, and when he stopped to look at me, I went on. "I still have questions, Pastor: the same questions that brought me down here in the first place. I can't go back to Rendezvous with those questions unanswered."

"No problem there," Pastor McAllan said, turning back to the fire. "The camp is long gone by now. They will have packed up. You won't be seeing them again for a couple of months."

"But the questions," I persisted. "How can I...?"

"How can you find answers down in this mud hole, by yourself? Do you expect some kind of revelation to come streaking out of the sky, like a bolt of lightening? Do you think if you sit here long enough, eating rat and drinking swamp water that God is going to say, 'Okay, he's earned a little enlightenment? Let's answer his questions' ?"

I started to protest, but realized that was exactly what I was thinking. In my mind, God was some kind of wizard, who from time to time sent his disciples out on quests. The ones who performed the best, or else suffered the most, were the ones who got ahead. Pastor McAllan could see my confusion and added, "Look, just walk with me awhile, okay? We'll talk, and we'll pray as we go. If you don't find what you're looking for, then I'll go on and leave you to work it out for yourself. Just give me a chance?"

I nodded, and started to pack. I had to admit, I wasn't going to miss this swamp.

But God chose the foolish things of the world to shame the wise; God chose the weak things of the world to shame the strong. He chose the lowly things of this world and the despised things—and the things that are not—to nullify the things that are, so that no one may boast before him.

I Corinthians 1: 27 – 29

Prayer: Lord, I can see that I am a product of my race, in that I have been led to believe that all things must be earned. Teach me again the wonderful mystery of Your grace and forgiveness. Show me that I do not suffer and contend in order to find Your favor, but because You have allowed these things for good.

Ask yourself: If grace were an earned thing, how much would you have to your credit by now?

October 11

Out of the Swamp

We moved slowly, partly because I still had not fully recovered from the fever, and partly because we were moving uphill through a trackless forest. After about an hour, we stopped to sit on a log.

Pastor McAllan tapped on the wood and said, "Did you ever wonder what killed this tree?"

"Of course not," I said, "This is the first time I've even seen it. How would I have wondered about it?"

"Would you have thought much about it, if someone had told you a few years ago that this tree was about to die?"

"Not hardly," I sniffed. "It's a big place. I couldn't keep track of every tree in the forest."

"I see," he said thoughtfully, "Then I guess some things are just none of our business."

"Wait a minute!" I exclaimed. "Are you trying to compare this dead tree with my son? The difference is, I loved my son. This is just a tree!"

"Do you think you loved your son any more than God does? Did you know how many hairs he had on his head? Did you see him as he was being formed in the womb? Did you see every day of his life and all the joy and grief he would experience before he was even born? Did you die a painful and humiliating death so that your son could live forever? Remember this, Friend: God wrote the book on love. If there's a reason for your son's death, it's not for lack of love on God's part. You'll have to look someplace else."

For I am convinced that neither death nor life, neither angels nor demons, neither the present nor the future, nor any powers, neither height nor depth, nor anything else in all creation, will be able to separate us from the love of God that is in Christ Jesus our Lord.

Romans 8: 38 – 39

....

Prayer: I have so much to learn about loving and being loved. Thank you for the opportunities You give me in this life to try and model the love You have for me. Forgive me when I fail, and teach me to love all the more because of my failures.

Ask yourself: What is the greatest thing a loved one has done for you?

October 12

The Next Lesson

As we struggled up the hill, working our way over, under and around the fallen timber, Pastor McAllan seemed totally unconcerned with the difficulties, instead talking to me as if we were sitting over a cup of coffee. "Tell me about your son," he said. "Was he an active toddler?"

"Was he ever," I said, my mind going back to those years. "He had two speeds: flat out fast or sound asleep."

"Did he go to kindergarten?"

"Yeah, there was a really good one right down the street from where we lived. He loved it. Extracting him from his friends was a daily challenge."

"Did you ever just let him stay overnight at the kindergarten?"

"No, of course not." I wondered where he was going with this.

"Why not? If he loved it so much, why didn't you just say, 'Well okay, you can stay'?"

"For one thing, the place was about to close," I said. "His friends were all going home. It was time to leave."

"Did you try to explain that to him?" "Sure, but, well, he was three years old. He couldn't have possibly understood."

"So you're saying that you made the decision to bring him home when it was time, even though it made him cry?"

It was starting to become clear to me. I stopped and turned to Pastor McAllan. "Are you going to tell me now that this world is a big kindergarten, and God's going to take us home when it's time?"

"Well, no analogy is perfect," he said. "But let's think about it: kindergarten is a place where a child can grow, have fun, and prepare for adulthood. If I read my Bible correctly, this world is a place where we're preparing for life in our real home, heaven. We work, we have fun, we love, laugh and cry, and in the process, hopefully we become Kingdom children.

"Only our Father knows when it's time to go home."

Then we will no longer be infants, tossed back and forth by the waves, and blown here and there by every wind of teaching and by the cunning and craftiness of men in their deceitful scheming. Instead, speaking the truth in love, we will in all things grow up into him who is the Head, that is, Christ.
Ephesians 4: 14 – 15

....

Prayer: You teach me, Father, that this world is not my home; that I am being prepared for eternal life with You. But like a child, I cry when I don't get what I want, and when I must go, or stay against my own will. Thank you for Your gentleness and patience. Train me up in the way I should go.

Ask yourself: Do you feel cruel when you prevent a child from doing something which may hurt him, but which is for his own good?

Life's Purpose Fulfilled

Pastor McAllan' image of the world as a huge preschool and God as our Father come to take us home sounded pretty silly on the surface. But the more I thought about it, the more sense it made.

"But why do some people stay here until they're old and gray, while others are taken before they even have a chance to experience life?" I protested.

"There's one assumption you're making which you might want to think through," he said. "From your point of view, life in this world is something everyone should experience before going on to heaven. I'd like to hear from someone who's seen both sides of life. The closest we can get is from the Apostle Paul, who was taken up for a glimpse. He wrote later, 'For me to live is Christ, but to die is gain.' He felt like there was no comparison, and he couldn't wait to move on. The only thing keeping him here was the work God had for him to take care of first."

I thought about that for a moment. "So, do you think everyone has a job to do, and when that's done, we can go to our real home?"

"I don't think it's as simple as that," he said, "but that may be part of the answer to the Big Question. Think about your son: what did he accomplish just before he died?"

"He saved my life: twice," I said. "Once when I got caught in a rip tide, and then when the lion was about to finish me off."

"If there's one thing I've learned on my own journey, Friend, it's the fact that we can't put God in a box; He's too big for that. But if it will help you deal with your son's death, consider the possibility that in God's perfect plan, he was saved and came to walk with you just long enough to bring you some joy, save your life and influence more people than you'll ever know around Rendezvous. That completed, God may have said, 'Okay son, let's go home'."

"If that's the case," I thought out loud, "then why am I still breathing air? Is there still something for me to do?"

For to me, to live is Christ and to die is gain. If I am to go on living in the body, this will mean fruitful labor for me. Yet what shall I choose? I do not know!
Philippians 1: 21

Prayer: Father, You know my heart; You know that the world is the only thing I think I understand, and because of that I see it as all important. Teach me about my real home, and help me do the work You have set before me in this life, in order that I might be better prepared for the next.

Ask yourself: Do you think God would place you on this earth with absolutely nothing to do for Him or His kingdom?

October 14

Back to the Trail

Midmorning found us back on the trail, not far from where the Rendezvous camp had been. We continued on to the site and found it empty, just as Pastor McAllan said it would be. Using the fireplace and some wood which had been left stacked nearby, we built a larger-than-normal fire, did laundry using water from the stream and hung our clothes up to dry.

Next on the agenda was lunch. It didn't take long to catch a couple of nice brook trout, and along with some potatoes we found in the garden, a feast was in the making. I watched the vegetables boil, but Pastor McAllan was watching me. "It's just not the same, is it?" he asked.

"What's that?"

"Rendezvous without the people. It's times like this that we really understand how important it is to have a family we can sit with, laugh with, cry with. I hope you don't miss the next one. If you get there, give everyone a special greeting from me."

"Why?" I asked. "Won't you be there?"

"My ministry is along this section of trail," he said. "A lot of people run into trouble around here. It's too far to go back, but it seems like an eternity yet to go. The mountain's not far away, and folks can always use a hand getting back down."

"Then there's the swamp," I said with a smile.

"Thank you," he said, looking at me.

"You're thanking me?" I asked, amazed. "Why?"

"Thank you for giving me the opportunity to share my testimony with you. Most people I meet here are not ready to hear something like that. It takes someone who's been there. God has His hand on you, Friend; I can see that clearly. He sent His Son to save you. He sent your son to refine you. You're going to do great things for the Kingdom. Just stay humble."

Now you are the body of Christ, and each one of you is a part of it. And in the church God has appointed first of all apostles, second prophets, third teachers, then workers of miracles, also those having gifts of healing, those able to help others, those with gifts of administration, and those speaking in different kinds of tongues.
I Corinthians 12: 28 – 28

....

Prayer: Thank You for Your Church, Lord. Thank you for allowing me to be a part of it: to share in the fellowship and the responsibility. Teach me how to serve Your people, so that I may serve You.

Ask yourself: What can you do within a body of believers that you could not do alone?

October 15

Separate Ways

I said good bye to Pastor McAllan this morning. He would be heading back down the trail, in the direction of the mountain. I still wasn't sure if I wanted to go back to Rendezvous or not; there were too many painful memories associated with that time. But I promised the Pastor that I would stay on the trail and keep moving forward. Perhaps I would find the answers I so desperately needed.

As we parted ways and left camp, I did learn one thing: my attempts to become a "heartless person" were futile. I was genuinely sorry to be leaving this man who had done so much for me, and who obviously cared about me. If I still wanted to conquer my grief by closing down all emotion, I knew now that it would be impossible. Hopes, fears, anger and joy were all intertwined into my very being. I could never destroy those without destroying myself.

But perhaps I could still compartmentalize: keep the daily activities of my life in one part and the things which hurt me in another. The need for such became clear when I stopped at noon for lunch. Before leaving Rendezvous, I had filled my backpack with vegetables from the garden. Rummaging through a pouch on the side, I felt something and lifted it out. It was the string of lion's teeth my son had made just before he died. Seeing it brought that terrible day back in a sudden rush of grief. Clutching the teeth, I stumbled over to the river, crying out in agony and intending to throw them away forever. But even as I drew back to throw, I knew I could not do it. Painful or not, this was a part of what my son was; a part of our lives together. To throw it away would be like killing that part again.

Wiping the tears from my eyes, I returned to the backpack and put the teeth in a seldom-used pouch, deep in the bottom of it, so that I would never again find it by mistake. Perhaps someday I would be able to take it out and remember without crying. But not today.

I thank my God every time I remember you. In all my prayers for all of you, I always pray with joy because of your partnership in the gospel from the first day until now, being confident of this, that he who began a good work in you will carry it on to completion until the day of Christ Jesus.

Philippians 1: 3 – 6

Prayer: What a blessing are the memories I cherish; and yet what pain they can cause, when they remind me of past suffering. Teach me to remember with You the things You want me to recall. Grant me "holy forgetfulness" when those memories would not serve Your kingdom.

Ask yourself: Do you think God would help you "forget" things which would be harmful in the recollection of them?

October 16

Joy and Guilt

The trail today led along the river, moving steadily but easily up a wide valley. To my left I could see broad meadows, and off in the distance were herds of deer and elk, feeding in the rich pastures.

When it came to time to stop for the evening, I had reached an area where beavers had dammed up the river in places, creating small ponds. Each pond came complete with a mound of mud and sticks in the center which I knew was the resident beaver's home. Accessible only from under the water, it was a safe and warm place to raise a family.

Just before sundown, as I sat and watched, a family of beavers came out of their shelter and swam to the far shore. Mom and Dad beaver set to work, gathering sticks to be used for food and building materials, but for the two young kids who came along, it was play time. They chased each other in circles, running as fast as they could on short, stubby legs. Then they wrestled, rolling together in the grass until they got too near the pond. One roll too many, and they both ended up in the water. They looked surprised at this new development, then overjoyed to find themselves in a whole new environment for play.

They continued to scuffle, and as I watched, I would laugh out loud when one would get the better of the other, only to find the tables turned in the next moment. Then I caught myself: how could I, a grieving father, laugh at something like this? Could I be so cold as to endure the agony I had just been through, then go on with my life as if nothing had happened? My joy turned instantly to guilt, and I put my head in my hands, uncertain of myself. Would my son approve of this light-hearted moment, or would he condemn my lack of respect for his memory? Would there ever come a time when I could laugh and not feel miserable for doing so?

I went to sleep, once again trying to shut out the emotions which somehow felt wrong. But I dreamed about baby beavers, playing in the water.

Blessed are you who hunger now, for you will be satisfied. Blessed are you who weep now, for you will laugh.

Luke 6: 21

....

Prayer: Father, I know that joy comes in the morning, and that there is a time for laughter, just as there is a time for weeping. Help me to know the times, and to be able to laugh when it is right to do so.

Ask yourself: Some cultures have a decided period for mourning, after which life is supposed to go on as normal. Does this sound good, or possible?

October 17

The Road to Healing

I've read that you know you're in grief when the fact of it is the first thing which comes to mind when you wake up in the morning. I woke with the sensation that my sleep had been good, my dreams pleasant. But immediately I felt that something was not good, and then remembered.

As I built the fire, prepared breakfast and packed my gear, I was quiet, almost sullen with myself. Where normally I would hummed a song or stopped to admire the beauty of the morning, I now kept my activities to the task of the day. As much as possible, I kept conscious thought away, knowing that exploring my mind would inevitably result in another discovery such as yesterday's of something which would trigger my grief again.

I've also read that the grief process can often take up to seven years to run its course. Recalling that, I could only breathe a sigh of relief and say, "Thank God that there is a process with a definable end to it!" Knowing that perhaps someday, I would be able to get up in the morning and enjoy a moment without feeling guilty about it gave me courage. With a second cup of coffee in my hand, I wandered back down to the pond. The beavers were nowhere to be seen, but I looked out over their home and remembered the enjoyment of last night's performance. I was proud of myself for being able to think about a pleasant memory without falling back into misery.

Such an ability would be necessary if life was to go on, I reflected. Sure, this cycle of grief might actually run its course in seven years or so, but are we guaranteed only one tragedy per lifetime? What happens if I get knocked flat again next year or the year after? Will I say, "All right; grief process number one (which we'll call gp#1) now has five years to completion, while gp#2 is just getting started. You'll have to go through gp#1 and 2 simultaneously for a while, then finish out #2."

I almost laughed at myself for such musings, then stopped when I considered the reality of what I was saying. As long as I live, grief will be a part of living. I'll have to learn to cope with it, or I may die from it.

While the child was still alive, I fasted and wept. I thought, 'Who knows? The LORD may be gracious to me and let the child live.' But now that he is dead, why should I fast? Can I bring him back again? I will go to him, but he will not return to me.

II Samuel 12: 22 – 23

....

Prayer: Comfort me in my grief, dear Father, then help me find a place in my heart where I keep it. Teach me to live in spite of past suffering, and to look ahead to the time when every tear will be dried.

Ask yourself: Can a person ever know real joy after experiencing great suffering?

October 18

Turning Outward

Walking along the trail today, I came across a thicket of blackberries, just ripe and ready for eating. Remembering the last such thicket I had found, and the bear who had been too busy eating to notice me until I had come way too close, I called out, then moved in. The berries were sweet and juicy, and I could see evidence that I was not the only one who enjoyed them. Footprints were scattered about, and I wondered if someone from Rendezvous had been here recently. A bird was also helping himself nearby, and when I moved in his direction, he flew off suddenly. But instead of flying clear, he struck another thicket and got caught in its thorny branches. Feathers were flying in all directions, and he chattered incessantly as he struggled to get free. "Hold on there, little guy," I said softly. "You're going to hurt yourself like that."

I reached in slowly, and as gently as I could took hold of his body then set about untangling the vines from around his wings. His heart was racing in fear, and I tried to soothe him with soft whispers. "There now, I'll just move that branch over, like that. Okay, now this one needs to come around here." Finally he was free, and I checked him over briefly to make sure nothing was broken. He seemed okay so I opened my hands and let him take to the air, chattering all the way and not stopping until he was well out of sight.

I went back to my own berry picking, enjoying the satisfaction of having done a good deed for the day. Then it occurred to me: that did feel good, didn't it? As long as I was intent on getting the bird free of his misery, I wasn't thinking about my own. Was this part of the healing process, I wondered? If I could get to the place where my thoughts and energies were directed outward, toward helping someone else, then maybe the pain I hold inside me would have a chance to heal. Maybe that helped to explain Pastor McAllan' dedication to helping guys like me. Perhaps by doing good for others, he's doing good for himself as well. It's an idea worth pursuing.

Let us not become weary in doing good, for at the proper time we will reap a harvest if we do not give up. Therefore, as we have opportunity, let us do good to all people, especially to those who belong to the family of believers.

Galatians 6: 9 – 10

Prayer: Lord, You teach us that the world will know us by the love we show one another. By that love, may we serve You and the purposes to which You have called us. And by that love, may we be a healing touch to those who are hurting.

Ask yourself: How is helping someone else also helping yourself?

October 19

Opportunity

With a bumper crop of blackberries, I could see that I would have to stay here for awhile. Some could be packaged for carrying, some boiled down into a sauce for cooking, and some would just have to be eaten right there on the spot. I picked a level place for a campsite, gathered firewood and settled into the day's work.

I had been picking for an hour or more when I noticed a figure up the trail, moving in my direction. Since the only other person I'd seen purposely moving in the wrong direction had been the evil man, I went to my backpack and drew out the sword. As he moved closer, however, I could see that it was a young man, about my son's age. His hair was long and unkempt, falling over one side of his face, so that I wondered how he could see where he was going. His backpack appeared light enough, but was obviously poorly packed, so that it pulled him to one side as he walked. He didn't see me standing by the trail as he approached – another indication of a poorly seasoned traveler – and I startled him when I called out, "Good morning, son."

He jumped, but tried to hide his surprise. "Morning," he said quietly, then started to move on past me.

"I don't see many folks going this direction on the trail. You're not lost, are you?"

"No, I'm not lost. Just going back, that's all," he said, avoiding my eyes as he spoke.

"That's quite a big decision," I said. "You sure you want to be doing that?"

"Yeah. I don't belong here. Anyway, I got things waiting for me back home. Gotta go."

He started to move on, but I couldn't let him go without trying to help. "Say, I've stumbled onto the mother of all blackberry thickets. If you'd be willing to stay awhile and help me pick and pack, I'll share them with you. How about it?"

He seemed to hesitate, started to move on, then thought again. "Yeah, okay, I guess. Not for long, though."

Long enough, though, I thought to myself with a silent prayer of thanksgiving to God for this opportunity to look beyond myself today.

Command them to do good, to be rich in good deeds, and to be generous and willing to share. In this way they will lay up treasure for themselves as a firm foundation for the coming age, so that they may take hold of the life that is truly life.
I Timothy 6: 18 – 19

....

Prayer: Thank you Father, for allowing me the wonderful privilege of taking part in Your plan to "call all men unto yourself". I know well that You can do all things without my help, but in Your love and mercy, You let me be a part of it. Praise You!

Ask yourself: Why do you think God would command His children to do the things which He, Himself could do alone?

Motivations

I learned that the young man's name was Gary, and as I suspected was the same age as my son. He had only been on the trail for a week, but had decided that it wasn't for him.

We picked berries side by side, throwing them into a sack between us. "What made you decide to start this trip in the first place, Gary?" I asked.

"A girl," he said with the hint of a grin on his face. "She decided to do this 'pilgrimage', as she called it. She asked me to come along, and I thought, hey, days all alone in the woods, nights under the stars: I could do that."

I smiled back at him. "But it didn't turn out to be like that, did it?"

"No way! First thing, she joins up with this group of folks like they were family or something. The next thing I know I'm surrounded by "brothers and sisters" who won't leave us alone. I tried to explain to her that this wasn't what I had in mind. She cried, and said there was a lot more to it than what I thought. Well, she was right about that. First chance I got, I grabbed my backpack and split."

My heart ached for him as he told of his frustration and displayed his ignorance. How could I help him, Lord? "What's waiting for you back home, Gary?" I asked after a while.

"Oh lots of things. I got friends. Girls, too. We hang around together."

"So there's no talk from them about traveling anywhere, right?"

"No way, man. We're staying right where we are."

"And in a few years, you'll be a middle aged man with middle aged friends, and you'll wake up one morning and discover that your life has gone nowhere."

"Whoa!" said Gary. "You're starting to sound like my old man."

"I guess I am," I smiled. "Sorry; I wanted to get you to think a few years down the track, that's all." I carried the sack of blackberries over to the campsite and dumped them into a pot for boiling. Gary followed me over and saw my sword.

"Cool blade," he said with a touch of admiration. "Where did you get it?"

"Tell you what, Gary," I said, picking the sword up and handing it over for him to hold. "If you'll stick around tonight, I'll tell you a story that will scare your socks off."

My brothers, if one of you should wander from the truth and someone should bring him back, remember this: Whoever turns a sinner from the error of his way will save him from death and cover over a multitude of sins.
James 5: 19 – 20

....

Prayer: Grant me an opportunity today to tell someone about Your mighty works, Oh God. Give me the words to speak and prepared hearts to listen, so that tonight there will be singing in heaven at the addition of a soul to Your kingdom.

Ask yourself: Who will you pray for today? Who will listen to you, as you tell of God's love and power?

October 21

The Call of the Road

By the time the evening was spent, I had shared with Gary stories of lions and evil men and demon warriors. I told him about nights spent in a cold river and days under a hot burning sun. I could see that the stories had captured his imagination, but he wasn't ready to be a part of them: not yet.

"So why do you do all this stuff?" Gary asked me as we settled into sleeping bags for the night. "Do you like being cut with knives, drowned in rivers and baked in deserts?"

I laughed at his summary, and said, "Well, when you put it that way, no, I guess I don't particularly look forward to the discomfort and danger. But it's like what your girlfriend said, there is more to it than that. Look in your heart and I think you'll see it. You weren't made to hang around the street corners the rest of your life, Gary. There's a part of you that wants to see things made right. You know the world isn't like it should be, and you know you're not all you were created to become. But as soon as you start thinking like that, something or someone comes along and tries to steer you away. That's the enemy of this world, Gary, and he wants to see to it that you never look at your own heart: that you never remember the way it used to be. Because, if you do, you'll start to discover what real life is all about."

I didn't know if Gary was listening to me, or if he was asleep already. Just before I drifted off, however, he spoke up. "Hey?"

"What?"

"How come I've never seen any of this nightmare stuff you're talking about?"

"Because you're no threat, Gary. To the enemy, you're just a poor unsuspecting victim who will go quietly to the grave. That's the way he wants it, and that's the way you're living it."

"Oh. Good night."

"Good night, Gary."

Be self-controlled and alert. Your enemy the devil prowls around like a roaring lion looking for someone to devour. Resist him, standing firm in the faith, because you know that your brothers throughout the world are undergoing the same kind of sufferings.

I Peter 5: 8 – 9

Prayer: There are times, Lord, when I know that the enemy of this world is attacking me, and I thank You for the strength you grant me during those times. There are other times, though, when I feel unhindered. Is that because I'm doing nothing for the Kingdom of God?

Ask yourself: Why would Satan bother you if you were no threat to his evil ways?

The Morning Light

It was quiet when I woke up this morning. I looked over at Gary's sleeping bag. He was lying on his back, his long hair an impossible tangle. He seemed to be sleeping, but as soon as I stirred, he picked up the conversation where he had left it.

"So you're saying that if I decided to turn on the trail and head back up, I might start seeing creepy things in the night?"

"It's different for everyone," I said. "Some things are scarier than others, and it's not always a foaming-at-the-mouth demon." As I said that, I remembered the mountaintop again, and decided Gary wasn't ready for that part of the story. "But you can be sure of one thing: the enemy won't like it if you turn back."

"Would you go with me?" he asked.

"I was hoping you'd ask," I said with a smile. "But tell me this: why would you want to go? Is it just the adventure?"

"No. I got plenty of adventure waiting back home." He raised up and looked over at me. "I didn't want to correct you last night, but my friends and I don't just hang around the street corners. We do lots of stuff. Dangerous stuff. The problem is, I know it's wrong, and I know I'm wrong for doing those things. Don't ask me how I know."

"I don't have to ask," I said. "I told you last night that the enemy of this world wants you to keep moving in the wrong direction. What I didn't mention is that the Creator of this world wants you on the right trail, and one way He does that is to convict your heart. The fact that you know something is wrong is proof right there that God is working in you. The next step is to do something about what you've learned."

We talked all through breakfast, and as we packed up the last of the gear along with equal shares of blackberries, I said, "So how about it, Gary? Are you ready to take a look at what your heart is showing you, give it to God and go with me today?"

"Yeah. Yeah, I am," he said with a sigh of relief. "Let's do it."

We kneeled together there beside the trail, and I led him in a simple prayer. He spoke in honest and straightforward language as he committed his life to Jesus. When he finished, he looked up at me and said, "What are we waiting for? Maybe I can catch up with my girlfriend!"

But I tell you the truth: It is for your good that I am going away. Unless I go away, the Counselor will not come to you; but if I go, I will send him to you. When he comes, he will convict the world of guilt in regard to sin and righteousness and judgment.

John 16: 7 – 8

Prayer: I thank you, Lord, because it is not mine to judge the world. By Your Holy Spirit, people come to know of their sin. All that I can do it try and live by the standard You have set for me, and in so doing to show others of Your great love. Help me to do that today.

Ask yourself: What would you say to the one who criticizes Christians for being judgmental?

A New Companion

Gary was a delight to travel with. His descriptions of the scenery we passed were so different than I would have imagined, it was a refreshing change. Seeing a waterfall on the other side of the valley, he asked, "Do you know where all that water comes from?"

"Sure," I said. "Aquifers under the ground collect water by percolation, where it travels down porous rock and into underground rivers, then..."

"No, no!" he said with a laugh. "You gotta think outside the box! Haven't you ever thought of the possibility that there's a little old man, just inside the mountain there, and he's got his hand on a big valve. Whenever people come along, he turns the valve open; we watch and go 'ooh!', then after we're gone he turns it back off to save water."

"No I never thought of it that way," I said with a smirk.

We walked along a few minutes more until the waterfall was out of sight. We stopped and listened, and hearing nothing, he mumbled, "Could happen."

At the end of the valley, the trail narrowed and started down a deep ravine. The river which had been flowing beside us was constricted into a raging torrent, rushing headlong over rocks and logs as it hurried to the bottom of the ravine. Once we had traveled down the steepest part, the trail cut back into a narrow valley to the right. "Do you remember this part?" I asked Gary.

"Yeah I guess," he said after a pause. "I don't remember it being this dark, though."

A chill ran up my back, and I unconsciously put a hand on my sword. "Stay close," I said to Gary. He seemed to sense my caution, and came up beside me. "How far does it go like this?" I asked.

"I don't know," he answered. "There's a lake down there eventually, where I spent the night. The next night was with you, so it must not be too far."

Two are better than one, because they have a good return for their work: If one falls down, his friend can help him up.

Ecclesiastes 4: 9 – 10

Prayer: Bless those who travel with me today, Dear Lord. May I be a joy to walk with, even as they make my travel more sweet. May we protect one another and encourage one another throughout the day.

Ask yourself: How is traveling with a fellow believer different than traveling with one who does not share your faith?

Barrier

We picked up the pace as the trail became narrower. The undergrowth, so close beside us, seemed to fly by as the hours passed. I couldn't see the sun, but I knew it must be moving toward late afternoon. Besides being dark and wet, there was no open space large enough for a campsite, so I was hoping we would break out to the lake soon.

Those hopes were dashed as we came around a bend in the trail to discover that a huge tree had fallen, blocking the way. Because of the undergrowth, we couldn't see either end. The trunk of the tree, covered with branches, rose at least ten feet above us. Gary turned uphill as if to climb.

"No, Gary," I said. "Never leave the trail; not if you can help it. Let's see if we can get over." Using my sword to hack away the smaller branches, I was able to get close enough to try and climb over the trunk itself. "Here," I said at last, "I'll give you a boost."

After much struggle, Gary was able to reach branches higher up and pull himself to the top. "Cool," he said. "This thing seems to go on forever in both directions. I can't see much straight down, either. Just a second."

He disappeared from view, and after a few sounds of cracking limbs, it was silent. "Hey Gary!" I called out. "How about giving me a hand?"

There was no response, and after several minutes, I decided to try and pull myself up. It was tough going, but I finally made it to the top. Looking down through the branches, I tried to see where Gary had gone. I started to call out, but hesitated when I heard a voice, definitely not his. I couldn't make out the words, but something in the way they were spoken told me that it wasn't a friendly greeting. I struggled more as the branches snagged on my backpack, but finally broke free and jumped the last six feet or so down to the ground. I found myself standing next to Gary, who remained unmoving, a pale expression on his face and staring up the trail.

There, not ten feet away, a snarl on his lips and pure hatred in his eyes, stood the evil man.

God has turned me over to evil men and thrown me into the clutches of the wicked.

Job 16: 11

....

Prayer: There are times I know, Dear Father, when I may have the opportunity to watch as a fellow traveler comes under attack by the enemy. Show me at that time what I should do, and how I can be used for the sake of Your kingdom.

Ask yourself: Would you be willing to step into the fight for the sake of a friend?

October 25

In the Gap

The evil man didn't even blink when I jumped down beside Gary. His stare was burning into the young man's eyes, and I could see that it was having the desired effect.

"What makes you think you have any right to be on this trail?" the evil man was asking Gary. But he didn't wait for an answer. "I'll tell you: you have no right. Everything you see here belongs to me: every thing and every body." I detected a quick glance in my direction, but the evil man still did not acknowledge my presence. Gary was his target, and he was not about to let him go.

"Turn around: now. Go back where you came from. I might choose to spare your miserable life, as long as you obey me. Otherwise..."

The evil man took a step toward Gary, and several things happened at once. Gary stepped back, then fell. I stepped forward, sword in hand, until I was directly between the two. The evil man stopped, and for the first time looked directly at me. His expression never changed, but he stood quietly as I heard myself speaking.

"Come no closer," I commanded. "You have no claim on this boy. Leave us. Now."

"But I do have every right to him," the evil man answered. "He admitted it himself: he only came along to be with his girlfriend." Something in the way he said it made the word sound dirty. "He is in my domain, and I will have him!"

"I question your claim to this boy," I said, not moving. "Especially since just this morning he claimed the blood of Jesus Christ for his forgiveness and acceptance into God's kingdom." The words seemed to have an adverse affect on him, so I took a step in his direction. "You can take up your claim with God's Son. Until then, if you want this man, you'll need to come past me first."

The evil man hesitated, then stepped back. Finally, he turned away, but just before going out of sight called back, "Be ready, boy. You won't always have a nursemaid around you."

I looked for a man among them who would build up the wall and stand before me in the gap on behalf of the land so I would not have to destroy it, but I found none.
Ezekiel 22: 30

....

Prayer: Help me know, Father, when to flee the enemy, when to resist, and when to attack. Use me, I pray, for Your Name's sake.

Ask yourself: What examples can you think of to illustrate one person "standing in the gap" for another?

Resolve

I remained where I stood for a long while, making sure neither the evil man nor one of his followers returned. I was aware of Gary behind me, getting to his feet and coming up close. I could hear his breath coming in short gasps.

"Is that as bad as it gets?" he asked after a few minutes.

"No. Do you still want to come?"

Gary was quiet for what seemed like a long time. His breathing finally slowed to a regular pattern, and he spoke. "Yes. I still want to come. You know why?"

"Why?" I asked.

"Because I saw the look on that thing's face when you used words like 'Jesus' and 'blood' and 'forgiveness'. There's nothing for me at home that could have faced up to something like that. I want to know more."

"First lesson:" I said, "He can't touch you, as much as he may try and convince you otherwise. As of your prayer this morning, you've come under the protection of Jesus Christ, God's Son. The evil man knows it, and that's a line he can never, ever cross over."

"Second lesson: he doesn't always have to touch you; not when he can convince someone or something to do the job for him. We live in a world broken by sin, and sinners come in all shapes and sizes. That's why we have to be prepared; and that's why we have to help each other."

"You helped me just now. Is that what you mean?"

"Sometimes. I knew lesson one, but you didn't. You may come across someone else who's forgotten it and needs help."

"One more thing," Gary asked. "Can you help me deal with lesson two?"

For he has rescued us from the dominion of darkness and brought us into the kingdom of the Son he loves, in whom we have redemption, the forgiveness of sins.
Colossians 1: 13 – 14

....

Prayer: I praise You, Father, for defeating Satan through the blood of Your Son, Jesus Christ. Forgive me when I forget that he is already a defeated foe, and act as though I am under his authority. Teach me to resist him, for Your Name's sake.

Ask yourself: Has Satan tried to convince you that you are living in his kingdom? What did you do?

October 27

Boot Camp

After the encounter with the evil man, Gary was more than ever motivated to learn. He wanted to know all there was about the journey: what could be expected, who he might meet, where it ended. I couldn't answer all his questions, but we started with the basics. I gave his footwear a careful scrutiny. "Those sneakers will have to go," I said. "They might be popular where you come from, but they just won't stand up to the trail's abuses. We'll be able to pick up something at Rendezvous, but that's not for awhile."

"What's 'Rendezvous'?"

"Never mind. We'll cover that later. Right now, let's use what you have to the best advantage. You've got plenty of lace here, so let's go back and strengthen this part, across the top of your foot."

We spent the rest of the day talking about foundations, and the importance of healthy feet. Gary wanted to add a few teasing remarks, but he saw that I was deadly serious and so kept quiet. By late afternoon, I was satisfied that he had the basics down pretty well. He tied and re-tied his shoes for me, then danced around the campfire, Indian style, pointing all the while to his shoes. "I guess I'm about ready to hit the trail now, right?" he said after a couple of laps around the fire.

"You're a lot more ready now than you were this morning," I agreed. "Of course, you're likely to travel in a big circle, unless you adjust that backpack."

"What do you mean? It feels fine to me."

"That's because you're body has compensated for the fact that it's over-weighted to one side. One of the first things I noticed when I saw you coming up the trail was that you were leaning to the left. A look at your backpack told me why."

As we laid all of his gear out in preparation for organizing and re-packing, I said, "Gary, this pack is like a lot of things in life. We get unbalanced with the things we think are important. It's not noticeable right away, and we adjust everything else to fit. The problem is, we're no longer walking in a straight line. There's a sermon in that illustration," I smiled at him, "but I'll let you work it out."

Enter through the narrow gate. For wide is the gate and broad is the road that leads to destruction, and many enter through it. But small is the gate and narrow the road that leads to life, and only a few find it.

Matthew 7: 13 – 14

....

Prayer: The farther I travel, Lord, the more I realize how a small mistake can lead to big changes down the road. Teach me how to stay in the straight way, on the path that You have laid before me. Correct me when I stray.

Ask yourself: How can even a small error in judgment result in serious consequences later on?

Off Again

With our footwear tightened up, our backpacks well-balanced and fully adjusted, Gary and I continued up the trail today. We spoke of the journey as we walked, and I noticed with surprise that I felt better. I still grieved for my son, but having the responsibility for helping this young man get started meant that there was not much time left in the day for dwelling on it.

"Why do people call you 'Friend'?" he asked when we stopped for a rest. "Don't you have a real name?"

I laughed at that. "Yes, I do have a real name, and maybe someday I'll tell you what it is. But I haven't been known by that name since I started this trip. It's like I became a new person when I started walking. People got to know me, then they gave me a name which seemed to fit who I had become. I'd like to think that 'Friend' describes who I am even better than the name on my birth certificate."

He thought about that awhile, then said, "I'd like a new name, too. Back home, I'm Gary the tough guy, Gary the sneak, Gary the going-nowhere. Ever since we prayed together, well, I feel like a new person. I don't want to be the old Gary, ever again." He picked up a rock and tossed it off the trail. "So how about it? Would you give me a new name?"

"You really amaze me, you know that?" I said. "What you've just told me is right out of the Bible, and yet you haven't even had a chance to read it yet. The Bible tells us that when we become a Christian, our old life is 'put to death.' And what's more, a lot of people back then did change their names to fit their new lives. I'd be honored to find a new name for you, but I'll have to give it some prayerful consideration.

"In the meantime," I said, getting up and putting on my backpack, "how about 'Talks-too-much-and-can't-keep-up-with-an-old-man'?"

"Very funny," he said, getting into his own gear. "Let's see who can keep up with who, shall we?"

The first thing Andrew did was to find his brother Simon and tell him, "We have found the Messiah" (that is, the Christ). And he brought him to Jesus. Jesus looked at him and said, "You are Simon son of John. You will be called Cephas." (which when translated is Peter)

John 1: 41 – 42

....

Prayer: You know the stars and call them by name; and You have known me since before I was born. Father, call my name, that I may hear and obey. Grant that my name may be a living testimony to You.

Ask yourself: What does your name mean? Has your life reflected that meaning?

October 29

The Lake

By late afternoon, we had reached the lake Gary had mentioned. It was a beautiful body of water, stretching at least a mile or more across, and lined with several varieties of evergreen tree. On the far side, a waterfall dropped off a cliff and into the water, and in the quiet of the approaching evening, we could just make out the distant roar.

The sound of bass jumping in the water also reached our ears, and we dug out fishing gear to see if we could snag a couple for dinner. "Biggest fish gets the prize!" Gary called out to me as he cast his line in the water.

"What's the prize?" I asked.

"You have to cook and wash up while I take a swim."

"You're missing a step there, son," I said. "First you have to catch the biggest fish."

We made several casts without a bite, then Gary gave out a yell as something took his bait. His rod bent nearly double as he reeled in the fish. Once when it jumped, I could see that it was a bass, and a beauty at that. Suddenly the fish darted to the right, and before I could move, had tangled itself up in my line. Both of our rods strained under the weight of the fish until Gary's line snapped, sending him backwards into the water. I wanted to laugh, but was too busy with the bass, who was now determined to free himself from my gear.

I knew he was only wrapped up in the line and would soon break free, but still reeled him in as carefully as I could. A blur of motion swept past me, as Gary raced out into the water toward the fish. Diving headlong, he went under completely for a moment, then camp back up clutching the struggling bass. It slipped out of his hands, he grabbed it again, then finally got a grip on its gills. Holding it up proudly, I congratulated him, then said, "Now, technically, I suppose I caught it, since it was on my line. And since you've already had your swim now, that just leaves the cleanup."

I watched Gary stepping out of the water with his prize, and said, "I think I understand now why Jesus chose fishermen for some of His disciples."

"Why is that?" he asked.

"They don't mind getting their feet wet in order to win the prize."

Early in the morning, Jesus stood on the shore, but the disciples did not realize that it was Jesus. He called out to them, "Friends, haven't you any fish?" "No," they answered. He said, "Throw your net on the right side of the boat and you will find some." When they did, they were unable to haul the net in because of the large number of fish.
John 21: 4 – 6

Prayer: Through the daily routines of life, You, Jesus, have taught us so much. Grant that I may see the world around me today through Your eyes, and see there all that You would show me. Then may I use what I have learned to be more like You.

Ask yourself: Look around you: is there an object or a scene which can be used to teach a deeper spiritual lesson?

October 30

A New Name

"There's nothing like charcoal-broiled bass, huh?" I said to Gary as we settled back after dinner. A moon was coming up over the lake, and the night was peaceful and still.

"Especially when you caught it yourself," he grinned.

"That's right," I agreed. "But don't worry; maybe you'll catch one next time."

He started to protest, but stopped when I held my hand up. "Just joking," I laughed. "Actually, I was quite impressed with your performance. So much, in fact, that I think I have a new name for you."

Gary sat up and looked expectantly. I went on: "When Jesus called Simon and Andrew to be His disciples, they were out fishing at the time. It must have been a pretty big deal, to go away and leave what was probably a lucrative business. But He said to them, 'Come, follow Me, and I will make you fishers of men!' And that's exactly what they did. Simon became Peter, the rock foundation of the church to come; Andrew was the faithful brother to the end, who brought people to Jesus. I see that kind of strength in you, Gary. You have a view of the world that says, 'Why does it have to be that way?' and then you set out to change it, even if it means running out over your head. Some of the best known and respected men in the world today are named 'Fisher'; but I'm afraid most of them don't even know the significance of those first fishermen/disciples. Maybe it's time we raised the standard... Fisher?"

He thought about it a moment, tried the sound of it a few times, then took the hook he had used to catch tonight's feast and stuck it onto a baseball cap he had dug out of his backpack. "Fisher it is!" he said with a grin. "I just hope I can live up to my predecessors' reputation."

As Jesus was walking beside the Sea of Galilee, he saw two brothers, Simon called Peter and his brother Andrew. They were casting a net into the lake, for they were fishermen. "Come, follow me," Jesus said, "and I will make you fishers of men." At once they left their nets and followed him.

Matthew 4: 18 – 20

....

Prayer: I stand before You, Lord, one of those "fish" that You said the disciples would catch. Help me to do the same for those who follow after me. Teach me to fish.

Ask yourself: How is evangelism like fishing?

October 31

A Heart for Fishing

We were up bright and early, and before the sun had cleared the trees were well down the trail, moving along the lake shore. "Fisher," as he had now come to be known, walked beside me when the trail allowed and asked a thousand questions.

"Oh, here's one," he said excitedly.

I smiled and said, "Really? You mean I haven't yet answered every question known to man?"

"No, I'm serious," he said. "You mentioned that Peter and Andrew were told by Jesus that they would be 'fishers of men'; what did He mean by that? Aren't those fish just poor unsuspecting creatures? Am I supposed to drag them kicking and screaming into the Kingdom against their will?"

"Good question, Fisher," I said. "I think a lot of folks may have that same idea: that spreading the Good News is somehow infringing on the rights of the rest of the world. As I read my Bible, though, I see a lot of reference in the Old Testament to fish as being those wicked men about to be caught and judged by God. Jeremiah, Ezekiel, Amos and Isaiah used the images, and I'm sure the disciples would have been familiar with them as well. But Jesus comes along and says, 'We need to save these people from coming judgment; get out there and find them; bring them in before it's too late.' Does that make sense?"

"Yeah, I think so," he said. "Just one more question though: do I use live bait or artificial lures?"

"That can be the topic of your first sermon," I laughed. "And I want to be there to hear it!"

But now I will send for many fishermen," declares the LORD, "and they will catch them. After that I will send for many hunters, and they will hunt them down on every mountain and hill and from the crevices of the rocks.
                                                                    Jeremiah 16:16

....

Prayer: Fill me, Father, with a sense of urgency for the lost. Remind me, I pray, that there are people dying every day without having given their lives to You. Again Lord, teach me to fish.

Ask yourself: Unbelievers would say that Christians are "pushing their religion" onto others. What do you think?

November 1

The Path Before Us

It was a pleasant day for Fisher and me, following the shoreline around the lake. The trail was level, and except for a few small streams which had to be forded, there were no major challenges. It was a good day for talking, and Fisher was making the most of it. We talked about his new decision to take up the journey, and about his life back home. He asked about my family, and about my own impressions of what we were doing.

"Friend," he said after we had taken our shoes off and waded across a small river, "I noticed that we opted to come straight across here, rather than go upstream where we might have been able to jump over rocks and cross without getting wet. I'm not complaining, mind you; I look forward to these chances for dipping my feet in ice cold mountain streams. But I wonder if it has anything to do with what you said just before we met up with the evil man. I was about to find a way around the fallen tree, but you stopped me, saying 'Stay on the trail if at all possible'. Is it against the rules to wander around?"

I laughed and said, "No Fisher, it's not exactly against the rules. It's just that I'm discovering that the trail is always the very best place to be. Every time I've gotten into trouble on this trip, whether it's looking for a shortcut or running away from something that scared me, leaving the trail has always brought me grief. I know, sometimes we have to step off, to gather firewood or enjoy a sunset. That's not what I'm talking about. What I mean are those times when you say to yourself, 'I know the trail goes that direction, but I don't like it, so I'm going to go in *this* direction. That's rebellion, Fisher, and God will call us to account for that. I admit, going around a fallen tree may not have made any difference to the trip, but I like to stay in the habit of keeping my feet on the path."

Fisher thought about that for awhile, then said, "I guess you're right, Friend. When you come to think about it, the evil man was waiting for me right on the other side of that tree. If he had met me up on the hill, where I was headed, who knows how things might have gone differently?"

So be careful to do what the LORD your God has commanded you; do not turn aside to the right or to the left. Walk in all the way that the LORD your God has commanded you, so that you may live and prosper and prolong your days in the land that you will possess.

Deuteronomy 5: 32 – 33

Prayer: I am such a sheep, Father. I know the trail is there before me, but so often I wander off to look for other enticements. Forgive me when I stray, and always come and find me, Oh Lord.

Ask yourself: Think of a time in your life when you strayed away from the path you knew God had for you.

November 2

No Outlet

Today we left the lake and started over a low-lying pass to the west. It was a fairly gentle climb, and by noon we had reached the top. The terrain was mostly level and marshy, with low-growing scrub bushes scattered around. I built a fire to cook lunch while Fisher unpacked what we needed. Looking around for a water supply nearby, he noticed a pool just a few paces away and went over to collect water for coffee.

"I don't think I'd drink that if I were you," I warned. "It might make you sick."

"Why is that?" he asked. "It looks okay."

"It's a stagnant pool; the water seeps in but there's no outlet for it. Without being able to flow, it builds up bacteria levels that could get dangerous. I just got over being sick from drinking swamp water and believe me: it's no fun."

"I guess you're right," he said. "I saw a small stream back down the trail a ways. I'll go there."

As Fisher left to get water, I looked at the stagnant pool. What was it about having an outlet that made water safe to drink? I thought of the Sea of Galilee and the Dead Sea: two huge lakes, one teeming with fish and the other a lifeless place where the only thing good is the plentiful supply of salt. The difference? Both had inlets, but only Galilee had an outlet.

As Fisher came back with containers of water, I said, "Okay, here's your next assignment: tell me why outlets are important. First example, a steam engine."

"Easy one," he said. "No outlet for the steam, big explosion. Happens all the time."

"Good," I said. "How about the human body?'

He wrinkled his nose and said, "Oh, we don't even want to go there."

"Okay," I laughed. "Then how about emotions? Do they need an outlet?" "If you mean emotions like anger, then yeah, I could see how holding it inside would make you crazy."

"Right on," I said, warming up to this impromptu lesson. "But what about all those other emotions, like worry, fear, happiness and love? Can a person keep those inside without expressing them?"

But if I say, "I will not mention him or speak any more in his name," his word is in my heart like a fire, a fire shut up in my bones. I am weary of holding it in; indeed, I cannot.

Jeremiah 20: 9

....

Prayer: Let Your Word burn within me, Lord, so that I cannot hold it in. Compel me to speak, and grant that my words may honor You and Your kingdom.

Ask yourself: Have you ever had a bit of news which you simply could not hold inside? How is that like the Gospel message?

November 3

Another Outlet

Fisher and I talked excitedly all through lunch about the need for venting one's emotions. Even passive things like worry are somehow able to build up inside, so that if they're not expressed they can make the situation much worse than before.

"So how can we provide an outlet for our emotions?" Fisher asked. "Can I turn myself into the Incredible Hulk and smash everything in sight when I get mad?"

"Obviously, that has drawbacks," I said thoughtfully. "No, I think there are acceptable and non-acceptable ways to vent what you're feeling. Not long ago, I was angry at God..."

"Whoa!" Fisher interrupted. "Can we do that? I mean, that sounds wrong, doesn't it?"

"What was wrong in my case was that I didn't understand what had happened, and I was holding God responsible. I still don't have all the answers, by the way, but what I'm coming to is a growing certainty that I *will* know, one of these days. In the meantime, I had to deal with the fact that my anger was making me hurt myself, and if anyone else had been around, I might have hurt them to."

"So what did you do?" he asked.

"I told God how I felt. I figured I couldn't hide what was in my heart from Him, anyway, so I might as well express it. I said to God that I didn't like what He was doing, or worse yet, what He wasn't doing. I admitted that I didn't know all there was to know, and that there had to be a perfectly good reason for what was happening, but at the moment, all I could do was express my anger, honestly and openly with Him."

"Do you think God accepted that as okay?"

"I think so. For one thing, He's leading me through all this with a growing sense of peace about it. I think if I had tried to sit on my anger at God and refused to talk to Him, then I might still be back there... in a swamp."

The LORD said to him, "Who gave man his mouth? Who makes him deaf or mute? Who gives him sight or makes him blind? Is it not I, the LORD? Now go; I will help you speak and will teach you what to say." But Moses said, "O Lord, please send someone else to do it."

Exodus 4: 11 – 13

....

Prayer: I read in Your Word, Father, of some who have told you of their frustrations and lack of understanding, and I shudder to think of doing such a thing. But I know that you see my heart perfectly, and you know the thoughts I hold there. Help me to present them to You, Lord, in a way that is not rebellious nor sinful, but rather a mark of the love between us.

Ask yourself: Do you think it is wrong to tell God that you are angry with Him?

November 4

Evangelism as Outlet

"There's one other illustration," I said as we made our way down from the pass and into the next valley beyond. "Not only is holding everything inside a bad thing for the holder, it prevents those good things from being a blessing to someone else. Take that water, for example." I pointed to a river forming up to our right as it made its way down the hill. The lowlands need that water, and if it just collected up here in stagnant pools, then everything in the valley would die."

"Not to mention the flood that would happen when the highlands couldn't hold it anymore," said Fisher. "And hey! I have another example. For the last couple of days, Friend, you've been filling me with truth about God that I never knew before. I'm learning all this great stuff, but you know what? If I don't find someone to tell it to pretty soon, I may just explode on you!"

I laughed. "You're really living up to your new name, you know that Fisher? I believe God has some great plans for you. I don't know exactly what those plans are, but I have a pretty good idea that it will involve being a "fisher of men": another word for evangelist."

"You think so?" he asked with a touch of anticipation in his voice. "I don't know. I *do* like to talk, that's for sure. And if you'll keep teaching me, I'll actually have something to say!"

"In that case, why don't we practice a bit? Tell me in your own words what you think Jesus meant when he said, 'Follow me and I'll make you fishers of men'."

Fisher warmed up to the task right away. "Well," he began. "It's like this: the ocean is full of fish, just like the world is full of sinners: that's you and me... and"

"Hold it!" I said, not wanting to make it too easy for him. "Are you saying I'm a sinner? I'm a pretty good guy, all in all."

"Yeah, but you see that's not what sin is, just doing good things" he answered. "It's all about relationship between man and his Creator..."

The miles melted away as I listened to a preacher in the making.

As iron sharpens iron, so one man sharpens another.

Proverbs 27: 17

....

Prayer: Send me people, I pray, who will "sharpen" me for service. And grant, Father, that I may help another in his own walk with You.

Ask yourself: Who have you "sharpened" lately?

Catching Up

We came to a grassy meadow in the valley today, and decided to camp for the night. It was an easy decision to make, because someone else had recently camped there, and had left behind a generous supply of firewood, a rocked up place for a campfire, and some very nice kitchen utensils carved out of wood.

"Looks like there were quite a few people camped here," I remarked. "Judging from what they left behind, they seem to be a hard working crew at that."

"My girlfriend made this," said Fisher, holding a spatula which had been made from a pine branch woven into a delicate design. "She's always making things with her hands. This looks like something she would do."

He sat there in silence for awhile, until I finally asked, "Are you looking forward to seeing her again?"

"Yes, and no," he said, still deep in thought. "I mean, yes! Absolutely. I'm anxious to see her and tell about everything that's happened. On the other hand, what if she doesn't like me? I mean, look at me! I'm nothing like that guy I used to be: the guy she knew and loved."

"But if I remember right," I said, "there was a major problem between the two of you. She was committed to God, and you weren't. How do think she'll respond, when she hears that you're now on the same page, spiritually?"

"Yeah, I guess you're right. But I guess we'll just have to get to know each other all over again, won't we? In the process, we may discover that we're not made for each other, after all."

"There's always that possibility," I admitted. "But look at it this way. Now the two of you have a common interest that you didn't have before: seeing this journey through to the end. You both have a common commitment to God, and a willingness to go wherever He leads you. It seems to me that you have a lot more possibility for a future than you ever had before. And if not, it's only because God has something even better in store for you.

"So if I were you," I said, lying back in the soft grass, "I'd take advantage of that river over there and try to wash off a few layers of grime." A few moments later, I heard a splash, followed by a yelp, as he jumped into the icy water.

Do not be yoked together with unbelievers. For what do righteousness and wickedness have in common? Or what fellowship can light have with darkness? What harmony is there between Christ and Belial? What does a believer have in common with an unbeliever?

II Corinthians 6: 14 – 15

Prayer: Guide me in my relationships, Lord. For those I have already made, may our faith be mutual and our love for You a thing we hold in common. As I consider future relationships, grant me wisdom before I make commitments.

Ask yourself: What special difficulties do couples face when one is an unbeliever?

November 6

Meeting Again

I didn't have to urge Fisher out of his sleeping bag this morning. He was up and blowing on the hot coals before it was light. By the time I was ready to climb out of my sleeping bag, he had already made me a cup of coffee and was packed and ready.

"Looks like a great day for a brisk walk," he said cheerily. "I'm ready to go, how about you?"

"Not until I've accomplished a few things, such as drinking this coffee and eating some breakfast. What's your hurry, anyway?" I asked with an all-knowing smile.

"Oh you know, just wanting to get going, that's all. It's such a beautiful morning, and the trail's calling me, and... is it that obvious?" he asked.

"Transparently so," I said. "But I guess I can't blame you. If those friends of yours are only a day's walk ahead of us, then we might just be able to catch up with them by tonight. I'd enjoy the company myself." I came out of my sleeping bag and stood up to get warm by the fire. "But I still want some breakfast before I..."

Fisher thrust something in my hands. "I took the liberty of making you a sandwich out of the leftover fish. You can eat it while we walk. Shall I hold your coffee for you?"

The birds had not even started their morning serenades by the time we were packed up and moving. The trail was mostly downhill, so we made good time, stopping only briefly for another leftover fish sandwich. I accepted it only because Fisher promised me a hot meal by evening. "Sandy's a terrific cook," he insisted. "She can take the simplest things and turn them into a feast."

"I believe you," I said. "Just look what she did with *you*."

He had to think about that for awhile before he caught on to my teasing. "She can also work wonders with tough old birds," he said under his breath.

The sun was disappearing over the mountains, and we were about ready to give it up for the day when Fisher stopped and said, "Do you smell anything?"

I stopped and sniffed. "Yeah. Smoke. With just a trace of tough old bird." Soon we could see the glow of a fire, and called out to let the camp know we were coming in. Even from a distance, I knew who Sandy was. She was stirring something in a pot until she saw us. There was a puzzled look on her face until she recognized Fisher, then dropping her spoon in the fire, she ran toward us with a shout of excitement.

Listen! My lover! Look! Here he comes, leaping across the mountains, bounding over the hills.

Song of Solomon 2: 8

....

Prayer: What an awesome blessing, to be created as man and woman, and to enjoy that special relationship. Grant me wisdom in decision making as it concerns the opposite sex, and bless our union, according to Your perfect will.

Ask yourself: Why do you think God created us as two sexes?

November 7

Getting to Know You

"Gary!" she called out as she ran to meet us on the trail. "Gary! I've missed you so much!" There was an embarrassed hesitation when Sandy arrived, then both laughed and hugged each other.

"Sandy, I want you to meet my Friend. In fact, that's his name. Friend, this is Sandy."

I took her hand and said, "Well, I have to say that you're everything Fisher said you would be." She raised a questioning eyebrow at that, and I corrected myself. "I mean, Gary, of course."

"Sandy, I just have to tell you before we meet the others: I'm not the same person I was when I left. I was so stupid to turn back. But, anyway, I met this man, and he helped me... a lot. Thanks to him, I finally understand what brought you out here. And I want to go too. It's like I've started a whole new life; which is why I have a new name now. Gary was the old guy. Call me Fisher."

Sandy went from joy to confusion and back to joy. Then she said, "Well Ga... Fisher, I can see we have a lot to talk about. C'mon, let's go meet the others."

The "others" were a group of ten travelers. From what I could discern, there were two married couples, three children and two more young ladies about Sandy's age. They were thrilled to see us, especially Fisher, and set about making a place for us around the campfire. I was served up an incredible meal of roast quail, potatoes and green salad, and when I commented on it, Sandy said, "We've got some pretty good hunter-gatherers in our group, and I've promised to cook whatever they bring me. Believe, me, it's not always this fancy!"

After dinner, Sandy and Fisher went out of the camp a short distance, to talk. One of the married men introduced himself as Aaron and asked about my journey. "I'm still fairly new to it," I said. "I began last January."

Aaron smiled and said, "Well then, that makes you the expert! We've all just started. I hope we can learn a few things from you."

My dove in the clefts of the rock, in the hiding places on the mountainside, show me your face, let me hear your voice; for your voice is sweet, and your face is lovely.
Song of Solomon 2: 14

Prayer: Lord, may I know the joy of a Christian home, where husband and wife share their faith openly and serve You without shame. Or, grant this blessing to my children, to my friends and loved ones, that I may rejoice in their happiness.

Ask yourself: Why do you think Christian marriages outlast all others?

November 8

Meet the Group

It was a pleasant night's rest, surrounded by soft conversations and the sound of children. I was reminded of Rendezvous, except that here, there were no "old timers" who had been on the trail for most of their lives. As it was, *I* was the old man to whom they came for questions about the journey. At first I was hesitant to answer their questions, thinking that I could not possibly know enough to be of any help. As we spoke, though, I could see that my few months' travel had taught me a great deal, and I was happy to share it.

"How did you folks decide to travel together?" I asked Aaron, as we sat around the fire.

"Reese and Amy, the other couple over there, had started reading their Bible for the first time since they'd gotten married. My wife, Patty and I were good friends, so we joined them. Next thing you know, we're all excited and wanting to do something about what we were learning. Sandy was our babysitter, and when we started sharing these things with her, she pulled her friends in to listen. By the time we had finished one book in the Bible, we were a close knit group, and a journey like this just seemed like the natural thing to do."

Aaron leaned back and kicked at the fire with his boot. "Then there was Gary. He was the odd one. He prayed together with us and everything, but we all knew that he only came along to be close to Sandy. But well, no one wanted to tell him to go back home. After a few days, he began to see that we were involved in something he didn't understand. As much as we liked him, I have to admit we all breathed a sigh of relief when he left us. What's happened to him, anyway? He seems like a different guy altogether."

"He is a different guy," I assured him. "He's a walking testimony to what God can do to a willing heart. I think you'll be surprised when you hear him talk." The sound of laughter carried into the camp from where Fisher and Sandy were sitting together in the darkness, getting to know each other.

Therefore, if anyone is in Christ, he is a new creation; the old has gone, the new has come!

II Corinthians 5: 17

....

Prayer: Thank you, Father, for Creation, both evident in history and evident in the lives we see re-born.

Ask yourself: Can you or someone you know testify to the life-changing phenomena that comes when a person gives his or her life to God?

November 9

A Child's Calling

Morning was a bustle of activity, with the three children, all under five years of age, running back and forth adding to the level of excitement. The two oldest were girls, Elisa and Jessica, and they were naturally drawn together, much to the aggravation of Greg, youngest child of Aaron and Patty and sister to Jessica. He spent most of the morning running after the two girls, with occasional rest breaks with Mom or Dad.

"There's one thing I've worried about," Patty said to me as Greg raced off again to join the girls.. "Aaron and I are 100% certain of our decision to take this trip. But when I remember that it could be dangerous, I feel guilty for bringing the kids along. I know God has called us; but does He call the kids too?"

Discussing our children was something I distinctly did not want to do, lest the pain in my heart found its way back to the surface. What could I tell them? That one of my children was at home with her mother and I grieved over them both? Or that my son had made the decision to come on the journey, and was now dead? Looking at Patty's expectant expression, I knew that I would have to tell them the whole truth – in time. But for now, I would share only what would be the most help for them today.

"God has a special place in His heart for children," I said at last. "The Bible is very careful to teach us the importance of raising our kids in the way they should go. As adults on this pilgrimage, we know for certain that this is the best, the only way. When our children are older, they'll have to come to that certainty on their own. But in the meantime, we would be poor parents if we kept them from what we know to be the way to life. That would be like the father who said, 'I'm not going to force my kids to eat healthy; I'll let them decide for themselves when they get older.' That's not to say that our children won't suffer while on the trail." I hesitated, afraid I was about to break down. "But how would we feel if they suffered while *not* on the trail?"

"God has called each of us here to a wonderful adventure; knowing that He loves our children even more than we do, I have to believe that He called them at the same time. Who knows?" I laughed. "Maybe it's the kids who have been called, and we're just along for the ride?"

He called a little child and had him stand among them. And he said: "I tell you the truth, unless you change and become like little children, you will never enter the kingdom of heaven. Therefore, whoever humbles himself like this child is the greatest in the kingdom of heaven.

Matthew 18: 2 – 4

....

Prayer: Father, You taught us to be like our children, and by that we know that You love them as we do, and even more. So I rejoice when you call me to service, because I know that our children are included in the call. Watch over and protect them, I pray, and may they be faithful to what You call them.

Ask yourself: What is it about a child that we are to become like?

Youth Group

Camp was packed, and everyone left in intervals, agreeing to meet again in the evening. The children and their parents were the last to be ready, and as slowest to travel, remained behind while the rest of us packed up. Fisher and Sandy had not stopped talking since daybreak; in fact, I think they may have talked all night. They started out first, moving at a fast clip, barely keeping up with their own conversations. By the time I was ready to go, Sandy's two friends – teenagers from the look of them – were getting their gear on as well. "Do you mind if we walk with you awhile?" they asked.

"Of course not, I'd love the company," I said. "You'll have to be patient with an old man, though."

As we started out together, I learned that their names were Heather and Brenda. They had been childhood friends with Sandy, and first came into the group because of her insistence. "We didn't know what Sandy was talking about when she tried to explain all this to us," said Heather. "But as soon as we started reading what she was reading, it all made sense. Brenda and I knew right away that this was what we wanted; and having Sandy there already was just frosting on the cake!"

"Do you all study the Bible together?" I asked.

"We try to," said Brenda, "but sometimes it's hard to participate. I mean, Patty and Amy are super, and I think their husbands are *so cool.* But you know, when they start talking about things like toilet training and life insurance and stuff like that, I'm just, like, well, whatever!"

"I think I understand," I said slowly. "What you mean is that everything they're interested in knowing more about is not exactly what you're interested in, right?" They nodded their agreement, and I made a suggestion. "How about you three girls and Fisher meet together separately once in awhile for a "youth" study? You know, look at what the Bible has to say specifically to your age group?"

"Do you think the others would mind?" Heather asked.

"I'll talk to them, if you like. Besides, you need to get ready for the youth at Rendezvous. I think they call themselves the "Trail Trekkers" or something like that."

With the news that there were other youth to meet, the girls were hopping with excitement. The rest of the day, we talked about the special challenges of being young. It made me forget my own "advancing age" challenges for awhile.

In the last days, God says, I will pour out my Spirit on all people. Your sons and daughters will prophesy, your young men will see visions, your old men will dream dreams.

Acts 2: 17

....

Prayer: Thank you for the energy, the idealism and the hopes of the young! Bless them, I pray, and keep them on the path for Your kingdom's sake. May they learn from the old, and teach it to the children.

Ask yourself: What specific qualities do young people have that neither the older generation nor the children possess?

November 11

Youth Leader

After a gentle climb for several hours, we came to a high point on the trail which looked over a huge forest, stretching out as far as we could see. There we met up with Fisher and Sandy, sitting on a rock and enjoying the view.

"Getting tired, are we?" I joked.

"No way," said Fisher, a huge grin on his face. "We just stopped to talk, and well, I guess the time just got away from us."

"Fisher's been telling me all about your journey," Sandy said to me. "We've got so much to learn. How will we ever be prepared?"

"I guess we can start by having some lunch." I suggested. If you guys could put together a small fire, I'd be happy to show you my specialty. I call it 'Biscuit surprise'."

"Sounds great," said Sandy. "What's in it?"

"That's the surprise," I said. "I'll make the biscuits: you find whatever you can to put in them."

As I unpacked my bag in preparation for cooking, the girls headed into the woods to look for anything edible. Fisher stayed behind to build a fire. "It's been such a fantastic morning," he said. "Sandy and I are so much alike, especially now that we have the same goal in mind."

"I've really enjoyed getting to know Heather and Brenda," I said. "But they need someone closer to their own age to help them grow. Are you interested?"

Fisher stopped what he was doing and looked over at me. "Do you think I'd be any good at something like that? I mean, I'm even newer at this than they are! What could I possibly teach them?"

"Teaching doesn't always mean that the teacher knows more than the student," I said. "Sometimes it just means being willing to take the initiative in learning together. Everyone grows in the process. God's given you a heart for people, Fisher, and I believe He will give you what you need to put that heart to work. Right now, you've got three young people who are eager to learn, and an old man willing to give some encouragement when necessary. How about it?"

Fisher grinned. "Just point me in the right direction!"

Don't let anyone look down on you because you are young, but set an example for the believers in speech, in life, in love, in faith and in purity.

I Timothy 4: 12

Prayer: Call from among the youth, men and women who will lead their peers into new levels of commitment and understanding. Guide them to firm foundations which will withstand all that this generation will throw at them. Bless them, that they may bless those who come after.

Ask yourself: Do you know a young person who could become a dynamic leader, given the proper training and encouragement?

November 12

First Lesson

Lunch was delightful. The girls had found mushrooms, Fisher produced some dried beef from his bag and I used milk powder and cooking oil to make gravy. Soon, we were all enjoying a feast we called "Biscuit surprise: ala beef and mushroom gravy".

"I could use surprises like this more often," I commented as I cleaned my plate with a piece of bread.

"Speaking of surprises," Fisher said to the group. "Let's all say what has surprised us the most so far on this trip." He was a gifted young man, I thought to myself, taking leadership as naturally as a fish to water. The girls jumped right into the conversation, each of them eager to contribute their own discoveries to the rest.

"I was surprised to hear that they're more young people," said Brenda "I can't wait to meet them!"

"I suppose you can all guess what I was surprised about," Sandy offered, looking over to Fisher as she spoke. "I started this trip with one boy; now I'm with another one, and they're both the same guy!" We all laughed, then Heather turned to me.

"I'd like to hear what your biggest surprise has been," she said.

"A lot of things come to mind," I thought aloud. "There have been times when I thought I'd die, but I didn't." Nervous laughter followed that. "Then there were times when I thought I knew what I was doing, but was surprised to find out how ignorant I was. I guess the biggest surprise of all has been the discovery that I've never been alone this whole trip. Even when there weren't nice people like you to travel with," I smiled at each one in turn, "God has never been far away. I have to admit, there were times when I forgot that fact. And if the truth be known, there have been times when I wanted Him to go away." That brought a few gasps of shock. "I'll tell you about those times later. But at the end of the day, there's nothing better than to be able to say, 'Good night, Lord,' and hear 'Good night, Friend,' from deep in my heart. He's with me every moment, waking or sleeping, whether I'm aware of it or not. To someone who doesn't know Him, that can sound like a pretty frightening proposition; but to those of us who *do* know Him, that's about the nicest surprise a person could ever ask for."

This is what the LORD says, he who made the earth, the LORD who formed it and established it—the LORD is his name: 'Call to me and I will answer you and tell you great and unsearchable things you do not know.'
Jeremiah 33: 2 – 3

Prayer: Oh Lord, You are truly the God of surprises. Each day brings new revelations of things which I knew nothing about. Grant me eyes to see them, I pray, and ears to hear all that You would teach me.

Ask yourself: How long has it been since you learned something you didn't know before?

November 13

Back Together

Our "biscuit surprise" lunch had turned into a lively discussion, carrying on late into the afternoon. So it was no surprise when the rest of the group caught up with us. Their coming was announced long in advance by the sound of children. A high pitched scream at first caused the hair on the back of my neck to stand up in shock, reminder of past encounters with the lion. After a moment, however, I could distinguish the cries of delight coming from Elisa and Jessica, followed by little Greg's cries of frustration at having been left behind again.

When the children, accompanied by their parents arrived at our lunchtime outlook, we all admired the scenery once again, asked the usual questions about the day's trek, then someone suggested that we stay here for the night. It was an easy decision. The children looked to be ready to stop, and Aaron and Reese had caught two rabbits which needed dressing out for dinner.

Before long, we were seated comfortably around a fire while the aroma of roast rabbit and sautéed mushrooms promised yet another feast to come. "Well guys," I said to the two men sitting across from me, "the girls told me you were quite the hunter-gathers. I'll have to get you to show me some pointers on the manly art of putting meat on the table."

Reese grinned in a shy sort of way and said, "Well, I was raised on a farm, so to our family every animal is either for workin' or eatin'. If they ain't good for one of those, then they're probably varmints."

"Is Amy a farm girl too?" I asked.

"Oh no," he chuckled. "We met at school. She was a little squeamish at first, when I started bringing things home for her to cook. I think she'd still be a vegetarian if she could. But you know, we had an interesting Bible study one night in Genesis. You know the part where God said He was giving us the animals for food?" I nodded and he went on. "The way I see it, if God gives you somethin', you probably better take it and be grateful."

Just then Amy straightened up from where she had been checking the roasting meat. "That may be so," she conceded, "but I don't see anywhere that I have to like it."

The fear and dread of you will fall upon all the beasts of the earth and all the birds of the air, upon every creature that moves along the ground, and upon all the fish of the sea; they are given into your hands. Everything that lives and moves will be food for you. Just as I gave you the green plants, I now give you everything.
Exodus 9: 2 – 3

....

Prayer: It is an awesome responsibility, Lord, to be given charge of every animal on earth. Help us honor that responsibility by caring for Your creatures as we should. Teach us, so that this world can be all that You made it to be.

Ask yourself: It has been said that Christians should make the best environmentalists. Why would that be true?

More on Meat

It was difficult for me to be objective about the theology of eating meat as I was enjoying the best roasted rabbit I could remember eating. The others were intent on following through, however, and kept bringing up questions as we ate.

Amy said, "I don't think it's right to kill animals for any reason. They're innocent creatures, and the Bible says we're supposed to take care of them."

Reese spoke up, "And taking care of animals means not being cruel to them, and letting them be used for whatever purpose God intended, including for food. Jesus ate fish, didn't He?"

Patty stuck up for Amy, "But fish are different!"

"Yeah, they're not cute like bunny rabbits!" Fisher laughed.

"Now wait a minute," I interrupted. "As Christians, you all agree that we have a responsibility to take care of the world God gave us. That includes animals and the environment. Can we do that without killing? What about weeding the garden, thinning the forest, or dare I suggest it, culling out part of an animal population so the rest will be healthy?"

"That's right," said Heather. "What about washing your hands? That's killing germs!"

"Actually," I said to Heather, "there are religious groups who have real concerns about that kind of thing. I don't know where the final answers lie, but the way I see it, like it or not we live in a world where life and death are, well, a part of life. It's a world broken by sin, and God's saying to us that the animals are now for our food, He may not be saying it the way it would have been in a perfect world, but He is telling us the way things in fact *are*. I don't think we're necessarily commanded to eat meat. If you'd rather stick with soy burgers and bean sprouts, I think that's okay with God. But given the world in which we find ourselves, it looks as though part of the Curse on the whole world includes the fact that things die, so that we can live. And when you think about it, it makes the whole picture of the crucifixion even more meaningful, doesn't it?"

> *By the sweat of your brow you will eat your food until you return to the ground, since from it you were taken; for dust you are and to dust you will return."*
>
> Exodus 3: 19

Prayer: Ever since You took animal skins to clothe Adam and Eve, we have been responsible for the death of Your creatures. Help us, Father, to endure the suffering of the curse we live under. Remind us again that the price has been paid and that there will be a new creation. May it come quickly, Lord.

Ask yourself: Look around you: can you see examples of death, which has resulted in making your life better?

Sacrifice

Moving from vegetarianism to Christ's death on the cross might have seemed like quite a jump, but in the context of the discussion was a natural development. "Think about it," I went on, "after Adam and Eve sinned, what was the first thing that happened?"

"They knew they were naked," Aaron said.

"Right. So what did they do?"

Jessica raised her hand as if in a schoolroom. "They sewed fig leaves together for clothes!"

"Five points for your class," I smiled. "Then what did God do for them?"

"He made them clothes out of animal skins," said Elisa.

"And what does that imply?" I asked.

"That animals died," everyone said softly.

"So the first result of sin was that the animal kingdom suffered. Later on, as Noah and his family got off the ark to a world devastated by flood and facing a possible famine, God said to them, 'Now, those animals you've been taking care of? You may eat them.' And so the process began which leads us all the way to standing rib roast and double cheeseburgers. Maybe it's not the way things used to be; but it's the way things are."

"So where does the crucifixion come in?" Sandy asked.

"People had to remember the consequences of their sin, so God told the people to take an innocent lamb, kill it in front of everyone, and remind them that sin led to this. Eventually, it was a regular part of Jewish worship: sacrificing animals in order to be forgiven of sin. Then Jesus came along, lived a perfectly innocent life, then was killed in front of everyone. God said, 'Okay, that does it; no more sacrifices are required; this One will be for all time and for all people. The Perfect Sacrifice.'

"Death came into the world by one man, Adam. Eternal life came through God's Son, Jesus Christ. Death is part of the curse, and it's by death we live. So if you wash your hands and kill a bunch of germs, or eat a rabbit, don't worry about it. Just thank God that we have forgiveness through the death of His Son."

When he is made aware of the sin he committed, he must bring as his offering for the sin he committed a female goat without defect. He is to lay his hand on the head of the sin offering and slaughter it at the place of the burnt offering.

Leviticus 4: 28 – 29

Prayer: Thank you Father, that I do not have to endure the sacrificial slaughter of animals, now that Jesus has paid the full price for my sin. But still I must live in a world broken by my sin. Cleanse me anew, I pray, and hasten the day when Your kingdom reigns on earth.

Ask yourself: Why do you suppose so many of the world's religions demand the sacrifice of animals as a part of worship?

November 16

The Two Shall Be One

The next morning, Fisher and the three girls were anxious to get started, so I suggested they leave ahead of us, and continue their discussion about Christian responsibility to the environment. They all had strong feelings for the topic, and I felt sure that it would be a lively day for them. Aaron and Reese asked if I would stay back and walk with them awhile, which I was happy to do. We let the ladies and children leave together, while we stayed back and cleaned up the campsite. Reese spoke up as we worked. "I'm sure you picked up on the fact that Amy and I don't always see eye to eye on every issue," he said. "In fact, it seems like we argue about a lot of things. Is that wrong?"

"Amy looks to me like she's a very strong young woman," I said as both Reese and Aaron nodded in agreement. "That by itself is not a bad thing, is it? You can be sure that she will be strong enough to take care of you and the family if needed, and I think you'll always know exactly how she feels. That's something every man would appreciate!

"The question I would have is this: have the two of you agreed on a chain of command?" They weren't sure of my meaning, so I explained. "If you can't agree on something, and a decision has to be made, will one of you back down and let the other take the lead? Everything in nature has a dominant and a submissive side. Even the human brain is divided into two parts, with one side taking precedence over the other. In cases where the two sides of the brain both try to rule, you have things like schizophrenia and bi-polar syndrome. In other words, there's either an agreed-upon chain of command or there's trouble."

"I guess it's like me and Patty," said Aaron. "We've never agreed about whether the ketchup goes in the refrigerator or the pantry. It was a real problem for awhile, until Patty finally said, 'Well, I think you're wrong; but because you're my husband I'll keep it in the refrigerator.'"

"Great example," I said. "But what if the issue is something more serious, like making a decision about your child?"

For this reason a man will leave his father and mother and be united to his wife, and they will become one flesh.

Genesis 2: 24

....

Prayer: What a wonderful institution is marriage! But what a formidable challenge, to learn the art of being one. Teach us how to love unconditionally, and to honor each other as Your Word commands.

Ask yourself: How can loving your spouse make you a better member of society?

The Tough Decisions

The question of where to store ketchup was easy enough to put aside, but when it came to critical questions about children, the struggles began. Reese had a fairly straight forward view of the problem.

"In my family," he said, "the man of the house made the decisions, and that was it. If my mom and dad were arguing about something, he'd let it go awhile, then he'd say, 'Here's what we're going to do,' and that was the end of the discussion."

"Did he ever make a mistake?" I asked.

"Yeah, I suppose he did. But like he said, *somebody* has to take the responsibility, right or wrong. I figure it should be the man."

Aaron was a little more pensive. "That sounds good, Reese. The problem in my family is, I know that Patty is smarter than me in some things. If I don't let her make the decisions about those, we could be in a lot of trouble."

"Well, let's look at this rationally," I said. "What does the Bible actually say about the role of men and women in marriage? It says that women are to be submissive, but does that mean that they're to be brainless door mats? I don't think so. Look at the President of the United States; he may not be the sharpest tool in the shed, but if he's a good president, he surrounds himself with people who *are*. Those people don't make the final decisions, but they advise the President, who in turn makes the decisions and lives by them, right or wrong. To me a good wife is a good counsel, who is ready and willing to offer the gifts she has for the good of the family. The wise husband will listen to her, then make decisions based on the best possible resources the two of them can gather. It's a partnership, where both husband and wife are vital to the success of the family, and in cases where an agreement can't be reached, then one of them has to be willing to be the final word and take the consequences."

"Can that final word ever be given by a woman?" Reese asked.

"I've seen families where it seemed to work," I said. But those were cases where the man, for one reason or another, simply wasn't capable of leading a family. By mutual consent, the woman took the initiative, and they moved forward. Maybe it wasn't the way God set it up to work, but then again, not much of the world *is* going like it should, is it?"

Wives, submit to your husbands as to the Lord. For the husband is the head of the wife as Christ is the head of the church, his body, of which he is the Savior. Now as the church submits to Christ, so also wives should submit to their husbands in everything.

Ephesians 5: 22 – 24

....

Prayer: In so many ways, Father, You have shown us by example how we are to live as Your children. Teach us anew, through the beautiful image of husband and wife, how to submit, to love, to honor and cherish.

Ask yourself: Why would wives object to the command to be submissive to their husbands?

November 18

Dropping the Ball

The question of men's authority in the world kept the conversation lively for the rest of the day. As we moved on down the trail, Aaron offered this opinion:

"I have to keep coming back to the Bible, Friend, where it says that men are to be in charge, make the decisions, lead the church..."

"And support the family, protect the peace, and fight the wars," I agreed. "But what does a woman do whose husband has deserted her? She gets a job, pays the bills and if necessary beats up anybody who threatens her children. I'm not saying this is the way it should be, but the sad fact is, we men have dropped the ball when it comes to some of our responsibilities. And when that happens, I can only thank God that our women are willing and able to pick it up and run with it."

"Okay," said Reese, "but you're talking about a case where a woman has to step in because some jerk of a man stepped out. But I know women who *want* to do those things, and will walk over a man to be able to do them."

"Now you're over my head," I laughed. "I sure wouldn't want to be the one who tells a lady Marine sergeant to go back to the kitchen. I think some things will just have to be worked out between God and the people involved. One thing I keep coming back to, though is this: when God made Adam and Eve, He said in essence, 'The big hairy one: he's in charge. The soft pretty one: she's going to help him.' That system, when it works, gives us a pretty good way of living. Sadly, we've taken the system and everything in it and twisted it around to try and fit our own selfish greed. Maybe if we could get together with our women and determine to follow God's lead, we could get back to where we should be. In the meantime, we just have to keep on loving, forgiving and working for the best."

"One more thought," added Aaron. "you mentioned at the beginning that it comes back to chain of command. If a man is living in submission to God, then it should be easier for his wife to live in submission to him. She may not agree with everything her husband does, but if she's convinced that he's walking according to God's plan, then she's better prepared to submit to her husband, and through him, to God."

Husbands, love your wives, just as Christ loved the church and gave himself up for her to make her holy, cleansing her by the washing with water through the word, and to present her to himself as a radiant church, without stain or wrinkle or any other blemish, but holy and blameless. In this same way, husbands ought to love their wives as their own bodies. He who loves his wife loves himself.
Ephesians 5: 25 – 28

Prayer: Through this passage in Ephesians, I understand, Lord, that the husband is not just to be boss over his wife, but also to be lover and protector. Teach our husbands this vital truth, Father; help them to live it.

Ask yourself: How can a husband be obedient to this command to love his wife as he loves his own body?

Drawing Conclusions

We all met together before dark in a beautiful clearing where the young people had stopped to wait for us. It had the makings of a great campsite, so we unpacked and settled in for the night.

After dinner, as we sat around the fire, it was evident to see that everyone had been involved in exciting discussions all day, and were anxious to continue them. Fisher began by telling us about the "environmentalism seminar" the youth had participated in.

"Basically," he said, "we decided that Christians are still under the command given to Adam to take care of things. That means protecting our resources, preserving wildlife and being responsible farmers. We're still talking about *how* we're supposed to do that, and especially in issues like killing animals, whether for meat or for population control. Given the realities of the day we live in, we think that God has given us a lot of freedom to make choices, but we'll be held accountable for the consequences of those choices. That means we have to stay in tune with the Holy Spirit's leading, every day, all day."

"Great conclusion," I complemented them. Turning to Reese and Aaron, I said, "Men, what have we decided today?"

Aaron said, "Well, first of all, we need to listen to our wives more..."

"I like *that*," giggled Patty.

Aaron smiled at her and went on. "We also need to let our wives be all that God intended for them to be: wise counselors, strong helpers and great lovers."

"I don't remember that last part," said Reese, "but I like it!"

"I know," said Aaron; "I just thought I'd throw that in."

"If I can speak for the fellows," I offered, "we also confessed that we've not been faithful to everything that God told us to do, and we want to say again how much we appreciate our women for taking up the slack and doing those things we've neglected. We hope that we can communicate better with the fairer sex, and in the process that we can all better understand where our duties and our boundaries lie. We've got the potential of showing each other, our kids and the world what God really had in mind when He put us together. I pray that we'll reach that fullest potential."

This is a profound mystery—but I am talking about Christ and the church. However, each one of you also must love his wife as he loves himself, and the wife must respect her husband.

Ephesians 5: 32- 33

Prayer: In all that I do today, Father, whether I am loving my spouse or caring for my pet, teach me how to do all things in honor of You.

Ask yourself: How is caring for a pet a picture of Christian obedience?

A Parting of Ways

I was awake before daylight, and thinking about this group to which I had become so close is so short a time. Gary-become-Fisher was an exciting young man whose life was transforming before my eyes. I had no doubt that he would continue to grow and develop as a dynamic Christian leader. His girlfriend, Sandy, seemed to be just what he needed to help keep him on track; and she obviously was a real mentor to the younger girls who traveled with her. The time spent with Reese and Aaron had been precious, and watching them relate to each other, to their wives and to their children was a real encouragement.

All that considered, it seemed to be time for me to move on. As much as I enjoyed the company of these new friends, and cherished the opportunities to talk with them about their faith and their journey, I knew that I needed to be stretching my own limits as well, coming to grips with my grief and trying to identify my own pilgrimage. This was something I would need to do alone, at least for the time being.

I rose out of my sleeping bag, packed as quietly as possible, then went over to where Aaron lay sleeping. Shaking him softly, I whispered, "Aaron? I'm going to head out this morning. I'll see you folks at Rendezvous."

Aaron mumbled for a moment, then as he understood what I was saying, sat up and started to speak. Then he thought better of it, reached out and shook my hand. "We'll miss you, Friend," he said at last. "I can't thank you enough for all you've done. We'll have some great stories to share when we meet again, huh?"

"You're right about that," I agreed. "Just stay to the trail, don't let anyone convince you to stop, and remember who you are... and *Whose* you are."

The moon was still shining brightly as I shouldered by backpack and started down the trail. I would miss these friends, but I would see them again soon. And we would all be stronger then.

Therefore, my dear friends, as you have always obeyed—not only in my presence, but now much more in my absence—continue to work out your salvation with fear and trembling, for it is God who works in you to will and to act according to his good purpose.

Philippians 2: 12 – 13

Prayer: Father, just as I cherish the fellowship of brothers and sisters in the faith, I also treasure the time You grant me alone: time to work out my faith issues and come to know You better. Grant me time alone today, I pray.

Ask yourself: What kinds of things can you do for spiritual growth alone that would be more difficult in a group?

Alone Again

After so many days of non-stop conversation, it was quite an adjustment to walk in silence again. I missed the camaraderie, but at the same time, the sounds of the forest returned, which I had not heard in awhile. It was good to listen to the early morning sounds of birds coming to life and the occasional chatter of squirrels as they went about their morning routines. As the sun rose over the mountaintop directly ahead of me, the before-dawn chill disappeared and in its place the subtle sounds of the earth as it warmed.

My heart was warming as well, as I thought back over the goodness of God, Who allowed me the opportunity to forget my own grief for a few days. Pouring myself into the lives of that small band of young pilgrims, I was reminded of the miles I had come, and the lessons which had thrust themselves upon me in the process. Whether I had realized it not, I was becoming a role model for those who came after me. In the simple observations I had made along the way, I was now the source of information, and dare I hope, inspiration for others who had yet to make those observations. If my life could accomplish nothing more than to help people like these to succeed in their own journeys, then it would be worth it.

But then I had to remind myself that my own journey was not yet over. Yes, I had learned a few things along the way, but no doubt there was much more yet to learn. I was not Charlie, the old man I had met at the beginning of my travel. He had seen so much more, and as a result had so much more to share with people like me. I would have to cover many more miles before I could hope to look through his eyes at the world around me. Could I do that? Could I go the places he had gone and come through to the other side? Could I experience yet more pain and grief in order to share the lessons learned with those who have yet to meet it?

My foot struck a rock in the trail, and I almost stumbled. Good timing, I thought to myself. I'm not as "old and wise" as those young people back there might have thought. In many ways, I'm still a babe in the woods, with an awful lot to learn.

Show me your ways, O LORD, teach me your paths; guide me in your truth and teach me, for you are God my Savior, and my hope is in you all day long.

Psalms 25: 4 – 5

....

Prayer: As long as I live, Father, I will never learn all there is to know about You, and who I am in Your Presence. Help me to redeem the time today, and become more of what You created me to be.

Ask yourself: What have you learned this week that you didn't know about yourself last week?

November 22

Same Crossing; Different Methods

The trail came to a river today: not a particularly large river, compared to what I had seen, but it ran through a steep, narrow canyon. From where I stood, it was probably less than fifty feet across to the far side. The first thing which caught my attention was a bridge made of rope. Three strands were anchored securely on both sides, so that a hiker could walk on the middle strand while holding on to the other two with left and right hands. I had seen bridges like this in pictures, but had never actually crossed on one. I took one step onto the middle rope, and decided that I would not make today my first experience, either. It sagged and twisted, so that I felt sure I was about to be thrown headlong into the bottom of the canyon. Stepping back off the bridge, I looked over to the right and saw another possibility. A huge tree grew at the edge of the canyon, and there tied firmly to a branch high up in the tree was a long rope. A smaller line was fastened to it and tied to the trunk of the tree, with about sixty to seventy feet coiled neatly at the base. Looking from the rope to the far side of the canyon, I could see what was expected: hold on to the rope, swing across to the other side, then those behind could pull it back to the tree by means of the smaller line.

Neither choice appealed to me. I didn't feel strong enough to swing across, nor adept enough to negotiate the bridge. As I studied the situation, I noticed a third option: the trail went down into the canyon by a series of switchbacks, then by jumping from rock to rock, it would be possible to cross the river before climbing back up the other side. Three choices: one requiring skill, another requiring coordination and the last requiring a lot of time and patience. As a young man, I would undoubtedly have taken the swing, then come back over the rope bridge, just for fun. It was with a depressing sense of acceptance that I started down the narrow trail. These days, I concluded, I would always opt for the safe, the sensible and the way which was the least physically demanding.

Finally standing on the far side of the canyon and looking back, I thought, at least I did make it to the other side, even if I took the old man's route. Was it wrong to avoid unnecessary risks for the sake of sensibility? Or if the truth be known, was I beginning to accept my own advancing years, taking care of my body in ways that in my youth would never even have occurred to me?

Remember your Creator in the days of your youth, before the days of trouble come and the years approach when you will say, "I find no pleasure in them"—
Ecclesiastes 12: 1

Prayer: Ever since the Fall of man, You have watched Your people grow old and die. I know that age will overtake me, and yet I rest in the assurance of eternal youth in the kingdom to come. Until then, help me to cope with my years, and to use my advancing age to bring glory to You.

Ask yourself: Does the thought of growing old disturb you, or fill you with anticipation?

November 23

Growing Old

I woke up this morning to a pain in my legs, and realized it was because of the climb down and back up the canyon yesterday. How was that possible? I've been walking every day now for almost a year! How could my muscles still complain about a little exertion? Moving slowly around the campfire to prepare a cup of coffee, I remembered my father's advice as I was contemplating the purchase of my first car. He said, "It's not the condition of the car; it's the miles traveled that's important. Any car can look good on the outside, but the road will leave its mark somewhere."

This morning, the road had left its mark on the muscles in my legs, and I had to admit that I wasn't in as good a shape as I thought I was. And the problem wasn't just exercise; my body was getting older.

I looked around a nearby riverbank and found a willow tree growing next to the water. Peeling off a little bark, I boiled it in hot water, then drank it as a pain reliever. Funny, I thought: not too long ago I would have seen a willow tree as the perfect source for sling shot material, taking the relatively soft wood and carving it into a masterpiece of weaponry which would be the envy of my friends at school. Now I look at the same tree and see a substitute for aspirin, a medicinal drink to ease sore, aching *old* muscles.

We kids would always snicker when Grandfather got up out of his chair with a "umph!" and struggle to get upright, sometimes taking two or three attempts before succeeding. His slow shuffle was an identifying characteristic which, if not an object of ridicule was at least a way of mimicking him. Grandpa, if you can see me now, I'll bet you're laughing. I never meant to make fun of you, and especially now as I see myself becoming what you were. How did you do it? How could you go day after day, in constant pain and unending reminders of your frailty? I don't think I can do that, but what choice do I have? I can fight it for as long as possible, but eventually my age will catch up with me. How does a person learn how to be old?

Better a poor but wise youth than an old but foolish king who no longer knows how to take warning.

Ecclesiastes 4: 13

....

Prayer: Father, You have shown us men in the Bible who died "old, and full of years". May my life be so blessed, as to not simply grow old, but to fill my life with years. Teach me wisdom and let me share it with the young. May I be even more useful to You in my old age as I was in my youth.

Ask yourself: Have you sat down and listened to an old person lately? What did they have to say?

November 24

Ageing Gracefully

Now there's a contradiction, I thought to myself as I moved slowly and carefully down the trail today. How could the terms "ageing" and "graceful" possibly go together? Getting old means tripping more often, running less, moving "sensibly". Gracefulness means shunning all those things for the sake of style and strength. I didn't see how I could possibly grow old and maintain any sense of style whatsoever.

But then I remembered Charlie, my old friend from earlier this year, who has gone on to be with the Lord. Looking back, I could now recall his stiff and painful gait as we walked together. At times we would move so slowly that we seemed to be going backwards, and there were even times when he would insist that I go on ahead rather than stay behind and shuffle along with him. I could recall those things now in retrospect, but at the times they were the farthest things from my mind. And why? Because the weaknesses of Charlie's body were insignificant compared to the strength of his character. He taught me more in a few short days than I could have learned in a lifetime of trial and error. When I think back to Charlie, it's that strength of character that I remember, and not the failing body.

But I'm not ready to have a failing body, and I have a long way to go before I have character like Charlie's. In fact, does character come naturally with age, or must I do something to earn it? Well, first things first, I decided. My body is not as young as it used to be, but then by the grace of God, it's not as old as it's going to get. The best I can do is take care of what I have, for as long as I have it. I stopped at regular intervals along the trail to rest, even though the "young man" in me was insisting that I could go farther. While I sat, I stretched my arms and legs to keep them as flexible as possible. Taking my canteen out of my backpack, I forced myself to drink, even when I didn't seem particularly thirsty. These were not indications of growing old, I told myself; rather, they were common sense practices which would keep me as young as I could be.

It may not be the best body in the world, I prayed, but it was the only one I would be receiving in this lifetime, and it was a precious gift. I would care for that gift to the best of my ability.

Teach us to number our days aright, that we may gain a heart of wisdom.

Psalms 90: 12

....

Prayer: Remind me today, Father, that usefulness in this life is not only a matter of physical strength. Teach me how to use what You have given me today, and to care for what I have. May my life today bear witness to Your power to use.

Ask yourself: Think of some the greatest contributions to mankind which did not require physical strength or speed.

Learning Wisdom

With the decision to take better care of my body, I was given an almost immediate affirmation: I felt better. I can't say that the aches and pains were any less, but my attitude toward them were much improved. After all, I had *earned* those sore muscles. Rubbing them, I brushed across scars I had picked up on the journey, and saw them in a new light. These were experiences which could never be gained from a textbook, and which cannot come instantly. I may not appreciate the coming frailty of old age, but I must learn to accept and appreciate the wisdom that can come with it.

But wisdom does not always come naturally, does it? I thought to myself. I've known old men and women who, in spite of their many years did not seem to have learned a great deal from them. That would be the real tragedy: to lose the blessings of youth but fail to gain the blessings of age. When that happens, people tend to turn inward, allowing bitterness to rob them of the joy which should be theirs. Instead of serving as a gold mine of wisdom from which the young can learn and grow, they become instead the picture of loneliness.

But I'm never really alone, am I? What does God call me? His child. Remembering that fact, I was able to see my ageing body in a new way. I live in a world under a Curse, and because of that, everything in it begins to die on the day it is born. I'm not as strong or as fast as I used to be, because that's what happens in a dying world. But God calls me His child, and says that He has a home for me in His kingdom. When I get there, I will no longer inhabit the degenerating flesh that I now call my body; I'll be what I am today, only without the burden. His child.

So in a sense, I'm moving toward what men have struggled for throughout the ages: eternal youth. The body that serves me, and occasionally fails me as I get older, is just a temporary condition. One day, I will cast it off and finally become all that I was created to be. Knowing that helps me put up with a few sore muscles today. And I hope it will help me to be a help for others who must face the same realities of age.

There are also heavenly bodies and there are earthly bodies; but the splendor of the heavenly bodies is one kind, and the splendor of the earthly bodies is another.
I Corinthians 15: 40

....

Prayer: What a glorious promise, Oh Lord, that one day we will throw off these mortal bodies and take on a new, heavenly body! I wait with longing for that day, but in the meantime, help me to care for what I have today.

Ask yourself: What do you think our heavenly bodies will look like?

November 26

Order and Ageing

After crossing the canyon, the trail was less demanding, winding through pine forests on fairly level ground. The sun broke through the treetops, bringing a kaleidoscope of color to the forest floor. As I walked throughout the day, I was able to think about this whole business of ageing and youth. One key element that kept coming back to me was the idea of order. A person begins young, grows old, then is brought into the kingdom, forever prime.

At least that's how it should be, I thought. A child is young, and that's right. We laugh at a baby's first faltering steps, not because we wish to ridicule, but because we rejoice that this young life is learning, step by step, how to move forward. When a child is old beyond his or her years, we call that "precocious" and think it cute... for awhile. When a child is tragically struck by a disease which accelerates the ageing process, we draw back in horror. And why? Because first, that child's life is cut short, but more to the heart of the matter, because a child is not, should not be old. The order has been tampered with.

By the same token, when an old person, full of years, begins to regress and start behaving like a child, we don't say it's cute; we say it's profoundly sad. And why? Because an old person should not live as though young. Once again, the order has been tampered with.

I could see where my thoughts were taking me, and I tried to change direction, but to no avail. The question of order in a person's life is never felt more deeply than when a child dies. Children should bury their parents: not the other way around. For the children of one who has lived a full life and is now laid to rest, it is a time of grief, but it's a grief tempered with the knowledge that this day would come. Generation replaces generation and life goes on. But how can my life go on, now that my child is dead? I know he's with the Father, and that I will join him some day, but in the meantime, I must live in a world where order has been destroyed.

As those thoughts stirred memories I had tried to suppress, my grief returned, and I stopped to cry.

May the LORD bless you from Zion all the days of your life; may you see the prosperity of Jerusalem, and may you live to see your children's children.
Psalms 128: 5

....

Prayer: With a grateful heart, Oh God, I can look around me today and see the order of Your creation. Thank you for allowing me a glimpse of my past and my future in the lives of those I see. Comfort us when we are denied that blessing, and we must grieve for one who has been taken prematurely. Touch us with Your gentle Hand and dry our tears.

Ask yourself: What comfort can you give to one who has lost a child?

In and Out of Shadows

I slept where I had stopped to grieve, and awoke with a familiar hollow feeling in my heart. Temptations offered back on the mountain came again to suggest that I didn't have to endure this; that if only I were to deny God's grace or lash out in anger, somehow my pain would be lessened. But I was surprised and vaguely pleased to discover that the temptations were not as powerful as before. With the sun's warmth coming through the trees, I began to feel that my life would somehow survive this ordeal. I knew that the slightest provocation would drive me back into the depths of grief, but for awhile at least, I could go on.

The trail was much the same as yesterday: level ground going through pine forest with splashes of light followed by sessions of shadow. The bright spots were pleasantly warm, while the shadows turned the trail suddenly cool and clammy. I found myself hurrying through the dark places while slowing down through the sunny spots.

An image came to mind as I walked, and that was of the forest floor as a picture of my life. The sunny places were the times when life was good: I relished the warmth of the day and even slowed down the pace to enjoy it longer. The shadows were those times when I was no longer sure of where I was or what was happening. Thinking about my son plunged me instantly into shadow; I had to watch carefully where I placed my feet, lest I stumble and fall. Returning to the sun, I would once again believe that life was worth living.

The only real surprise in this image was the fact that my grief was not a single valley through which I must pass. Emerging into the light did not mean that the darkness had passed, never to return. While the shady places might grow fewer and farther apart, they would always be there, and I might find myself back in darkness without a moment's notice. But as the songwriter so aptly explained, "Be encouraged by the sight; where there's a shadow, there's a light." The dark places are only there because the light has not reached them. If there were no light, if there were no hope, then shadows themselves would not exist. All would be darkness only.

So I will welcome the times of shadow, if for no other reason than that they remind me of the great Light I'm moving toward.

The LORD is good, a refuge in times of trouble. He cares for those who trust in him.

Nahum 1: 7

....

Prayer: Just as there is joy, I know full well that in my life will also be times of sorrow. You have told me already, and I praise You for Your honesty. Prepare me for such times, I pray. May my days of shadow be just as much a time for rejoicing as my days of trouble, for You are with me.

Ask yourself: Can you rejoice in God's Presence, even when you are sad?

An Unexpected Friend

I was walking through the forest this morning when I heard a mournful sound. It was reminiscent of a child's cry, but more animal in nature. It seemed to be coming from somewhere off to the right, so I turned that way, stopping every few steps to listen.

After a hundred yards or so, I came to a canyon. The rock where I stood was the top of a cliff which dropped down into a thickly-wooded area. The howling sound was coming from that direction, but as I stepped closer to the edge, I saw that the source was directly below me. About ten feet down, a narrow ledge jutted out, and there sat a dog.

It looked to be no more than a puppy, maybe four or five months old. It had the markings of a Labrador, however, and the size of his feet told me that he had a lot of growing to do yet. He was sitting, facing out to the canyon below, and every few moments would give out a long, low howl of despair. Somehow, he had fallen to the ledge and was hopelessly trapped.

"Hey there fella," I called down to him. He jumped in surprise, looked up at me, then exploded into a flurry of enthusiasm. I was afraid that he would back off the ledge in his excitement, and tried to calm him down as I thought about what to do. "Whoa, whoa," I said softly. "Sit still, now. I'll get you up, but you have to be patient, okay?"

I knew he didn't understand my words, but he seemed to be comforted by them, and obediently sat for as long as his puppy temperament would allow, then jumped up again, placing his front paws on the rock as if to climb up to greet me properly. I stepped back out of sight, which led to another series of howls, and tried to formulate a plan for rescue. I had some rope, but how could I get it around him?

First we try the simplest, I thought. Taking a length of rope and putting a loop in one end, I lowered it over the edge. If I could get him to step into it, I could pull him up fairly easily. The first attempt failed, however, when he saw the rope as an offer to play. He grabbed it, shook it, then began to chew on it until I had to pull it back up for fear he would ruin it. Several more tries proved what I knew all along: this was not going to work. I would have to go down there if I ever hoped to rescue him.

Defend the cause of the weak and fatherless; maintain the rights of the poor and oppressed. Rescue the weak and needy; deliver them from the hand of the wicked.
Psalms 82: 3 – 4

Prayer: Lord, how often have I been like that poor dog, trapped and helpless, with no hope of rescue? Praise You for Your mercy and love for me, that You would come to where I am and bring me back to safety! As You have loved me, may I love others.

Ask yourself: Why do you think a person naturally feels a desire to help the helpless?

November 29

To the Ledge

Three problems presented themselves: first I would have to get myself down to the ledge safely. Then I would have to get the dog back to the top. Implied in that task was the third problem, which was getting myself safely back up. Could I manage to carry a squirming bundle of energy in one hand while pulling myself up a rope with the other? Not a chance. The dog would have to go separately.

Looking through my backpack, I found a shirt which would work as a crude sling, and tied it to the end of a length of rope. That was lowered down to where the dog now danced in delight on the ledge, with the excess rope passed around a nearby tree up above. The other end of the rope I tossed down to the ledge as well.

Taking another length of rope, I tied off one end to the tree, put a few knots in it for gripping and tossed it down to the ledge. After a few deep breaths, I lowered myself down into the waiting maelstrom of excitement, as the dog bounced around my legs in joy. A few moments of getting acquainted, and I was ready to tie him into the sling. He was quite happy about this until I actually started pulling on the other end of the rope, gradually lifting him to the top. He struggled for a moment, then froze in uncertain fear as he was carried up. Arriving at the top, he was more than willing to scramble to safety, then disappeared out of sight, returning occasionally to look down at me with a mixture of confusion and delight.

Now comes the hard part, I thought, taking a firm grip on the knotted rope and giving it a tug. Would I be able to pull myself up? Thoughts of ageing these past few days had left me fairly uncertain of my physical abilities. But there's nothing like the fear of being stranded on a narrow ledge to add a dose of adrenalin. The climb back up was easier than I thought it would be, especially with the one-dog cheering section which encouraged me on. Pulling myself over the edge, I was greeted to a proper welcome which only a delighted puppy can give.

I untied the sling and let him run, then led him to a nearby stream where he helped himself to a huge drink and an impromptu swim. A few more turns around the meadow, and he was finally ready to come sit at my feet and get better acquainted.

The Word became flesh and made his dwelling among us. We have seen his glory, the glory of the One and Only, who came from the Father, full of grace and truth.

John 1: 14

Prayer: Lord, You knew that we could never save ourselves, and so You came in the form of a Man; You dwelt among us and taught us the way to salvation. Praise You for the unspeakable gift!

Ask yourself: Why is it better for missionaries to go live among the people to whom they minister rather than simply dropping Bibles to them from airplanes?

Like a Dog on a Ledge

After a drink, a swim and numerous circuits at full speed around where I sat, the puppy was now ready to think about food. He looked as though he hadn't eaten in several days, and I could only imagine how long he had been trapped on the ledge. Had it not been for his mournful wailing, I would never have found him, nor would anyone else, I was certain. Falling from the ledge would have definitely proved fatal, and climbing back up unaided was not an option. "You're a lucky dog," I said as I dug through my backpack for something to eat.

But then again, one lesson this journey was teaching me was the fact that all things work together for a purpose. Was he meant to fall off the cliff, so that I would find him, or was this simply an example of God using the willing (in this case, myself) in order to rescue this animal from his own clumsiness? Either way, it was a good experience for both of us, I thought. I had the joy of doing something worthwhile, with the added encouragement of finding that my ageing body still had a bit of strength left in it.

As he enthusiastically dug into some dry bread, I thought about the image of his plight, and what I could learn from that. In a lot of ways, his situation was a mirror to mankind, wasn't it? By this dog's poor choices, and by Adam's decision to sin, they both found themselves in dire straits, doomed to die unless rescue came. I found the dog, but was unable to convince him to work with me on pulling him up. For that matter, he had neither the understanding nor the skill to strap himself into the sling which would pull him to safety. Adam and all of us who followed him were similarly stranded, with no way of pulling ourselves out of the position we'd fallen to, even if we had been thrown a lifeline. Just as I had to lower myself down to the hapless puppy, Jesus had to come personally to sort out our predicament and show us the way to salvation.

In my case, coming to the ledge meant a certain amount of risk on my part, as I could have found myself stranded, or else slipping and falling to my own death. At that point the analogy breaks down, because with Jesus, it was far more than a risk: death was certain.

I only wish I could demonstrate my gratitude with such a demonstration of joy as this puppy is able to produce.

I will not leave you as orphans; I will come to you.

John 14: 18

....

Prayer: Lord, there are so many, like that puppy, who are stranded and alone. Show me how to reach out to them, or if necessary, to go where they are and bring them to safety in You. Rescue them, I pray, for Your Name's sake.

Ask yourself: Who do you know today who waits stranded and lost? How can you help that person?

December 1

Choosing a Name

Finally having eaten his fill, my new friend now lay at my feet, contented. Whenever I stood up to move around, however, he would jump up and follow, determined to keep me within easy reach. I couldn't imagine where he had come from, but where he was going seemed to be clear, at least to him.

"So, you think you want to tag along with me?" I said, giving his ears a scratch. "In that case, you need a name." He looked up at me in anticipation. Even though he couldn't understand my words, he was obviously committed to whatever I had to say. The puppy in him was still ready for a romp without a moment's notice, but something in his genetic make up told him that I was now "top dog".

What was it about domesticated animals? I thought to myself. The wild creatures I had come across on the trail saw me as either predator or trespasser, in either case someone to be avoided at all costs. A few, such as the lion, had entertained the notion of man as mortal enemy, and any meeting of the two would result in a battle to the death. But to a select group of those in the animal kingdom was given the unique privilege of living and working alongside man, each one bringing to the partnership special skills, allowing things to be done which would have been difficult or impossible otherwise. From the horse to the hunting falcon; from the pig who digs for truffles to the faithful dog, these creatures offer services in exchange for food, security and companionship.

At this point in my journey, a good companion would be welcome, I decided. But every companion needs a name: what would fit this young Labrador puppy? Seeing his eagerness to serve, I was reminded of Onesimus, the runaway slave befriended by Paul and eventually sent back to his master. Had this dog run away, or was he just lost? Did he have a master somewhere looking for him, or was he born in the wild, never a part of the man/dog partnership? Wherever the truth lay, I had at my feet a willing servant, who as the name Onesimus implies, could be "useful".

"Onesimus," I said aloud, to which he perked up. "That's rather a big name for such a little dog. What do you think of "Onessy?" As if in reply, he jumped to his feet and ran in circles, barking for all he was worth. It's a good feeling, to have a name.

I appeal to you for my son Onesimus, who became my son while I was in chains. Formerly he was useless to you, but now he has become useful both to you and to me.
Philemon 4: 10 – 11

....

Prayer: Having been rescued, we are all now bought with a price and owe our allegiance to You, Father. May we be useful to Your Kingdom and bring honor to Your Name.

Ask yourself: Does the thought that you are "owned" disturb you or relieve you?

December 2

Learning to Obey

With a name comes responsibility, and as new master, I had to teach Onessy how to get along in his new world. We started with simple commands like "Come" and "Stay". The first was easy, since the pup wanted nothing more in life than to come to wherever I happened to be. "Stay" proved to be much more of a challenge, however, since it went against everything Onessy was committed to.

I began by breaking a piece of dried beef up into tiny pieces, to use as a reward. Whenever he would obey, I would praise him enthusiastically and give him a piece of meat. Getting him to stay in one place while I walked away might have been an impossible task if I hadn't thought finally of taking a length of rope, tying to him, then looping it around a tree behind him, carrying the other end with me. That way, by pulling on the rope, I was actually pulling him away from where I stood. And, by holding the rope securely, I could prevent him from coming directly to me. Of course, if he ever figured out that by going back around the tree, he could have come anytime he wanted to, the lesson would be over. But he never did figure that out.

By evening, he was getting the idea, and we actually had a few successes before I decided to call it a day. That night, after I made dinner for both of us, I put his on the ground, then held onto him while he watched it like a prize hunting dog. "Stay," I said quietly. He knew what he was supposed to do, but just couldn't bring himself to obey. I held him back, talking to him all the time. "Onessy, stay... stay... Okay, you can go!"

I loosened my grip a fraction, and he was off like the bullet from a gun. When he had finished with his own dinner, he came to see if I wanted all of mine. I placed a bit of meat on the ground, looked at him until he made eye contact with me, then said, "Onessy, stay... Okay!"

Dinner over, we cleaned up the camp, and made preparations for bed. For Onessy, there was only one place: On top of my sleeping bag, curled up on my feet. He had the satisfied look of a dog who knew he had done well today. There were still a lot of things for him to learn, but we were well on the way, and he knew it.

A lot like me, I thought as I pulled the covers up around my neck.

Take my yoke upon you and learn from me, for I am gentle and humble in heart, and you will find rest for your souls. For my yoke is easy and my burden is light."
Matthew 11: 29 – 30

....

Prayer: I know the question, Lord, is not whether I have a Master, but rather, Who my Master is. What a joy to know that You own me, you love me, and you teach me all that I should know!

Ask yourself: What has God taught you lately? Did the lessons come easily?

December 3

Learning to Work

The next morning, after a breakfast for two, interspersed with some review of yesterday's lessons, Onessy and I were ready to travel. He had taken to the task of learning so eagerly, that I felt he should also have a chance to share in the workload. Taking the shirt I had used for a sling yesterday, I designed a few modifications using my sewing kit, and fashioned a "doggie backpack". It fit snugly over his shoulders, with a small pocket on each side big enough to carry a few miscellaneous items, such as cooking equipment and extra rope. It wasn't a heavy load, but I could feel the difference in weight when I lifted my own backpack into place.

As for Onessy, he couldn't have been more thrilled if I had offered him a bone. He had to get used to the straps at first, and we stopped several times to make adjustments. By mid day, however, he was marching ahead of me, wagging his tail, and I was certain, wearing a smile. He loved to work, as if knowing that by his efforts he was making me happy.

By evening, we stopped to camp, and I removed his pack. He ran in circles awhile, then rolled over and over, scratching his back in visible relief. Then he came to me as if to say, "Did I do all right?"

"You did great, Onessy," I praised him. "Extra rations for you tonight."

Work is not a bad thing, I decided, watching how it had brought pure joy to this young dog. Even in the Garden of Eden before the Fall, work was a part of living. We all need work to do, whether for measuring our progress, toning our muscles, or simply serving our Master. It's a shame that work is so often associated with punishment, when it was originally intended as part of the "good" world we lived in. The difference, I suppose, is what God described in the Curse, that work now involves thorns and sweat, pain and failure along with the satisfaction of a job well done.

"Well Onessy," I said as we settled down to sleep. "I hope we both work well, rest well, and enjoy the task." He wagged his tail and laid a head on my knee. He was tired, I could tell, but his sleep would be well-deserved.

Now the LORD God had formed out of the ground all the beasts of the field and all the birds of the air. He brought them to the man to see what he would name them; and whatever the man called each living creature, that was its name. So the man gave names to all the livestock, the birds of the air and all the beasts of the field.
Genesis 2: 19 – 20

....

Prayer: Praise You for work, Oh God! Thank you for giving me something "useful" to do today. Help me do it with all my might and mind, so that at the end of the day, I will have Your smile.

Ask yourself: What is it about work that makes us happy? What about it makes us discontented?

December 4

Helping to Defend

I felt it before I heard it: Onessy's low growl as he lay across my feet. I put a hand down to reassure him and discovered that his head was up and motionless. He was staring intently into the darkness and the growl was becoming more audible by the second.

"What is it, Onessy?" I whispered, straining to hear what he had detected. I saw and heard nothing, but knew that a dog's senses were more acute than my own. I slipped out of the sleeping bag and reached over to take my sword from the backpack. When I stood up, Onessy stood as well, and became more aggressive. The hair stood up on the back of his neck, and the growl was now a full-throated warning.

"Who's there?" I shouted into the dark. "Speak up before I let the dog loose."

A rustle in the grass, the snap of a twig, then two men stepped into the faint light given off by the coals left in my campfire. "Who are you?" I challenged them. "And what are you doing here in the middle of the night?"

The men were armed with clubs, but didn't seem all that eager to use them, especially with the sight of a man with a sword standing alongside a possibly vicious dog. One of the men spoke. "Seems to me, we should be asking you that question. This property belongs to the king. You're trespassing."

"What king would that be?" I asked. "I serve only one King, and He created all that you see."

The other man gave a low "humph!" and said, "Just as I thought. He's one of *them.*" Looking over at me, he said, "We serve a different kind of king, stranger: the kind you can see with your eyes. You've come onto his land, and if I were you, I'd start moving on right now."

I could see these men weren't prepared to carry out any challenges immediately, so I mustered what courage I could and answered them back. "I move as my king leads me. Not until then. If your king has a problem with that, then I would invite him to come tell me so. Until then, it's late. I'll bid you two good night."

They seemed uncertain for a moment, then exchanged glances and backed away. "You'll see us again, stranger. You can be sure of that."

They disappeared back into the shadows, and I allowed myself to breathe again. Onessy seemed to relax as well, so I felt certain that they had gone. "Thanks, fella," I said, patting him on the back. "It looks like you're good for more than hauling a pack."

Though one may be overpowered, two can defend themselves. A cord of three strands is not quickly broken.

Ecclesiastes 4: 12

....

Prayer: I know that as I journey toward the Kingdom, I will have to defend myself from time to time. Thank you, Father, for fellow travelers who will stand by me. Bless them, I pray, and protect them.

Ask yourself: Why do you suppose God would provide you with friends who help protect you, rather than simply protecting you Himself?

Willing Ownership

I wasn't ready to make a run for safety, but then again, I had no desire to stay in the area any longer than necessary. Whoever this "king" was, who my midnight visitors spoke about, he seemed to be willing to challenge my right to the trail. Better to move on, I thought.

But first, a small ceremony was in order. I had a spare belt in my backpack, so I cut it to fit Onessy, inscribe his name on it, and then as a final touch, fastened onto the collar one of the four lion's teeth I carried. "For bravery, faithfulness and a willingness to serve your master," I said as I buckled the new collar around his neck. "May this lion's tooth serve as a symbol of your valor, the collar as a mark of ownership. By your devotion, you have demonstrated your willingness to be called 'Onesimus', otherwise known as 'Onessy': my dog and faithful friend."

He sat as still as a young pup could sit, wanting to dance for joy at this attention, but my demeanor communicating to him that now was the time for restraint. With a pat-on-the-head salute and a "good boy", he sprang back into action, running around the perimeter of the camp and announcing with loud barking his new status to the surrounding forest.

Just as we all want work to do, I believe that in our heart of hearts, we want a Master as well. We may talk of freedom, but what we really desire is freedom with boundaries. I can be at peace and know real joy when I know how far I can go and when I must stop. What a joy to know that I am not my own: that I have been bought with a price, and that my Master is loving and good.

Onessy knows how to show his joy at such status. Maybe I can learn from him.

But if the servant declares, 'I love my master and my wife and children and do not want to go free,' then his master must take him before the judges. He shall take him to the door or the doorpost and pierce his ear with an awl. Then he will be his servant for life.

Exodus 21: 5 – 6

....

Prayer: Father, I may yearn for what I think is freedom from time to time, but in my heart I know that I can only be free while under Your authority. Grant me a lifetime of service to Your kingdom, and then take me to be with you for eternity. Never let me go.

Ask yourself: How is a fence around a young calf an instrument of freedom for him?

December 6

Fog

The trail led along a canyon to my right, with a range of mountains running along to the left. As we walked, I watched for signs of this "king" the men had spoken of, but could see no indication of permanent settlements along the path. Perhaps up in the high country, there might be something, but if there was, it was hidden from view. Once when we stopped to rest, I thought I heard the sound of drums carried on the wind, but could not tell how far away they were, nor from which direction they came. Just as well, I thought, cinching up my backpack and adjusting the straps on Onessy's rig; I had no desire to meet anyone along here who had chosen to settle and stay. And the fact that one of the men last night had referred to me as "one of those" left me with a vague sense of dread. Apparently someone lived nearby: someone with a leader they called "king" and someone with no regard for travelers like myself. If I never met up with them, that would be okay by me.

The trail began a long, gradual ascent, apparently headed toward a low-lying pass I could just see in the distance. We walked steadily for several hours, then reached the saddle of the pass by late afternoon. I was anxious to get back down to a lower altitude before making camp for the night. The air seemed cool and slightly damp. A fire would feel good.

As we got to the point where I could see to the other side of the pass, however, I was dismayed to see that fog had completely filled the valley ahead. The edges were lapping up to the top of the pass where I stood, and as we started down, it became increasingly difficult to see where we were going. The path was running across hard packed shale which left no trace of our passing. For the first mile or so, trail markers showed me the way to go, but as the fog got thicker, I could no longer see them. I strained my eyes to see evidence around my feet of a path, but with the coming darkness that was now impossible.

I had two choices: I could stop right where I was and wait until morning when, hopefully, the fog would lift and I could see my way; or else I could keep moving downhill in the hope that I was still on the trail. As much as I feared losing the trail, I feared more the thought of staying here, with no wood for a fire and no place to lay a sleeping bag. I decided to keep moving, however slowly.

Keep me, O LORD, from the hands of the wicked; protect me from men of violence who plan to trip my feet.

Psalms 140: 4

....

Prayer: On the days when I cannot see my way forward, grant me wisdom, Lord. Shall I move? Shall I stop and wait? Let You Holy Spirit guide me in the path I should follow.

Ask yourself: What can you learn in times of complete darkness?

December 7

Ready to Lead

I walked slowly for a mile or more, straining my eyes through the fog, in hopes of seeing a trail marker. As time passed, however, and darkness began to settle in, I became more and more convinced that I had gotten off the trail and was now headed away from it. The thought horrified me, and I stopped to consider staying where I was until morning when, hopefully I would be able to see better.

Onessy was right beside me, ears pricked up, sniffing the air. "What do you think, boy?" I asked, giving his head a pat. "Shall we wait it out til morning?" His tail wagged in response to my words, but he never took his eyes off an imaginary point in the distance which seemed to have caught his attention. He stood stock still another moment, and then as if some inner decision had been made, he gave a loud bark and took off running.

"Wait Onessy!" I cried. "Stop! Come back!" His answer was another bark, followed by another, this time farther away. I started off toward the sound, my thoughts conflicted. If I followed him, we might both become hopelessly lost. On the other hand, if I let him go, then he might become lost from me, a thought which brought a wave of sadness. Finally, I considered the possibility that he might have heard or smelled something and was moving toward it at full speed. I remembered the men I had met the night before, and had no desire to stumble in their camp.

Well, I concluded, there comes a time when a man must either lead or let himself be led. There in the fog, with nothing more than a dog's enthusiasm to guide me, I decided to become a follower. Striking off in the direction of the sound, I hurried as fast as I could over the hard packed shale. I stopped every few moments to listen, adjusting my direction to keep following Onessy's path.

The next time I stopped, I heard another sound coming from the direction I was going. A metallic rattling, like pots and pans, and the occasional sound of voices carried through the fog. Onessy was no longer barking, but I wasn't sure what that meant. I started to pull my sword out, just as a precaution, but as I set my pack down to open it, a familiar aroma swept across the fog. I stood up, not willing to believe what I was sensing, but after a few more whiffs, it was unmistakable: Lizzie's stew.

When he has brought out all his own, he goes on ahead of them, and his sheep follow him because they know his voice. But they will never follow a stranger; in fact, they will run away from him because they do not recognize a stranger's voice.
John 10: 4 – 5

....

Prayer: Lord, teach me when to lead and when to follow. Show me those who are worthy of leadership, and guide me to lead even as I am led by You.

Ask yourself: What are the marks of a good leader? What makes a good follower?

December 8

Rendezvous Relocated

I moved as swiftly as I could through the fog, following the heavenly scent of Lizzie's cooking, interspersed with the sounds of people at work. The light of a roaring fire appeared first, and then I could make out the shapes of men and women as they moved about the camp. Onessy had found a comfortable place next to the fire, and was enjoying the attention of several girls. As I moved closer to the group, he turned and looked at me with a wag of his tail, his teeth firmly gripped around a huge bone. Lizzie was the first to notice me and called out, "Well, well, well! It looks like the mystery of the Pilgrim Pooch has been solved. Come up to the fire and warm yourself, Friend. Supper will be ready soon."

It was good to see everyone, especially since only moments before, I was contemplating a fireless night on a fog-bound mountainside. I looked around and saw a few familiar faces, as well as several I had not seen before. Everyone was working feverishly, setting up tents, gathering wood, unpacking crates and arranging tables. "Am I earlier than usual?" I asked, looking around at all the activity. "I've never been here to see the place actually being set up."

Ralph appeared out of the crowd and gave me a handshake that quickly turned into a hug. I noticed he was wearing a sword and a somber expression. "Welcome back, Friend. We've been praying for you every day since you left. I know we'll all want to hear about what happened, as soon as we get settled."

Hank came up behind Ralph, also wearing a sword. "The reason we're still unpacking is because we had to move camp," he said, barely disguising his anger. "We were all set up about ten miles back, when these *thugs* showed up and told us to move on. I said we should have stayed right there and had it out with them, but the group decided to move."

"I think I met the same guys," I said. "And so, then you made the right choice to leave. Something's not right about that place; the farther we are from them the better."

"Well, we may not have heard the last of it yet," said Lizzie as she stirred the pot. "Do you know Steve, the site manager of the camp? He's gone back," Lizzie said. "He decided to go have a word with whoever's in charge. That was two days ago, and we haven't seen him since."

Remember the words I spoke to you: 'No servant is greater than his master.' If they persecuted me, they will persecute you also. If they obeyed my teaching, they will obey yours also. They will treat you this way because of my name, for they do not know the One who sent me.

John 15: 20 – 21

Prayer: You have told us, Lord, that Your Church will be persecuted. I see evidence of that fact today, and I grieve for Your people. Please surround the Church with Your Holy Presence and protect her with Your mighty arm. Grant courage and faithfulness to Your people, for Your Name's sake.

Ask yourself: Why do you think some people have a natural hatred of the church?

December 9

Persecution

At the news of Steve's going to talk to the "king" of that area, I felt a cold chill run up my back that didn't come from the fog. Whoever those men were that came to my camp the night before, they seemed to have a base of power located nearby. Furthermore, they knew about travelers like us, and most certainly did not hold any good will for us.

"I didn't meet Steve along the trail," I said, "so that means he must have turned off to find where those men lived."

"Not only did they tell us we couldn't stay where we had camped," Hank continued, "they said if they caught us drinking out of the stream or gathering any food in the area, we'd have to answer to them. I mean, how can they say that? This place doesn't belong to them, any more than it belongs to us. What gives them the right to tell us what we can do?"

"They *don't* have the right," I said to Hank. "But sometimes people claim territory that's not theirs. They hold onto it by force, and subject everyone within it to their own laws."

"Then why don't we just go back there and tell them so?" said Hank, his anger building by the minute. "We've got weapons. We're trained, and we're *right.*"

I waited for a minute to see if anyone else was going to answer that question, but everyone seemed to be looking to me. "The reason we don't go back there, Hank," I answered, "is because we're not here to right every wrong we come across on this journey. There's a lot of rebellion going on all around us; but those people are not rebelling against *us*. They're rebelling against God. Sometimes, God may direct us to go and confront the evil doers. Ralph and I were sent to a town where the enemy had blinded everyone into believing a lie. But until we get a word from God on this, I believe we need to stay out of their way and keep to the path."

A few heads nodded in agreement, and I could see the relief in their faces, as if some kind of decision had now been made. Were these people looking to me as their leader?

All this I have told you so that you will not go astray. They will put you out of the synagogue; in fact, a time is coming when anyone who kills you will think he is offering a service to God. They will do such things because they have not known the Father or me.

John 16: 1 – 3

Prayer: Show me, Father, where I must stand and fight and where I must back away from those who would persecute Your Church. Whatever I do, may it be done by Your Spirit's leading and by no other. Grant me courage, either to fight or to refrain.

Ask yourself: Do you think the church should be immune to the laws of the land in which it sits?

December 10

Emerging Leadership

Lizzie handed me a bowl of stew, which seemed to indicate that the impromptu meeting had come to a close. The crowd went their separate ways, leaving Lizzie and me by the fire. Onessy had found a comfortable place to chew on his bone.

"Lizzie?" I asked quietly. "What's going on here?"

"Sit down," she said. "You eat, and I'll fill you in."

For the next hour, she told me about the side of Rendezvous which I had never seen before: the side where issues are discussed and decisions affecting the whole group are made. "Steve is a good site manager," she said. "He's hard working and well-liked. But his strength is in the day to day operations. He can size up a campsite and tell you where everything needs to go quicker than I can unpack a cook pot. But when it comes to complex issues like relationships between people, he has trouble. Whenever Pastor McAllan is in camp, we do fine; but now that he's gone, we miss his leadership."

"Just now, you brought a taste of that leadership back to the group, and I'm sure you felt the relief from everyone when you spoke up. We need more of that, Friend. We need you."

"What are you saying, Lizzie?" I asked, dumbfounded. "Do you have any idea what I've been through since I left Rendezvous? I've been fighting back feelings against God that a traveler shouldn't feel. Do you know that when I came back down from the mountain, I went into a *swamp* to avoid seeing you folks again? A leader needs to be someone who's strong in his faith. He needs to be sure of himself. He needs ..."

"He needs to be honest, and straightforward," Lizzie interrupted. "He needs to have the courage to open his heart before God, and then to act upon what he's shown. He needs to be someone like you." She smiled, and looked over at Onessy. "He needs to have the ability to love unconditionally, and to make friends with the friendless."

Onessy looked up, wagged his tail, and went back to his bone.

Be shepherds of God's flock that is under your care, serving as overseers—not because you must, but because you are willing, as God wants you to be; not greedy for money, but eager to serve; not lording it over those entrusted to you, but being examples to the flock.

I Peter 5: 2 – 3

....

Prayer: Today I lift up the leaders to You, Oh Father. Bless those who take responsibility for Your church. Protect them and keep them in Your perfect will. Use them for the ongoing of Your kingdom and guide them in the way they should go.

Ask yourself: What can you do for a church leader today?

December 11

Learning the Job

By morning, the fog had lifted around the camp, revealing a beautiful clearing surrounded by tall pine trees and a stream nearby. But my mind was still clouded with confusion as I thought about everything I had heard the night before. Lizzie had asked me to pray about leading the Rendezvous team, a job I hardly felt qualified for.

Steve had still not returned, after deciding to go back down the trail to talk with the men who had forced the camp to move. Tents were still being set into place this morning, and people were shifting supplies from one to the other. Lizzie and the ladies who helped her had served up breakfast for everyone, and I helped them wash up.

"Lizzie," I said as we dried utensils and put them back into their proper containers, "I never asked you about the actual running of Rendezvous, because frankly it never occurred to me. I guess I thought this place just sort of happened. Seeing you folks working so hard now makes me a little ashamed of myself that I didn't appreciate you more."

Lizzie laughed and said, "That's the best compliment you could give us, Friend. If we're doing our job well, then travelers like you don't have to concern yourselves with all the details; you can just enjoy the place, learn a few things, and leave here with God's blessing. There's a lot that goes on behind the scenes around here, but a person has to be called to it, just like you were called to take this trip in the first place."

"So I guess that answers my first question," I said. "I'm on this journey because God called me to it, and I've learned the hard way what happens when I get off the trail and lose sight of the goal. If coming onto the Rendezvous team meant forsaking that call, then I'd have to be pretty sure about it."

"You're right about that," Lizzie smiled. "That's why we only ask people whom we already feel God is calling to the job. Everyone on the staff here has prayed about it, and we all feel that calling for you. The last thing to consider is what you, yourself feel about it. The way we understand it, God's call comes to an individual and is confirmed by the body of believers. If anyone along the way has doubts, then we all need to back up and look again."

Brothers, choose seven men from among you who are known to be full of the Spirit and wisdom. We will turn this responsibility over to them and will give our attention to prayer and the ministry of the word.

Acts 6: 3 – 4

....

Prayer: Today Father, I lift up those who choose our leaders. As a part of Your Body, guide them in all wisdom and understanding, so that they will call upon Your people to lead Your Church. May they be of one mind and one Spirit, so that all they do will bring glory to Your Name.

Ask yourself: How should a church elect its leaders?

Time and Space

"There's one thing I really don't understand, Lizzie," I said as we walked around the camp. "Each time I leave Rendezvous, I leave you and the others behind packing things up, getting ready to move. And yet, you always seem to be in front of me on the trail, setting up as I arrive. Do you guys know a shortcut?"

Lizzie laughed and said, "Oh my! That would be a secret worth sharing, wouldn't it?" She thought a minute, then said, "Let's look at your visits to Rendezvous this year, shall we? The first time was with Old Charlie. You left ahead of us, then lost the trail back at the canyon. By the time you were back where you needed to be, we had already arrived and set up.

"The next time you left, Ralph caught up with you, and you and he left the trail again to go rescue those dear people who had been deceived in settling down. Once again, we passed directly to the next Rendezvous site, and were ready for you when you got there.

"The last time you left us was with your son." She hesitated, stopping to look at me. "That journey to the mountaintop once again took you away from the direct route we followed to the next stop. I believe last night you said something about 'going to a swamp' rather than come join us, am I right?"

"Oh Lizzie, you're right," I said. "Every time I've left you, I've left the trail for awhile, either because of my own mistakes or else because God sent me. Meanwhile, Rendezvous has moved forward, steadily and without swerving, always where it needs to be."

"That's the goal," she said, taking my hand in hers. "We want to be here for the travelers who so desperately need this place for refreshment, encouragement and support. It's not always easy to make that happen. That's why we need strong leaders like you."

The elders who direct the affairs of the church well are worthy of double honor, especially those whose work is preaching and teaching.
                                                                    I Timothy 5: 17

Prayer: Thank you, Father, for giving to some the awesome responsibility of leading Your church. May I honor them in all that I do, and never fail to pray for them in all matters, encouraging and supporting them. Use their ministries for Your glory, I pray.

Ask yourself: Do you think it is right to pay a church worker for his or her service, or should it be volunteer only?

December 13

Meeting the Staff

After the morning meals, a meeting was called of all Rendezvous staff. As everyone gathered in the big tent, I was impressed again with all the responsibilities required to make this place a success, and with all the people willing to be a part of it. Frank was there as head instructor for defense, having left Hank with his class. Dr Artinian represented the medical staff and Jennifer the nurses. Lizzie came in, surrounded by her team of cooks. Dozens more filed in, and from their dress I assumed they were wood gatherers, equipment movers and set up specialists. The only staff person missing was Steve, the site manager, which troubled us all. Lizzie made her way to the front of the group and called the meeting to order.

"I guess because I'm the oldest in the group, you expect me to take charge." She smiled as several 'amens!' and 'go grandmas!' came back in reply. "Actually, the only reason I'm doing this is because Steve is still not back. We need to keep praying for God to watch over him." She paused as we all thought about that, then went on. "In the meantime, I want us to consider something that's been in our thoughts for some time now, and that is, extending the invitation to our brother here to join our Rendezvous team as overall coordinator and spiritual leader. Steve shared with us all that this was only to be temporary, until a suitable person could be found. We've all come to know and love our Friend here this year; and we've struggled with him as he's had to face some of the most heartbreaking and difficult challenges a person could experience. He'll be the first to tell you that he feels unworthy for the job, which as we all know is the first criteria before we even ask someone!" Everyone laughed softly at that.

"So there you have it," she said. "Friend, we believe God is calling you to come and lead us. If you agree with us, then how about it: will you come?"

I was quiet a long time, wondering what to say. Finally I stood up and looked over the crowd. "I spent most of the morning since I woke up trying to think of ways to tell you I couldn't accept this offer." A few faces looked up in surprise. "But after seeing you now, and hearing Lizzie, and most of all, after hearing my own heart, all I can say is, God must really love a challenge, to call someone like me to something like this!"

Who serves as a soldier at his own expense? Who plants a vineyard and does not eat of its grapes? Who tends a flock and does not drink of the milk? Do I say this merely from a human point of view? Doesn't the Law say the same thing? For it is written in the Law of Moses: "Do not muzzle an ox while it is treading out the grain."
I Corinthians 9: 7 – 9

Prayer: In the joy of the Spirit, I praise You my God for Your Church and all those who serve in it. I also remember that serving also involves daily decisions and logistical support. Teach us how to remain in the Spirit while dealing with the needs of the day. Bless those who lead, physically as well as spiritually.

Ask yourself: When should a person volunteer his services to the church and when should he expect to be reimbursed?

December 14

Taking Charge

I decided to spend my first day as Rendezvous leader in visiting all the team members while they were at work, to better understand their individual tasks. Onessy was delighted to see me getting out of bed before daylight, and was at my heels when I stepped out of the tent. The wood gatherers were already at work, blowing on the hot coals of the cook fire and getting it ready for breakfast. Next, they divided into teams of three and went in different directions around the camp in search of wood to replenish what had been used the day before. I stayed at the fire to join the cooks. Lizzie might have appeared old and frail, but this was her element, making sure that every separate part of the meal was ready at the appropriate time. With breakfast cleared away, she started a huge pot of stew cooking, which gave me a chance to excuse myself and go to the medical tent. Doctors and nurses were hustling from one side to the other, taking care of patients, cleaning equipment and scheduling procedures for the day. Dr Artinian saw me come in and insisted on taking a look at my old injuries, whistling in amazement at how well they had healed and sending me out with a clean bill of health. Next stop was Ralph's defense training class. He was showing them the basics of using whatever is at hand, be it sword, stone or length of rope. "And of course," he said in a voice loud enough for me to hear, "we mustn't forget the classic 'fishing rod' maneuver." When some of the class members asked what he meant by that, he said, "Ask Lizzie during story time tonight, and she'll tell you all about it."

After a visit with the supply staff, the tent set up crew and the laundry and wash up team, I was finally ready to come back to the fire and enjoy a cup of Lizzie's coffee. "It all looks great," I said to her as I sat down. "The only class I didn't see was 'Foundations'; are they meeting?"

"Not at the moment," Lizzie said. "Ralph had to take over full time for the defense class, which left us with no teacher for the beginners. One of the wood gatherers has really impressed me, though: a young woman named Sybil. I'll point her out to you tonight if you'd like to talk with her about it."

"Thanks for that, Lizzie. I'd appreciate any suggestions you can give me."

Our talk was interrupted when someone shouted, "Travelers coming in!" I looked back down the path and saw a group of what looked like nine adults and three children. I recognized Fisher, carrying one of the children. They all looked tired and frightened.

It was he who gave some to be apostles, some to be prophets, some to be evangelists, and some to be pastors and teachers, to prepare God's people for works of service, so that the body of Christ may be built up until we all reach unity in the faith and in the knowledge of the Son of God and become mature, attaining to the whole measure of the fullness of Christ.

Ephesians 4: 11 – 13

Prayer: I am reminded today, Lord, that many jobs are required for the proper operating of Your church. May I remember them all, and pray for them all, as your faithful servants.

Ask yourself: What is a job in the church that often goes unnoticed?

Fisher's Tale

When the group came into the camp, I could see that they had had trouble. Their clothing was torn in places, and a few cuts and scratches were visible. The children were either asleep or walking in stunned exhaustion. Aaron was supporting his wife as she limped along beside him. Another man whom I didn't recognize had an arm around one of the girl's shoulders, helping her walk.

"Fisher!" I called out. "Here, let me take the child. Come around by the fire. Listen everybody," I called out to the new arrivals, "right over there is a medical tent. Some of you look like you could use some attention. Go right inside and see a nurse by the name of Jennifer. When you've been treated, then come back out here and we'll organize some food for you."

Fisher stayed behind with me, even though he seemed as much in need of a doctor as the rest. I had him sit down and gave him a cup of coffee to warm up. One of Lizzie's helpers took the child I was holding and went to the medical tent with him. After a few drinks of coffee, Fisher was able to take a breath and speak. "After you left," he began, "we moved slowly but steadily. We stopped early to camp, and were just getting settled in when a group of men came up to us. They said we were trespassing and would have to go with them. Aaron tried to explain that we were just passing through and would stay on the trail, but one of the men hit him from behind with a club. He went down, hard. Reese and I started to fight back, but there were too many of them. We had to do what they said.

"They led us off the trail up the mountainside. I remembered what you said, Friend, about leaving the trail. I really didn't want to go with them, but..."

"You did the right thing," I assured him. "If you had tried to fight, then the women and children would have been in danger. What happened after that?"

We walked for a long time, then finally came to a settlement of some kind. They had built a fort-looking thing out of logs, and there were men armed with clubs and a few swords standing all around. I looked at their faces and saw nothing but pure *hatred.* All hope we had of finding any understanding from those people disappeared when we came into the fort. There was a big open area right inside the gates, and in the middle was a gallows. A body was hanging there... a man.

Lizzie gasped from behind me, and I heard her whisper, "Steve!"

But Stephen, full of the Holy Spirit, looked up to heaven and saw the glory of God, and Jesus standing at the right hand of God. "Look," he said, "I see heaven open and the Son of Man standing at the right hand of God."

Acts 7: 55 – 56

....

Prayer: It grieves my heart, Oh Father, when I remember that even today, men, women and children are giving their lives for the sake of Your Church. I know You are grieved as well, and I pray for comfort, and where possible, for protection.

Ask yourself: Do you think there are more or less martyrs today than there were in the past? (Consult the Christian Almanac)

Imprisonment

As Fisher spoke, the rest of his group began filing back to the fire, one by one. There were no major injuries, they said, just cuts and bruises, made worse by hunger and exhaustion. Lizzie dished up stew as each arrived, and Fisher continued to tell the story.

"The man who had hit Aaron pointed with his club to the body on the gallows and told us, 'That's what we do with your kind'. I asked him to tell what he meant by 'our kind', but he wouldn't say. He just went on and on about how they had claimed this land for their own; that they had the strength to keep it, and that their king was the only one worth following. Reese couldn't keep quiet with that, and said that we were followers of the One True King. He didn't get far after that, because several men jumped on him and started beating him up. The girls were screaming for them to stop, the kids were crying, and Aaron and I were pinned to the ground by some other guys. Finally they stopped and pushed us into a building toward the back of the fort. When they closed the door and locked it, we realized it was a jail. The only window looked out toward the gallows, so we took a shirt and hung it up to hide the view.

"We didn't know what else to do except pray, so that's what we did. We stood in a circle facing each other and prayed until after dark. Then Sandy started singing a hymn. The rest of us joined in, and we sang for an hour or more. We heard a guard outside yelling for us to stop, and when we didn't, the door opened up and this guy steps inside and closes it behind him. In a loud voice, he hollers, 'What did I tell you about singing?' Then in a soft voice, he added, 'I want to help you. Listen to me.'

He said that his name was Rodriguez, that he had been sickened when the man outside had been hung, and that he wanted to leave. He told us to be ready to escape later on, then left with another angry shout of 'Now keep quiet, or you'll get more of the same!'

"We stopped singing, but our prayers intensified."

Some faced jeers and flogging, while still others were chained and put in prison. They were stoned; they were sawed in two; they were put to death by the sword. They went about in sheepskins and goatskins, destitute, persecuted and mistreated—

Hebrews 11: 36 – 37

Prayer: Father, if I must face persecution, then grant me the faith to stand. May I endure what I must, for the sake of Your Name, and use every opportunity to bear witness to Your love and power.

Ask yourself: Why do you think the church grows stronger in areas where it is most persecuted?

Escape

Fisher continued his story: "After the guard named Rodriguez left us, we kept on praying until sometime in the middle of the night. Then the door opened again and he stepped inside. 'Everyone is asleep,' he whispered to us. 'It's my turn to stand guard, and I'm going to lead you out of here. Be very quiet and follow me.' The kids were asleep by then, so the ladies picked them up and carried them. Our backpacks had been taken, so there was nothing else to carry.

"When we got outside the jail cell, it was almost as dark as it had been inside, with just a little light from a fire over near the gallows. Rodriguez led us behind the building to a place in the wall. 'I've been working on this for weeks, waiting for a time to use it,' he said, and taking a grip on one of the logs, lifted it up and pulled it in, making just enough of a gap to squeeze out of. Aaron went out first, then whispered back for the rest of us to come. First, the ladies, then Reese went through, but just as I was about to slip out, somebody from up on top of the wall shouted that we were getting away.

"One man ran up to us swinging a club. Rodriguez blocked it and made a swing with his own. Then two more men were on us. I picked up the club the first man had dropped and used it like you taught me, Friend." He smiled and looked over at me. "We pretty much took care of those three guys, but there were more coming, and we could hear shouts from all over the fortress. Rodriguez and I slipped out and ran with the others as fast as we could go, back into the woods.

"I thought we should be heading back downhill, toward the trail, but instead we started up a narrow canyon. 'This doesn't look good,' I told him, but he said to trust him. Soon we came to what looked like the end of the canyon, but just as I was about to say, 'I told you so,' Rodriguez pushed some bushes away to reveal the entrance to a cave. We all went inside while he pulled the bushes back in place. Moving farther in, we felt the narrow passage opening up wider. I heard the sound of a match being struck and turned back to see Rodriguez lighting a candle. He led us on until it opened up into an area big enough for all of us to stand upright and move around. A spring flowed out of the back wall, and over to the right, I saw stacks of boxes."

Fisher took a deep breath, another sip of coffee, then turning to the stranger who had arrived with the group, he said, "Rodriguez, how would you like to take it from there?"

The jailer called for lights, rushed in and fell trembling before Paul and Silas. He then brought them out and asked, "Sirs, what must I do to be saved?"

Acts 16: 29 – 30

....

Prayer: Lord I lift up today those who persecute Your Church. Open their eyes, I pray, that they may see the error of their ways and the beauty of Your light. Help us, the persecuted to be a constant example of Christ's love, so that by our lives they may find the way to salvation.

Ask yourself: Can you pray for the enemy who wants to destroy you?

Rodriguez

The stranger had finished while Fisher spoke, and handing the empty bowl over to Lizzie with a word of thanks, he remained standing by the fire and spoke to the group. His English was heavily accented, but easy to understand. He said, "My name is Rodriguez Ortega. I began this journey six months ago, after my wife left me. She said that I had become cruel and unloving, and now that I look back on those days, I can see that she was right. I was angry at everything and everybody. No matter what happened in my life, I blamed it on someone else. Even when my wife left, I convinced myself that it was she who had the problem. I broke a few things around the house, then walked away.

"I lived on my own for a few weeks, taking part time work when I could get it, but usually ending when I would lose my temper and hurt someone. Then one day I met some men who seemed to be as angry at the world as I was. We hung out together, not doing much except complain about things, and if we got the chance, stealing something.

"Then we heard about some guys who had gotten together and were living up in the mountains. Stories said that they ruled the place like a small country, doing whatever they wanted. This sounded good to me, so I came up into the mountains to find them. They found me first, and after a few fights they took me in. We lived like a gang, robbing anyone who passed by. It was perfect for me: I could be as angry as I wanted to be.

"After awhile, though, I started getting tired of being angry. I remembered my wife, and how she had loved me when we first met. I wanted to go back to the way it was, but by now I knew I couldn't leave this gang of men. They would kill me if I tried. So for weeks, I planned my escape. I knew the men patrolled the trail, and would soon catch up with me if I just ran away. So I looked until I found a hiding place nearby: a cave with a hidden entrance. I smuggled food and candles into it, and made a place in the wall of the fortress where I could crawl out. My plan was to sneak away at night, stay in the cave until they stopped looking for me, then move on.

"I was planning to leave next week, but then the man you call Steve was brought in. They had tied him up, and were trying to keep him quiet, but he kept shouting about how God loved them, and how they were welcome to come and join him in a fantastic journey. But the more he talked the angrier the men became. They picked him up and carried him to the gallows. But even as they put the rope around his neck, he was saying over and over, 'You don't have to do this. God loves you. God loves you.' His last words were quieter, but I heard them clearly. He said, 'Lord, please forgive them.'"

By faith he left Egypt, not fearing the king's anger; he persevered because he saw him who is invisible.

Hebrews 11: 27

....

Prayer: Lord, help me to keep my eyes on You when I stand before those who hate me. May my words and actions point only to Your throne, and may my life or my death be useful to Your kingdom's work.

Ask yourself: Do you think Jesus' prayer for forgiveness of his executioners was answered?

December 19

A New Life

Rodriguez held back tears as he spoke. Someone offered him a place to sit, but he remained standing by the fire. After a few deep breaths, he continued. "When I watched that innocent man die, I knew that I didn't belong there: not anymore. I still held anger in my heart, but this was different. If that man had been just another victim we found on the trail, I might have accepted it, but his words kept coming back to me. 'God loves you; please forgive them.' Now, more than ever, I wanted to know about that kind of love, that kind of forgiveness.

"I had never prayed in my life. I had never used the name of God, except as a swear word. But I knew that I had to speak to Him. I slipped away from the men and went back to my hidden cave. I sat in the darkness for a long time, not knowing what to say, or how to say it. Finally, I just whispered, 'God? Are you there?'

"Something happened; I can't explain it. There was no big light, no sound that I could hear, but *something* moved in my heart. For the first time in my life, I felt like I wasn't alone. And it was a good feeling. The anger which had been so much a part of my life just melted away in a moment. I cried tears of joy. I laughed out loud. I tried saying the words again and again: 'God, are you there? God, are you there?' I knew I should be saying something else, but I didn't know what to say.

"It was coming to evening, so I had to return to the fortress before they closed the gate, or else they would come looking for me. I went back determined to find out more about this God, and to move up my plan to escape. But when I got back, more people had been brought inside." He looked over at Fisher and the others. "Those people.

"I knew what I had to do. I couldn't stand by and watch them die. It was late, so they were thrown into the jail we had built. I volunteered for the late night guard duty, and tried to let them know that I would help them. The others thought I was coming in to beat them. When I came inside, they were standing in a circle, holding hands." Rodriguez turned to Fisher. "You were singing a song I had never heard before, but the words I can never forget: 'God be with you till we meet again'.

"I knew at that moment, that whatever happened, I wanted to be a part of that circle."

Then he looked at those seated in a circle around him and said, "Here are my mother and my brothers! Whoever does God's will is my brother and sister and mother."

Mark 3: 34

Prayer: In the midst of trouble, Father, You give us family to comfort and be comforted by.

Ask yourself: Have you ever had to leave a group you knew was a bad influence on you?

December 20

The New Traveler

Reese was the last to leave the medical tent. His head was wrapped in a bandage; and he was being led by his wife, Amy. They joined us around the fire and Rodriguez continued his story.

"Reese was the worst hurt, having been beaten. After we entered the hidden cave, we made him comfortable as best we could, then I told them that we must stay there at least two days, until the men stop looking for us. The one you call Fisher surprised me when he said, 'Good; that's about how much time I need to tell you a wonderful story!'

"Fisher, and all of you," he said, looking around at Reese and Amy, Aaron and Patty and the three girls, "all of you helped make it the most wonderful two days of my life. I heard things I had only dreamed about. I learned about the God who does love me, and takes care of me. I learned that my anger was just a sign that God's love was not in my heart. If you had told me these things anywhere else, at any other time, I would not have believed you. But there was something about that cave, closed off from the rest of the world, that forced me to listen. When I did, God spoke, and I heard for the first time.

"Fisher prayed with me, and his words sounded just like the words Steve had spoken before he died. He told me that God loved me, and had forgiven me, and that my anger no longer had any place in my life. I prayed, too, and I asked God to take control.

"God did take control, and in ways I could not have imagined. Once, we heard searchers coming close to the entrance to the cave. They were close enough to hear their voices, and I was afraid. But I heard Sandy whisper a prayer. She said, 'God, blind their eyes so that they won't find us.'

"The men stayed close by for a long time, talking, then moved away. After awhile, I crept out to see if they were gone and was horrified to see that the bushes I had used to hide the entrance had all been blown away, leaving our path inside in plain view. They had to have seen it... unless they were blind.

"Their eyes were blinded; my eyes were opened. And it was all by the same God."

Jesus said, "For judgment I have come into this world, so that the blind will see and those who see will become blind."

John 9: 39

....

Prayer: Just as mysterious as is the opening of my eyes to see Your truth, Dear Father, is the way You prevent others from seeing. Thank you for Your wonderful care; in Your time, I prayed, may those who do not now see the things of Your Spirit be blessed with the vision to see, and believe.

Ask yourself: Can you think of a time when someone failed to see something which would have resulted in a threat to yourself or to God's people?

December 21

New Beginnings

After hearing all that happened, we prayed around the fire, thanking God for calling Rodriguez into our family, and for using him to rescue our friends. We mourned for Steve, praising God for his courage and faithfulness, while praying for strength and comfort to go on without him. After that, we found sleeping accommodations for everyone and got them settled for the night.

The next morning, Fisher and his grouped all joined me for breakfast. They looked a little haggard, but the night's rest had been good for them. As they ate, I got them organized for the day.

"First of all, let me welcome you officially to Rendezvous," I said. "This place is for you, and we'll do everything we can to help make your journey this year the best God wants it to be." Looking directly at Reese, I said, "Some of you will want to go back to the medical tent for a quick check up by Dr. Artinian. He's a good man, and he'll want to make sure you're recovering properly.

"For the kids, we have some great play groups forming up near that tree over there. If you moms will take them and introduce them, I'm sure they'll have a great day. Next, I want you to visit the supply tent over there," I said, pointing behind me. "You'll find clothes, packs, and enough gear to help you replace what was lost. Take everything you need; there's no charge. Finally, when you're all settled and re-outfitted, come back here and let me introduce you to the course everyone here goes through. It's called "Foundations," and it will give you all the basics you need for the rest of your journey."

Lizzie looked up from the fire and asked, "Who's teaching that, Friend?"

"I spoke to Sybil last night, and she's willing to take it on if someone will help her. Fisher here has had the course one-on-one with me. I'm sure he'll be ready and willing to jump right in, am I right, Fisher?"

He looked surprised at first, then broke into a big grin and said, "Sure; love to!"

As the group dispersed in different directions, Sandy stayed back to admire Lizzie's cooking. I saw a match made in heaven. "Lizzie," I said, "One of Old Charlie's last requests was that you take on an apprentice to help you with the cooking: someone to whom you could entrust your secret recipes. Let me introduce you to Sandy, a girl who can turn whatever you give her into a feast fit for a king. All she needs is a little wisdom from someone like you.

"Sandy," I said with a smile. "This dear lady can cook like anything; but what's even more important comes between courses. Pay close attention to her."

Are all apostles? Are all prophets? Are all teachers? Do all work miracles? Do all have gifts of healing? Do all speak in tongues? Do all interpret? But eagerly desire the greater gifts.

I Corinthians 12: 29 – 30

Prayer: Thank you for such a diversity of gifts in Your Church, Father. May I learn to better appreciate them all, even as I learn and apply what I myself have been given to do.

Ask yourself: What would you say are your spiritual gifts?

December 22

Vengeance is Mine

Onessy had found his place at Rendezvous with the children. Staying with me as I went to check on Play Group, I could see him looking at all the activity going on, and it wasn't difficult to read his mind. "What about it, fella?" I asked, giving his ears a scratch. "Can you behave yourself with those boys and girls?" He seemed to know what I was suggesting, and started bouncing in one place, whining with delight. "Go on," I said, pointing to the field. That was all he needed. He was off in a blur of motion, running to the first group of boys and jumping from one to the other. They screamed with delight and started throwing a ball for him to chase after. The girls soon joined in and it was all about Onessy from then on.

Ralph stepped up to join me as I watched. "How's the defense class going?" I asked. "Hank seems to be doing well as assistant."

"Maybe too well," he said, and when I asked him why, he went on. "Hank and the others are still upset about Steve. They're thinking we need to get up a group and go back there. From what I hear, we'd have a pretty good chance against those guys. They're not very well armed, and they operate more out of anger than any special training."

"What do you think about the idea?" I asked.

"You're in charge of Rendezvous," he said. "That means you're also the last word on what the defense team does. If you give the word, we'll be ready."

"That's not what I asked, Ralph. I asked you what you think about the idea."

Ralph stood quietly for a few moments, then answered. "It's not the same as before, is it? When you and I went to that village alone, we were going there to convince some travelers to come back to the journey with us. These men who killed Steve are not travelers; they never were. As much as I'd love to go back there and teach them a thing or two, something keeps telling me that it's not for us to do."

"I have the same feeling," I said. "I really, *really* want to wreak vengeance on those guys. And part of me says that I have a responsibility to do that, for the sake of the next travelers who pass that way. But try as I may, I can't seem to find a peace for that decision. And as long as that peace doesn't come, then we stay away from them. Agreed?"

"Agreed," he said. "But I don't have to like it."

It is mine to avenge; I will repay. In due time their foot will slip; their day of disaster is near and their doom rushes upon them.

Deuteronomy 32: 35

Prayer: You know my heart, Oh Lord; and You know that I always seek justice, or should I say, vengeance. Forgive me for desiring what belongs to You. Help me to keep my emotions in check, and to act only at the leading of Your Holy Spirit, and not upon my own will.

Ask yourself: When was the last time you were tempted to "take the law into your own hands"?

December 23

Rodriguez Returns

The Foundations class was going well. Sybil was a natural when it came to teaching, and everyone loved her. I could see that Fisher was settling in to his role as assistant, drawing on the things he had already experienced in order to teach the importance of the basic concepts of the journey.

"Now I know that you all learned to tie your shoes in kindergarten," he was saying to the group. "You can do it good enough to get you through a normal day, with maybe one or two stops to re-tie. But let me tell you, when you're running for your life through underbrush in the dark, the last thing you need is a loose bootlace." That brought a few chuckles, then he went on. "But we're not just talking about footwear, are we? This class is called "Foundations" for a purpose. I started out on the trip for all the wrong reasons. I was here, and I was moving forward, but I had no idea about why, and for Who. The first time things got a little rough, I was going the wrong way; and if it hadn't been for a good Friend," he looked in my direction, "it could have been fatal. Let's tie those laces once more, and as we do it, let's talk about the things that are fundamentally important, okay?"

Rodriguez was the first to talk, as he adjusted his laces. "I was the biggest fool of them all," he said. "I let little things rule my life, making me angry, making me hurt people for no good reason. I lost my friends, I lost my wife, I lost my reason for living, and if it hadn't been for you people, I would have lost everything." He stood up, gave his laces an approving nod, and said, "And that's why I have to go back."

Everyone looked up, startled, but before anyone could speak, he said, "I've done some real bad things back there. I know God has forgiven me, and that's wonderful. But I have to try and make things right. I'm going to go back, and talk to those guys. I know a few of them feel just like I did; they're just afraid to speak up. Maybe if I tell them what God has done for me, they'll listen.

"What they'll do is *kill* you, Rod," said Fisher. "You won't have a chance to say a word before they have you up on that gallows. You'll die, and it'll all be for nothing."

"Maybe I will die," he said. "I don't know. But if my death can make one of those guys back there think about his own life, then maybe things will turn around. Anyway, I'm going. Thank you for praying for me." He paused, then said, "God bless you," and walked back to the fire where his gear was already laid out.

When we heard this, we and the people there pleaded with Paul not to go up to Jerusalem. Then Paul answered, "Why are you weeping and breaking my heart? I am ready not only to be bound, but also to die in Jerusalem for the name of the Lord Jesus." When he would not be dissuaded, we gave up and said, "The Lord's will be done."

Acts 21: 12 – 14

....

Prayer: We know well, Father, that obedience to You may result in suffering and death. And yet You give us courage and allow us the blessed opportunity of following You, even to death. May our sacrifice be acceptable to You.

Ask yourself: What people, ideals or things would you be willing to die for?

A Blessed Eve

There was a different aroma around the camp today: something besides wood smoke and Lizzie's stew. It stirred a forgotten hunger in me, and I followed it until I found Lizzie and Sandy, up to their elbows in flour. They had set up a huge table, and were laughing together as they mixed up mountains of dough. "What's going on here?" I asked. "It looks like you're getting ready to feed an army."

"Not an army," Lizzie said. "Just a small band of warriors. We've got crews out gathering berries for pies. Sandy's friends Aaron and Reese came in this morning with two wild pigs they had caught." She pointed to a smoldering heap of coals nearby. "They're roasting nicely underground. Then we have another group of volunteers scouring the supply tent to see what they can find in the way of canned goods."

"But why all the fuss?" I asked. "You don't need to work so hard, after all."

"It's a joy, believe me," she said, wiping a bit of flour off her nose. "Especially with this wonderful girl you sent me." Sandy grinned and kept working the dough. "And besides, Friend, I think you may have forgotten what today is. Am I right?"

I thought about it. "To tell you the truth, I haven't thought much about what day it is this whole trip. I know it must be December, so..." I thought a bit longer, then it came to me. "Christmas?"

"Christmas Eve, to be more exact," said Lizzie. "A time for celebration. Sandy and I will take care of the food. We're counting on you to make the place look like the season. How about it?"

I looked around and saw Clarence, one of the woodcutters. "Hey Clancy!" I called out. "I need a Christmas tree. A *big* one!" He looked surprised for an instant, then called out to a couple of other guys to lend a hand. Running down to the Foundations class, I said to Sybil, "Classes canceled for the rest of the day. I need you guys to decorate! Hank, go down to Play Group and see if the kids will make something that will hang on a tree." Last stop was the main tent, where the set up people were busy doing regular maintenance on the guy ropes. "Big meeting here tonight," I called out. "Make sure everything's ready!"

So Joseph also went up from the town of Nazareth in Galilee to Judea, to Bethlehem the town of David, because he belonged to the house and line of David. He went there to register with Mary, who was pledged to be married to him and was expecting a child. While they were there, the time came for the baby to be born, and she gave birth to her firstborn, a son. She wrapped him in cloths and placed him in a manger, because there was no room for them in the inn.
Luke 2: 4 – 7

Prayer: On this night we remember the birth of Your Son, Jesus Christ. We celebrate with You, Oh Father, that most precious of nights, when You came to earth to save us.

Ask yourself: Why do you think Jesus came first as a baby; why not as a grown man?

December 25

A Child is Born

The evening was unforgettable. Clancy set up a beautiful blue spruce down at the front of the meeting tent, and the Foundations class took responsibility for seeing that it was decorated. The children had strung brightly colored berries and flowers, and someone cut aluminum foil into thin strips, then hung them on the tree like icicles.

The sounds of Christmas music were filling the air long before dinner, so that by the time we were all gathered, there was no doubt as to what day it was. Lizzie and Sandy organized the kitchen team into a thing of beauty, serving up baked ham with all the trimmings, and topped off with a table full of pies.

We sang Christmas carols until late, then divided up into small groups to pray. We thanked God for the wonderful gift of His Son, Jesus Christ, and for the mystery of Christmas. We prayed for each other, and for friends and loved ones who were not with us. I prayed especially for my wife and daughter, and missed them so badly it was like a physical pain in the pit of my stomach. How I wished they were here with me!

This morning, Christmas Day, we gathered again in the meeting tent to sing carols and celebrate the season. I was asked to say a few words as Rendezvous leader, so as I stood up, a silence fell over the crowd.

"Those of you who know me well can attest to the fact that I'm not very good at speaking," I said. "On a day like today, we'd all rather have Pastor McAllan here to bring us a Christmas message, but I know that he's where God wants him this morning. Let's remember to pray for him, wherever he is, and whatever he's doing.

"Christmas is a time for gifts, and from the joyful sounds of the children that woke me up this morning, I can see that you parents have not forgotten your duty. I want to thank you too for the wonderful notes of encouragement I found when I got up this morning. There's no gift any greater than the loving support of a family like this. And why do we do it? Because that's what God did for us on that Christmas day so long ago. He bent down to give us the most precious gift He could give: His only Son. And so to remember that, we gather in places like this, we sing praises, we pray, and we exchange gifts with a "Merry Christmas!" from the heart. We don't have much out here on the trail, so our gifts can't be very lavish, but I hope they express what God expressed to us on the first Christmas: love, and joy, and good will for all.

"Merry Christmas everyone!" I looked at the back of the crowd and saw Rodriguez standing at the doorway, his arms filled with candy, toys, tools and clothing.

When they saw the star, they were overjoyed. On coming to the house, they saw the child with his mother Mary, and they bowed down and worshiped him. Then they opened their treasures and presented him with gifts of gold and of incense and of myrrh.
Matthew 2: 10 – 11

Prayer: Just as the magi brought gifts to the Baby Jesus, so we offer our gifts to You, Oh Father. May our offerings be acceptable, and may they bring joy to Your heart.

Ask yourself: Why do we give gifts to each other at Christmas?

December 26

Unexpected Gifts

At the sight of Rodriguez standing in the doorway of the meeting tent, everyone came to their feet to welcome him and shout for joy. A path in the crowd was opened, so that he could make his way to the front. Laying down all the things he had been carrying, he stepped up beside me and shook my hand. "Merry Christmas, Rod," I said. "We didn't know if we would see you again. What's happened the past two days?"

Rodriguez smiled at me, then turned to wave at everybody in the tent. Great cheers rose from the people, and it was several minutes before it was quiet enough for him to speak. "Hello everybody," he said at last. "It's good to be home."

This brought another session of cheers, until he finally put his hand up for quiet, then said, "As you know, I had to go back to those men. I wanted so badly to tell them what I had found, to give them a chance to join us. As I went back, I prayed for wisdom, and for courage. I have to tell you, though, I was scared. I knew they wouldn't be too happy about my helping you folks escape.

"But I remembered something Fisher told me while we were hiding in the cave those two days. He said there's a place in the Bible where it's written 'Greater is he who is in you than he who is in the world'." He looked out over the crowd until he spotted his friend. "Hey Fisher!" he called out. "You have to tell me where that verse is!

"Anyway," he continued, "As I got close to the fortress, I expected to be spotted at any moment, but there was no one. In fact, there was no one anywhere. The gates were standing open, and there were clubs and swords laying all over the ground, but not one person. I stayed there all night, expecting them to come back from a raid, but they're gone. I looked through the storeroom and found a few things the kids might like." He pointed to the pile on the ground in front of him. "These were things that were stolen from travelers. There's plenty more back there, if you guys would like to come back with me and get them."

I led the crowd in another prayer of thanksgiving for Rodriguez's safe return, and for the apparent end of the threat. We asked for God's mercy on those misguided souls, and for the safety of future pilgrims who pass along this way. All in all, it was a most blessed Christmas.

You, dear children, are from God and have overcome them, because the one who is in you is greater than the one who is in the world.

I John 4: 4

....

Prayer: Remind me today, Father, as I look about me and see the enemy on every side, that You live in me. There is no power greater than Yours, and I could be in no better place than here. Calm my fears; show me Your power.

Ask yourself: Why do you think the enemy of this world thinks he could ever overcome the power of God?

Return to the Fortress

After meeting with Ralph, I decided to leave part of our defense team back at Rendezvous, in case they were needed. The rest of us took the ten mile hike back to the fortress to see what Rodriguez had described. It was just as he had reported: Personal items were strewn all over the ground, evidence that their owners had dropped them where they stood. But where had they gone? There was no sign of a struggle, no bloodstains, no indication of anything but a quick and complete desertion of the fortress.

We considered the possibility that a band of demon warriors had dispatched the men, like had happened at the castle a few months ago, and like they had tried to do with us at Rendezvous once before. But that theory was put aside for two reasons: first, demons would have left a gruesome mess behind, and second, these men would have been considered allies, since they attacked and killed pilgrims. There was only one possibility that made sense, and that was the fact that God had dealt with this situation directly. In our anger and desire for revenge, we had all wanted to come back personally, but were led in no uncertain terms that this was not our battle. And yet, we knew that God had protected us in the past, even by supernatural means, and no doubt would have been able to handle this band of thieves just as easily.

Whatever the means, they were gone, and would no longer be a threat to passing travelers. We gathered around the gallows (which incidentally no longer held Steve's body) and offered a prayer of thanks to God for His mighty Hand.

The storerooms were indeed filled to overflowing with all kinds of food, utensils and supplies of every description. It was decided to carry back all we could, then burn the fortress so that it would never be used again.

As the smoke rose from the ruin, I knew the people back at Rendezvous would see it and know that a tyrant was finished. God was still the only True King, and His Kingdom would outlast anything man could ever hope to establish.

At dusk they got up and went to the camp of the Arameans. When they reached the edge of the camp, not a man was there, for the Lord had caused the Arameans to hear the sound of chariots and horses and a great army, so that they said to one another, "Look, the king of Israel has hired the Hittite and Egyptian kings to attack us!" So they got up and fled in the dusk and abandoned their tents and their horses and donkeys. They left the camp as it was and ran for their lives.

II Kings 7: 5 – 7

....

Prayer: What a marvelous truth, that the battle is and always has been Yours, Oh God. Occasionally, You allow us to witness it or even take part in it, but let us not forget that it is You who wins the victory.

Ask yourself: Finish reading the passage in II Kings (above) and consider the decision of the men to go back to the city and tell the news. How is this like evangelism?

December 28

A Bible for Rodriguez

Sorting through all the supplies we had carried back from the fortress proved to be a massive job. There was clothing of every shape and size, tools for every job, food enough to outfit our kitchen for weeks. We began by sorting things into general stacks, and then went back to sort those into more specific categories. Heather and Brenda, Sandy's friends, were happy to tackle the pile of clothes, placing them into bundles for men, women and children. Sandy and the kitchen crew went through the food. Aaron and Reese knew more about tools than anyone else, and I was left with the pile that didn't fit any of the categories.

There was money, which we placed into the Rendezvous benevolent fund. It would be used to help travelers who needed help. Watches and other jewelry were catalogued and set aside, in the hope that either their owners or family members might be identified some day. Besides all that, a small stack of books was left to sort through, and I started into it. Most of them were journals, and I decided to start a Rendezvous library with them. Looking through them and reading of the travels of fellow pilgrims was an encouragement, and I wanted as many people as possible to share in these life stories.

One rather large, black book caught my attention, but when I opened it up, I saw that it was written in a language I couldn't understand. I thought I knew what it was, but to be sure, I called Rodriguez over. "Hey Rod," I called, "can you read this?"

He looked at me for a moment, then at the book. I watched as he opened it up, then as a huge tear fell from one eye. He read, "Jehovah es mi pastor; nada me Faltará." He looked up at me and said, "The Lord is my shepherd, I shall not want. It's a *Bible*, Friend. And it's written in my own language."

"Then it must be yours. Guard it well, and read it often."

Rodriguez nodded silently, clutching the precious book closely. He turned and went outside, where I saw him sit down under a tree and begin to read.

Now there were staying in Jerusalem God-fearing Jews from every nation under heaven. When they heard this sound, a crowd came together in bewilderment, because each one heard them speaking in his own language. Utterly amazed, they asked: "Are not all these men who are speaking Galileans? Then how is it that each of us hears them in his own native language?

Acts 2: 5 – 8

Prayer: What a glorious thought, that my simple and faltering prayers are transformed into my heart's cries before Your throne! Hear my prayers, Oh God, and not just my words.

Ask yourself: Where did languages come from? Do you think God understands them all?

December 29

Separations

Fisher came to see me this morning. He thanked me for appointing him as assistant Foundations teacher. "That's such a great class," he said. "Sybil is a fantastic teacher, and she's letting me try new methods as we go. Some of them work, some are best forgotten, but we're all getting smarter in the process, so it can't be all bad!

"Thanks too for introducing Sandy to Lizzie. Working with that sweet lady is the best thing that could have happened to Sandy. She's doing what she loves to do, and more than that, she's learning so much wisdom from Lizzie."

"I'll tell you a secret," I said to Fisher. "Lizzie is getting at least as much a blessing from their friendship as Sandy is. She knows she's not getting any younger, and has prayed for someone who could work with her and learn the craft, but until now the right person has never come around. Sandy's a real answer to prayer."

"There's one other thing I wanted to ask you about," said Fisher. As you know, our group started with Lizzie and her friends, meeting with Aaron and Reese and their wives. It's been fantastic, and the things we've learned together have been unforgettable. But, and you probably know these things better than I do, married couples with children have their own special needs. In a lot of ways, they shouldn't have to be burdened with our own issues."

"I'm sure they don't mind it," I said. "I've never heard them complain about you."

"No, they never would. And that's why I want you to talk to them, and encourage them to leave us here when it's time to move on. I want to stay and get ready to teach the next Foundations class; and I know Sandy will never be convinced to leave Lizzie. That just leaves Heather and Brenda. Is there something they can do around here?"

"They seemed to fit right into the Play Group," I said. "I'll talk to them and see if they're interested." As Fisher went back to his class, it occurred to me that everyone was finding a particular place of service: each a perfect fit. Maybe that's what the different gifts are about: different talents for different jobs, but one ministry.

Every day they continued to meet together in the temple courts. They broke bread in their homes and ate together with glad and sincere hearts, praising God and enjoying the favor of all the people. And the Lord added to their number daily those who were being saved.

Acts 2: 46 – 47

....

Prayer: Lord, You have called us to fellowship. Thank You for making it possible through Your Church. Give each of us a job to do which matches our own gifts, and as we serve, may our love and respect for one another grow.

Ask yourself: Is it possible for someone to be a part of the church and have no responsibility whatsoever?

December 30

Nearing the Goal

There was an air of excitement all over the camp today. Tomorrow is the last day of the year, and that means the end of this year's journey. Individuals were sitting alone, catching up on journals, small groups were gathered in tightly packed circles, going over the events of the past year and comparing notes.

I decided to walk a ways out of camp to be alone and think. This would be the end of a one year commitment I had made to God. I had left my family in shock, struck out alone and determined that by this time tomorrow, I would either be fully committed to the journey or else I would go back to the way it was.

I knew now that I could never go back: not after these past twelve months. There had been too many valleys, too many mountains, too many encounters to believe that life could ever be the same as it was.

I had known from the beginning that making it to the goal at year's end was never guaranteed. I thought back to those I had known and loved whose "early pickup" had taken them from the trail and brought them face to face with God. Old Charlie, Jonathan... my chest tightened and a lump came to my throat... my own son. But in spite of fire, flood and enemies that I could never have imagined, here I stood, one day away from the end. For what purpose I could not say, God had protected my life and brought me from the very edge of despair to this time of fulfillment.

And what next? I thought. Am I prepared to make another commitment for another year? There are certainly enough people counting on me to do just that. Lizzie, Ralph, Hank, Fisher, Sandy and all the people at Rendezvous are assuming I'll be with them the day after tomorrow, to begin a whole new journey.

I love them like my own family. Whatever I decide to do, I hope they're not disappointed with me.

Jesus replied, "No one who puts his hand to the plow and looks back is fit for service in the kingdom of God."

Luke 9: 62

....

Prayer: May I never look back on what I used to be, except to give You praise for what You have made me today. Keep my eyes firmly fixed on what lies ahead, and lengthen my stride.

Ask yourself: Do you find more blessing in looking forward or in looking backward? What you do the most?

December 31

The End of the Journey

The day had been spent in packing. Tomorrow, the Rendezvous camp will be moving on to the next location, about three months away. Everything would have to packed carefully and orderly. Without Steve as site manager, it was left to me to coordinate the efforts. But of course, since I had never done it before, I was at a complete loss. Lizzie came to my aid, suggesting ways to organize the job which were, of course, the tried and tested ways we should have been following all along.

After dinner this evening, we gathered in the big tent for one more time of worship. Brenda and Heather brought the children up to the stage for a musical performance which left no dry eye in the house. Someone led off in a praise song which was quickly picked up by the entire congregation. That song led to another, which led to another. An hour turned to two, and no one wanted to see it close.

Finally, I stood at the front and waited until it was quiet again. I had no idea what I was going to say, but opened my mouth to speak, trusting God to give me a voice. "Brothers and sisters," I began. The impact of what I had just said struck me afresh, and I was left speechless for a moment. "What a privilege it is, to call you family," I said at last. "And in every sense of the word, that's what we are, isn't it? We've shared joy and grief, pain and pleasure, tremendous bounty and immeasurable loss. And in the process, we've become knit together as no womb could ever duplicate. We can honestly say to each other, 'I love you', and know that the words can never be degenerated by what the world might make them out to mean.

"Ours is a love which is like the peace that the Father gives us: that surpasses human understanding. It's a love that Jesus promises us: enabling us to run to our Creator and cry out, 'Abba!'"

"Daddy!" Every head in the place turned to the back of the room to see who had interrupted. I peered over the heads of those standing between me and the doorway, but all I could see was a rippling of bodies, as something raced past them in a direct line to the stage. When she broke out of the crowd, I saw that it was my own daughter. I fell to my knees as she ran into my arms with another cry of "Daddy! Daddy!"

I held her so tightly I thought she might break, my eyes so clouded with tears that I thought I might have gone blind. But when I felt a hand on my shoulder, I knew before looking up that it was my precious wife. She came to her knees to join me there; the three of us lost in the unspeakable joy of reunion.

I knew I should say something, but I knew that it would be impossible for some time. I looked around and saw Fisher standing nearby. A brief nod was all it took. He stood up to face the congregation and said, "Just as we cry, 'Abba! Father!' so the Father takes us into his loving arms, never to forsake us; never to leave us. We leave this place tonight with a sense of completion, but at the same time with a sense of anticipation. The year is finished, but the journey is not. As long as there is breath in our bodies, as long as a heart beats, we are called to move forward toward that day when every tear will be dried and every tongue will confess that Jesus is Lord and Savior. In His Name we pray. Amen."

Believe in the Lord Jesus, and you will be saved—you and your household

Acts 16: 31

Prayer: Father, I cannot express my joy at what You have done for me this past year. Through trial and victory; through mountains and valleys, You have been my ever present Help. By Your Hand, I have been brought safely to this New Year's Eve, and I look forward to what lies ahead tomorrow. Grant me courage to face whatever may come. Use me to further Your Kingdom, Oh Lord, and hasten the day when Your kingdom comes to earth. I love You, Lord; help me to love You better. Amen.

Ask yourself: If you had known one year ago what you would be feeling today, how would that have affected your journey? What will you decide tomorrow concerning the upcoming year?

Epilogue

There's a smell of waterproofed canvas in the air. The new year has begun, and each step is accompanied by the creak of new leather and the rhythmic rattle of essentials, finding their way to the lowest reaches of my backpack.

A quick glance over my shoulder confirms that I am not alone. My wife is close behind, a new pilgrim with a new commitment to the path ahead. Beside her, my daughter moves gracefully, a quick smile at each of us before settling into the pace next to the Labrador known as Onesimus. We don't know what lies ahead, but we do know Who waits. We will trust each day to Him.

Index to Scripture References

I Chronicles 16: 11 – 13	April 2
I Chronicles 4: 10	July 23
I Corinthians 1: 27 – 29	October 10
I Corinthians 11: 23 – 24	February 16
I Corinthians 12: 13	April 11
I Corinthians 12: 28 – 28	October 14
I Corinthians 12: 29 – 30	December 21
I Corinthians 15: 40	November 25
I Corinthians 3: 2	July 21
I Corinthians 3: 6	February 18
I Corinthians 4: 10	May 29
I Corinthians 9: 7 – 9	December 13
I Corinthians 9: 25	July 25
I Corinthians 9: 27	January 2
I John 1: 7 – 9	April 19
I John 2: 10	June 18
I John 2: 13 – 14	June 14
I John 4: 4	December 26
I Kings 19: 10	May 24
I Peter 1: 10 – 12	May 2
I Peter 2: 24	July 19
I Peter 3: 15	July 31
I Peter 4: 16 – 17	August 6
I Peter 5: 2 – 3	December 10
I Peter 5: 8 – 9	October 21
I Peter 5: 8 – 9	January 29
I Samuel 16: 7	May 6
I Thessalonians 5: 3	February 5
I Timothy 1: 15 – 16	October 8
I Timothy 4: 12	November 11
I Timothy 5: 17	December 12
I Timothy 5: 18	July 27
I Timothy 6: 11 – 12	June 2
I Timothy 6: 18 – 19	October 19
II Corinthians 12: 10	June 27
II Corinthians 4: 18	June 5
II Corinthians 5: 17	November 8
II Corinthians 6: 14 – 15	November 5
II Corinthians 9: 14 – 15	January 25
II Kings 19: 29 – 28	August 24
II Kings 2: 16	February 21
II Kings 7: 5 – 7	December 27
II Peter 2: 15	March 23
II Peter 3: 11 – 13	May 5
II Samuel 12: 22 – 23	October 17
II Samuel 19: 4	September 18
II Timothy 2: 15	February 13
II Timothy 4: 17 – 18	April 5
II Timothy 4: 5	August 3
II Timothy 4: 6 – 7	August 15
Acts 16: 29 – 30	December 17
Acts 16: 30 – 32	June 13

Acts 16: 31 – 33	February 1
Acts 2: 17	November 10
Acts 2: 46 – 47	December 29
Acts 2: 5 – 8	December 28
Acts 21: 12 – 14	December 23
Acts 26: 16 – 18	May 12
Acts 28: 26 – 27	February 29
Acts 6: 3 – 4	December 11
Acts 7: 55 – 56	December 15
Acts 9: 18 – 19	May 26
Colossians 1: 10	December 31
Colossians 1: 13 – 14	October 26
Colossians 3: 8	July 5
Daniel 4: 30 – 31	February 6
Deuteronomy 18: 10 – 11	September 5
Deuteronomy 21: 6	March 22
Deuteronomy 30: 19 – 20	March 28
Deuteronomy 32: 35	December 22
Deuteronomy 32: 7	September 30
Deuteronomy 5: 32 – 33	November 1
Ecclesiastes 1: 1 – 2	September 26
Ecclesiastes 11: 8	February 4
Ecclesiastes 12: 1	November 22
Ecclesiastes 3: 1 – 3	October 1
Ecclesiastes 4: 12	December 4
Ecclesiastes 4: 13	November 23
Ecclesiastes 4: 9	October 23
Ecclesiastes 4: 10	April 6
Ecclesiastes 7: 14	August 16
Ecclesiastes 7: 15	June 20
Ephesians 4: 11 – 13	December 14
Ephesians 4: 14 – 15	October 12
Ephesians 4: 17 – 18	May 21
Ephesians 4: 26 – 27	August 22
Ephesians 4: 26	August 8
Ephesians 5: 25 – 28	November 18
Ephesians 5: 32 – 33	November 19
Ephesians 5: 22 – 24	November 17
Ephesians 6: 10 – 12	April 17
Ephesians 6: 13	May 17
Ephesians 6: 17 - 18	April 7
Exodus 16: 3	January 23
Exodus 20: 9	February 19
Exodus 21: 5 – 6	December 5
Exodus 3: 19	November 15
Exodus 4: 11 – 13	November 3
Exodus 9: 2 – 3	November 13
Ezekiel 22: 30	October 25
Ezekiel 27: 3	September 2
Ezekiel 34: 12	June 22
Galatians 6: 2 – 5	May 27
Galatians 6: 9 – 10	April 8
Galatians 6: 4	July 4
Genesis 1: 1 – 2	June 3
Genesis 1: 25	September 28
Genesis 1: 28	June 6

Genesis 1: 31	February 20
Genesis 2: 15	May 4
Genesis 2: 19 – 20	December 3
Genesis 2: 24	November 16
Genesis 22: 2	August 12
Genesis 22: 8	August 26
Genesis 3: 17b – 18	January 7
Genesis 3: 6 – 7	February 22
Genesis 32: 30 – 31	July 17
Genesis 6: 5 – 6	January 6
Genesis 9: 5	January 9
Genesis 9: 2	January 8
Hebrews 11: 1 – 2	January 4
Hebrews 10: 25	August 2
Hebrews 10: 23 – 25	February 11
Hebrews 11: 1 – 2	August 19
Hebrews 11: 13 – 14	August 20
Hebrews 11: 27	December 18
Hebrews 11: 36 – 37	December 16
Hebrews 11: 8 – 10	April 25
Hebrews 11: 13b – 16	January 3
Hebrews 12: 13	March 7
Hebrews 12: 2	September 1
Hebrews 12: 1	January 5
Hebrews 13: 20 – 21	April 13
Hebrews 13: 5b	September 23
Isaiah 11: 6	March 26
Isaiah 11: 8 – 9	April 18
Isaiah 26: 19	September 20
Isaiah 26: 2	January 21
Isaiah 30: 20 – 21	January 22
Isaiah 30: 26	October 3
Isaiah 33: 5 – 6	March 4
Isaiah 35: 8	January 15
Isaiah 40: 31	July 10
Isaiah 41: 17	March 27
Isaiah 47: 12	September 8
Isaiah 49: 8 – 10	March 29
Isaiah 54: 16 – 17	April 22
Isaiah 6: 8	August 1
Isaiah 65: 25	May 9
James 1: 2 – 4	January 11
James 1: 15	May 30
James 2: 19	September 13
James 4: 7	June 28
James 5: 19 – 20	October 20
James 5: 13 – 15	February 12
Jeremiah 1: 5	September 24
Jeremiah 16: 16	October 31
Jeremiah 17: 7 – 8	May 7
Jeremiah 20: 7a	October 9
Jeremiah 20: 9	November 2
Jeremiah 23: 3	February 9
Jeremiah 33: 2 – 3	November 12
Jeremiah 4: 19	September 21
Jeremiah 7: 23	August 27

Job 10: 20 – 22	September 19
Job 10: 15	September 29
Job 16: 11	October 24
Job 19: 25 – 26	February 24
Job 20: 29	August 30
Job 23: 16 – 17	March 13
Job 26: 8	March 15
Job 3: 25 – 26	August 29
Job 32: 15 – 16	August 10
Job 32: 9	June 16
Job 36: 24	July 8
Job 38: 11	June 1
Job 41: 1 – 2	June 9
Job 41: 1 – 4	June 10
Job 7: 16	September 27
Job 9: 27 – 28	August 18
Job 9: 23 – 24	June 21
John 1: 1 – 5	September 14
John 1: 14	November 29
John 1: 41 – 42	October 28
John 10: 4 – 5	December 7
John 10: 3	July 20
John 13: 34 – 35	May 28
John 14: 1 – 3	February 27
John 14: 18	November 30
John 15: 16 – 17	Prologue
John 15: 18 – 19	May 18
John 15: 20 – 21	December 8
John 15: 5	February 23
John 16: 1 – 3	December 9
John 16: 7 – 8	October 22
John 21: 4 – 6	October 29
John 3: 8	March 17
John 5: 3 – 4	March 2
John 8: 43	May 22
John 8: 44	September 9
John 8: 31 – 32	April 15
John 9: 39	December 20
Jonah 1: 15 – 17	June 8
Jonah 4: 5 – 6	March 31
Jonah 4: 8 – 11	April 1
Joshua 24: 14 – 15	May 8
Leviticus 16: 9 – 10	August 31
Leviticus 26: 12	September 4
Luke 12: 25 – 26	April 26
Luke 12: 4 – 5	April 16
Luke 12: 20 – 21	February 7
Luke 15: 7	July 14
Luke 18: 29 – 30	January 26
Luke 19: 43 – 44	April 24
Luke 2: 4 – 7	December 24
Luke 6: 21	October 16
Luke 6: 46 – 47	October 2
Luke 9: 62	December 30
Luke 15: 21 – 23	October 4
Malachi 3: 6	August 7

Mark 10: 15	April 12
Mark 14: 27 – 29	March 19
Mark 3: 34	December 19
Mark 4: 37 – 38	March 18
Mark 9: 36 - 37	March 25
Matthew 10: 22	September 7
Matthew 10: 28	September 12
Matthew 10: 34 -36	May 19
Matthew 10: 8	January 31
Matthew 10:16	February 14
Matthew 10:29	June 19
Matthew 11: 28-29	Prologue
Matthew 11: 29 – 30	December 2
Matthew 12: 33	August 21
Matthew 12: 46 – 50	January 28
Matthew 13:15	March 20
Matthew 16: 17 -18	April 21
Matthew 17: 4	March 21
Matthew 18: 2 – 4	November 9
Matthew 18: 21 -22	July 12
Matthew 18: 5 – 6	May 14
Matthew 19: 11	July 28
Matthew 2: 10 – 11	December 25
Matthew 23: 37-38	May 20
Matthew 28: 18 -20	May 15
Matthew 4: 18 – 20	October 30
Matthew 5: 14	July 29
Matthew 6: 14 – 15	July 13
Matthew 6:16	January 24
Matthew 7: 13 – 14	October 27
Nahum 1: 7	November 27
Philemon 4: 10 – 11	December 1
Philippians 1: 21	October 13
Philippians 1: 29 -30	August 4
Philippians 1: 3 – 6	October 15
Philippians 2: 12 – 13	November 20
Philippians 3: 13 – 14	January 1
Philippians 4: 12 – 13	April 4
Philippians 4: 4 – 7	May 1
Philippians 4:13	August 14
Proverbs 1:29-33	February 8
Proverbs 15: 31	April 29
Proverbs 15:28	January 27
Proverbs 15:30	July 7
Proverbs 16: 19 – 20	October 6
Proverbs 16:18	October 5
Proverbs 16:25	March 12
Proverbs 17:17	May 13
Proverbs 18:24	July 16
Proverbs 20:2	February 10
Proverbs 20:29	April 9
Proverbs 21: 16	April 27
Proverbs 22:3	January 20
Proverbs 22:6	November 4
Proverbs 25: 11	July 6
Proverbs 27: 10	January 30

Proverbs 27: 9	July 2
Proverbs 29: 23	July 3
Proverbs 3: 5 – 6	June 17
Proverbs 4: 11 – 12	April 23
Proverbs 4: 25 – 26	June 4
Proverbs 8: 33 – 34	August 9
Psalms 1: 1 – 3	February 25
Psalms 1: 1	September 6
Psalms 1: 3	February 26
Psalms 10: 11 – 12	September 22
Psalms 102: 6 – 7	March 16
Psalms 103: 1 – 5	July 22
Psalms 106: 36 – 37	September 10
Psalms 107: 37 – 41	September 25
Psalms 112: 1 – 2	June 12
Psalms 115: 15 – 16	September 16
Psalms 119: 25 – 26	August 17
Psalms 119: 30 – 31	August 28
Psalms 124: 7 – 8	June 7
Psalms 127: 3 – 5	July 9
Psalms 128: 5	November 26
Psalms 140: 4	December 6
Psalms 140: 7 – 8	June 25
Psalms 140: 1 – 3	February 3
Psalms 141: 4	September 3
Psalms 143: 8	January 17
Psalms 144: 1	June 26
Psalms 147: 3 – 4	June 30
Psalms 147: 4 – 5	January 13
Psalms 18: 28 – 29	April 3
Psalms 18: 34	June 23
Psalms 19: 1 – 3	January 10
Psalms 20: 7 – 8	February 28
Psalms 23: 1 – 3	May 25
Psalms 23: 4 – 5	May 16
Psalms 25: 4 – 5	November 21
Psalms 25: 8 – 9	April 28
Psalms 27: 9	September 17
Psalms 27: 13 – 14	January 18
Psalms 28: 5	February 2
Psalms 30: 2 – 3	July 1
Psalms 31: 24	April 10
Psalms 32: 6 – 7	March 10
Psalms 33: 20	January 19
Psalms 37: 14 – 15	April 20
Psalms 37: 23 – 24	March 3
Psalms 38: 17 – 18	July 11
Psalms 39: 4	August 11
Psalms 4: 4 – 5	August 23
Psalms 4: 8	June 29
Psalms 40: 1 – 3	May 3
Psalms 42: 1 – 3	March 24
Psalms 46: 10 – 11	January 16
Psalms 46: 6	August 25
Psalms 48: 14	March 1
Psalms 49: 4 – 5	March 8

Psalms 53: 4 – 8	March 6
Psalms 55: 18	June 24
Psalms 56: 3 – 4	March 9
Psalms 61: 2	March 14
Psalms 77: 18 – 19	March 11
Psalms 8: 3 – 5	April 30
Psalms 8: 5 – 6	March 30
Psalms 81: 5	March 5
Psalms 82: 3 – 4	November 28
Psalms 86: 11 – 13	April 14
Psalms 90: 12	November 24
Psalms 93: 3 – 4	May 31
Revelation 12: 10	February 15
Revelation 2: 10	August 5
Revelation 21: 4	January 14
Revelation 5: 13	July 30
Revelation 5: 4, 6	September 15
Romans 1: 20	July 24
Romans 1: 25	January 12
Romans 10: 15	July 26
Romans 11: 3	May 23
Romans 12: 10 – 11	May 11
Romans 12: 4 – 5	July 15
Romans 15: 5 – 6	August 13
Romans 16: 23 – 24	October 18
Romans 5: 1 – 3	October 7
Romans 5: 3 – 4	July 18
Romans 8: 38 – 39	October 11
Song of Solomon 2: 14	November 7
Song of Solomon 2: 8	November 6
Timothy 4: 1	September 11
Titus 2: 2	February 17

Printed in the United States
18848LVS00002B/55-102